SWA

The Aggressor Series
Volume III

FX HOLDEN

SWARM

(sw**ɔ**ˑm)

noun:
A swarm or fleet of Uncrewed Aerial Vehicles is a
set of aerial robots, i.e. drones, that work together to
achieve a specific goal.
©Science Direct

Contact me:
fxholden@yandex.com
https://www.facebook.com/hardcorethrillers

Novel three of five in the Aggressor series

With huge thanks to my fantastic beta-reading team for their
encouragement and constructive critique.
*Bror Appelsin, Juan 'Pilotphotog' Artigas, Mukund B, Johnny Bunch, Jim Bennett,
Robert 'Ahab' Bugge, Marshall Crawford, Barry Conroy, Kelly Crunk, Ted
'Bushmaster 06' Dannemiller, Glenn Eaves, Julie 'Gunner' Fenimore, Brett Fidler,
Dave Hedrick, Dean Kaye, Thierry Lach, Brad 'Bone' McGuire, Alain Martin,
Barry Roberts, Omar Badman Salam, Andy Sims, Claus Stahnke, Lee Steventon,
Julian D Torda.*

And to editor, Nicole Schroeder,
alexandria.edits@gmail.com
for putting the cheese around the holes.

Books in the Aggressor Series:
1. AGGRESSOR
2. BEACHHEAD
3. SWARM
4. MIDNIGHT *(out April 2024)*
5. FINAL *episode to be released June 2024.*

Also by FX Holden: The Future War Series
(each is a stand-alone story)
1. KOBANI
2. GOLAN
3. BERING STRAIT
4. OKINAWA
5. ORBITAL
6. PAGASA
7. DMZ

China outpacing U.S. in warship production, Navy secretary warns

Fox News, Feb. 3, 2023: The United States is falling behind the People's Republic of China in the production of military ocean vessels, according to the head of the U.S. Navy.

Secretary of the Navy Carlos Del Toro spoke Tuesday at the National Press Club in Washington, D.C.

During his remarks, he warned that the Chinese military was producing warships at a greater pace than the U.S., jeopardizing American supremacy on the seas.

A Pentagon report projects a 460-ship Chinese fleet by the 2030s.

Last year's report emphasized that the People's Liberation Army Naval (PLAN) fleet was the largest in the world, with a battle force of 350 ships, compared to the U.S. Navy's 293.

This year's report lists the PLAN as having 355 battle force ships (the U.S. fleet now stands at 294 ships).

Expert's warning to U.S. Navy on China: Bigger fleet almost always wins

CNN, Jan. 17, 2023: As China continues to grow what is already the world's largest navy, a professor at the U.S. Naval War College has a warning for American military planners: In naval warfare, the bigger fleet almost always wins.

Writing in the January issue of the U.S. Naval Institute's Proceedings magazine, Sam Tangredi says if history is any lesson, China's numerical advantage is likely to lead to defeat for the U.S. Navy in any war with China.

Tangredi, the Leidos Chair of Future Warfare Studies at the U.S. Naval War College and a former U.S. Navy captain, looked at 28 naval wars, from the Greco-Persian Wars of 500 B.C. through recent Cold War proxy conflicts and interventions. He found in only three instances did superior technology defeat bigger numbers.

Contents

Area of Operations
& Tactical Maps

The Pacific Theater

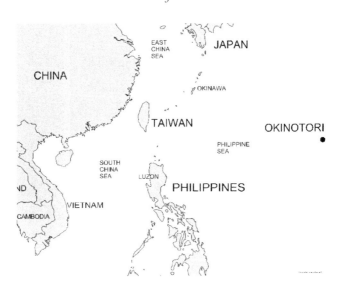

Taiwan and the South China Sea

Taiwan showing key locations

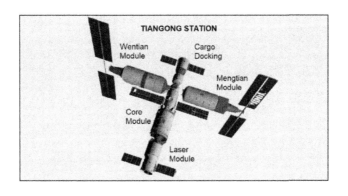

Tiangong (Heavenly Dragon) Space Station
with Small Modular Reactor docked

Aggressor Series Recap

On day 60 of a Chinese blockade of Taiwan, the US Air Force has a private military contractor—Aggressor Inc.—fly hypersonic anti-ship missiles into the besieged island at the same time the US president announces a multinational "Berlin Airlift"–style operation to supply Taiwan with food and medicine. China reacts with a heavy hand, shooting down a UK cargo plane and embarking its troops, seemingly to attempt an invasion of two Taiwanese islands just off the coast of China.

The US and Taiwan are prepared—in fact, the administration of US President Carmen Carliotti has been waiting for this day—to provoke a military face-off against communist China that will weaken its ability to wage war for generations. The two nations trade hypersonic missile attacks on their vulnerable carriers, with both sides being forced to withdraw them, even as the US Coalition floods land-based aircraft into the theater and begins attacks with strategic bombers based in Guam, the Philippines, Japan and Australia. The pride of the Chinese fleet, the carrier *Fujian*, is badly damaged and limps to safety in neutral Papua New Guinea.

Aggressor Inc. remains in the thick of the action as the US begins stage two of its plan to weaken China and lands Marines in the South China Sea to destroy key Chinese military installations. The US hopes to fix in place a large part of China's navy and air force in the South China Sea so that it cannot be used in a Taiwan invasion. China retaliates with an attack on US subsea cables off the California coast, resulting in the loss of a Chinese submarine but giving fuel to a political push by the US president for a mandate to send US ground troops to Taiwan to aid in its defense. Her cause is ironically helped by a failed assassination attempt, which kills several members of her inner cabinet but gives her and her anti-China rhetoric a massive rise in public support.

It seems almost nothing can stand in the way of her plan to use Taiwan as the rock "upon which I will break the back of communism forever." But the first signs of the conflict spinning out of control emerge as China and India clash on the Indian-Himalayan border and as Australia, unhappy to see the Chinese flagship on its northern border, ignores the neutral status of Papua New Guinea with a combined sea and air attack on *Fujian*.

Then China rocks the well-laid plans of the US president and her inner circle as it launches its invasion of Taiwan, not with human troops but with hundreds, then *thousands*, of autonomous Tianyi "killer drones," programmed to destroy military vehicles, installations, civilian infrastructure and transport hubs.

China is on the offensive at last, but not in the way Taiwan or the US Coalition expected. This is not the air or ground war they prepared for. Aggressor Inc. is tasked with destroying a Tianyi launch site but suffers heavy losses, and the mission proves ultimately futile as more Chinese Tianyi launch sites are brought online.

Taiwan and its US Coalition allies seem to have no counter to the Chinese drone invasion. But what is China's next move?

Cast of players

COALITION
Washington
US President Carmen Carliotti
NSC ExCom members: Vice President Mark Bendheim, Homeland Security Secretary Janet Belkin, Defense Secretary (nominee) Dan Caulfield, Chief of Staff HR Rosenstern, Chairman of the Joint Chiefs General Earl Maxwell
Director, China Joint Wargaming Council (JWC), James Burroughs
Assistant Director, JWC, Julio Fernandez

68th Aggressor Squadron, AGRS (Aggressor Inc.)
Lieutenant Karen 'Bunny' O'Hare, P-99 Black Widow flight leader, 68th AGRS
Captain Anaximenes 'Meany' Papastopolous (USAF Reserve), CO, 68th AGRS
Captain Charlene 'Touchdown' Dubois, F-22 Raptor flight leader, 68th AGRS
Second Lieutenant Lukas 'Flatline' Fibak, P-99 pilot, 68th AGRS

Taiwan
Lin Hungyu, fisherman, robotics engineer
Sergeant Mason Jackson, 1st Battalion, 8th Marines
Sergeant Wu, Corporal Jerome Xu, Airborne Special Service Company, Yun Chi Tuan 'Thunder' Squad

US Space Force
Colonel Alicia 'The Hammer' Rodriguez, 615th Combat Operations Squadron, Space Launch Delta 45
Colonel Dan 'Tug' Boatt, Director of Operations and Lead Pilot, 615th Combat Operations Squadron Skylon Program, Space Launch Delta 45

Captain Sally Hall, Assistant Director and pilot, Skylon D4 'Tiger,' 615th Combat Operations Squadron Skylon Program, Space Launch Delta 45

Technical Sergeant Caleb Levi, crew chief, Skylon D4 'Tiger,' 615th Combat Operations Squadron Skylon Program, Space Launch Delta 45

USAF 492nd Special Operations Wing

Captain Rory O'Donoghue, 18th Flight Test Squadron, AC-130X 'Outlaw'

Lieutenant Robert E. 'Uncle' Lee, copilot, 18th Flight Test Squadron, AC-130X 'Outlaw'

AUKUS submarine *AE1*

Commander Gary McDonald, Royal Australian Navy submarine, HMAS *AE1*

Lieutenant Carla Brunelli, Executive Officer, RAN submarine HMAS *AE1*

LCS-30 USS *CANBERRA*

Officer of the Watch, Lieutenant Daniel 'Dopey' Drysdale

Watch Supervisor, Chief Petty Officer Hiram Goldmann

Sonarman Elvis 'Ears' Bell

CHINA
PLAN *Fujian*

Colonel Wang Wei, Air Wing Commander, PLA Navy carrier *Fujian*

Major Tan Yuanyuan, PLA Navy Intelligence, PLA Navy carrier *Fujian*

Lieutenant Maylin 'Mushroom' Sun, Flight Leader, Ao Yin Fighter Squadron, PLA Navy carrier *Fujian*

PLA Strategic Support Force (Space)

Senior Colonel Liu Haiping, Taikonaut, People's Liberation Army Astronaut Corps, Tiangong Space Station

Lieutenant Colonel Zhu Boming, Taikonaut, People's Liberation Army Astronaut Corps, Tiangong Space Station

Captain Chen Yuqi, Taikonaut, People's Liberation Army Astronaut Corps, Tiangong Space Station

Port Aeon

Captain Andrei Rafalovik, Port Aeon detachment, PLA Ground Forces 71st Air Defense Brigade

Taneti Tito, Liquor Merchant, Port Aeon, Kiribati

Operation Reunion Staff

Chief Engineer Lo Pan, National Defense Science and Technology Innovation Bureau (NDSTIB)

June 2038

1. The battle of 1135 Wilson Boulevard

He was old and slow. He'd never felt so old nor so slow. He'd run down six flights of stairs, hit ground level and found a locked door.

What kind of parking garage has fire stairs that are locked at street level?

A derelict parking garage, that's what. He could only go up again because if he stayed here, he would be killed for sure. But if he went up again, he'd probably be killed too. Maybe he could go up one level and jump to the ground?

James Burroughs took the stairs two at a time, even though his legs were burning. The last time he had done any running was a Boston half-marathon when he was 30 … 20 years ago now. He got to the second floor, stood by the metal door, tested whether he could open it. It opened a crack, but it opened with a creak. He'd left his would-be killer on the fifth floor, gone up, run across the sixth-floor roof parking and down the stairs on the other side. Chances the killer would be right outside? Not zero.

He listened. No sound in the concrete and metal stairwell. Put his ear to the crack in the doorway. No sound outside. Easing the door open just wide enough to slip himself through gave a screech like a bird of prey calling, but he was out and running again, headed for the nearest railing. He hit it so fast he nearly tipped over. Looked down. It looked about 20 feet and dropped onto unforgiving concrete. If he jumped here, the least he would break was his ankles. He looked up and down the path below for bushes, an awning, anything that might break his fall without breaking his back.

A bullet smacked into the concrete by his waist. He lurched away from it, ducking down, and ran for the stairwell again, heaving the door

15

open, another bullet smacking into the iron frame with a heavy metal whang.

He pulled the door shut and hesitated. Up or down? No, not down. But he got an idea. He took off a shoe, threw it on the landing down to the next floor, then began running up the stairs again. Bait. Maybe the killer didn't know the street-level door was locked.

If Burroughs didn't get shot, he was going to die of a heart attack, that was for sure.

He hadn't heard a gun. A gun going off inside an empty garage— shouldn't it make a noise? That wasn't good. His attacker was using a silenced weapon. Burroughs was no expert on assassins, but he was pretty sure being pursued by one using a suppressor was Not A Good Sign.

He got to the roof again. He had to make for the other stairs, hope that the exit door on the ground floor on that side wasn't locked. He hadn't tried it because in his panic, he'd run up …

He had to stop and breathe. The roof had parking spaces in rows around the outside and a large central air-conditioning and elevator room in the middle. He ran for the air-conditioning room, or hobbled, really, since he had only one shoe. Which was stupid, running in one shoe, so he took the other off and heaved it down to the other end of the parking garage roof, where it clattered into the guard wall. Let his attacker think he'd gone off the sixth-floor roof, why not?

Which … He looked up. If it had been a long time since James Burroughs had done any serious running, it was even longer since he'd done any climbing. But if he could get one foot on that exhaust duct … another on the fan outlet just above it …

He clambered up the outside of the air-conditioning room and rolled onto its roof. It was covered in discarded tubing and cables, and he lay there a moment, panting, listening for the sound of the stairwell doors opening.

How the hell did he get here?

16

He lay still, looking up at the dark sky, retracing the breadcrumbs …

The Chinese Foreign Ministry spokesperson on the flat-screen TV on a wall of the Joint Wargaming Council's Pentagon offices was a small, thin, hawk-nosed woman with slicked black hair. She didn't so much speak to the camera as screech, and she'd been doing a lot of screeching at the camera since Taiwan unleashed its opening missile barrage at Chinese invasion forces several weeks earlier.

She'd screeched about "unprovoked aggression," which was more than a little ironic given China had Taiwan under naval blockade and had just shot down a US Coalition relief flight. More than passingly hypocritical, given it had marshaled 300,000 troops on the coast opposite the rebel island. And a little less than credible given that the target of the Taiwanese strike was the 5,000 PLA Navy Marines China had just embarked on landing ships to assault the Taiwanese islands of Kinmen and Matsu.

She'd screeched about "acts of war" as a US air coalition moved in to defend Taiwan and the US landed its own Marines on two of the atolls China illegally occupied in the Spratly Islands chain in the South China Sea, ejecting the Chinese troops there. She'd railed against a "stab in the back" from India, which had lost 200 troops defending an outpost on the Chinese border in the Himalayas from a Chinese "defensive action."

She had become apoplectic about Coalition attacks on the Chinese aircraft carriers *Shandong, Liaoning* and *Fujian*, not mentioning the Chinese attacks on the USS *Enterprise* or USS *Bougainville* task forces. And she had announced in shrill tones that China was ejecting a handful of US diplomats in protest over the "unwarranted attack on a peaceful Chinese research vessel in international waters" five miles off the coast of San Francisco.

But she was not screeching now. She was giving the cameras a thin-lipped smile, almost a leer. "… And so it is with great pleasure that we announce the leaders of our great nations have signed the Shanghai Declaration of Friendship, Cooperation, and Mutual Assistance"—she held up a leather-bound folder, opened it and flourished it at the camera—"which will usher in a new era of equal footing and mutual respect; win-win cooperation between a global alliance of equals; multi-polarization of politics, economics and culture; and an international order based on an understanding that outdated global governance structures must be reformed …"

"And so the Shanghai Pact is born." JWC Director Burroughs sighed.

"We called it," his deputy director, Julio Fernandez, pointed out. "China has been trying to pull together a NATO-like coalition with the Eurasian republics for decades, and an East-West conflict over Taiwan was always going to be a strong catalyst."

"We *didn't* predict Russia joining," Burroughs said. "Iran, Syria, North Korea, Venezuela, the Organization of African States, yes, but Moscow as junior partner to Beijing?"

"What choice do they have? Russia is a busted flush. But they won't spin it that way," Fernandez replied, "Any more than the UK regards itself as a junior partner in NATO." His brow furrowed. "This puts China in a formal defense alliance with three other nuclear-armed states—four, when Iran inevitably goes nuclear, with their help …"

Burroughs held up a finger. He was reading the subtitles as the Chinese spokeswoman continued. "… announcing that next week, the combined maritime and air forces of Russia and China will be conducting joint drills focusing on anti-submarine and sea assault operations in the waters of the Okhotsk Sea and Russian Kuril Islands."

Burroughs whistled, but Fernandez shook his head. "No, we called that too. China started moving its invasion troops out of range of our air attacks weeks ago. They have gathered 300,000 troops up north at Qingdao and have been marching them on and off landing vessels for two weeks. We said they would probably stage some kind of exercise to show they were still serious about invading …"

"Not a *joint* exercise," Burroughs said. "Not supported by Russian cruisers, amphibious landing ships, bombers, fighters, submarines …" He walked to a map of Southeast Asia taped to a wall and festooned with multicolored pins, pointing to an island chain that stretched from just off the coast of Hokkaido, Japan, all the way to Russia's Kamchatka Peninsula. He stabbed his finger down on an island about a hundred miles northeast of Japan in the Kuril Islands chain. "We've been hearing noise about Russian naval vessels and troops arriving at Iturup. It's an almost perfect small-scale replica of Taiwan. Russia plays blue, defends the island, while China plays red and practices invading. They televise it to the world, and the Taiwanese government is supposed to realize resistance is futile." Burroughs was moving into role-playing mode, second-guessing China's next moves. "I've already got them on the ropes, hiding in caves in the hills while my killer drones roam the countryside unchecked …"

They were in a small cubicle in the office in a wing of the Pentagon that the JWC had been assigned when it was

19

formed. Twenty academics and analysts were crammed into the space, divided into cubicles with a single central meeting room. Burroughs sat himself on Fernandez's desk. "Puts Japan on the back foot too, with exercises just off their coast. Do they *really* want to support the US against a China-Russia-North Korea pact? Let's play it through …"

That was as far as the idea got. From the cubicle next to them came a moan, and one of the DIA analysts supporting the JWC pushed back his chair, hands holding his head like it was going to explode. He was staring at his laptop screen. "OK, that's not good …"

Burroughs looked up. "What is it?"

He gestured at his machine as though it were to blame for his mood. "Just did an analysis of Chinese space force launches since the conflict began, compared with prior years." He turned his screen to show them a graph. "The red bar shows the last three months."

Burroughs studied it. "So, they've launched more military satellites. That's to be expected …"

"Four hundred and thirty-two more?" the man said, pointing out that the scale on the left of the graph did not start at zero. "They've been running at a launch a day, either from Jiuquan, Xichang, Taiyuan, Wenchang or their new Yellow Sea Maritime Launch Platform. Every bird they've sent into space has deployed an average of five satellites."

"That is an intense launch program," Fernandez agreed. "Did we know they had that much capacity?"

"Yeah, they've been mass-producing those low-cost Tianlong-3 rockets supposedly for 'commercial launches,' so they've been ramping up in plain view. But no one in our intelligence community has done a study of what the implications would be if China *militarized* that commercial capacity, and began launching continuously, overnight."

"Until now," Burroughs pointed out. "Because ... why are you working this angle, Elijah?" The man was one of Burroughs's borrowed Space Force analysts, a young Floridian called Elijah Carmody.

"Because I read yesterday that China is launching its super-heavy Long March 9 today, with a 150-ton military payload. Their biggest yet. And then I started thinking, I wonder how many other military payload launches there have been since Taiwan kicked off ..."

Fernandez was studying the data on the screen again. "That's 90 launches. You've confirmed every one of those Tianlong-3 rockets was carrying a military satellite?"

Carmody sat back in his chair. "Not all. About a third are confirmed by either signals, cyber or human intelligence; the rest I extrapolated based on the launch proximity and rocket type." He looked defensive. "Even if you only take the confirmed payloads, that's still 120 new military satellites—minimum."

"But not ..."—Fernandez leaned forward, reading off the screen—"432."

"No, but ..."

Burroughs could see where Fernandez was headed. The new analysis wouldn't make the daily report to the National Security Council Executive Committee. It wasn't solid enough. Yet. "It's good work, Carmody," Burroughs said. "Try to get a higher level of confidence on the payloads. Meanwhile, start thinking about *why* China would need that much additional mil-sat capacity. Is it to handle new capabilities? Is it for redundancy? Try to find a strategic development that it would support, and I'll take it to ExCom."

"So we just go with Shanghai Pact today?" Fernandez asked him. The ExCom meeting was only two hours away.

"Shanghai." Burroughs nodded. "And how it changes the game."

"I won't say thank you for that update, General," US President Carmen Carliotti said. Following the death of half her cabinet, Carliotti had redrawn her ExCom.

The attempt on Carliotti's life had claimed the Vice President, the Secretary of Defense and the Homeland Security Secretary, and Burroughs's predecessor at the JWC, Michael Chase. All cabinet members had been replaced with new appointees from her own party, with one exception; the Chairman of the Joint Chiefs, General Earl Maxwell, had been brought in to replace the Defense Secretary, as Carliotti's pick for the new Defense Secretary had not yet been confirmed. Security at the White House had been intensified, and NSC meetings had moved back into the West Wing basement. Their ExCom meeting had been delayed while the president was briefed by Homeland Security on their ongoing investigation into the bombing.

Interestingly, Carliotti had also invited the Speaker of the House of Representatives, David Manukyan—an opposition politician and vocal critic of US involvement in the Taiwan conflict—to join the NSC ExCom. On the back of the assassination attempt, Carliotti had won a vote in both houses of Congress that gave her a mandate to send US troops to Taiwan, despite Manukyan's opposition. Faced with the inevitable, he had agreed to join ExCom "in the interests of national unity," though he made clear at every opportunity that his stance would not change; war with China was a folly to which he and his party would remain opposed.

General Maxwell had just run through the situation regarding the autonomous drone attacks on Taiwan's defense and civilian infrastructure and the Coalition troop "surge." Taiwan's ground-based radar coverage was at 30 percent of pre-war levels, with the gap being filled by Coalition AWACS aircraft. Fixed anti-air and anti-ship missile platforms were at 20 percent while mobile units had been withdrawn to bunkers—every time they emerged, they were being hit. It wasn't that they couldn't kill the Chinese drones; the problem was they were simply being overwhelmed by the constant flood of predatory drones China was able to land with each of its 'Tianyi' mother ships.

Fifteen percent of Taiwan's remaining fighter aircraft had been destroyed on the ground, and the rest were now operating out of the Philippines and Japan alongside Coalition aircraft. Fifty percent of the Army's light armor and tactical vehicles had been destroyed or damaged, along with an as-yet-uncounted number of police and emergency services vehicles. Major shopping centers and rail and transport routes were closed, electricity substations and water pumping plants had been targeted, and the capital, Taipei, was rationing water and electricity for essential services only.

It was a sobering situation, an invasion by any other name, without Chinese troops even setting foot on the island.

"There is good news, ma'am," Maxwell said. "Our troop surge is going to plan. We have air superiority over the western Pacific and secure sea lanes from Okinawa and Luzon. The landing of Coalition troops on Taiwan at the ports of Keelung City near Taipei, and at Hualien on the west coast, is proceeding to plan, and our air defenses around these ports are ensuring we can get our troops safely ashore without losses."

Burroughs had in fact read that Coalition troops were pinned down in Taiwan's ports, unable to move out in numbers without their convoys being hit by the Chinese drones. Their only success in the last two weeks was to establish a Marine base inland in Chiayi, in the center of the island. But on the west coast facing China, the part of the island most exposed to invasion, they'd proven unable to penetrate south of Taipei without suffering significant losses to drone strikes. Jamming attacks did not work against the fully autonomous drones, and mobile "anti-air" systems like missile-armed Strykers and Bradleys were being overwhelmed by both the volume of drones China was deploying daily and the fact they moved around at street level, making them almost impossible to detect in an urban environment until they were right on top of their "prey." They were also quick to attack anything that looked like a soldier with a MANPAD or rifle, even civilians carrying pipes or brooms were at risk.

The picture was nowhere near as rosy as Maxwell presented, but Burroughs chose not to pick an argument with the General.

"We have 30,000 Marines ashore already, and when the 82nd Airborne finishes deploying at the end of this week, the total number of Coalition troops on Taiwan will be more than 50,000," Maxwell continued. "Finally, we are having some success in the South China Sea …"

"Glad to hear it, but it's the politics that have me worried right now," Carliotti said. "My last call with Taiwan's president, he's hanging tough, but his cabinet sounded pretty shaken. Our troops are stuck in the cities were are landing them in, so our 'surge,' General, isn't changing the picture on the ground."

Maxwell looked pained. "We're focused on securing the big population centers like Taipei first, Hualien and Chiayi, and then …"

"But Taipei is *not* secure, General," Carliotti pointed out. Burroughs was glad he wasn't the only one who had been reading the briefings. "President En-le said his prime minister and cabinet ministers have requested permission to operate as a government in exile from Japan. So far, he refused, saying if they flee, as Commander in Chief of the Armed Forces, he will depose them and impose martial law." She surveyed the people around the table. "I'll say it inside these four walls: All the Coalition troops in all the ports on Taiwan won't help if we can't get on top of this drone scourge and start securing potential Chinese invasion points." She rubbed her eyes, seeming tired. "And now we're facing this new unholy alliance with Iran and Russia and North Korea, and I don't know who else. Mr. Burroughs, how will China leverage this new pact?"

Burroughs was ready for the question. "Ma'am, China is playing a very long game," he said. "It's about Taiwan, but it's about much more, and the Shanghai Pact is China moving all its pieces into place …"

"A measure we *forced* them into," Manukyan said, right on cue.

"The Axis of Evil rises again," quipped the Homeland Security Secretary, Belkin. She winked at Burroughs, which unsettled him. In his few interactions, he'd learned she liked to make light of serious topics, to play peacemaker in disagreements, but she was the kind of person who worked a room in coffee breaks, often taking an opposite position in private to the one she had taken publicly moments before. He didn't trust her. What the hell was that wink supposed to mean?

Manukyan missed the wink and piled on. "It does, Madam Secretary, it does! And yet, Madam President, you are determined to continue this foolhardy 'surge'? Even though now we're facing off against *three* nuclear-armed states?!" Manukyan continued, a note of hysteria in his voice. "Madam President, I hope you can see now why I simply cannot, I will not, support US troops on Taiwan soil. You are turning a limited conflict over Taiwan into a full-scale war that will be our ruin."

"Mr. Speaker, if we do not face China down here and now, we will have to face an even stronger China later," Maxwell warned. "And that, sir, is a fight we do not want."

Carliotti intervened. "Sorry, Mr. Burroughs. You were talking about China's 'long game'?"

"Yes, Madam President," Burroughs said. He pointed at the large LCD wall screen and pulled his tablet from his leather portfolio. "May I?"

Rosenstern nodded. "Please."

Burroughs connected to the screen, logged into the JWC cloud and brought up a map his team had prepared. It was China, but not as anyone in the room knew it.

"What is this?" Carliotti asked.

"*This* is China at its last historical peak, during the Qing dynasty, 1644 to 1912," Burroughs said. "When the Chinese ruled not just mainland China as we know it today but inner and outer Mongolia, Tibet, Taiwan and parts of Russia, while all of East Asia, from Korea, Vietnam and Thailand to Laos, Burma and Nepal, were tributary states." He clicked to highlight the outer boundary. "China ruled over a third of the

Asian landmass. When the Chinese premier talks about 'The Great Rejuvenation of the Chinese Nation,' *this* is his benchmark. Qing dynasty China."

"China can't achieve control over a third of the Asian landmass without it resulting in nuclear war," Secretary Belkin said to Burroughs, pointing at the screen. "Why would they not think this unbridled ambition will result in global Armageddon?"

Burroughs swiveled in his chair and turned to Speaker Manukyan rather than Belkin. "Mr. Speaker, I said China is playing a long game, bigger than Taiwan. Your position is that we should *not* go to war with China over Taiwan?"

"Damn right," Manukyan said. "Both parties still support the One China policy, last time I checked. 'Render therefore unto Caesar the things which are Caesar's.'"

Burroughs nodded. "What about if China moved on Nepal and Tibet?"

"Some Buddhist temples on hilltops? Not worth fighting World War III for, no," Manukyan said.

"Burma, Laos, Thailand, Vietnam?" Burroughs continued. "If China threatened war, or actually went to war with those nations and installed friendly governments?"

"Vietnam was the perfect example of why USA should never get involved in other people's wars," Manukyan said. "A pointless waste of American lives."

General Maxwell looked like he wanted to reach across the table and throttle Manukyan, but he maintained his calm.

"I see. And let's say … South Korea?" Burroughs asked. "The north is already a tributary state to China, but if China attacks Taiwan and both China and North Korea move on South Korea next, should we support them as we are supporting Taiwan now?"

Carliotti and Maxwell both looked like they wanted to say something but were waiting for Manukyan's answer. He hesitated, but then his face hardened. "We already fought one war in Korea. It cost us 40,000 dead and 100,000 wounded and ended in stalemate. So no, never again. We can support these nations against any aggressor economically and with arms, like we did in Ukraine, but we cannot fight their fight for them. No sir." Manukyan looked directly at Carliotti. "I say no, and ever no."

"Thank you, Mr. Speaker." Burroughs gave the Homeland Security Secretary, Belkin, a wan smile. "There you have it, Madam Secretary. You can see why China might believe there *is* a pathway by which it could return to its Qing dynasty power *without* the risk of nuclear war with USA. China's leadership feels it simply needs to chip away. It is not daunted by the sight of a few Coalition troops on Taiwan. It expects that as our losses to missile and autonomous drone strikes on Taiwan mount, sooner or later, our willpower will buckle, and we will load our troops back onto their ships and bring them home again. The Shanghai Pact is another pressure point supposed to hurry us on our way and make an invasion unnecessary."

"Wait. You don't think China *will* invade?" Carliotti asked. Burroughs paused. She sounded surprised, almost … *disappointed?*

"Madam President, I'm sorry if my predecessor didn't already make this clear. China has mobilized its Eastern and Northern military command to demonstrate that it *could* invade, if it chose to, but the launch of this massive and continuous autonomous drone campaign indicates it thinks it can win back Taiwan without having to do so."

Manukyan stood. "Madam President, China is not playing your game; it is playing its own. You have put tens of thousands of our young men and women in harm's way for a cause that is already lost and …"

Carliotti held up her hands in a gesture that could be interpreted either as an attempt to get the Speaker to shut up or a gesture of defeat.

"A lot to think about. Thank you, Mr. Speaker. Thank you, Mr. Burroughs," she said, with typical understatement. "HR, can I ask you to get together with State and examine the full ramifications of this 'Shanghai Pact'?"

"Madam President," General Maxwell intervened. "This new alliance does not change the calculus militarily …"

"Not militarily, perhaps, but politically, General," Carliotti said. "So, HR, please, pull together a proposal for how we should respond if our allies see Russia and China patrolling the Taiwan Strait together and start to panic." She smiled at Burroughs. "Or North Koreans jumping out of Chinese airplanes over Taiwan."

The General gritted his teeth, held back the comment he clearly wanted to make and just nodded instead. "Any assistance you need, Mr. Rosenstern, please just ask."

The meeting broke, and Burroughs was in a hurry to return to the Pentagon to see if Elijah Carmody had gotten any further with his satellite launch analysis. The heavy lift rocket on its way to the Chinese Space Station had piqued his interest.

"James, wait up," a voice called as he began hurrying down the corridor to the back of the building, where his driver would be waiting.

He turned and saw Rosenstern walking toward him. *James?* HR Rosenstern had never called Burroughs by his first name before. This couldn't be good.

Rosenstern pointed to one of the empty briefing rooms off the corridor. "Join me? Won't keep you long." Usually the basement would be filled with assorted hangers-on and flunkies, either preparing to brief the NSC or debriefing after they'd done so. But after the bombing, the Situation Room and the rooms adjoining it had been swept for explosives and given added security, and all non-essential personnel were banned, their access to the basement revoked. The only persons cleared to enter the basement were the members of the NSC ExCom and their Secret Service details, and even ExCom members were scanned and searched on entering. Anyone else on the ExCom agenda joined by video link only.

They slipped into a small meeting room, and Rosenstern closed the door. So the conversation was so confidential it couldn't be overheard by other ExCom members? Burroughs's level of concern doubled.

"So here's the thing," Rosenstern said. He wasn't one for small talk. "I've set up a task force, all the usual agencies, to investigate the Raven Rock bombing. It reports directly to me, and it needs a China expert. Special adviser, if you like."

Burroughs tried to keep up, thinking immediately of potential candidates, but a thought intruded. "They're assuming China was behind the attack?"

"No. And that's the problem," Rosenstern said, frowning. "FBI is coordinating the task force, and they've convinced themselves it's domestic terrorism. They just told the President they're no longer looking at a China angle."

"Makes sense," Burroughs allowed. He had been party to a couple of briefings on the bombing investigation. "The

30

attackers were recruited via an online 'Patriot' forum, all vets or ex-cops with a hate on Carliotti and everything from drug to money problems. Maybe it was domestic terrorists, and there *is* no China angle."

"No, it was China," Rosenstern insisted, as though it were an immutable fact. "But it's going to be damn near impossible to prove, which is why I want someone from JWC inside the task force, looking for Chinese connections, shining a light in any corners where China's agents might hide. Chinese influence groups, China-leaning individuals, corporate links, think tanks, all that good stuff … Get the FBI back on track."

"I can't find what isn't there," Burroughs said, not quite comfortable with the direction the conversation was taking.

"And we won't find anything if we *don't* look," Rosenstern said, sounding frustrated. "I'm not asking you to invent evidence. Whoever did this infiltrated the construction crew a *year* earlier to plant explosives inside the complex. They had National Guard uniforms, weapons, vehicles, up-to-date credentials. Nearly half a million dollars was transferred into their bank accounts before the attack. Those who didn't die in the complex or down in the tunnel committed *suicide* rather than be captured. That sound like some half-assed bunch of domestic terrorists to you?"

Burroughs had to admit it didn't. There must have been some kind of state actor behind the attack. But assassinating the US head of state just didn't *feel* to him like the kind of thing China would do either. Russia, maybe. But China, no. Still, there was a first time for everything. "I'll find someone for your task force," he told Rosenstern.

Rosenstern put a hand on his arm. "You misunderstand. The President wants *you* on the task force. Because if you tell us there's no China angle, we'll believe it."

Burroughs blanched at the thought. He had only ever had limited dealings with law enforcement agencies—as senior analyst on DIA's China desk, he'd been invited to speak to the Secret Service, FBI and DEA more than once—and what he'd learned was theirs was a world so far removed from his, he was better not even thinking about it.

"You got a deputy at JWC, Harvard guy ..." Rosenstern clicked his fingers, not giving him time to say no. "What's his name?"

"Julio Fernandez. He'd be perfect for this kind of thing," Burroughs said, unashamedly throwing Fernandez under the bus. But Burroughs was Princeton, not Harvard, so he did it without a trace of guilt.

"Yeah, no. He can take your chair at ExCom so long as you are on the task force. And I'll see that you still have access to all the resources of the JWC. Use them as your back-office team for this." Rosenstern let go of his arm, looked at his watch and patted Burroughs's shoulder. "Alright, good. Someone from the task force will be in touch with details. Call me later; you'll have questions."

And he was gone.

Burroughs stayed, still backed up against a desk, thinking. He did have questions, about a dozen of them already. But he also had a couple of conclusions he could draw from the brief conversation.

One, he'd just been removed from ExCom. He'd barely had time to settle in among the president's inner circle of advisors and cabinet secretaries, but now he was out.

Burroughs had to assume Rosenstern was acting with Carliotti's approval.

So one door had closed, but another had just opened up for him. Rosenstern clearly saw something he liked. He wanted Burroughs on his task force. "Chair of the White House Joint Wargaming Council" looked pretty good on his resume, but so would "Special Adviser to the Task Force Investigating the Raven Rock Bombing."

That had to be A Good Thing, right?

"JWC says China is not going to invade, HR," President Carliotti said the moment Rosenstern returned to the Situation Room, checking his messages. She was sitting alone, chair reclined, shoes off, staring up at the ceiling. She favored jackets that buttoned at the throat over matching trousers, which HR had told her had ironically a Chairman Mao look about them, except that they weren't Army green, they were usually shades of red. Right now, the jacket was unbuttoned.

Carliotti was feeling the heat. "If China *doesn't* invade ..." Carliotti said.

"Maxwell has a plan for ensuring that they do," Rosenstern reminded her. "In the meantime, I'm more worried about Manukyan." He held up his cell phone. "His campaign to impeach for 'abuse of power' is gaining momentum." He sat down at the table again. "My sources tell me he's got most of his party with him now, and the doves on our side could tip a vote in the House in his favor. The Chinese cyberattack and sub fiasco off California helped us win the mandate for the surge and a bounce in the polls, and so do our successes in the South China Sea ... The Senate is solid, but you're maybe 15 votes short in the House."

"So he can't win, but we definitely don't need the headache of an impeachment vote passing in the House. We have to pull the trigger on Manukyan," Carliotti said.

Rosenstern nodded gravely. "We do."

Carliotti sat up again. "When could you get him the briefing?"

Rosenstern looked at his watch. "About an hour from now. We'll make it look like a special update for all NSC members."

"And he'll leak it."

"If he's true to form."

"Secret Service is still ready for a full-court press when he does?"

"They lost six agents in one day in the Raven Rock attack, and the people who matter are convinced the Speaker had a hand in it. Secretary Belkin has all the pieces in place to move as soon as the leak hits the wires."

An hour later, Speaker of the House David Manukyan looked up in irritation as one of his aides knocked on his door. He was preparing a speech for a donor event at which the media would be present, and it was a great opportunity to once again make the case for Carliotti's impeachment for abuse of power.

What he'd heard at ExCom that afternoon hadn't changed his mind; if anything, it gave fuel to his fire. Taiwan's own government was about to flee the island? War against *three* nuclear-armed nations? There could be no victory in a war with China, only economic ruin and humiliation. Any sane person could see that.

"Sir, a flash communication for you. NSC members' eyes only."

Manukyan held out his hand for the envelope. He insisted all communications be printed for him, whether they arrived via encrypted digital channels or not. He'd made a special agreement with the bureaucrats at Homeland Security that everything printed for him was numbered, accounted for and shredded at the end of each day.

He waited until the aide left the room and closed the door, then opened the envelope with interest. Their last ExCom meeting was less than a couple of hours old. What could have happened in the interim?

TOP SECRET/HCS-P/SI/ORCON-USGOV/NOFORN

EXCOM INTELLIGENCE: SUPPLEMENTARY BRIEF 23 JUNE 2038

At 1530 hours the US president took a call from the President of the Republic of China (Taiwan). The Taiwanese president advised that the Taiwan war cabinet had unanimously voted to propose an immediate ceasefire with China, with a view to initiating reunification negotiations.

Taiwan's president said he immediately relieved the Prime Minister and his cabinet of their offices and placed them under guard. They will be charged with sedition. He intends to announce a State of Emergency in coming hours and declare martial law. He has requested the support of Coalition troops to maintain order in the capital, Taipei.

The US president expressed her regret at these events and said the US would need to consider its position as the implications of these developments extended beyond the current conflict.

The two presidents agreed to speak again tomorrow.

//ENDS

Manukyan slapped the page down on his desk. "Consider its position? Use *our troops* to support a coup?!" he railed out loud. "What the hell is there to consider? This benighted fiasco is over!"

His aide stuck his head through the door. "Did you want something, Mr. Speaker?"

Manukyan waved him away and reread the brief. He needed to wedge Carliotti so she couldn't do anything precipitous while she was "considering." The header on the memo showed it had been sent to the entire NSC, which was currently 24 members strong. That gave him all the plausible deniability he needed.

He reached into a drawer and pulled out the burner cell phone his most trusted journalist had given him. From the same drawer he pulled a pile of SIM cards and stuck one in the phone—no easy feat for hands that trembled with the effects of newly diagnosed Parkinson's disease, but needs must.

He took a photograph of the memo, then opened the encrypted app he used to communicate with the journalist, logged in and posted the photograph. He didn't like to leave it entirely to his intermediary to come up with their own interpretation and always tried to guide them. Usually they followed his lead, which was what made it such a beneficial arrangement. Underneath the photograph he wrote:

Taiwan capitulates, PM proposes ceasefire and reunification negotiations. President to declare martial law. Anarchy on Taiwan with US troops in the crossfire.

Commentary: With Taiwan's own elected government seeking peace, there is no justification for the further involvement of US forces in the China-Taiwan conflict. President Carliotti should withdraw our troops.

Approach for comment: members of Congress Gregory-Brown, Burleigh and Sarkissian.

Manukyan hit "send," then pulled the SIM card out of the cell phone. The shredder beside his desk was capable of destroying more than paper. He started its metal teeth whirring and dropped the SIM card into it. The NSC memo followed.

He put the burner phone in his jacket pocket. It would end at the bottom of a well on his neighbor's property later tonight as he took his daily walk with his dog.

He returned to his speech with newfound optimism. *This benighted fiasco is over.* He wasn't sure how he'd hit upon that form of words, but he liked it. He had the conclusion of his speech; now he just had to fill in the rest.

House Speaker Arrested, Property Searched

NBN Breaking News: Speaker of the House of Representatives, Congressman David Manukyan, has been questioned by the Secret Service and his North Potomac property searched in relation to "willful retention and transmission of information related to national defense."

A Secret Service spokesperson confirmed Speaker Manukyan was detained and questioned by Secret Service agents overnight. It is not clear whether he has been or will be charged with an offense.

Speaker Manukyan appears to have been the subject of a complex sting operation. A copy of the search warrant obtained by NBN states that:

"The named individual (Manukyan) is suspected of leaking secret national security information to journalists over a longer period. Yesterday, false information contained in a briefing provided to Speaker Manukyan alone appeared on the website of a major national newspaper the same evening. Speaker Manukyan is the only possible source of that false information."

NBN Breaking News has been unable to obtain a comment today from Speaker Manukyan or his staff.

NBN's security correspondent, Arshad Iqbal, speculated that the "false information" may relate to a headline item on the Washington Record website last night citing an anonymous source "inside the administration" who claimed Taiwan's government had asked China for a ceasefire and opened reunification negotiations.

A Taiwanese government spokesperson subsequently denied the report.

Sitting at his dining table with coffee, whole-grain toast and a boiled egg in front of him, HR Rosenstern flicked through the headlines covering the Manukyan arrest and put his cell phone down.

He held his hot egg with a napkin and tapped the top of it with a spoon, crushing it before lifting it off to show the yolk inside. Perfect. But then HR Rosenstern never left anything to chance, not even his breakfast egg. He always chose large eggs and boiled them for exactly four minutes and 35 seconds, standing over the pot with a spoon so that he could scoop the egg out at just the right moment. Not a second more or less.

He dropped a pinch of salt onto the egg, and a single twist from the pepper grinder. He was already enjoying the prospect of the coming conversation as he ran his spoon around the inside of the eggshell.

Then he picked up his cell phone.

"Ah yes, HR Rosenstern for Speaker Manukyan. Yes, I'll hold …" He dug out the plump egg and dropped it onto his hot, buttered toast, watching with satisfaction as the yolk spread evenly over it. "Ah, Mr. Speaker. No, I …" he winced and held the phone away from his ear. When the man at the other end stopped shouting, he tried to take up the call again. "No, Mr. Speaker, I did not call to gloat. I called to offer you an olive branch. A 'get out of jail free' card, if you will …"

Rosenstern laid it out for Manukyan. Manukyan would drop his campaign to impeach Carliotti, and his opposition to the surge, and Rosenstern would make the Secret Service investigation go away.

Manukyan huffed and puffed, but in the end, he caved. As Rosenstern knew he must.

He put down his phone, took a bite of his toast and smiled. The fix was in. The last meaningful opponent of the Coalition troop surge had been neutralized.

It was going to be a good day.

Lying on the roof of the air conditioning room on the sixth floor of the abandoned parking garage, heart beating fast, out of breath, Burroughs was having a weird flashback - to the time he and his wife to be had been making out on the back porch of her house when her father had woken up and come into the kitchen for a glass of water. They'd frozen. Then, the back door had begun to rattle as he unlocked it. They'd both bolted around the side of the house, backs pressed up against the wall, hearts pounding, waiting to be discovered. He remembered how his wife had taken his hand and squeezed it. Her father stayed on the porch, taking in the air, then went back inside, and they'd started giggling.

He wished she were here now to squeeze his hand and let him know it would be OK. Or no, actually not. Better she was a million miles away from whatever was happening right now.

He heard the roof access door from the stairwell creak open, heard it click shut again. Then silence.

A soft voice, speaking into the darkness.

"Did you jump, Mr. Burroughs? Climb down the outside of the building, maybe? I don't think so." He heard feet walk to the guardrail where he'd thrown his shoe. "The first shoe was inspired. The second is boring."

From over by his shoe, his attacker raised his voice. "There is no way out of the building, Burroughs. I locked the place down and turned off the alarms, so we won't be interrupted. Now I know you won't believe I just want to talk, so I'll do you a deal ... get this over with, and I'll let your body be found. Your children can weep at your funeral, your life insurance will pay out, they won't have to quit college and get food delivery jobs or sell drugs to survive. Or ..." The voice was coming closer. "... or you make me search all over this building, I still kill you, but I'll take your body with me. I know a place not far from here you will never be found. Your kids will wonder for the rest of their unhappy lives what happened to you, but your insurance company will be happy because you'll just be missing, not dead. They won't have to pay your next of kin a cent."

The voice stopped immediately beneath him, waiting. "You're going to keep hiding. What kind of father are you, Burroughs?"

2. The battle of the Eastern Pacific

"Nomad Two, Nomad Leader is 60 kilometers from release waypoint," the CO of the 68th Aggressor Squadron, former RAF pilot 'Meany' Papastopolous, said to his wingman, Second Lieutenant Lukas 'Flatline' Fibak. "I have four targets on the ELINT download, locked and boxed. Confirm you have sync."

Sweeping in toward the Taiwanese coast from their base in Okinawa, Japan, the two P-99 Black Widows of the 68th were each carrying six Joint Air-Surface Standoff Missiles, or JASSMs. The Widow was, in essence, a stealthy missile truck, developed specifically for the war in the Pacific that the USA had known it would one day be fighting again. It could carry a large payload of air-to-air or air-to-surface ordnance, equivalent to the venerable F-15EX, and had double the range of an F-35 Panther.

"Good copy, Nomad Leader," Flatline replied. "Four targets locked and boxed here; ordnance armed and allocated."

"Switchback from Nomad Leader. Ready to poke the hornet's nest, Touchdown?"

"Primed to bring the hurt, Meany," Captain Charlene 'Touchdown' Dubois replied. Dubois and her flight of three F-22s were about 20 kilometers ahead of Meany and Flatline. Their role was to probe China's air defenses north of Shanghai, identify the defensive combat air patrols in the coastal sector south of that city and engage them from long range.

The aim of the attack wasn't to create a hole in what had become known as the Great Air-Wall of China. That would take more than the paltry mission package of five aircraft that

Aggressor Inc. was bringing to the game. But since the US president's announcement that the Coalition would be committing significant ground forces to the defense of Taiwan, Coalition air operations had intensified in an attempt to regain superiority over the Strait.

They were only five aircraft, but five aircraft were enough to do the job they had been assigned—their last before they were pulled off the line and transferred to Misawa Air Base on Japan's Honshu Island, to rest and refit after more than a month of constant combat.

Meany ran his eyes over the tactical plot on his targeting screen. The mission was to take out a Chinese forward command-and-control outpost on the coast south of Shanghai in advance of the day's operations. China's command centers had proven very difficult both to identify and to destroy.

Having learned the lessons of wars like Ukraine and Syria, China had developed hard-wired optical-fiber quantum-encrypted comms networks that ran between every major city and military installation. These gave off zero electromagnetic emissions and were impossible to intercept, even if you put a physical tap on the fiber cable—doing so just collapsed the quantum encryption, scrambling it and letting the sender know it had been intercepted. For mobile communications, China used quantum-radio-based low-emission virtual command posts comprising four light tactical vehicles, or LTVs, that could be parked anywhere in a 5-square-mile area as long as they had line of sight to one another. One vehicle managed local communications via laser-optical digital data transfer. The other three managed air, ground and naval defense coordination, relaying information from front-line units to commanders far in the rear for analysis and direction.

They never stayed in one location for very long. Their electronic emissions signatures were so low they were very hard to lock on to. Knocking out all four units across such a large area took multiple precision strikes that were hard to achieve, and if you didn't knock out all four units, the remaining units could simply take over the roles of those that were destroyed. And because they were purely "virtual," even if you did achieve a total takedown, no senior officers were lost since they were all safely ensconced in bunkers hundreds of miles from the coast.

But they weren't *completely* invisible to US electronic warfare aircraft and satellites, and once located, they could be targeted. The trick was to provoke them to radically increase their emissions profile, which they had to do when an air strike went in. That was Touchdown's job.

Meany could see his missile release waypoint approaching. He could see the air search radars of Chinese frigates and destroyers hugging the safety of the coast 200 kilometers away, none of which had a lock on the Aggressor stealth aircraft. He could see the Chinese fighter aircraft ahead of them that Touchdown's flight of F-22s had identified. Experience told him there would be more that they could not see—China's stealthy J-20 and J-31 fighters.

He had downloaded the last known locations of the four LTVs as four painted electronic signature blobs on his targeting screen. All that remained was to pinpoint their current positions and ensure they were up and emitting radio energy.

The stage was set.

"Alright, Touchdown, wake them up," Meany said.

Switchback flight leader Charlene 'Touchdown' Dubois was worried.

Not about the 20-plus Chinese fighter aircraft she could see roaming the coast 150 kilometers ahead of her. Nor about the 20 or more stealth fighters she *couldn't* see, which would be anywhere between her and those she *could* see. She was worried about Jack 'Magellan' Chang, the Republic of China Taiwan Air Force pilot embedded with the 68th Aggressors and now flying about 5 kilometers off her port wing.

He was coming up on 20 combat sorties, or about 60 hours, in just under a month. Every pilot in the 68th had been flying from day one of the conflict, but none of the others were flying and fighting for their country's survival. None of the others had volunteered to cover for every single slot in a mission that couldn't be filled because other pilots were fatigued, sick or suffering from the effects of constant high-g maneuvers. As flight leader, Touchdown had access to the data from his combat AI downloads post-mission, and they showed Magellan was relying more and more on the F-22's recently upgraded AI to fly and land for him—a sure sign of fatigue.

But no one in the 68th had more skin in this fight than 'Magellan' Chang.

"Switchback flight, maintain separation. Sending target data now," she said, tapping the icons on her main screen that were the known enemy aircraft the Aggressors, the Navy AWACS aircraft behind them and Taiwan's low-frequency ground radars had detected. The targets were automatically distributed between the three fighters in her flight. The closest was 180 kilometers out, the farthest 220. Inside the engagement envelope for their AIM-260 missiles but not optimal. She wanted to be inside 200 kilometers before they let fly, give the Mach 5 missiles less than 90 seconds to run, increase the chances of surprising their targets.

But they were up at 40,000 feet to give their missiles a shorter run time, and it increased their chances of detection if there was a Chinese stealth fighter lurking in their sector.

"Switchback Two has data sync," her wingman said.

"Switchback Three has sync," Magellan said. He sounded alright, but then, he always did when their mission was about to get kinetic. No one could accuse him of not being on his game when the missiles started to fly.

Touchdown checked the surrounding sky, then ran her eyes over the radar and satellite data. *No new signatures.* Her screen showed the two other aircraft had armed their missiles and were actively tracking the targets she'd given them. Each F-22 carried six AIM-260 medium-range missiles and two shorter-range Peregrine dogfighting missiles.

They had about 24 potential targets and only 18 longer-range missiles to throw at them. But the math was the math.

They crept closer to the Chinese coast. *Two ten kilometers, two oh five, two hundred, one ninety.* "Nomad, Switchback, we are in position," she told Meany. "Switchback pilots, you are free to engage. Two, stay on my wing as soon as your missiles are away. We'll change heading, then we're going to keep pushing in. Three, take overwatch."

"Two copies."

"Three copies."

One eighty kilometers. Her thumb caressed the firing button on her flight stick. "Fox three," she called. The doors of her payload bay snapped open, and her missiles dropped out in pairs, lit their tails and streaked away toward the horizon, trailing thin white vapor. Contrails that would point back to the aircraft that fired them, if there was an unseen enemy within visual range as they passed. Left and right of her, she saw the contrails of the other Aggressor pilots' missiles following hers.

Down on the coast south of Shanghai, the Chinese command center was about to get very, very busy.

Touchdown didn't need to keep a radar lock on the targets herself while they were flying; they would guide themselves based on the target's projected position, only lighting up their own radars once they got 20 kilometers, or about 10 seconds, from their targets.

"Breaking left to 180," she said, putting her machine into a gentle banking turn to take it away from the scene of the crime.

"With you, Switchback Leader," her wingman told her.

"Three going high," Magellan said.

Jack 'Magellan' Chang eased his stick back and pushed his throttle forward, and his Raptor rocketed to 30,000, then 40,000, to 50,000 feet.

He was bone-tired. But he kept his fatigue at bay when he was in the cockpit with a fuel made of cold fury. Though he admired the commitment of his Aggressor Squadron hosts, like a lot of Taiwan's pilots, Magellan had very personal reasons for pushing himself beyond, and they weren't all fed by blind patriotism.

Magellan's uncle, Lin Tang, had been at home in Dunhua on the first day of the attacks by the killer drones, which had already earned the media nickname *shārèng jīqì*, or "slaughterbot." A slaughterbot had poured 20 mm cannon fire into a busy shopping center across the road from his apartment, and Tang had run outside to help the wounded.

Where he had been gunned down by a second drone coming in to finish the work of the first.

At 50,000 feet, he started weaving back and forth, trying to locate any threats before they …

A tone sounded in his ears, and his eyes darted to his radar warning receiver screen. *Airborne search radar.* Off to starboard. No lock on them yet, but it wasn't one of the aircraft on his own tactical plot.

Chinese stealth fighter. And where there was one …

"You seeing this, Switchback Leader?" he checked, holding his course for the moment, trying to get some separation between him, the launch point of their missiles and the new contact.

"Got it, Magellan," she replied. "Move to bracket."

Every second they stayed broadside on to the Chinese fighter was another second they might be seen, but he wanted to get south of it, help Touchdown set up in the north so they could engage it from two directions. "Roger that. I'll come back around. You can push in and try to lock it up."

It was a deadly game they had been playing with China's stealth fighters since the first day of the conflict. And it was best played at standoff range, with long-range missiles, not like this, where they had to get within 100 kilometers, ideally within 50, to engage with their Peregrine missiles. In stealth vs. stealth combat, the pilot who saw their enemy first was usually the winner. Against the larger J-20, the small and nimble F-22 had an advantage in radar cross-section and a comparable scanning array radar. It would usually find the J-20 first and could get to knife-fighting range before it was seen.

"Contact, bearing two seven nine, altitude 32,000 feet, range eight nine, heading … headed right for me," Magellan said. "I have a solution—ready to engage. Uh, AI signature analysis says it's a Gyrfalcon."

J-31 Gyrfalcon. Dammit, Touchdown cursed inwardly. The newer Gyrfalcon was a near rivet-for-rivet copy of America's F-35, with the main differences being two engines instead of one, which made it more vulnerable to attack with heat-seeking missiles from the rear. So …

"Light it up and pull it toward you, Magellan," she ordered. "I'll bring us around behind. Switchback Two, arm a Peregrine in infrared seeker mode."

Her hand tightened on her flight stick as she swung her machine around and pointed it at the new enemy. They could only see one Chinese stealth fighter right now.

A Gyrfalcon *never* hunted alone.

Meany watched Touchdown's missiles converge on their targets as his Black Widows moved closer to the Chinese coast. He had taken his flight down to sea level, and they had armed their JASSM-E missiles. Above them, signals detection satellites were passing over the Chinese coast, waiting for the Chinese mobile command post to break out of its low-emissions state to try to coordinate a response to their attack.

The first of the American AIM-260 missiles reached a target. What had been an orderly pattern of patrols along the coast in the sector surrounding the Chinese command post became one of chaos as the remaining 17 Chinese pilots broke in all directions, missile warnings no doubt screaming in their ears.

"Come on, Colonel Whoeveryouare, wake up down there," Meany muttered. It was the waiting Meany hated most: those deadly seconds as you drew closer to the enemy, the curvature of the earth between you and them flattening out and the chances of discovery increasing exponentially. All he needed was …

"Signature lock," he said with satisfaction, watching as a satellite overhead squirted data to them and the four red and yellow electronic signature blobs resolved themselves into four clean targets, each about 10 kilometers from the other. A single bomb or artillery strike wouldn't be able to take them out altogether, but that was why his Widows were aloft.

He got to work allocating his JASSMs. "Nomad Two, take the two in the north; confirm your targets," he ordered. He boxed the two southernmost mobile units, not much bigger than a Humvee in reality. Hitting each vehicle with 2,000 lb. warheads was probably already overkill, but someone wanted 100 percent surety this CP would be blinded in advance of the day's operations, so he'd been ordered to send eight missiles downrange in the first attack and save four in case a follow-up attack was needed.

"Targets locked," Flatline intoned.

Meany did a last check of the tactical environment. Touchdown and her F-22s were hunting to the south now. She'd stay on task until the target was down and he called her back. No ground or naval radars in their neighborhood, no sign of Chinese fighters nosing into Taiwan's airspace right now.

Get to work, get home, Meany told himself. It was hard not already to be mentally on the way to Misawa Air Base and a long overdue pint of Asahi lager.

He had four targets, four green lights on the missiles in his payload bay. He checked his altitude and eased his stick back, lifting the Widow to its launch altitude of 5,000 feet.

"Rifle," he announced, thumbing the missile release button. The Black Widow pursuit fighter was no F-22. More like a cut-down B-21 bomber than a fighter plane, it was basically a 50,000 lb. stealth-coated, delta-shaped flying wing. Nonetheless, he felt the thump and rode the bump as four JASSMs dropped from the belly of his machine.

"Rifle," Flatline repeated. Eight cruise missiles pulled away in front of them. Each pilot rolled their machine onto a wingtip and began a slow circle—they had to remain on station until the strike went in and the targets winked out of existence. The JASSM-E was GPS-guided for its initial run but then homed on the electronic signature of its target in its—literally—terminal phase. The satellites overhead would tell them the second the Chinese command post went dark.

"Radar on my six!" Magellan called out. "Missile launch; evading!"

Touchdown's flight had gone from hunter to hunted in the blink of an eye. One moment, they were setting up their attack on the Chinese Gyrfalcon, seconds away from launching; the next, her number three was spiraling down from 50,000 feet, missiles from an unseen foe screaming toward him, and the Gyrfalcon they had been tracking had spun on its axis and was trying to set up a firing solution on *them*!

"Vertical break, going high," Touchdown said. She firewalled her throttle, pulled her machine into a near-vertical

50

climb as her number two did the opposite and dived for the deck.

She watched on her tac screen with satisfaction as Magellan dodged the missiles chasing him and hauled his machine around in an aggressive turn to put his nose on his attacker. "Fox two," he called, loosing a short-range missile.

"Engaging," Touchdown announced as she rolled her machine onto its back, pulled back her throttle and bracketed her target with her radar at the same moment as he locked her up. "Fox two," she said, even as her radar warning receiver began warbling a warning in her ears. "Evading."

She'd done her job though—gotten the Chinese pilot's attention, allowed her number two to slip in low, under his guard.

"Fox two," Magellan announced.

Touchdown turned her attention back to Magellan. She worked her radar frantically, filling the air ahead of him with radar energy, trying to find his attacker. *There.* A Gyrfalcon, down low. The Chinese had used their own tactics against them, baited them up high with a decoy and attacked them with a punch to the groin. But she had him now.

"Magellan, break. I'm engaging," she told the Taiwanese pilot.

"Copy," he said with a grunt as he complied.

She was boring in on the Chinese fighter behind Magellan. Sixty kilometers out. *Missile to active radar guidance mode. Lock.*

Fire.

Her attention split like a fairground mirror. She had her eyes on the sky, on her tactical screen, on her instruments as she hauled her machine around the sky, saw the missile from her number two go wide, the Chinese pilot off her starboard quarter successfully avoiding him, heard her wingman fire again. Saw Meany and Flatline launch on the Chinese command post. Saw Magellan's machine rise from 10,000 to 30,000 feet in the space of seconds, saw her own missile closing on his attacker.

Kill!

She shoved her throttle forward again, pulled her nose around and trained her radar on the same target her wingman was targeting.

The Chinese pilot "lost his bottle," as Meany would say. Her screen showed him flip like a dime in the air about 50 kilometers away and put his nose down as he bolted for the Chinese coast. She checked the targets they had fired on 100 kilometers away. Where there had been 20, she saw 15 or so now. Someone would tell her how many kills they'd scored at some point later. The only one she was sure of was the last. That Gyrfalcon pilot, if he or she survived, would be swimming home.

"Switchback flight, form on me," she said. They'd done their job, dealt some pain, drawn the heat. They had to get out of Dodge before the officers of that command post marshaled their reserves and sent them after her like a pack of hounds baying for her blood.

Meany was studying the same tactical plot as Touchdown, but with different emotions: relief that his fighter screen was pulling back now, unscathed. And tension as his JASSM attack approached the Chinese coast. Any second now they would switch to "home on emissions" mode and zero in on the four Chinese command post vehicles, which should've been frantically trying to coordinate air defenses in the sector south of Shanghai.

"Looks like we got off cheaply," Flatline observed. "You know any good bars in Misawa?"

"Fat lady hasn't sung yet," Meany told him. "Head in the game, Nomad Two."

But he didn't blame Flatline for wanting to celebrate already. They'd had several hard weeks on the line. Lost two pilots—Flowmax and O'Hare. And for what? China had launched a new kind of drone mother ship at Taiwan, one that was almost impossible to intercept and that scattered autonomous bots all over the island. They roamed at will, attacking with impunity, and self-destructed when their ammunition was expended. Microwave weapons could bring them down, but Taiwan didn't have enough of the vehicle-mounted HPM cannons to make a difference. Taiwanese troops engaged the slaughterbots with Man Portable Air Defenses, or MANPADs, but every day a thousand new bots were sent across the Strait, and Taiwan didn't have enough MANPADs to meet the onslaught.

The 68th Aggressor was being pulled off the line to rest and refit in Misawa, but Meany seriously doubted they would be redeployed. Coalition air- and submarine-launched missile strikes were preventing the Chinese from assembling their invasion fleet, but that seemed like a hollow victory. He'd heard the Taiwanese "war cabinet" had lost two members to killer bot attacks and was considering suing for peace. It felt to him like China was about to get exactly what it wanted, without a single Chinese soldier setting foot on Taiwan.

Park those thoughts, pilot, Meany told himself. *You still have a job to do.*

Their attack was 50 kilometers out. The JASSMs were homing on the enemy's emissions now.

But as he watched and waited, the four targets on hilltops south of Shanghai disappeared. One second, they had been there, on his tactical screen. The next, they were *gone*. Meany had seen radar and radio signals go dark if the operators thought they were under attack, but this was different. All four units dropped off the grid simultaneously.

Then a small warning in the lower right corner of his heads-up display got his attention. *Battlenet link lost … battlenet link lost …*

Meany frantically went through the procedure to reconnect.

"Uh, Nomad Leader, I've lost …"

"Me too," Meany told Flatline. "Wait one."

Their missiles had only 10-minute-old GPS targeting data now. And GPS targeting data was next to useless against a target that relocated on a random schedule. The missiles could home on the target's radio emissions using onboard passive sensors, but frequency-hopping Chinese radios and the use of mobile relay stations meant a precision strike could only be delivered when signals were triangulated by an electronic intelligence, or ELINT, satellite overhead. JASSMs took their targeting from the P-99 Widows, which in turn took their targeting from overhead satellites. The Widow pulled down the data and then bounced it up to another satellite, which bounced it to the JASSMs to give them a real-time target to steer on. Without their battlenet link, the E in the JASSM-E missiles was redundant.

Meany called back to the mission controller on an AWACS aircraft circling northeast of Taipei.

"Uh, Lamprey Control, Nomad flight leader. My missiles are running blind, and we seem to have lost our link to the battlenet," he said. "Nomad is rebooting …"

"Copy that, Nomad. We seem to have heavy Chinese downlink jamming on your allocated satellite. I can't get bandwidth on a backup for you inside the next 20 minutes."

Meany thought fast. Their missiles were outbound. Time to target … four minutes. "Uh, won't help, Lamprey. Our ordnance is on the way to the target, and if it misses, the target will just shut down and hide. Nothing more we can do here without that link. Request permission to RTB."

"Nomad, you are cleared to RTB. Mission abort is approved," the AWACS controller said. "Lamprey out."

Bugger me sideways, Meany thought to himself. He reached for his radio control. "Switchback, Nomad Leader. We're done here, Touchdown. Bug the hell out. See you on Okinawa."

"Good copy, Nomad. Switchback flight is bugging out," Touchdown replied.

Meany was waiting on the apron as Touchdown taxied her Raptor to a halt in front of him. He stretched his muscles wearily. Roomy as it was for a normal pilot, the cockpit of the P-99 Black Widow was cramped for a man who used an exoskeleton bolted to his legs to get around.

He didn't complain. He was still flying, which was more than he'd expected when the doctor in the hospital in Crete told him he was paralyzed from the waist down after ejecting from his RAF Tempest fighter over Syria. Let alone that he'd be flying a sixth-generation multirole fighter not a million miles different in task and purpose to the World War II Beaufighter his great grandfather flew against the Japanese over Burma.

He locked his exoskeleton into a knee-bent posture that allowed him to wait comfortably as Dubois popped the canopy on her Raptor. She handed her helmet to the airman on the ladder before climbing down herself.

She looked worried. "That's starting to happen too often for my liking," she said. "Either China is getting better at satellite jamming, or our battlenet link is getting less stable."

"We'll have to wait to hear the results of the strike," Meany said. "We might have gotten lucky." He shifted his weight and started moving back toward the ready room. "Anyway, not our problem anymore. We're off the line."

She fell into step beside him, which wasn't easy considering his stride was augmented by his exoskeleton. "You been to Misawa before? How's the local food?"

"I hear it's good, but we won't get to try it," he said. "We're not going to Misawa after all."

"You just said we're being taken off the line, so where? Philippines? Guam?"

"No. Joint Base Hickam, Pearl Harbor," he said. "I just got word our war is over. Officially, USAF has advised it has sufficient assets in theater now and no longer has need of our services. We'll relieve our guys doing Aggressor training for units rotating through Hawaii on the way to Taiwan."

Touchdown should have looked happy at that news. She didn't. "Are you kidding me? We have the highest kill-to-loss ratio in the entire theater, and they 'no longer need our services'?"

"I said that was the official version," Meany told her. "Unofficial version is that there's a General at INDOPACAF who isn't happy a private contractor is showing better results than his regular fighter wings."

Touchdown shook her head sadly, then fixed him with a glare. "What about O'Hare? We're just going to leave the theater without …"

"Aggressor Inc. doesn't leave people behind," Meany told her. "Dead or alive. There's an Aggressor Inc. aircraft at Taichung Air Base waiting for her. If she's alive, she can fly it out herself. And if not …"

"It'll fly her body home? That's some consolation, Meany."

"Yeah, well, sometimes there's no way to sugarcoat it," he replied.

3. The battle of the Killer Bees

Bunny O'Hare wasn't dead. But that was about the only thing she knew for sure.

Eyes only half open, brain fogged. *Just sleep*, a voice was saying. Her own voice. Good advice.

She slept. Dreamed she was floating. She batted her arms helplessly, like a turtle flipped onto its back. Then her head went under. Boots dragged her down. Dragged her deeper. She flapped to the surface again, managed to pull in some air, coughed water from her lungs as she tried to pry her boots off with numb fingers until finally just kicking them free.

Laying with arms outspread, head tilted back, looking up at the stars in confusion. The dam—had she fallen in the dam near the homestead?

Ah, no.

She let her eyes close. She could taste saltwater.

The sea.

She'd bailed out into the sea off the Chinese coast. It came back now. How long ago? She remembered hitting the water, chute separating, looking for her seat and raft … nothing. Vest around her neck inflating. Pulling her hundred-thousand-dollar helmet off and watching it sink into the Taiwan Strait. Then nothing. Must have blacked out. Now she was awake again.

Her limbs were responding, but she couldn't feel her extremities. She was swaddled in something. Her brain regressing back to babyhood now? She rolled her head, moaning with the pain in her neck. OK, that wasn't normal in a dream. She blinked her eyes. Low gray light. Dark walls. Cabinet with … medicines?

58

Closed her eyes again, concentrated on what she could hear. Nothing. No, not nothing. Voices, somewhere outside the room.

And a smell. Smells. Vomit and cleaning fluid.

She tried flexing her fingers, wiggling her toes. She could feel them, but they were bound. Her hands bound at the wrist, arms by her side. Feet bound by the ankle, a couple of feet apart. She twisted slowly. That hurt. Tied to something. A belt or rope across her waist too.

She tried to lift her head, but the pain nearly made her scream. She saw her feet, a door beyond. No light coming through the door, so it must be dark in the corridor outside.

Then she heard voices. Speaking Mandarin.

She tried to muster her fogged thinking into the good, the bad and the ugly about what this all told her. The good: She'd been rescued. If the smell and surroundings were anything to go by, she was in a hospital or clinic of some sort. She was alive and more or less well, potentially lifelong neck injury aside. The bad: She was strapped to a gurney hand, foot and waist and couldn't even scratch herself. The ugly: The voices could be Taiwanese, which would be good, but they could also be Chinese, which would be bad.

That mystery was about to solve itself. The door opened, and she tried to raise her head again to get a look at whoever was coming in.

Nurse, she decided, letting her head slump back down onto the bunk she was tied to. The woman was in her 60s, Asian, green military uniform. Her face was lined and serious behind a face mask. So she was right; she was in a medical facility. But whose?

The woman loomed over her, looking nervous. She had a cell phone or some kind of device in her hand.

59

"Wh—" Bunny tried talking, but coughed painfully instead.

She had lifted her head again as the coughing spasm swept through her, and the nurse put a hand under her head to support it, then lowered it down again as the coughing subsided. She spoke rapid-fire Mandarin into the cell phone and then held it down by Bunny's ear for her to hear the translation. Bizarrely, the voice from the phone had an Irish accent. She saw now the woman was holding a flask of water, and she waved it near her face.

"Stay still; you might be injured. You are safe," the device said. "Have some water."

Bunny wasn't sure she believed her, but she lifted her head again and the nurse cradled it as she drank, washing the putrid taste from her mouth. Bunny realized now the vomit she could smell was probably her own.

She managed to clear her throat. "Why ... where am I? Why am I tied up?" The nurse held the device out to her so she could repeat her question.

When it had finished translating, the nurse spoke into the device again. "You are in Navy Clinic Penghu Island. You came in unconscious and vomiting, developed a bad fever, and you have been moving too much, so we tied you down in case you had spinal injuries."

"Which navy?" Bunny asked.

The nurse frowned and held the device down to her again. "Taiwan Navy. You were rescued by a couple of fishermen." Now she smiled as he spoke, and the device translated. "Your rescuers are outside. Each pilot they bring in gives a $100,000 reward. They have been waiting two weeks for you to come around. They will be very happy to see you. A live pilot is better than fish."

60

Better than fish? One of the nicest things anyone had ever called her. "I'll lie still," Bunny said. "You can untie me." Bunny tensed. Would she? If this really was a Taiwan Navy facility, she should. But if it was Chinese and the woman was lying …

The nurse put down her device and undid the belt around her waist, then started unstrapping her wrists and ankles. When she was done, Bunny lifted herself gingerly up onto her elbows.

"Would you like to meet the men who saved you?" the nurse asked.

"Uh, sure," Bunny said. She didn't exactly feel like entertaining, but if her rescuers had been waiting two weeks for her to come around, then the least she could do was greet them and say thanks. Though she still wasn't entirely convinced that she wasn't in a Chinese facility and the people about to be invited in weren't PLA interrogators.

The nurse was gone for several minutes. Then the door opened again, causing Bunny to blink at the light behind the two figures walking into her room.

The door closed behind them, and she knew the nurse had been telling the truth.

The two men stank of fish.

The older of Bunny O'Hare's rescuers was from at least six generations of fishermen, and he knew the temperamental seas of the Taiwan Strait better than he knew his own wife's mind. His name was Lin Zhiwei, and he had bigger worries than whether his tiny island would be able to withstand the Chinese onslaught its war-hungry leaders had triggered with their "preemptive act of self-defense."

Zhiwei's family had been fishing in the Taiwan Strait when the waters were controlled by the Tower Ship vessels of the Han dynasty. They fished all the way through World Wars I and II, they helped smuggle arms to the Kuomintang army, and then they helped ferry the Kuomintang soldiers and their officers to Taiwan when they fled from Mao's forces. As American and Chinese ships harried each other up and down the Strait through the latter part of the 20th and early 21st centuries, they fished.

But it was Zhiwei's fear that he would be the last fisherman of the Lin family. His only son, Hungyu, showed no interest in the life his father led. Zhiwei had tried to tempt him with the promise of a boat of his own. Together with his brother, Hungyu's uncle, they had formed a cooperative of eight boats, strong financially but also big enough to stand against the Chinese marauders who plundered their waters and tried to scare them away. With nine boats, they would be even stronger, once the fury of war had passed over them. The commercial opportunity hadn't appealed to Hungyu, nor had the appeals to his family heritage. Hungyu had helped his father on his boat until he was old enough for university, and then he had left their house in Dongshi and moved to Taipei to study robotics.

He had started with a vague idea that he might find an alternative way to farm the seas than the large commercial fish farms that lay waste to square mile after square mile of coastal seabed, or the trawlers, like his father's, that turned the waters of the Strait into aqueous deserts, so devoid of fish stock that Chinese and Taiwanese fishermen had fought for control of the seas with their very lives, even before the war had broken out.

No wonder his father spent his nights searching for a fortune falling from the skies, like a man with gold fever spending his last dollar on a mule and a pickax.

Hungyu had a different vision of his future. He had started by studying underwater robotics, even filed his first patent in the field of commercial fish farming, after he identified that ocean trout could be trained to school around robotic "alpha" fish emitting the same sound frequency through their gills that wild trout emitted when they found a food source. Though he never got to test it, his hypothesis was that a school of his robotic fish could be sent out into the ocean to attract wild fish and then lead them into captivity. No more men in boats dragging their nets through the sea, destroying everything they caught, just a few of his robotic "alphas" leading school after school of the desired species into pens for harvesting.

He never tried to get his patent into prototype testing because his wandering mind became preoccupied with another application of robotics to the tendency of wild animals to form schools or flocks. He became fascinated with the swirling dance of starlings and their ability to form flocks containing thousands of birds that twisted and turned through the sky as though they were a single living organism. They did it with a speed that could not possibly involve verbal communication since the birds in the center of a flock of 1,000 birds, surrounded by 2,000 beating wings, could not possibly hear a chirped command, and in any case, researchers had found none.

Hungyu learned that in a similar fashion to his alpha trout, each of the super-flocks was led by just a few alpha birds, whose movements the others copied slavishly by watching only the movement of the birds immediately around them.

The alpha flew up and left, those behind him did the same, and 1,000 others followed until a new alpha took up the fight, broke away in a fashion compelling enough to pull the birds near him with him, and the entire flock turned again, following a new leader. He developed AI algorithms that mimicked the action of starlings in microdrones, and awed his PhD supervisor when he took him out to a field and showed him 1,000 microdrones spinning and turning through the air like a flock of starlings.

"Amazing," his supervisor said, awestruck, watching the dense cloud of drones stretch, split, coalesce, break into two and then reform again, over and over. "You have recreated one of the wonders of nature." After a few more minutes of watching the cloud of drones swirl and dance, his supervisor put his hand on Hungyu's shoulder. "But to what end, Hungyu? What application does your research lend itself to, other than simple entertainment?"

Hungyu wasn't disheartened. Simple entertainment was not to be underrated. Hungyu registered his second patent based on creating a 3D moving diorama with his flocking drones, and in addition to earning him his PhD, it earned him a tidy sum of money when he sold the patent to a large American theme park conglomerate. They had just opened a theme park outside Taipei, and he enjoyed seeing the videos people posted of multicolored flocks of his microdrones swirling over the spires of the theme park's fantasy castle.

It wasn't long after that the drums of war began beating. His father returned, shaken, from a fishing voyage in the company of his consortium of boats in which one of the boats had nearly been sunk in a collision with a Chinese coast guard vessel after being surrounded and isolated by a larger number of Chinese fishing vessels. "War is coming," his

64

father told him. "We will have to move our boats into the seas east of Taiwan, but the Chinese fishing fleets are there too, and there are no free berths in Keelung or Kaohsiung. We will have to sail two days just to get to the fishing grounds, and our countrymen will not be happy to share their catch with us." If he sounded glum after that incident, he became even more so after China announced its blockade and started using its navy to turn back any boat or ship that tried to leave Taiwanese territorial waters.

Hungyu had been working on a commission from the theme park people who wanted him to evolve his flocking algorithm so that the microdrones could create "3D cinema in the sky." His heart wasn't in it. Mimicking a few static images was one thing; having his flock generate a cinematic experience frame by frame was quite another. He found himself spending more time playing chess with his despondent father than working on the theme park commission. But the threat to his island home galvanized him.

He began wondering whether his technology could have any military application. One of his former grad school friends was working at Taiwan's Defense Technology Development Office (DTDO) and he invited him out for a beer. After they were caught up, he put his idea to him.

"Swarming drones are nothing new," the guy told him. "Sorry. We have a half dozen systems already deployed. Another four or five in development …"

"But what's the biggest dynamically maneuvering swarm you've launched at a target simultaneously? Twenty, 50 drones?"

His buddy had smiled. "That's classified, but … yeah, you're in the ballpark."

"Because more than that, you can't coordinate," Hungyu speculated. "You either use radio signals to synchronize them, which can be jammed, or give them laser-based comms, which can't be jammed but can be degraded by simple dust or smoke or tinfoil chaff." He leaned forward over the table. "My flocks use a mimicry-based algorithm and just follow their leader. And I'm not talking 10, or 20, or 200. I'm talking 1,000. The tech is scalable; there's no reason you couldn't take it to 5,000, or 10,000!"

"Microdrones," his buddy said, after a moment's thought. "With tiny colored flashing LEDs, right? What would happen if you put your algorithm into a modern kamikaze drone, quadrotor, 20 lb. warhead …?"

He paused. "They wouldn't be maneuverable enough to flock," he admitted. "Not with the algorithm as it is."

His friend gave him an encouraging pat on the shoulder. "You're bringing a solution to a problem we don't have. Our problem isn't how to make our swarms bigger. So let's come at this the opposite way; I'll tell you our problems, and you can think about how your algorithm can solve them."

"Alright," Hungyu said, pulling out the notepad and pen he carried with him everywhere.

"We're in an arms race, with every advance we make being met by a counter technology that requires a new generation of drone." He drew a line in beer with his finger and put his fingertip at the start of it. "2000s: Israel started using drones to assassinate terrorists. Terrorists started sending drones into Israeli settlements. Israel built Iron Dome to shoot down rockets and missiles, had to find a new solution to bring down small, low-flying drones.

"2020s: Ukraine used commercial hobby drones for artillery spotting and dropping hand grenades into Russian foxholes. Russia replied with Lancet kamikaze drones and massed drone attacks on Kyiv. Both sides eventually got smart and developed better jamming systems that brought the radio-controlled drones down or messed with their GPS so that the only things that could get through were dumb, inertially guided drones with the accuracy of a Grad rocket, but a Grad could carry a bigger warhead, so they went back to lobbing rockets and artillery shells at each other.

"2030s: Syria. Iranians and Syrians launched the first real drone swarms at the Israelis—not just a few drones all fired at once but small groups, using laser comms to coordinate their strike, distributed intelligence to choose targets and prioritize. The Israelis tried using pulsed lasers to take them down, and that worked alright, until they found themselves facing swarms of 20 at a time. The US came up with high-powered microwave systems that fried their insides and dropped anything that got close. So everyone started hardening their drones against microwave attack, and we're building more and more powerful microwave emitters to burn through. We're still flying the big legacy drones like the Fantom, Okhotnik and Chongming using satellite commands, which can't be jammed from the ground, but they're vulnerable to aerial jamming, so keeping a solid link to an uncrewed fighter aircraft with satellites that can burn aerial enemy jamming—that's a whole other arms race ... and we haven't gotten to undersea drones yet."

He kept going until Hungyu was worried his pen would run out of ink. Then he drained the last of his beer and put his glass down. "If your flocking algorithm and microdrones can solve any of those problems, give me a call, and I'll let you buy me another beer."

It was Hungyu's turn to be despondent. Taiwan's defenders had problems, a multitude of them. None of his ideas seemed to solve any of them.

He pitched a couple of other ideas to his buddy, got nowhere, so he tried sending his ideas to other contacts, in the Navy, Army, Air Force and finally, in desperation as the shooting war started across the Strait, just to random mil-tech mailing addresses he found on the internet. Eventually, his buddy called him. "Hungyu, you have to give it up. I know you want to help, but you know what people at DTDO are starting to call you? Bird man."

"Bird man?" Hungyu frowned.

"On account of you have no flocking idea what you are talking about," his friend said. "Look, a million people would wish they were you right now. You have this sweet deal with the theme park people, and blockade or war, it doesn't stop you working. They just want your AI code, right? So leave the warmongering to us, and go back to the entertainment business, alright, brother?"

The war however, had other ideas. When the combatants started using hypersonic missiles against each other's aircraft carriers, Taiwan's government issued a national mobilization edict. All men and women between 18 and 60 were ordered to report for military service unless they were engaged in a critical occupation.

Hungyu did not want to go into the military, but theme park AI coder was not on the critical occupation list. Fisherman was.

Which was how Hungyu found himself aboard his father's fishing boat, cruising the Taiwan Strait, looking out for Chinese warships or drowning Coalition pilots.

Not that he ever expected, when they found this one, that she would be five foot eight, with a platinum buzz cut and covered in tattoos.

The two men were nervous, and the older man pushed the younger one forward.

"Uh, I am Hungyu Zhiwei, and this is my father, Lin," the young man said in English. "We are glad to see you alive."

I bet you are, Bunny thought wryly. *A hundred thousand dollars glad.* "Karen O'Hare," she said. She held her hand out, suddenly realizing how weak she still felt. The young man shook it tentatively. They sat awkwardly in chairs at the side of the room, like they didn't really know what else to say.

"The nurse told me you guys pulled me out of the sea?" Bunny asked. "Thanks for that. I guess I was in bad shape."

"You had swallowed some water," the younger man said, in what was probably polite understatement. "We got you breathing again, but you were not conscious when we brought you here."

"Thanks, again. Can I ... What is the date?"

"It is June 11."

"And when did you rescue me?"

"May 28."

Bunny lay back on her bed. Two weeks. She had been here two damn weeks! "I need to get back to my unit," she said to no one in particular.

"We will take you to the mainland," the young man said. "It is why we waited."

Bunny got up on an elbow again. "That's very kind. But a helo would be faster. If I can get a message to my unit, they will send ..."

"No helos," the old man said. Clearly he had been following the conversation, even if he wasn't confident joining it until now.

"Look, if it's about the reward, I'll make sure you get paid," Bunny said.

The young man looked confused. "That is not why. The hospital here can vouch for the fact we rescued you. We are 60 kilometers from Taiwan island. There are no helicopters, no aircraft. No navy boats or ships are making it through to Penghu anymore."

"But a fishing boat can make it?" she asked, dubiously.

The young man nodded. "The military can explain. When you are able to walk, we can take you to the harbormaster."

They stood and gave her a little bow, then withdrew. Could she believe them? The situation in the Strait had deteriorated so badly that the Taiwan Air Force couldn't get a helo across 60 kilometers of water to rescue her? They were right about one thing; she needed to speak to someone in the military.

She spoke to the nurse again, got some food, then waited impatiently for a doctor to come and sign her out. While she was waiting, she tested her legs, pacing around her room. She was sore, and weak, felt like she'd been in a head-on car crash.

But she was alive.

The doctor was clearly in a hurry and didn't do more than give her chart a cursory check before peering into her eyes with a small flashlight, listening to her breathe, and having her bend and stretch for him. "You need an MRI," he told her. "We can't do that kind of thing here."

"What I need is a telephone or radio," Bunny told him.

He didn't look sympathetic. "Report to the Navy, at the harbormaster's office," he said, signing her chart and walking out.

Her two guardian angels were hovering in the corridor outside when she emerged from her room in a badly fitting Taiwan Navy uniform that someone had left on a chair for her. At least they had saved her boots for her; they were dry now, but they had a smell that could wake the dead.

Hungyu handed her a snack bar and a bottle of water. "Navy harbormaster?" he asked.

"Yes, please."

Walking outside the clinic, she saw she had been in a blue-roofed two-story building alongside a dock. A few fishing boats and a tug were tied up at the dock. Uniformed Navy personnel moved quickly between buildings, glancing nervously up at the sky.

Then she saw why. From a point across the harbor, there was the *whoosh* of a missile launch. A contrail of white smoke curved into the sky before exploding in the distance. She could see all the way across the harbor to a few streets with buildings, and then the sea on the other side. It was a very *small* island.

The only military vessel to be seen was what might once have been a corvette or patrol boat. It was about 100 meters out into the harbor, down by the head, half-submerged with steam or thin white smoke trailing into the air from its stern.

She wouldn't be getting back to Taiwan on that one.

In the harbormaster's office, a Taiwan Navy Lieutenant Colonel confirmed what the fishermen had told her—she wasn't going to be choppered anywhere, and he warned the two fishermen they shouldn't try to leave the islands either.

"Chinese autonomous drones—what the media are calling 'slaughterbots'—are hitting anything smaller than a main battle tank that moves on the mainland," he said. "Anti-air capabilities are at 30 percent; anti-ship at 40 percent. Aircraft are getting destroyed on the ground as soon as they land."

"We got out," the younger Taiwanese fisherman insisted. "We can get back again."

"I need to contact my squadron," Bunny told him.

"We have had no communication with the mainland for a week," the harbormaster told her. "Undersea cable was cut. The Chinese are jamming our radio."

"We will take you back," the young fisherman said again.

"I can't stop you. You can try." The Lieutenant Colonel shrugged. He looked out the harbormaster's office window, down at the motley ranks of the fishing vessels lining the dock. "And you can die. The drones leave most small boats alone, but I heard of boats smaller than yours being attacked."

"I don't understand," Bunny said with a frown. "Can't Taiwan's air defenses deal with these drones? The main island is crowded with radar-guided cannon systems, ground-to-air missiles, truck-mounted microwave, armor-mounted laser …"

"We haven't seen them on Penghu yet," he said. "Not important enough, I guess. I can only tell you what I was told before we lost communication. They went after the anti-air missile batteries first, drones armed with 20 mm guns. Then they started hitting anti-ship batteries and tactical vehicles, police, fire trucks and anyone carrying anything that even *looks* like a shoulder-launched missile …"

"Couldn't we jam them?"

"Normal EW attacks didn't seem to work. We think they're autonomous, no radio or satellite links to jam. We hoped armor-mounted laser and microwave units might be able to take them on, but the second wave of drones coming over included some armed with Hongjian anti-armor missiles. The missile-firing drones were going after low-flying aircraft, armor, and military shipping." He looked through the window at the empty skies. "So no helos. And you'd be crazy to risk sailing a boat between here and the mainland."

"What about our bounty?" the young fisherman asked in English, for her benefit. "Can you sign for delivery of the pilot?"

The Lieutenant Colonel looked pained. "Not my area. You'll have to sort that out with Southern Sea Area Command, Kaohsiung. Or the US military."

"Which means we're back to 'How do we get to the mainland?'" Bunny guessed.

He nodded. "That's your problem to solve, I'm sorry. But come back here if you decide you need a billet."

They left the office and stood in a stairwell. Her two rescuers conferred among themselves, and even though Bunny couldn't understand a word, she could sense they were between a very bare rock and a very exposed hard place. At last, something was agreed.

"We need to deliver you back to your people to claim our reward," Hungyu told her.

"I'll sign whatever you need me to sign. You don't need to risk your lives again," Bunny told him. There was no question in her mind she would take the chance if it was offered, but she couldn't ask the two fishermen to put themselves on the hook if they didn't want to.

"He doesn't trust the authorities to pay us," Hungyu said, a resigned note in his voice. "But maybe if you vouch for us?"

"Of course," Bunny said. "Least I can do."

They made their way down to the dock to the men's boat. It was about 20 meters long and shaped like a shoe, with a bluff bow and a small box-shaped wheelhouse in the stern. In the wheelhouse, Hungyu unfolded a map, pointing to a small U-shaped island off the Taiwan coast, not much more than an atoll. "We are here, Magong City. Our port is Dongshi, the closest port. We will go to Dongshi. Two hours sailing."

Outside, she heard another missile launch. She suddenly felt very, very tired again. *If we live that long,* she grimaced inwardly.

They met their first hunter-killer drone about 5 kilometers offshore.

The fishermen had wanted to wait until night, thinking it might offer them some protection, but Bunny convinced them the sort of drones the Navy Lieutenant Colonel had described would almost certainly have infrared night vision, so there was no reason to delay their journey.

Hungyu steered the boat from the wheelhouse, which Bunny could not help but notice had what looked like a 20 mm shell hole in the roof. Following it down, she saw an exit hole in the side wall of the wheelhouse and then a hole in the deck outside. Hungyu watched her walk around the boat, and when she returned to the wheelhouse, he shrugged.

"China airplane," he said. "It missed."

His father sat on the bow with a pair of binoculars, scanning the sea over iron sights with a rifle that looked like it was left over from the 1949 civil war. Bunny stood beside Hungyu, watching the seas behind them. Killer drones weren't their only worry. If Taiwan's air defenses were down, the only thing keeping the Chinese air armada at bay were the Coalition fighters flying out of Okinawa and Luzon in the Philippines—and the holes in the wheelhouse showed that gaps in that line were inevitable.

But there was only so much a pair of Mark I eyeballs could do if she actually spotted a supersonic Yingji anti-ship missile spearing in from behind them. There would barely be time to yell "jump!" between when she saw the contrail and when it hit.

She heard a shot from up ahead and spun around. The old fisherman had his rifle raised to his shoulder, firing at what looked a lot like a seabird in the distance. She ran forward as he was working the bolt on the old rifle, and pushed the barrel down. "Wait," she said and reached for the binoculars on the deck beside him.

It wasn't a gull. His eyesight was better than Bunny credited. He'd taken a pot shot at a barrel-shaped quadrotor drone the size of a large dog, about 200 feet in the air. And it was moving toward them. Slung under its belly was a box magazine that looked like it held a three-by-three configuration of small missiles—Hongjians, probably, if the Lieutenant Colonel on Penghu had been right, smaller but similar in design to the American Hellfire.

"Put the rifle down," Bunny said. "Hide it."

"I can hit it," the old man insisted.

"Maybe, maybe not," she said, keeping her eyes on the drone as it closed on them. "It could have launched on us by now, but it hasn't. It's coming for a closer look, and I'm betting it's looking for weapons."

The old man put his rifle back on the deck and pulled some fishing net over it. Bunny noticed he kept his hand near it though.

The drone kept a good 100 meters out from the chugging fishing boat and made a circle. Bunny could see a set of cameras above the missile turret, and they were trained on the Taiwanese vessel the whole time. Bunny wondered whether there were human eyes watching the video feed from the drone or whether it was just an AI matching what it saw against a simple database.

She hoped it was the latter, actually. A human might be tempted to put a missile into the wooden hide of the fishing boat just out of boredom or spite or because they needed the practice. An AI would be governed by a strict set of rules, with little or no freedom of action.

Bunny heard a whistle and snapped her head around. Hungyu was pointing. On the opposite side of the boat, standing off at about 200 meters, a second drone was approaching. Any question of using the old man's blunderbuss to take on the Chinese drones was out of the question, and he slowly pulled his hand away from it.

The second drone was armed with a rotating-barrel autocannon, an ammunition belt hanging out of a box under the main body of the drone and feeding into the weapon.

Interesting, Bunny thought. *Did that first drone call the second, or did it just happen to be in the neighborhood?* The first possibility implied they could communicate with each other somehow, in which case it should have been possible to jam them. But the Navy Lieutenant Colonel said jamming wasn't working. The second possibility was just as worrying, as it implied there were a large number of the things aloft, if two of them could stumble on the Taiwanese fishing boat in the space of just a few minutes. "Stay calm, everyone," Bunny said.

Then, suddenly, it was over.

The first drone pulled higher and moved away south. The second completed a circle around them, just as the first had, and when it was satisfied it had reached the same conclusion about them, it pulled away too, heading north.

Hungyu yelled something short and sharp at the old man before turning his attention back to the wheel. Bunny hadn't learned enough of Taiwanese Mandarin to know what he said for sure, but she could take a guess.

"You old goat, you nearly got us killed."

She'd been burning pure adrenaline since leaving the clinic on the Penghu Islands, but the minute the drone threat was past, her legs went from under her, and the fishermen lay her on a bunk down below.

She was sleeping when they reached the port of Dongshi and had to be carried off the boat with her arms around the two fishermen's shoulders. The medical clinic in the tiny town took her in, put her on a drip and got her on her feet again within a couple of days. The clinic's head doctor told her, "You are suffering from fatigue, exhaustion. You should eat and drink. Sleep. Stay calm and quiet."

Calm and quiet. Right. That's going to happen.

There was only a token military presence at the small fishing port, and the Army unit she approached was more interested in watching the sea for an invasion than lending her their radio, but at a police station, she was finally able to get on an encrypted video call to Meany at the 68th AGRS.

She was surprised to learn they had been pulled back to Hawaii. It reinforced to her how long she'd been out of play.

"You look like shit, O'Hare," Meany said with a smile after the video link opened and Bunny gave him the abbreviated version of what had happened to her.

"See how you look after getting shot down, fished out of the sea and attacked by killer bots," she replied. "Any word on Flowmax?" The last time she had seen or heard from the Aggressor pilot with a determination to tempt fate had been moments before he flew his machine into a missile that was aimed at Bunny, somewhere over the Chinese coast off Xiamen.

Meany lost his smile. "MIA. He might be in a Chinese hospital or prison, so we're trying to stay positive. After all, *you* came back from the dead."

O'Hare had seen Flowmax's machine dissolve in a ball of flame and metal, so she couldn't share his optimism.

"Look, I'm stuck in a fishing village on the west coast," Bunny told him. "Army says I should just stay put. Local police say the roads are being patrolled by these killer drones, and they're tagging anything that looks vaguely military, including anything the size of a delivery van and up. I might be able to pay someone to take me to Taichung in a passenger sedan, but a Navy Colonel I talked to on Penghu said nothing is flying …"

"Nothing flying? Coalition fighters are flying nonstop," Meany told her. "Look out your window, you'll see the biggest air battle since World War II. But he's probably right that nothing is getting off the island right now. We are trying to keep air superiority over the western approaches because half the US Marine Corps plus the 82nd Airborne are being landed on the west coast. That's our priority. Those drones—

78

Taiwanese call them 'slaughterbots'—are pretty much roaming uncontested outside of our landing zones, and that means no rotary aircraft available to lift you out. There aren't enough MANPADs in the entire Taiwan arsenal to bring them down, and anything mounted on wheels or tracks is being taken out the moment it leaves cover …"

Bunny was thinking hard. "How about you get me a satellite link and a couple of Valkyries?" she suggested. "I can escort an uncrewed quadcopter in and out myself." She could understand no one on the Coalition staff wanting to lose more pilots trying to rescue her, but if she could get control of a couple of uncrewed Valkyrie drones and an uncrewed transport helo, maybe she …

"*No one* is getting satellite time right now," Meany told her, shaking his head. "Undersea cables between Japan and the US West Coast are still at half capacity; satellites are doing all the heavy lifting. There's no spare bandwidth for anything but absolutely critical air operations."

That set her back. She knew uncrewed aircraft—Navy F-47s, Sentinels and Stingrays, Air Force Valkyries and Ghost Bats—filled nearly a third of the Coalition inventory in the theater. No satellite capacity meant they were effectively *grounded*.

"Look, if you can get yourself to Taichung somehow, Aaronson ordered the Aggressor Inc. Gulfstream left in a bunker there to wait until you or Flowmax either turned up, or washed up …"

"That's dark. But tell our kind owner the gesture is deeply appreciated. I'll get myself there somehow."

He leaned toward the camera. "My advice, not that you'll listen to it? Don't do anything reckless, O'Hare. Sit tight, rest up. Marines and Army will get the slaughterbots under control, and then you can get out of there, alright?"

"Alright, alright …" she said through gritted teeth.

Not alright, she was thinking as she cut the call. She could hang around long enough to sign the sheaf of papers the fishermen had downloaded and have her photo taken so they could collect their finders' fee, then what? The two of them were in the room next door, talking animatedly with some police, and she rose, leaning against the doorframe. They were all gathered in front of an old LCD TV screen, which had just been showing static until now. The Chinese drones hadn't just gone after military targets; they'd also hit infrastructure like power and water pumping stations and communication towers.

But someone had found a channel that was still broadcasting, and she joined them in front of the screen.

A TV news reporter was speaking excitedly into a microphone and pointing at something in the distance. The camera zoomed shakily in, and Bunny saw a drone like those that had buzzed them offshore. This one had an autocannon slung under its belly on a gyro-stabilized mount. As she watched, the camera pulled back to show two men in camouflage fatigues, crawling through dry brown grass between some palm trees on what looked like a major ring road, empty of traffic. One of the soldiers had a large anti-materiel rifle cradled in his elbows as he crawled. The other had a scope of some kind.

A sniper team.

"Where is that?" Bunny asked.

Hungyu looked back at her. "Caixia Road," he said. "West."

"In Dongshi? How far?"

80

"Yes, about 2 kilometers."

Bunny was a hammer looking for a nail to hit, and she was apparently not the only one.

As she watched, the camera stopped panning. Even the excitable reporter shut up for a moment as the rifleman put his weapon to his shoulder and settled his cheek to his scope.

The rifle bucked, the drone about 200 meters away jumped, and then it started spinning out of control toward the ground. When it hit, it lay there for a moment.

Then it *exploded*.

The room erupted with cheers, but Bunny pulled Hungyu aside. "I need you to take me there," she said.

"There?" he asked, looking over his shoulder at the TV doubtfully. "Why?"

"I want to get a look at whatever is left of that Chinese drone," she said. The TV picture was showing the two-man sniper team on their feet again now, and doubling back toward the cover of some buildings. She pointed at the screen. "And I need to talk to *them*."

4. The battle of Tiangong Space Station

"Can you repeat that please, Wangchang?" Taikonaut Liu Haiping said, trying not to let concern bleed into his voice. He didn't want to worry his crew. Yet.

"Uh, yes, I said the trajectory is different from the pre … from the predicted trajectory." The disembodied voice was unrecognizable after being squirted through 200 kilometers of atmosphere and space, but Liu dearly wished he knew who he was talking with. He knew most of the members of the Wangchang Tiangong mission control team personally.

"That is what I gathered, Wangchang. So we're still waiting for impulse burn?"

"Confirmed. Range is 5 kilometers, range rate is 10.5 meters per second."

Whoever he was speaking with sounded nervous. Nervous was not a good vibe when the object approaching your very fragile space station had a mass of 150 tons and was currently closing at 40 kilometers an hour, relative. He kept the crosshairs of their docking camera centered on the module as it approached. The process was entirely automated, managed by AIs aboard the module and Tiangong itself, but he had the ability to abort the docking if he wasn't happy.

And right now, he wasn't happy.

"What are you seeing, Wangchang?" he asked.

"Uh, range four point two, range rate ten decimal seven three meters per second."

Liu frowned.

"Range rate should be decreasing," the taikonaut at his elbow, Captain Chen Yuqi, said, stating the obvious. "Not increasing."

"Keep your voice down; the mic is open," Liu snapped. He was showing his tension now. It would not do. "Don't want you going viral on WeChat again, Yuqi," he joked in a whisper, trying to lighten the mood. Chen had become an unwitting social media sensation after a cargo mishap in which she failed to secure some caged mice and was filmed trying to recapture them as they bounced around one of the lab modules. As Liu watched, the approaching module drifted suddenly out of view.

"Uh, Wangchang?"

"Tiangong, we are performing a retrograde up maneuver, so we're going to get back on the right trajectory," the voice said with forced confidence.

"Wangchang, I just lost visual."

"No, we're still locked on with the core, so, um, it should get much better. We should get better alignment."

He checked the numbers running in the corners of the docking screen. What he was seeing was always a few seconds ahead of what they were seeing on the ground since Wangchang was taking its feed from Tiangong's radar. "Wangchang, I don't like these numbers."

It was the biggest cargo module China had ever tried to dock at its space station, and only the third launched by the massive new Long March 9 heavy-lift rocket.

"Right. Right now, my camera is blurred, so I can barely see any parameters," the mission controller said.

"You have to call it," a voice from behind Chen said. "Abort." It was her third crew member, Zhu Boming. A former fighter pilot, he was the one among them prone to snap decisions. Each of their psych profiles had been weighed against the other before they had been sent into orbit. Zhu's quick decision-making was essential in a crisis, but he acted

83

without taking in all available information. Chen was a pessimist who called herself a realist, who talked about everything in scenarios and could never have enough data. Not surprisingly then, their commander, Liu, was somewhere between them, but his pitfall was he allowed personal relations to cloud his decisions, and he had a tendency to want everyone to feel consulted and included. China's National Space Agency had tried to train that out of him and had mostly succeeded.

But only mostly.

"Chen, your thoughts?"

"Wait until it is 2 kilometers out," she said. "They might be able to get it back on trajectory with this burn."

The mission controller broke in again. "Colonel, please prepare to start the timer as soon as the retrograde burn is complete."

Chen leaned toward the mic. "Wangchang, that is your job, not ours."

There was a pause. "Yes. Uh, at completion of the retrograde maneuver, I will start the timer."

Chen cursed under her breath. "Who is this idiot?"

Liu ignored her. "Wangchang, we still have good telemetry here, and a good lock between the module and the core."

"Copy, Tiangong. The timer has been started. Reverse maneuver is in progress."

The module drifted into view on their docking video screen again and slowly centered itself in the crosshairs.

"Right, so, we have completed the burn, and we are back to our regularly scheduled trajectory. So no worries," the mission controller said, sounding quite pleased with herself. "You can initiate the dock activation command and start the dock test ..."

The next few minutes felt busy but consisted largely of monitoring the feed from the two AIs to make sure nothing unexpected was taking place. But after the off-nominal approach, Liu kept his hand near the abort switch. Flight engineers would be spending the next few days working out why the module's planned and actual trajectories had deviated.

"Closing rate zero-decimal-five meters per second," the mission controller announced. "Docking in 10 seconds."

The three taikonauts braced themselves, felt the thud of the new module slotting into place against the cargo service dock, then let out the breath they had all been holding in anticipation of disaster.

"Uh, that's docking complete, Tiangong. You are clear to integrate. Begin leak checklist."

"Good copy, Wangchang, we ..."

The station shuddered.

A piercing alarm sounded through the station.

"The hell!" Zhu yelled. He had opened a hard contact data link to the new module and was looking at the numbers running across his screen. "Its thrusters are firing! We're tumbling."

Liu looked at what the cargo module AI was telling him. It showed nothing wrong.

"Two degrees, attitude degrading. We're *tumbling*," Chen confirmed. Once again, it was superfluous information. They could all see the two flat floors and semicircular walls of their core module rotating around them. "AI is engaging Hall thrusters!"

Their core module was fitted with a ring of Hall-effect thrusters, which it used to adjust its orbit. But they were built to nudge, not to fight against an out-of-control cargo module trying to spin them like a top.

85

"Ten degrees—slowing, but we're still losing attitude control," Chen said.

Zhu grabbed a handhold and pulled himself to one end of the command module. "Where are you going?" Liu asked.

"Wentian module," he said without stopping. "We can use the thrusters on Wentian to counter the spin."

"You'll have to do it manually," Liu warned. "AI has no control over Wentian. And Wangchang won't be able to get a control link until …"

"I know. That's why I'm moving," Zhu said, his head disappearing into the central docking and Extra Vehicular Activity, or EVA, ring. His feet followed.

Liu watched him go. He was right. Using the thrusters on the lab module was their best option to correct their tumble. "Wangchang, we have lost attitude control. The cargo module …" Liu reported.

"Cargo module thrusters are firing erratically," the mission controller said in a high-pitched voice. "We are working out how to shut them down from here."

"You do that. Meanwhile, we are going to manually counter the roll using thrusters on Wentian. Copy," Liu said.

"Good copy. We won't be able to assist with that, Tiangong—not until you come back over and we can get a command link. That's uh … eight minutes."

"Tell us something we don't know," Chen muttered. Then she looked over her shoulder at Liu. "Probably a *good* thing they can't help.

Moments later, Zhu's voice came over the intercom. "I'm in position, thrusters online. What's the tumble rate?"

Liu checked the readout. "Still two degrees per minute. We're 15 degrees off nominal, heading to 20." Losing attitude control wasn't going to kill them fast, but if the spin damaged their solar panels or comms antennae, or ripped something else off its mounting, it could kill them slow. Countering a rogue cargo module *wasn't* one of the 300 crises they had trained for.

"Two-second burn?"

"Roger, let's see what two seconds does."

"Hope Two's docking ring holds," Chen said, her tone clearly conveying she thought it wouldn't.

"Captain Chen, stow your pessimism until we regain control of the station, please."

"Aye Colonel."

Zhu counted down. "Starting burn in three … two … *one* …"

They heard and felt nothing. But Liu saw the rotation slow on his screen and even reverse by a couple of degrees. "That did it. Back at 15 degrees off nominal. But it will keep degrading unless you keep firing."

"You mean a longer burn?" Zhu asked. "Five seconds, maybe?"

Liu thought about what Chen had said about the docking ring holding. "No, we don't want to stress the connector." He opened the channel to Wangchang.

"Mission control, how long now?"

"Six minutes, Tiangong, we'll have a command link up in six minutes."

He checked the attitude. It had deteriorated to 18 degrees off nominal again. He opened the station intercom again. "Zhu, give me a two-second burn every 30 seconds for the next six minutes starting now. That will hold the tumble. Got that?"

"Two seconds every 30. You got it. I'll count it in each time. That's three … two … one …"

Six minutes can be a lifetime when you are floating in an out-of-control shipping-container-sized tin can 400 kilometers above the earth. Zhu had just counted in his 13th two-second thruster burn when they finally heard the words they were hoping for.

"Tiangong, Wangchang. We have a command link, and we have succeeded in shutting down the module's propulsion system. You should see ..."

Liu was staring at his readouts. Their Hall thrusters were still firing, but the attitude was ... *rolling back toward nominal.*

"We have regained control, Wangchang. Thank you."

"Don't thank *them*," Chen said. "They should be thanking us. We just saved their gazillion-yuan space station!"

Three hours later, they had regained full attitude control, run a systems validation to ensure there was no damage and completed their integrity checks. They were ready to equalize pressure and crack the hatch into the new module.

"Alright," Zhu said, floating over the door. "Let's see what's shaken loose." He thumped the cargo module door release.

The door swung toward them, and they peered inside. It looked nothing like a normal cargo delivery. A typical payload was bagged in shockproof, padded bags and fastened to the tubular walls of the cargo module with Velcro straps.

But 150 metric tons was far from a normal delivery for Tiangong. To Liu's eyes, the module seemed larger in the cramped confines of space than it had on the ground. But it had a familiarity about it bred from more than 100 hours of intensive training.

Three harness stations sat in the middle of the module, facing a bank of screens and keyboards. But it was the instrument station at the far end of the module that had their attention, not least because it was the reason they had been so tense when the module misfired. They had only seen a mockup and run simulations; they had never seen or used the real thing because it would have been impossible on earth.

They propelled themselves over to it.

"They didn't take our advice on the display or the power modulation control layout," Chen observed.

"We were brought in too late," Liu said. "No time for spec changes."

"I don't care," Zhu said, cracking his fingers theatrically. "Just let me at it."

The operation of the power system at the end of the module was his responsibility, and he ran a diagnostic routine, checking the results on the instrument display. With a tap on the panel like he was patting a dog on the head, he announced the results. "Power systems nominal. Most importantly, for our own health and welfare, the shielding held. Lady and gentleman, welcome to our new module: Light of the Heavens."

Liu smiled. They had come up with the nickname of the module themselves. Their suggestion had been warmly embraced by the program's director. The Tiangong station's other two modules were called "Dreaming of the Heavens" and "Quest for the Heavens."

Then came the moment the mission psychology team chief had prepared Liu for. Zhu turned to the wall opposite the three workstations. Fitted to the curve of the bulkhead was a smooth rectangular box about the size and shape of a notepad. The moment the module had connected with the space station, it had started drawing power, so the box was already pulsing with golden light, indicating it was ready to boot up.

Zhu floated over to it, his face lit by the golden glow. "So this is the thing that is going to make taikonauts redundant."

"Taikonauts will never be redundant," Liu said in a relaxed tone he had practiced many times. "The ultimate goal of our space program is to put a man on Mars."

"And woman," Chen said quickly.

"And woman."

Liu grabbed a handhold and pulled open a drawer beside the workstations. From it he unfastened a small package and read the label. Then he looked at his watch. "I need to perform the system reset in one hour." He studied Zhu and Chen. Naked curiosity had kept them on their feet, but they looked exhausted. No one slept well in space. Sleep consisted mostly of longer or shorter cat naps rather than solid blocks. "Take some downtime if you want it, guys. Report back in 50 minutes."

"I'll take that offer. Might be the last nap we get," Chen said, not joking for once. "Ever."

Colonel Alicia 'The Hammer' Rodriguez would have killed for a beer at that moment. It would have gone nicely with her plus-sized portion of humble pie.

Rodriguez had bragged to the Joint Chiefs that the 2-megawatt ground-to-space laser under the command of her 615th Combat Operations Squadron would be able covertly to disable or destroy the Chinese Long March 9 rocket payload, "no problem, sirs."

And it should have been able to. Every test they had done using the Modular Efficient Laser Technology (MELT) test platform against de-commissioned US satellites had either destroyed them outright or caused a catastrophic malfunction.

Interdicting the Chinese space station module had become a critical mission after human intelligence from several highly placed sources indicated the payload was definitely military. The exact nature of the payload wasn't known, but if the customer was the People's Liberation Army, the US did not want the 15-ton module to arrive at the space station intact. Not in the current political "environment." A deniable attack vector was needed, and Rodriguez promised she would deliver it.

The failure was especially embarrassing since requesting priority routing from the St. Lucie Nuclear Power Plant 100 kilometers away required the Florida governor's approval, which the Pentagon was always reluctant to request, and Rodriguez didn't have that many political cards to play.

Her weapons engineering team would be poring over the data from this attack for weeks, but that didn't help her now. The Chinese cargo module launched from Wangchang had apparently docked with the Tiangong space station without incident, so their covert attack had done little more than warm the insides of the Chinese cargo module.

She could use all kind of excuses—the atmospheric conditions were against them, they'd been given insufficient time to prep the attack, there had been fluctuations in the laser pulse frequency due to power grid issues—but that was not her. 'Hammer' Rodriguez didn't do excuses. She had five years at the helm of the 615th Combat Operations Squadron precisely because she *owned* her failures. And was quick to address them.

91

She was already on the line to the Pentagon, joining a conference call with officers one, two and even three levels above her rank. She stayed silent, letting others dissect the problem, until it was time to find solutions.

"We need to deploy Skylon," she said. She spoke directly to the defense secretary nominee, Dan Caulfield, who had just asked the Joint Chiefs for options. She had not waited to be asked her opinion. "If China militarizes its space station, we need to be able to respond instantly."

"That platform is still under evaluation," a US Navy Admiral pointed out.

Rodriguez sighed. Yes, the Skylon spacecraft had been under evaluation by Space Force for three years. But it had been in service with the Royal Air Force for six years already. Rodriguez had, over several years, screamed in frustration at how long the US was taking to approve the purchase of a technology their British allies had already deployed. She tried pointing out that it had taken nearly 10 years for the US Marines to adopt the tried and tested RAF technology of the AV-8B Harrier "jump jet", dragging their feet in approving it even after it had almost single-handedly won the Falkland's War for Britain.

A combined-cycle, air-breathing rocket-propulsion-engined spacecraft, the Skylon could launch from any airport with a long runway and power itself at Mach 5.4 into low earth orbit within 20 minutes. The version being tested by the US, and already in service with the UK, could be fitted with a half dozen mission-dependent modules.

It wasn't just Space Force evaluations holding the US purchase of the Skylon back; it was the "not made in the USA" attitude of US Congress funding mechanics. The UK had just agreed to a deal by which all US Space Force Skylon aircraft would be built, and launched, in the USA, but party politics were still delaying the approval.

It drove Rodriguez nuts. She had a weapons system already in use with another nation, under trial by the USA, but she was unable to access it at a time of national emergency. The Skylon could take out anything China launched—hell, it could take out that entire damn space station if it was allowed to.

"Admiral, 'that platform' is sitting on a runway at Vandenberg Air Force Base and could be launched at three hours' notice. It can be tasked with any mission you can think of."

"Any one of my *Constellation* class frigates can take down that space station with an SM3 missile in a third of that time," the Admiral said dismissively. "We've just seen what happens when we rely on unproven technologies."

"You use a missile against the Chinese station, you create a debris field that would take out hundreds of satellites, including those of the US and our allies," she pointed out. "Skylon can target specific points on the space station with directed energy weapons that will disable it *without* creating a debris field. Or if you wanted, we could send it up with a payload of Marines and hijack the station completely. I have a rapid reaction force trained and ready to go. Just make the call."

The Navy Admiral was apparently not a man who was used to being challenged, let alone forcibly disagreed with. Even on the video screen, Rodriguez could see him redden. The meeting was being chaired by her own boss, the Commander of Delta 45, Brigadier General Chris Panhagen, and he stepped neatly into the awkward silence.

"Thank you, Colonel, the Skylon option is noted," he said. "You can return to your post-mission review. We need to understand why our energy weapon attack failed. We'll leave you to it."

Her connection was cut. A more junior officer would be worrying about her career right now.

Alicia Rodriguez was worried about something a little more important: the survival of her nation.

It wasn't just the physical and mental state of his crew that motivated Senior Colonel Liu Haiping to send them to their quarters for some well-earned rest.

He had a task to perform that none of the others had been briefed on or needed to know about. He'd called it a 'system reset' for simplicity, but it was much more than that.

Moving himself through the station, alternately pulling and gliding, he entered the station's central core module. When he got there, the first thing he did was check the bio-signs being transmitted by sensors in Chen and Zhu's sleeping bags.

Heart rate, body temperature and breathing all indicated they were in their bags in the crew rest zone, either dozing or trying to.

The mission psychology chief had spoken with him after he had been briefed on the next element of the mission. A political commissar was present too, weighing his responses. "You will be giving the AI complete control of every system on Tiangong. With that, goes the power of life and death." The psychologist looked at Liu as though sizing him up. "How do you feel about that, Taikonaut Liu?"

"If it is necessary, it is necessary," he'd replied.

"A Taikonaut will no longer be sole commander of Tiangong," the psychologist pointed out. "You will share authority."

"I will have an override code," Liu pointed out.

"Which you cannot share with the crew," the psychologist said. "If you are incapacitated, you have to trust that the AI will pass the code to your second in command. And that the AI will act on the code if ordered to do so. There are situations in which it has been programmed to ignore an override order. For example, if the order conflicts with critical mission priorities."

This statement caused the commissar to lean forward. Liu weighed his response carefully.

"I am aware of this. I have been briefed on all of the relevant situations and they are highly unlikely," Liu said. "Plus, the same AI has been used on nuclear missile submarines for years. It has been proven …"

"It has not been proven in space. Every new technology implementation carries a risk of failure, you know that. Denial is not a healthy response," the psychologist said.

"I am not in denial, but perhaps I have more faith in our technology than you do, doctor? I couldn't go into space if I didn't have that faith."

That conversation had taken place before he was sent into space. It had also taken place before the rebels on Taiwan had attacked China and war had broken out with Taiwan and her "Coalition" partners. That reality had increased the urgency of their new mission and accelerated the timeline for the launch of the new module. But it had also increased the possibility that if he was about to screw up their life support, a rescue mission might not be possible in time.

And might not even be prioritized since, as Zhu had crudely pointed out, the humans aboard Tiangong were about to become largely redundant.

Focus, Liu, he told himself, shaking off the anxiety he had insisted to the psychologist he didn't feel.

From the small package he had taken from a drawer in the new module, he pulled out the case containing the computer motherboard and associated processors that were going to change life aboard Tiangong forever.

He put on cotton gloves, then held the card up in front of his eyes. It looked like a pretty normal computer motherboard, and the spin-qubit quantum processors at its center seemed little different to the last-generation silicon CPUs they were replacing. He suddenly remembered a TV broadcast from 2021, and the stalactite-like tower of golden tubes and wires that was China's first ever quantum computer. It had amazed and intrigued him as a schoolchild.

This new motherboard was 10 times more powerful, and only about 12 cm by 12 cm. Twenty pins were arrayed along one edge, ready to slot into the station's comms motherboard. The logo of a Chinese quantum computer manufacturer was printed on the top of the processors, which were a glowing gold color, the international indicator that a processor was quantum-based.

Liu had heard many boasts in his time in the People's Liberation Army Astronaut Corps, and the small conglomeration of quantum dots, spin fields, magnetometers, resonators and detectors in his hand did not seem capable of living up to the job of being his 'decision support partner'.

But the motherboard was also the key to enabling the larger unit mounted inside the Light of the Heavens module to take full control of Tiangong's systems and relieve the crew of a huge percentage of their workload.

He opened their systems and sensors' mainboard access panel. The new board was slightly bigger than the old, and he had to move a few wires out of the way before he made the swap.

He touched his throat mic and opened a ground link. "Wangchang, I am ready for system reset. We will lose communications. Please mute all system alarms at your end. I will do the same here."

"You are clear for system reset, Tiangong. All preparations are in place here."

He took a deep breath, calming himself. If this went wrong …

If it goes wrong, you can just put the old board back in, he told himself. *And you have a backup for that, so stop worrying.*

He was, among other things, about to kill their air, water, energy and sensor management systems. The only analogy he could think of was an old-time deep-sea diver deliberately severing his air hose to the surface in order to replace it.

"Good copy, Wangchang. Tiangong out."

He opened the comms panel. Then he muted the system alarms via a switch inside and disconnected the power supply to the main and to the backup board.

The emergency reserve power supply to the life support system kicked in seamlessly. Apart from a millisecond-brief flicker of the lights, without an alarm sounding, he doubted Zhou and Chen would even have noticed, but he turned to check on their bio-signs, just in case.

Both still seemed to be resting.

The comms panel beside him was also dead. It was usually blinking with various status lights, scrolling text messages, backlit control panels and video call screens. Even the long-wave ham radio they used to talk to students across China was down. They couldn't see or hear anyone on earth, and couldn't electronically see or be heard.

Liu Haiping was not used to being invisible, and he realized with some surprise he didn't like it. He'd gotten used to being a media megastar. Millions clicked on every social media image or utterance he sent out into the world. Despite only being in his early 30s, he was the highest-ranked taikonaut in China's space program, darling of politicians and pop stars. He was the former test pilot who was going to take the first Chinese manned mission to *Mars*.

Assuming he didn't screw up on Tiangong. Crewing China's space station was not the ends; it was the means. When he had interviewed for the space program, he had been asked by dull-witted bureaucrat after dull-witted bureaucrat, "What is your motivation?" Each time, he had pulled from his pocket a 4 cm by 4 cm image he had taken with his cell phone, through the lens of a telescope his father had set up in their backyard. "This," he had said, and handed it to them.

He remembered one particular dimwit, in party uniform. He had taken it and frowned. "What is it?" he asked, handing it back.

"Mars," he'd replied. "One day, I will go there."

He was already a decorated pilot, having fought in the South China Sea conflict over Pagasa Island. His fellow pilots sometimes mistook his single-minded ambition for arrogance or base self-promotion. They didn't know him. They hadn't been there, those summer nights in his backyard with his high school teacher father, the two of them peering through the tiny lens of his "borrowed" school telescope as he told Liu the stories that Liu told to schoolchildren today whenever he was on a PR tour.

"The Westerners think Mars is named after the Roman god of war," he told them. "But in China, we know differently. Since ancient times, long before the Romans, Mars was known to Chinese astronomers as Yinghuo, the Fire Planet. It was something to be feared. If it was in retrograde during a birth or death, it was a bad omen. Chaos would follow the child born in the shadow of Yinghuo." Then he would smile. "*I* was born in the shadow of Yinghuo."

"What do you see, Haiping?" his father asked him when he was 12, stepping away from the telescope. He put his eye to it, thinking his father wanted him to describe the image through the lens. "It … is pale red. Nearly pink. I see craters …" He tried to guess what his father wanted him to say, repeating what he'd been taught. "It has a very thin atmosphere. It looks dry, but there is ice water under the crust. I see …" He concentrated. He couldn't really see anything else through the lens of the primitive school telescope, but he wanted to please his father. "I think I can see our Mars rover," he said. It was a lie, but his father indulged him, leaning to the eyepiece and clicking his tongue. "Yes! I think you are right. I can see it too."

Chinese taikonauts had orbited Mars in 2033, just as China planned. China's Mars habitation module—Heavenly Garden—was remotely deployed in 2037, ready for a crewed mission planned for 2039. It was a mission Liu Haiping would lead. His father had told him so, when he was 12.

"Do you know what else I can see, Haiping?" he'd asked after assuring him he could see the Chinese rover. "Here, look," he said, pulling his son back to the eyepiece.

He looked but saw nothing new. "What, father?" Liu asked.

"I can see *you*," he said. "I can see the future. I am standing here, in this backyard, with this telescope, and you are waving to me, and I am so proud I *explode*," he said, then swept the boy up in his arms and swung him around. "And my soul flies up to the stars and we dance together up there, just you and me."

He'd tried telling a journalist that once, but the man hadn't understood. No one did, really.

"Tell me, Liu Haiping," the journalist had said. "The thing all my followers are wondering … why would anyone want to make a one-way trip to Mars? You already know that if you reach the surface, there is no way to get you back. You would have six months of oxygen, no more. You would do your experiments, and you would die. What can possibly motivate you to want that?"

He had rehearsed the answer with the Space Agency media relations team, and it was supposed to be something about "advancing science for the good of the motherland." But instead, he'd replied, "My father died two years ago. I promised him as he was dying that we would dance in the stars together."

Taikonaut wants to dance in the stars, had been the heading on the viral post the journalist had recorded. The post hadn't even mentioned his father, perhaps someone judging that part of the story was too maudlin. And yes, he *was* terrified of the idea of making a one-way trip to a cold and lonely death. But his father was waiting there. He knew it. So he wouldn't be dying alone. Not at all.

But he had to get there first.

A small warning screen got his attention and pulled him out of his reverie.

Comms break, it said, with red, blinking insistence.

No shit, he thought.

Gently, he pulled the old motherboard out and let it float beside him. Even more gently, he pressed the new card into place and checked the fit. The new processors on the card were clear of any obstructions, and the card itself seemed to be seated firmly.

There will be no noticeable difference, he'd been briefed. *Even after system reset. Not until you start the system validation routine.*

Well, we'll see. He reached for the power switch and powered the system back on. There was a slight hum that hadn't been there before, but it went quiet after a couple of seconds. He expected the system reset to start automatically, as it had in the rehearsals earthside. But it didn't. The status screen in front of him stayed blank.

A moment of involuntary panic overtook him. Life support was still running on backup power. No indication of a system restart.

He pulled a keyboard off a Velcro panel on the wall. *Manual restart.* That was his next move. He hit the three-key combination to execute a manual reboot.

The system status screen flickered. Boot code began running down the screen. Finally, a simple text prompt appeared. *System validation required. Do you want to proceed? Y/N.*

Yes, most definitely yes, he thought, hitting the "Y" key on the keyboard.

The lights flickered again as power was restored and normal life support systems began operating again. More code ran down the screen and then disappeared, replaced with a new graphic interface. It showed the same sensor and instrument readings as it had previously, but now it included a small, postcard-sized window with oscillating points of golden light inside it, like the one inside the laser module.

And there you are, Liu thought. *Diguo Bazhu, otherwise known as "Empire Dominator."*

He tapped on the glowing golden lights.

"This is Mission Commander Liu Haiping, logging in …" he said.

The response from speakers over his head was instant. "Hello, Commander, may I come aboard?"

He felt like he was inviting a vampire over the threshold: a vampire that he was about to give the ability to shut down life support systems throughout the station, as he had just done. And more. But it wasn't like he had a choice. Not a real one.

"Uh, yes, welcome aboard, I guess," Liu said, feeling awkward.

"Please set your personal override code," the AI requested.

This was what he couldn't let the others see or hear, and why he'd sent them for a rest. He'd chosen a code based on the planned date for China's Mars mission. "Mars Two Zero Three Nine."

"Thankyou. Your override code is Mars Two Zero Three Nine. You may also choose to give me a working name and a visual avatar, Commander." Avatar? He had no desire to personalize the AI at this point. The golden points of light were quite mesmerizing to watch; they would do. Neither did he feel like giving the entity a name. "No avatar. Your name will simply be 'Tiangong,' like the space station," he continued. "Please disable any personality routines. You may begin supervising sensors, propulsion, environmental and …" Liu hesitated. It was not a phrase he had ever imagined he would be using. "… and weapons systems."

102

If Liu Haiping had a polar opposite, it was former USMC Colonel Dan 'Tug' Boatt.

Where Liu was driven, Tug never exceeded his self-determined maximum effort threshold. Where Liu was intense, Boatt was chill. And very few people followed Tug on social media because all he posted were photos of his dog, reviews of whatever new whisky he was drinking, or sometimes—if he was really changing it up—a photo of the whisky bottle with his dog in the background.

The only time he'd been interviewed by a journalist was for *Leatherneck Magazine*, when he became the first Marine Corps aviator selected for Space Command's 615th Combat Operations Squadron after six years at the helm of the United States Naval Test Pilot School at Naval Air Station Patuxent River.

Asked if he "had any advice for aspiring astronauts," he said gruffly, "Sure. In space it is easier to fail upwards."

The reality was that unlike Liu Haiping, who had dreamed of going to the stars from 12 years of age, Tug Boatt had only taken the role of director of operations and lead pilot for the Skylon project because of Hammer Rodriguez.

They'd met at the Aviation Safety Officers' Course at the Naval Postgraduate School in Monterey, California, in about 2030. Rodriguez was headed to Alaska to head up some top-secret Navy project, and he was headed to Patuxent River. They discovered on that course that they had complementary personalities and a shared love of whisky—or bourbon, in her case, but he could work with that—and dogs.

Both were divorced, and neither was looking for a new partner. It was a match made in heaven.

She'd called him just after he'd attended what felt like his hundredth Test Pilot graduation ceremony.

"Tug, the 615th has been asked to help test a new platform, and I'm putting together a team," she said. "I need someone to head it up." If she'd intended that to set a hook, it didn't work. The idea of starting up a new unit wasn't that enticing. "I don't know, Rodriguez," he said. "I got a sweet setup here. I live in Hollywood, you know that?"

"Hollywood, Maryland?"

"Sure. We get crab and oysters every Wednesday in the galley. I run the bar at the Cedar Point Golf Club, with the finest selection of single malts in the state. I got a banjo, a porch overlooks Cuckold Creek and a US government–issue shotgun to keep the mosquitos away."

"Sounds like paradise," Rodriguez replied. "How's the surfing there?"

Tug was a Californian, who grew up surfing the beaches of San Clemente. Rodriguez knew damn well he had to drive three hours from Pax River to find a surf beach. "Better than it is where you are, at Cape Canaveral," he said.

"This job isn't based at Canaveral," she told him. "Too hush-hush. You'll fly out of Vandenberg AFB. You can finish work, jump in a Hummer and be surfing inside 30 minutes," she said. "And no mosquitos."

"Yeah, I don't know … 615th is Air Force …"

"Space Force."

"Same difference. I'm an incarnated leatherneck, you know that. You Air Force types tend to be more …"

"Uptight?"

"Right. Like they would probably object to a guy having his own still."

"You are a full Colonel now, but you still brew your own moonshine?"

"Finest bootleg whisky, I prefer to call it. Won a prize at the local fair."

"Hard to compete with that. Did I tell you the test platform is a *space* plane, and the mission is to create the first unit of Space Marines?"

And that was how Tug Boatt got lured into the Skylon program. The rest—setting up the squadron, recruiting the pilots (well, he *stole* most of them from the Royal Air Force), putting the British machine through its paces—that was history.

It hadn't been boring.

The Skylon was already in service with RAF 11 Squadron. Starting as a concept on a drawing board at British aero-engine designer Reaction Engines in 1982, it had staggered from concept to prototype, was scrapped completely in the late 1980s, reinvigorated with a new design in the 1990s and finally took wing when Boeing and Rolls-Royce bought into the redesigned hydrogen-fueled SABRE engine in the early 2020s. The Skylon D2 was a half-size single-stage-to-orbit prototype that took to the skies in 2025, followed closely by the full-scale D3 commercial suborbital "spaceliner" in 2030 and finally the orbital D4 version delivered to the RAF in 2032.

The D4 could take off from the ground like an aircraft, deliver a 33,000-kilogram payload to a 400-kilometer low earth orbit, then land at specially prepared airstrips either at RAF Lossiemouth, the European spaceport in Kiruna, Guiana Space Center or Vandenberg. Using interchangeable payload containers, it could be fitted to carry satellites and weapons modules or, with a specialized habitation module, could boost a personnel payload of up to 30 "astronauts" into orbit, making Great Britain the first nation that could theoretically put a platoon of light assault Marines into space. It wasn't a capability the UK had pursued.

But it was all of these capabilities, and especially the last one, that had gotten the attention of US Space Force and which the pilots and personnel of the 615th Test Unit had been exploring for the last year. So far, they had completed six flights with Marines in the payload bay.

On the last flight, the four Marines they had taken up with them had completed a spacewalk during which they tethered and captured a disused satellite, wrangled it into the Skylon's load bay and returned it to Earth.

Tug had flown that mission himself and was poring over the data with his copilot, former RAF Captain Sally Hall. The Skylon had a crew of two—a pilot and a systems engineer. Tug was no engineer, so he'd been sure to recruit the best, and Hall was a physicist, electrical engineer *and* astronaut who had more than 200 hours in the D4.

The two of them were trying to work out whether to increase the number of Marines carried for a satellite capture mission. Four had been sufficient, but six would be optimal.

Tug's cell phone was on the table between them, and it started buzzing. He picked it up and frowned. "It's the boss," he told Hall. "Better take it—she gets tetchy I don't answer straight away."

"I'll get tea," Hall said, giving him space. He watched her go before picking up. The back of her T-shirt read "Say That To My Face." No one in the 615th Team Skylon wore uniforms unless they were flying or out on the flight line. Their two D4s were kept under wraps in a hangar in a remote southern corner of the airfield, and Vandenberg's single long

SE-NW aligned runway was perfect for keeping their takeoffs and landings discreet because it fired the Skylon straight out over the Pacific. It was public knowledge Space Force was conducting evaluations of the Skylon out of Vandenberg, but they didn't need to make life easy for prying eyes.

"Colonel," Tug said, picking up the call. "What's up?"

"You might be, very soon," Rodriguez replied. "I just told a subcommittee of the Joint Chiefs that you could have a D4 airborne inside three hours. Did I lie?"

She was serious, Tug could tell from the lack of banter. "No ma'am," he said. Their crews had given the two suborbital space planes nicknames, of course, and they'd stuck. The long, sleek aircraft resembled something you'd see in the sea rather than the air, so they'd named them after sharks. "Mako is still being turned around after its last mission, as you know. But Tiger can be ready for a test flight inside three hours if I give the order now." He needed to know how to configure the machine though. "What's the mission?"

"Undecided," Rodriguez said. "And it won't be a test. It will be a combat mission. Are your people ready if they need to be?"

Tug had asked himself that question a few times since things had kicked off with China over Taiwan. He was pretty sure every Army, Navy, Marine and Air Force officer worth their stripes had done the same. "They are, ma'am," he said. "Uh, with your permission, I need to get about a thousand pieces into place if you're thinking of sending us to war. I assume I can start the wheels turning, just in case?"

"That would be wise, Tug," she said.

"Alright then. Anything else?"

"I want you in the pilot seat for this first mission," she said. "Who should we have riding shotgun?"

Hall chose that moment to come back in, two steaming mugs of tea in hand. She didn't drink coffee, and that meant Boatt didn't get coffee either. The front of her T-shirt said across her chest in small print, "If You Can Read This … Back The Hell Up."

She saw Tug looking at her with a smile on his face. "Oh, no. What?"

He kept smiling. "Captain Hall just volunteered, ma'am."

5. The battle of the Eastern Pacific

"The plan is the plan," Meany said.

"The plan sucks," Flatline repeated. "Chunks of suck."

"There is no tanker available for us to pull fuel from mid-Pacific," Meany repeated. "So we're going the long way around – Kadena to Guam, Wake, Midway, Hawaii."

"With respect, you mean there is no tanker available to Aggressor Inc., because the moment we land at Hickam, we stop being Air Force Reserve and start being a private contractor again, so how we get to Hawaii is our own problem," Touchdown said bitterly.

"Air Force has more than enough problems of its own without worrying about us," Meany pointed out. "We are close to losing air superiority over Taiwan. Ten to 20 percent of Chinese slaughterbot mothership launches from the mainland are getting through air defenses and air patrols, and each mothership is dropping another 20 slaughterbots on Taiwan." He fixed Flatline with a glare. "So we need to fight our way to Guam? We've got a golden ticket out of the slaughterhouse, Flatline; we have nothing to complain about."

Touchdown was studying the flight plan on a tablet. "Stripped clean of everything but wing tanks, my F-22s will only have about 240 gallons in reserve when we reach Guam. With four AIM-260 missiles, we'll be arriving on fumes. That leaves no margin for fighting our way to Guam."

"That's why you're not taking four missiles. Your payload is two medium-range CUDAs," Meany told her. The cut-down CUDA weighed only half as much as a long-range AIM-260. But it had only half the range.

"Better and better," Flatline muttered.

109

"Flatline and I in the P-99s will be your missile trucks," Meany told her. "If you spot them, we'll swat them. You won't even need ordnance."

He'd sounded more confident back then than he felt right now, 1,000 clicks away and halfway across the Philippine Sea between Japanese Okinawa and American Guam. They'd arrived at Okinawa with one P-99 and three F-22s after losing Flowmax and O'Hare over the Strait. USAF made a second P-99 available—an ex-Japan Air Self Defense Force evaluation machine—but they'd lost another pilot when Jack 'Magellan' Chang told them he was staying on Taiwan and returning to his old unit. They'd brought two fresh F-22 qualified pilots in from Arizona … 'Cyber' Neumann, a former German Air Force pilot, and 'NextGen' Diaz, a former Puerto Rican National Guard pilot. Neither had gotten much combat experience before the order to relocate to Hawaii had arrived.

Ordinarily, even in contested airspace like they'd have to cross, he would be confident. Three fifth-gen F-22s and two sixth-gen P-99s backed by US air and satellite recon assets would normally be a formidable package. But the F-22s had been essentially de-fanged to give them longer range, with the longer-endurance P-99s carrying the missiles for them. A Black Widow in "beast mode" could carry 12 air-to-air missiles internally in stealth mode, and 16 if external pylons were used—four more than the venerable F-15EX. But the coming flight would also test the Widow's endurance, so Meany and Flatline were only carrying internal ordnance to lower their drag coefficient.

It wasn't their missile loadout that dented Meany's confidence. They had 30 missiles between them. And they could use passive electronic and radar sensors to detect and avoid Chinese ships and aircraft, *if* those ships and aircraft were radiating. And they'd have to be damn unlucky to fly within visual range of a Chinese warship that wasn't using its radar. But a Chinese J-20 Mighty Dragon or J-31 Gyrfalcon fighter had optical infrared sensors that rivalled those on Meany's Widow. Their experience in combat over the Strait was that a J-20 could pick up a moving aircraft at ranges up to 300 kilometers in optimal daylight conditions, and 200 at night.

What worried him was that China had recently started putting a lot of resources toward shutting down the air highway between Taiwan and Guam along which the US Coalition was moving aircraft and supplies.

So they were making the job as hard as they could for long-range Chinese patrols probing the Philippine Sea. They were flying at night, at subsonic speeds that would keep their aircraft skins cooler. The Widows were using their exhaust gas cooling systems to further reduce their infrared signatures. The Raptors didn't have that technology but would have their exhaust ports shielded from any aircraft looking at them from the west, where Chinese fighters were most likely to be patrolling. They were flying low, under 1,000 feet. It cost a little more fuel but made it harder for movement detection algorithms to pick up their silhouettes against the sea. And they were flying dark, all radar and radio emissions locked down so that not an erg of energy would give them away. It meant they had to stay within visual range, since they used laser optical comms to "speak" with each other instead of radio.

One hour flight time down, two to go.

The downside of not using radar, Meany reflected as he picked up the ghost of an aircraft emission somewhere ahead

111

of them, was you only had imperfect vision about what the hell was out in front of you.

"Bogey ahead. Bearing left 10 degrees," Meany said over their interplane laser link. He began banking gently to drag their formation around to the new heading. He was on point, with the four F-22s tucked in behind him in a loose diamond, a couple of kilometers' separation between them, and Flatline playing tail-end Charlie another few kilometers farther back.

Another emission signal, this time to their left. A new contact. "Wait one," Meany said, voice not hiding his consternation. "I've got a second bogey on the new bearing. Going to have to come right see if we can …"

A *third* contact announced itself, now to the right of the other two. Their separation was such that there was no way around them; they would have to try to pass *between*. "Damn. Three bogeys now. We'll have to thread the needle."

"I see them now. Too much to hope they're friendly?" Touchdown asked.

He was getting no IFF signal off the bogeys, so they were either not American or not wanting to announce their presence either.

"Nothing in the preflight intel about Coalition aircraft in this sector," Meany responded. "So we hope for the best and prepare for the worst. Missiles hot, emissions cold, ladies and gentlemen."

He flipped to his weapons arming screen and tapped the icon that brought his six long-range AIM-120 missiles online. He knew Flatline would be doing the same. Three targets, 12 missiles. He wasn't as confident now as he had been a couple of hours ago, but you couldn't hate the math.

There weren't three Chinese fighters ahead of the Aggressor Inc. pilots. There were *eight*.

What Meany could see were three last-century J-15 Flying Shark fighters of the PLA Navy flying out of the newly occupied Pratas Island, south of Taiwan. A former Taiwanese possession 400 kilometers from the southern tip of the island of Taiwan, Chinese Marines had quickly displaced the small Taiwan Coast Guard force on the island and taken control of its airfield, from which it was trying to achieve air dominance over the airspace between Taiwan and the Philippines.

It was probably the most heavily bombed PLA Air Force base in the conflict, receiving daily attention from Philippine-based Coalition fighters and submarine-launched cruise missiles. But as quickly as the Coalition cratered its runway and destroyed any aircraft parked there, China repaired the holes and flew in new machines and pilots.

One of those pilots was 24-year-old Lieutenant 'River' Deep Wong. A Hong Kong university graduate, River had been undergoing conversion training for the J-31 Gyrfalcon when the conflict over Taiwan had kicked off. He and his fellow trainees expected Taiwan would capitulate in the face of imminent invasion, and the fight would be over before they saw any action.

Instead, the Kuomintang rebels had launched an ineffectual spoiling attack, and the prospect of a real war was upon them. River's conversion training had been accelerated, and with just 10 hours behind the stick of a Gyrfalcon, he was sent first to Lingshui Air Base on Hainan and then to the besieged Pratas, or as China called it, "Dongsha," Island. By fast motorboat, not by airplane.

He spent his first 36 hours sheltering in a bunker, emerging only to shovel sand back into bomb craters. To his

113

astonishment, one of the holes still had an unexploded bomb at the bottom of it. It had been more like a mole tunnel than a crater, and he'd leaned on his shovel as engineers examined it. They'd decided they would just fill the bottom of the hole with concrete and then cover it over.

"What if it explodes?" River had asked a nearby engineer. "While we're shoveling?"

"It's under a concrete cap and about four feet of sand already, so it should explode downward," the man said. "Probably." But River noticed the engineers retired quickly to their bunker, leaving the airmen to fill the hole.

The mission he was flying now was his first combat sortie. The rumor among the pilots on Dongsha was that their unit—3rd Brigade 'Flying Stingrays'—had already seen 19 aircraft destroyed and six damaged, most of them on the ground but at least six, and four pilots, in air-to-air combat. None of the Flying Stingray pilots grumbled at being ordered to take a machine up, though. More than a dozen squadron personnel had been killed and twice that number wounded in Coalition air attacks. Dying in the cockpit taxiing on a runway or in an aerial engagement was much preferred to being buried alive in a bunker under the sand.

River was flying one of the aircraft Meany *couldn't* see. The five J-31 Gyrfalcon stealth fighters of the Flying Stingrays had been sent out into the Philippine Sea hunting Philippine Coast Guard vessels. The ex-Australian Navy Cape Class patrol boats were proving a headache for the PLA in more ways than one. Flying through the water at 30 knots, they were able to harass and deny passage to Chinese navy vessels in disputed waters because the Philippine Navy had up-gunned them by adding US-made 'Skua' tail-sitting vertical launch drones to the boats. A Skua drone could launch off the fantail of a patrol boat carrying a single 1,000 lb. glide bomb, a Very Lightweight Torpedo or a swarm of 20 Locust kamikaze drones. They couldn't trouble a determined task force or flotilla but were proving a threat to single warships or commercial vessels trying to transit Philippine waters. Which was exactly why Australia had gifted the Philippines its entire flotilla of retiring Cape Class boats in the 2020s.

They were also annoyingly good at rescuing downed Coalition pilots, using their Skua for reconnaissance and to drop rafts. At least 10 vessels were known to be operating in the Philippine Sea between Luzon and Taiwan, and according to media reporting, they had rescued more than a dozen Coalition flyers.

China hadn't declared war on the Philippines in this conflict. Yet. But that wouldn't stop it sending a message to its less powerful neighbor about the price of choosing the wrong side.

The small, 200-foot Cape Class vessels, with their low-profile, sharply angled hulls, were proving hard for China's maritime patrol aircraft to detect. Not least because the Philippine Coast Guard hid the Cape Class boats among its ubiquitous fishing fleets, ostensibly to protect the fishermen but also to make the job of identifying and attacking them a real headache. Which was why the Flying Stingray Gyrfalcons had been dispatched to hunt them. Their AI-supported scanned array radar could sort fishing boats from patrol boats from more than 50 ki"lometers away, and their precision-guided Eagle Strike anti-ship missiles could be guided by data link all the way to their targets so that the chances of a collateral kill were small.

The were down at 15,000 feet, combing an area of ocean east of Luzon along the flight line from Guam to Okinawa. A favored route for Coalition aircraft being ferried into the theater—hence their escort of J-15s overhead—but also a favorite patrol point for the Philippine Coast Guard vessels loitering in case they were needed to effect a sea rescue. The Stingray pilots had each been assigned an area of ocean 50 kilometers wide and 100 deep to search. Apart from a US Navy destroyer flotilla, which he'd been ordered to give a wide berth, River had so far found only fishing and commercial vessels. For a "combat" patrol in a supposedly hot war zone, there was a distinct lack of combat. He'd seen more action dodging Coalition bombs and missiles on Dongsha.

Unless …

"Stingray Leader, I have a possible Coalition aircraft on DAS, bearing two seven seven, altitude 1,000, range 40 clicks, airspeed estimate … 620 knots." He tried to keep his voice calm. At that speed and altitude, it had to be a fast mover: a Coalition fighter or bomber.

"Target identification?" his flight leader asked.

He checked his heads-up display. "None yet. Still too far out for an ID."

The voice of his flight leader came back with barely disguised impatience. "At 40 kilometers, you should be able to identify *type*—piloted aircraft, UAV, cruise missile. Adjust your algorithm, Deep."

River cursed. A noob mistake. Like radar, you should start your AI analysis wide and then narrow your search. He adjusted his AI settings and got an answer. "Fast mover, piloted."

And then things got suddenly very, very real. "Four more contacts, same general bearing, altitude and speed!" he said, nearly shouting. "Pushing data."

"Data sync confirmed," his flight leader said. "Allocating targets. Stingray pilots, we have five incoming aircraft. They aren't Chinese. Prepare to engage as soon as we have an AI ID." He directed the next order to River. "Stingray Four, climb to 20; close to identification range."

"Stingray Four, copy," River said. The cloud of contacts was off his left wing, and he swung his machine around carefully, keeping his optical infrared sensors in play as he pushed his throttle forward and began climbing out. Looking at his tactical screen, he saw the other Gyrfalcons swinging around to face the enemy too, three aircraft on his portside and one, his flight leader, on his starboard. All were already in missile range, but River was closest. River heard his flight leader ordering their J-15 escorts to begin actively searching for the unidentified aircraft too. They were unlikely to be able to see them yet if they were stealth fighters, but they could prove useful decoys in the opening few seconds of any engagement.

Come on, come on ... River said under his breath, urging the AI to make the call. They had to be American, British or Australian fighters, right? What else could get so close without the J-15s seeing them? Thirty clicks out now. The scattered dots that were the enemy aircraft were still the size of pinpricks on his screen, but each pinprick was a data point being fed to his PL-15 missiles and shared with every other fighter in his flight.

He just needed a damn ID!

"Chinese J-15s, bearing zero two zero, 35,000 feet, 45 clicks!" Meany said. "I'm getting painted by search radar now—no lock, but I think they're suspicious." He thought

117

fast. The Chinese naval fighters would be flying from land bases, probably in the Spratly Islands or Hainan. They'd be at the limit of their range this far out in the Philippine Sea. "Touchdown, adjust southeast. Flatline and I will take the bogeys out. You go around the guy at the far end of the line."

"Roger, I see them now. Breaking southeast."

"Flatline, take five clicks starboard separation. Engage on my mark," Meany ordered.

Meany was about as close to the Chinese fighters as he wanted to get in his fat-assed Widow. The J-15 was old but nimble. He didn't want to get into a knife fight with one.

He cued up his AIM-260s, put them into active radar-seeking mode and locked them onto the radar signals from the Chinese fighters.

"In position, boss," Flatline told him. "Targets locked."

"We shoot and break southeast behind Touchdown," Meany told him. "On my mark … fox three!"

At the precise moment River's AI gave him an ID on the enemy aircraft, their formation began to split. Four fighters— all F-22s—broke left and headed straight for his flight leader! The two others, both P-99 Black Widows, according to his AI, swung right and aimed themselves at the J-15s.

So the decoy action hadn't worked! The Americans had seen both the J-15s and their Gyrfalcons and were moving in to engage!

River panicked. The Black Widow was the most formidable airborne killing machine the Americans possessed. Like its namesake spider, it usually struck before you even knew it was there, and its bite was deadly. Its name was already legend among Chinese pilots; anytime a missile appeared out of nowhere headed right for them, the first thought of a Chinese pilot was "Widow!"

But he was close enough to *see* them. Close enough to *strike*. He allocated two of his missiles to the two Black Widows, the other four to the F-22s sliding away to his right. "Stingray Leader, Stingray Four engaging. Launching missiles!"

Touchdown heard Meany order the attack, then an alert began screaming in her ears. Icons began flashing in her helmet display, demanding her attention. She swiveled her head. Twenty kilometers to starboard, a series of icons showed a volley of Chinese missiles, *inbound.*

Not from the J-15s.

She spun her machine to face the threat, seeing with satisfaction that Cyber and NextGen were doing the same without being ordered.

"Meany, we are defensive. Probable Chinese stealth fighters at my three o'clock," she said. She brought her radar online. She couldn't kill what she couldn't see.

Fifteen seconds until she had to maneuver to save her life.

She worked her radar with her left hand, tightening the grip on her flight stick with her right. She heard Cyber and NextGen signal they were maneuvering. *I know you are there, ratface,* she muttered under her breath. *Show yourself . . .*

The missile warning in her ears changed from a warble to a scream. A target appeared on her radar screen, and faster than she could think, she thumbed her trigger, launching one of her two CUDA missiles at it. As she rolled her machine on its side and slammed into a neck-breaking turn, her payload bay doors flipped open, her missile was flung out, and it accelerated away behind her.

She'd waited too long.

River's multimode PL-15 missile ignored the small spray of decoys in the air behind Touchdown's Raptor and went instead for the juicier target: the flaming-hot nozzles of her twin Pratt & Whitney engines.

Not only had River's precipitous attack given away the Chinese stealth fighter's position, but he'd also made a second newbie mistake in watching his missiles track toward their targets rather than set himself up to defend against a counterattack.

So when Meany and Flatline launched a second volley of missiles down the bearing to the Chinese Gyrfalcons, River Deep was punching the perspex over his head with unsuppressed joy at the sight of one of his missiles merging with at least one of the American Raptors.

His shout of joy died with him as Flatline's AIM-260 blasted through his Gyrfalcon like it was soft cheese.

Meany didn't register Flatline's kill, nor what had happened with his own first or second volleys. From the moment he launched on the Gyrfalcons, with at least one Chinese missile coming for him, he had only one thought.

Get lower!

He bunted his nose down, felt his vision redden, saw his altitude drop away as he bullied his machine down from 5,000 to less than 500 feet above the sea. He nudged his yaw pedals with his exoskeletal feet, pointed the nose of the Widow directly toward the missile that was diving down on him, forcing it to burn fuel as it maneuvered to stay on an intercept course. He didn't have to deploy decoys; the Widow did that automatically, pumping a stream of radar, heat and laser-dazzling decoys into his wake.

None worked.

The Chinese missile kept tipping over, steering ahead of Meany until it was pointed almost vertically at the sea, aimed precisely for where he was going to be five seconds in the future.

He grunted, skidding his machine into a desperate flat turn across the wavetops. One last chance. In the fuselage behind his head was a last-ditch Air Trophy defense turret. As the Chinese missile closed to within 100 meters, the turret popped out, locked its sensors onto the incoming missile and fired a spray of explosively formed penetrating lead slugs in the direction of the threat.

They missed.

River's missile avoided the rain of metal by pure luck, made one last micro-adjustment to its course … and dived into the waves 50 feet *behind* Meany.

"Luck be my lady," Meany muttered to himself as he brought his machine around and started scanning the sky, his instruments, and the horizon around him, for whatever else might try to kill him.

Touchdown knew exactly what, or more accurately who, was trying to kill her.

Her own machine.

The Chinese missile had detonated right in the opening of her portside exhaust nozzle, causing the engine to flame out.

It also took out her port elevator. She could see it was still physically there, but her own eyeballs and a dozen warning lights told her it wasn't responding to control inputs. There was probably other damage too, but in terms of what was going to kill her, that was the most immediate. She'd reflexively punched the machine's emergency flight control initiator the moment she'd sensed the aircraft getting away from her. It monitored a thousand flight surface, avionics and engine inputs that she didn't even have access to, and inside a couple of seconds, it had her flying straight and level again. Her starboard engine was laboring hard just to keep her airborne at—she checked her altimeter—2,000 feet.

She had no idea what had happened to her other pilots. "NextGen, Cyber, report," she said.

"Still here, Captain," NextGen Diaz said.

"On your starboard wing," Cyber Neumann reported. Looking back over her shoulder, she saw him now, above and about a half kilometer behind, floating above the ugly trail of black smoke she was trailing in her wake.

"Don't worry about me," she snapped at him. "Those Chinese fighters …"

"Bugged out, ma'am," Diaz told her. "Meany and Flatline took out two J-15s and a Gyrfalcon. You bagged a fourth with your snapshot. The rest look to have scrammed for home."

Meany's voice came over the radio again. He and Flatline had closed to visual range and were coming up behind the Raptor flight. "Uh, what's the thinking here, Touchdown?" he asked. "Can you get some altitude?"

"No, my starboard engine is redlining just holding this altitude."

"I never heard of a Raptor that made it home on one engine," Diaz interjected. "Not ever."

"Park it, Diaz," Meany ordered. "You and Cyber get back on course for Anderson Air Base with Flatline. I'll stay with Touchdown."

"Roger that, boss," Flatline said and turned his machine toward Guam. He didn't question the order or add anything else. What else was there to say?

Meany dropped down beside Touchdown's wing, looking across at her machine. Then he carefully lifted himself up and over it, inspecting it from the starboard side before falling back behind and surveying the damage to her elevator and engine port.

"It's bad, Touchdown," he said, falling in on her wing again and looking across at the pilot in the cockpit of the Raptor. "Diaz is right. There's no Raptor ever made it down on one engine. And we've still got … uh, 800 kilometers of open water ahead of us."

"Well hell, pop your canopy and I'll jump over," Touchdown said. "Oh, wait, the Widow doesn't have a canopy. There goes that great idea."

"But seriously …" Meany said gently.

"But seriously? I'm not punching out in the middle of the Philippine Sea Meany; not as long as this machine can fly straight and level."

"Can you change heading?" Meany asked, concerned that every minute they flew on the wrong heading was taking them farther from Guam. "Don't disengage emergency flight control, just drop a nav point two points off your nose on the …"

"I know how not to kill myself, dammit!" Touchdown said. "Who is the Raptor flight lead here?"

123

Meany held his tongue. He eased his machine back and watched as, nudge by nudge, the Raptor yawed around until it was pointed at Guam again. It flew ugly, but it still flew.

Touchdown came back on the radio. "The plan is, fuel allowing, we get ourselves to Guam, and I punch out over a beach resort, and by the time I'm out of my harness, you are standing there with a Mai Tai and an impressed expression on that British po face."

"You get that machine anywhere near Guam, I'll have the whole damn Navy waiting for you, woman," Meany promised.

"The whole damn Navy? What kind of girl do you think I am, sir?"

They might have made it too. But as Touchdown had foreshadowed, the fuel burn rate of a Pratt & Whitney F119 running in the red zone just a few thousand feet above sea level was worse than two engines in a cruise state at 20,000. Much worse.

About one forty kilometers northwest of Guam, her fuel warning lamp began flashing that she had less than a minute of fuel remaining. Touchdown patted the instrument panel in front of her fondly. "Been nice knowing you, boy," she said softly. Then she began tightening her harness.

Dawn lit the horizon on her left, soft and pink. It looked like it was going to be a nice day. Somewhere else.

Meany was still off her port wing, but he'd only just arrived back. He'd lit his tail and powered ahead of her until he was in radio range of Guam and had, as he'd promised, organized a suitable Navy reception for her.

Between their position and Guam, at around 10-kilometer intervals, just about every available vessel, Coast Guard, Navy or merchant marine was strung out along her flight path, waiting for her to jump. Holding station off her starboard wing was a Boeing Scan Eagle maritime surveillance drone. Two Coast Guard Sikorsky Jayhawks were hovering 10 kilometers ahead of her, where they'd calculated she should jump.

When Meany had filled her in on the preparations, she'd laughed. "Wait, no Mai Tai?"

A Navy destroyer flashed under her nose. Soon she saw the bright orange blobs of the two Coast Guard helos in the distance, hovering left and right of her flight path.

Her signal to eject.

She made one last check of her instruments, then reached for the ejection handle below her thighs. "Hey, Meany, if I die, tell O'Hare I know she stole my makeup."

Meany's voice resonated with fake surprise. "Really? Those are your last words?"

No, they are not, Touchdown was thinking. *But you don't want to hear what I really want to say.*

She pulled the handle.

Meany watched from above and to her right as the canopy flew off the crippled Raptor and Touchdown's ejection seat blasted into the early morning sky.

Deploy, please deploy, he urged her parachute.

He watched one of the Coast Guard helos wheel around as the doomed Raptor passed it. He didn't watch to see the fighter fall into the sea because his eyes were fixed to Touchdown's ejection seat tumbling through the air.

Then the parachute was streaming out behind it, it swung violently downward like a child's swing, and it began

125

dropping toward the water. The Coast Guard Jayhawk was hovering like a cat waiting to pounce.

Meany had been told to clear the area as soon as Touchdown punched out, but he'd had to see that chute. It was no guarantee she'd make it. She could have hit her head on the way out of the cockpit. The bell crank on the ejection seat could malfunction when the chute opened, pinning her to the 200lb seat all the way to the bottom of the sea. Her life vest could malfunction. She might be bleeding, attracting sharks.

He thought of all that and more as he piloted his Widow reluctantly onward and left her fate in the hands of the Coast Guard helo crew.

One more pilot down.

Aggressor Inc. was not having a good war.

6. The battle of AC-130X 'Outlaw'

Ninety-three hours. That was how long it was going to take the crippled Chinese flagship, the PLA Navy *Fujian*, to crawl through the south Pacific northeast of Papua to the waters of the Chinese-aligned nation of Kiribati and the PLA Navy–leased port there.

Ninety-three tortuous, terrifying hours for Lieutenant Maylin 'Mushroom' Sun. Indonesia's navy, its government outraged that the Chinese vessel had been attacked from within what it regarded as its exclusive economic zone, agreed to attach two of its *Martadinata* class stealth frigates to sail in close formation with the *Fujian* to protect it against air and surface attack, on the condition it sailed to a neutral port and did not attempt to return directly to Chinese waters.

Mushroom spent every minute of every hour of the voyage waiting for the next attack to come. Their enemy had shown no reluctance to ignore international law and the rules of war before; why should it start now?

But it seemed the US-led Coalition drew the line at attacking neutral Indonesian aircraft, and with Indonesian frigates sailing in close formation and Indonesian Rafale fighters circling, *Fujian* and its remaining escorts, the air warfare destroyers *Dalian*, *Haikou* and unarmed fleet tender *Taihu,* limped northeast toward Port Aeon on Kiritimati Island in Kiribati—a non-aligned nation in name only. Port Aeon and the World War II–era airfield beside it had been rebuilt from the seabed up with Chinese Belt and Roads loans.

But the target destination took them farther from China and closer to the main enemy, with Hawaii only 1,200 kilometers away—no more than the distance between New York and Chicago.

Wild rumors began circulating about what would happen with *Fujian* and its crew when it reached port. So when they reached Mushroom's ears, she took the first opportunity that arose to confront *Fujian*'s Air Wing commander and acting captain, Colonel Wang Wei. *Fujian* was still incapable of flight operations, but that didn't stop her surviving pilots from running simulator drills while the crew's engineers and mechanics fought to get the deck catapult working again.

Wang had come to the pod deck to watch the afternoon training session, and when it was done, Mushroom levered herself out of her pod and rolled straight over to him.

"Colonel, what will happen to *Fujian* when we reach Kiribati?"

Wang straightened from the screen he had been reviewing and saw other eyes and ears had also tuned in to the conversation. "Ah, Lieutenant," he said. "Tell me what you have heard." He smiled. "If I can address any misunderstandings, I will."

Mushroom had lost most of the inculcated deference for PLAN leadership drummed into her at flight academy. Most of it had melted away in the heat of a hypersonic missile in the Philippine Sea. Then the last of it dissolved in the tears she shed for the comrades she lost off the coast of West Papua.

"People are saying that our damage is too great to be repaired, that we cannot hope to defend *Fujian* so far from home and so close to the main enemy," she told him. "And so *Fujian* will be scuttled if we reach Kiribati."

"*When* we reach Kiribati, surely, Lieutenant," Wang corrected her sharply. "Not *if*."

Mushroom wasn't deterred by his tone. "So it is true?"

"If we are ordered to scuttle *Fujian* on arriving at Port Aeon, we will," Wang replied, then he softened his tone. "But we have not been so ordered. Tell me, do you know the story of the American carrier *Yorktown*?"

Mushroom vaguely remembered a conversation with Wang at the funeral of the pilots and crew killed in the last attack on *Fujian*, in which he mentioned the American vessel, but … "No Colonel, not in this context."

Making sure anyone in earshot could hear, he stood with his hands behind his back, his shoulders wide. "*Yorktown* was part of a two-carrier task force sent to ambush Japanese ships on their way to New Guinea, but its commander gave their position away, and the Americans were attacked. *Yorktown* was bombed, its flight deck crippled, fires four decks down. The Japanese considered it sunk, but *Yorktown* made it back to Pearl Harbor, and within *two days* it had been repaired and sailed to join the Battle of Midway, where its pilots sank the Japanese carrier *Soryu*."

Mushroom began to see his point now, but she was wise enough to let him finish.

"*Fujian* will dock in Port Aeon with *Dalian* and *Haikou* at its side. Our Navy and Air Force will resupply us with ammunition and drones. Our proximity to the main enemy will be our strength, not our weakness. We will deny the surrounding airspace to the adversary and put up an air defense so determined that any attack against us will result in their humiliation." He pulled himself erect. "And we *will* repair our catapult, so that we can put aircraft in the air once again and force our enemy to bring the battle to us, until we have expended every last shell, every missile and every life that *Fujian* has to give."

The entire pod deck had gone silent. Fire swelling in her breast, Mushroom began applauding, and soon every last man and woman in sight was clapping and cheering too.

Eight hundred kilometers south of *Fujian*, watching the data feed from a drone circling the *Fujian* Strike Group well out of range of its missiles and the Indonesian Rafales escorting it, was the pilot whose job it was to find a way to finish *Fujian* off, before it reached Kiribati.

And he was fuming.

Because as far as he could see, the *Fujian* was a problem without a real-world solution, unless his Pentagon masters were willing to throw everything they had at the problem and to wear the political consequences.

For a start, *Fujian*'s air defenses had been bolstered by the addition of two of Indonesia's most capable warships, bringing its picket strength back up to four air and submarine defense vessels, while Indonesian fighters flew defensive patrols overhead. Secondly, the two Indonesian ships were almost welded to the port and starboard flanks of the Chinese carrier. No matter how accurate an attack on the *Fujian* was, whether by air or sea, it would be almost impossible to deliver without damage to the Indonesian frigates.

The carrier was vulnerable—two attacks so far had proven that—but now it was sailing behind a political *and* diplomatic shield. Indonesia was keen to see the Chinese carrier out of its own waters, but they were also determined that nothing more would happen to it on their watch. Indonesia wasn't a part of the new "Shanghai Pact," but running a blocking tackle for *Fujian* was a shrewd political move intended to earn Jakarta a big favor from Beijing.

The tight escort also ruled out an attack by a wolf pack of *Virginia* class submarines.

So Captain Rory O'Donoghue of the 492nd Special Operations Wing, 18th Flight Test Squadron, had been tasked to shadow the Chinese strike group from outside the range of their aircraft and missiles and look for "air attack vulnerabilities." To do it, he had one of the most storied aircraft in the US inventory.

The first flight of the first machine in its line had taken place in 1955. The first model of the type Rory was commanding took wing in 1966. The actual aircraft Rory was flying in had rolled off the production line in Marietta Georgia in 2015 as an AC-130J Ghostrider before being returned to the manufacturer in 2028 and reconfigured into the newest AC-130X variant.

Rory's crew had named their machine "Outlaw" after a Special Operation in which they had disobeyed orders and landed on a highway in Syria to rescue a Delta Force unit after a reconnaissance operation gone wrong.

They'd recovered the Delta Force team, and though their AC-130 was damaged by ground fire, it got them home. Each of them got a written reprimand in their files and were docked a month's pay. "Outlaw" was born and became the unofficial name on the machine's 781 maintenance binder.

Despite being one of the oldest aircraft types still flying, Outlaw was also one of the few crewed aircraft with the legs to be able to shadow the Chinese carrier across the Pacific and the capability to do what Rory was about to do.

He had been ordered to probe the Chinese task force for vulnerabilities, and despite the near impossibility of the task he'd been assigned, he was about to do so.

With prejudice.

"Sir, you asked to be alerted to anything unusual, whether it appeared to be a threat or not …" Wang's air defense watch officer said hesitantly.

With *Fujian*'s superstructure gone, so was its bridge, and Wang was commanding *Fujian* and its strike group from the Combat Information Center, or CIC, two decks under the flight deck.

"Yes. Put it on screen," Wang told him, pointing to the large central wall-mounted LCD that dominated the CIC's forward bulkhead. A single map replaced the multiple windows of information there, showing *Fujian* and its escorts about 100 kilometers out from their destination: Port Aeon, Kiribati. About the same distance east was a chain of Indonesian islands, the largest of them a Manhattan-sized island called Jamdena. It was here the watch officer had drawn a box around the shape of a blue aircraft symbol.

"Indonesian air traffic control radar reported a return from a large, slow-flying aircraft just north of Jamdena, on a northerly heading. It did not respond to air traffic control instructions and descended to sea level before disappearing from radar."

Fujian was about to enter the stage of its voyage where it was most vulnerable to a follow-up air attack, either out of Australia in the south or Hawaii in the north. They were halfway to Kiribati, about 3,500 kilometers from Australian bases in the north of that country, and 4,000 kilometers from Pearl Harbor. Technically still inside the range of Coalition stealth fighters using aerial refueling, but more importantly, well within the 11,000-kilometer range of American stealth bombers.

The vast distances of the Pacific were a problem for their Indonesian Rafale escorts, which also had to rely on airborne refueling to stay with the strike group. The Indonesian fighters were now passing between the US-aligned Marshall Islands to the North and non-aligned Nauru to the south, and were at the limit of the coverage they were able to provide from their base at Jayapura. It had only ever been a paper-thin diplomatic cover, not a serious military one, and it was about to be withdrawn, leaving *Fujian* out on the open seas. Their missile defense teams were already on high alert, and they still had the support of their Indonesian Navy compatriots, but a single American stealth bomber or submarine with a bellyful of cruise missiles, if it got close enough …

"Satellite assets, what do we have?" he said urgently.

"None in position, Colonel."

Wang cursed. They would not be able to begin seriously to repair their catapult and launch surveillance aircraft until they docked in Port Aeon. He was not only crippled; he was near-blind too.

"Latest from Indonesian Air Force?"

"They have two Rafales on patrol overhead, which just announced they are bingo fuel and returning to their tanker. We are not expecting another patrol."

"Get onto the Indonesian Air Force. Request they urgently investigate the contact," he said, turning to his executive officer, or XO. The man was newly promoted—*Fujian*'s former XO having died on the bridge—and still had the look of a deer in the headlights every time Wang addressed him. "XO, contact *Dalian*; order them to move out another 10 miles and scan that vector, optimize search for stealth aircraft. Let the Indonesian vessels know we are moving to general quarters and suggest they do the same. Sound general quarters."

A large, low-flying aircraft ignoring air traffic control? It *could* be drug smugglers. Or it could be serious trouble.

Rory's Outlaw *was* east of the *Fujian* Strike Group. But it was nowhere near where Indonesia's air traffic control radar had "identified" it. What the Indonesian civilian radar had picked up was the radar "ghost" from a LongShot electronic countermeasure, or ECM, drone launched from Outlaw after it left Australian airspace off Darwin.

The LongShot was a long endurance drone or ordnance mother ship controlled by Outlaw that could launch its own fleet of smaller drones. Drones like the small ECM drone circling off the coast of Indonesia's Jamdena Island—designed to create a radar signature that made it *look* like a much larger aircraft.

Rory's Outlaw had survived multiple Red Flag and special operations in contested airspace because it was rarely where its enemy thought it was, and by the time they realized that, Outlaw had done its job and was long gone.

They'd wasted four valuable hours getting their ISR package together for this mission, and the Chinese strike group was getting closer to the protection of Port Aeon by the hour. On an operation like this, Rory left the piloting to his copilot while he took the role of Mission Crew Commander.

His electronic warfare officer, or EWO, was tracking the radio signals from inside and around the *Fujian* Strike Group. He couldn't break their encryption, but by tapping into satellites overhead, he could triangulate their positions. His

EWO's voice came over the radio. "Indonesian fighters are pulling out. We have clear air over the strike group. Window is open, boss."

Chinese planners had been right; there was no Coalition appetite to make an enemy of Indonesia. A real attack on *Fujian* right now had not been authorized. But Rory was about to give the *Fujian* Strike Group a hell of a shock and see how it responded. He checked the tactical plot, then addressed his combat systems officer.

"CSO, launch LongShot One Locusts at Chinese destroyer contact F-1. Weapons, you are clear to launch LongShot Two."

Rory's machine had a cowgirl riding a LongShot drone stenciled on its nose. Like the Outlaw it was named after, the AC-130X had multiple tricks up its sleeve. Outlaw could carry six of the dispensable LongShot drone mother ships, each configurable for different missions while she was in flight. Like its forerunners, the AC-130X could travel far and loiter for a long time, but unlike earlier marques, it was no longer limited to firing large bore guns or dropping glide bombs on its targets. It could strike from "over the horizon," and could make itself look like a squadron of fighters or a flight of cruise missiles. It could launch pinpoint assassination strikes on moving vehicles or broad area strikes on troop concentrations. The new capabilities made Rory's old, fat, slow gunship a very, very dangerous enemy to a wounded carrier strike group.

Circling 20 nautical miles northwest of where Indonesia's radar thought it saw Outlaw off Jamdena Island, Outlaw's LongShot One mother ship launched the rest of its payload.

These were also small ECM drones, but they were not configured to look like Outlaw to adversary radar. They were configured to mimic the electronic signatures of F-35 Panther fighters.

Fifty miles east of the *Fujian* Strike Group, the swarm of 20 ECM drones rose from wavetop height and started radiating electronic energy. After one minute, they killed their emissions and dived for the sea again, banking south this time.

"Contacts detected by *Dalian*—adversary stealth fighters!" Wang's air warfare watch officer, or AWO, said, nearly shouting in alarm. "Classified F-35s, bearing eight zero, altitude 5,000, range 50. Twenty-plus bandits. On-screen."

The large tactical map showed a cloud of blue dots to their east. So the Australians were coming at them again, caring nothing for diplomacy.

"Contacts lost," his AWO said. "*Dalian* has nothing on radar."

Wang cursed. He could not strike what he could not see. The Australian fighters could have, probably had, already launched their cruise missiles at *Fujian*. If he was lucky, *Dalian* and *Haikou* would pick them up 20 miles out, in plenty of time to intercept.

But if they were not lucky …

He studied the tactical map intently. To their immediate left was the Indonesian island of Wetar, covered in tropical jungle and volcanic mountain ranges. It would mask the approach of terrain-following missiles from that direction until they were within … 5 miles of *Dalian*. "XO, order *Dalian* to jam down that bearing. Prepare short-range interceptors and HPM batteries. It is unlikely they will …"

"Contact reacquired by *Dalian*!" the AWO announced. "F-35s, bearing 120, altitude 2,000, 45 miles. Still 20-plus bandits."

Another cloud of blue dots, a little farther south this time.

"*Dalian* engaging!"

Wang nodded with satisfaction. Already on alert, already forewarned, the air defense teams on *Dalian* had been quicker this time. Twenty HHQ missiles appeared on screen, spearing out toward the Coalition F-35s.

Which disappeared.

"Contacts lost again," his AWO announced. "Missiles moving to search-and-track mode."

The attack wasn't wasted. The interceptor missiles, having lost the data lock from *Dalian*'s radar, would start using their own radars to find and attack the Coalition aircraft down the bearing they had been fired.

But was this the same group they had first identified or a second squadron altogether? They were so close, it almost had to be, didn't it?

"Chinese destroyer engaging," Rory's EWO advised. "Swarm has gone low, turning east again. LongShot One returning."

So the Chinese had taken the bait. "How many missiles?"

"Estimate 20," his EWO replied.

Twenty missiles the Chinese wouldn't have in later combat. Their chances of finding and hitting the tiny ECM drones were minimal. He wasn't satisfied though. "Where is LongShot Two?"

His EWO drew a box around the strike group, with *Fujian* at its center. "Approaching ingress waypoint."

"Release your swarm as soon as LS2 is picked up on Chinese radar," Rory ordered. "Bring her straight back to mama, and get ready to bug the hell out before another Indonesian air patrol rolls in."

LongShot Two, or LS2, was also armed with a swarm of 20 ECM drones, this time configured to mimic the older F-15EX multirole fighter, itself a formidable "missile truck." It was hugging the surface of the sea, and Rory's intelligence was that *Fujian*'s pickets could pick up a low-flying stealth aircraft anywhere from 20 to 50 miles out from the carrier. The appearance of 20 "F-15EX missile trucks" at point-blank range was intended to put ice in the veins of the Chinese commander. In "beast mode," an F-15EX could carry 28 250 lb. glide bombs, so 20 F-15s could theoretically "pop" up to 20,000 feet and send more than 500 bombs gliding toward *Fujian* and its escorts.

More than once, Rory and his mission planners had speculated about what they could have achieved if Air Force had just granted them the assets they were simulating. Two squadrons of F-35s, two of F-15EXs, and the *Fujian* problem might have been solved.

Of course, that might also have pulled Indonesia into the war, but Rory was a warrior, not a politician. He tended to favor high-explosive solutions to complex problems.

Dalian's interceptor missiles had reached the estimated position of the Coalition fighters, and the data they were sending back indicated two kills. *Two! Out of 20 aircraft detected!*

Had the rest turned away? Fled? Had the Coalition been serious about its attack, or was it yet another damned feint?

"New contacts! Designating 'Group Two.' Bearing southeast, altitude 1,000, range 45, heading west-southwest. AI says … F-15s."

Wang narrowed his eyes. Not stealth aircraft, but using nap of the earth to hide. Inside cruise missile range, but they had not launched …

"Engage immediately. They're trying to launch iron bombs," Wang predicted. "Hit them before they can." Optically guided iron bombs would be harder for *Fujian* and its pickets to intercept, but the aircraft launching them were much more vulnerable. He had just ordered his people to initiate a slaughter. He shook his head. Whoever had ordered this attack had no respect for the lives of their pilots.

And it would not succeed. He heard his XO bark out the orders. "*Dalian* and *Haikou* to engage Group Two. Launch all ready long-range missiles." *Dalian* should still have 50 long-range HHQ-9 missiles in its vertical launch cells. The older *Haikou* would have 28. He was leaving the strike group vulnerable to the F-35s lurking out there somewhere, able to defend itself only with short-range interceptors and close-in weapon systems, but the threat from the American missile trucks could not be ignored.

"Whoa." Rory's EWO whistled. "Chinese are engaging the swarm from LS2. AI estimates *70-plus* missiles fired."

"Are the Indonesians supporting?"

"Doesn't look like it. That's just the Chinese pickets."

Rory slapped his thigh. The Chinese were swatting gnats with baseball bats. His first swarm of EW drones was turning south and would soon drop themselves into the waves.

"Alright, ladies and gentlemen," he announced on the ship's intercom. "We've seen all we need to see. Pilot, RTB. Loadmaster, prepare to recover."

The $4 million LongShot was theoretically a "low-cost attritable" drone, but it could dock with a drogue and be recovered in mid-air via Outlaw's loading ramp, reloaded and reused.

And Rory had a feeling he'd be needing all the airframes he had.

Wang's crew was celebrating. The Coalition F-15 attack from the south had been driven off, several destroyed. The remaining Coalition fighters had disappeared from radar south of the island, apparently too afraid to press their attack.

Fujian had survived to fight another day.

So why didn't Wang *feel* like it had been a victory?

Too much didn't add up. Why hadn't the F-35s in the east pressed their attack? They had disappeared from radar well within cruise-missile-launch range. If *Fujian* was the target, a blizzard of cruise missiles should have been fired from that sector.

There had been 20 F-15s detected in the southeast. Only seven had been destroyed, their interceptors reporting they had locked on a target in the milliseconds before it disappeared. Why had the rest not pressed their attack? What he had seen of the Coalition pilots so far in this war did not indicate they were reluctant to seek combat.

And the action could not have been a feint. It would have required dedicated tanker resources and considerable coordination. To lose so many multi-million-dollar aircraft and pilots in a probing action far out in the Pacific would be indefensible in any Air Force.

Unless … He turned away from the map and to his AWO. "What was the average airspeed for the Coalition aircraft?"

The man had been slapping one of his fellow officers on the back and frowned, turning to his console and consulting his support AI. "Uh, nothing on the first group, Colonel— the contact was only brief, and then we lost them." He typed another query. "We had a decent lock on the second group. They were flying at 400 knots."

Four hundred? The cruising speed of a fighter like the F-15 should be more like 500 to 600. "What is the optimal airspeed for an F-15 deploying a small-diameter bomb or LRASM missile?"

The man typed again. "It's a range. Anywhere between 300 and 800 knots, Colonel."

Three hundred? And the F-15s had been logged at 400. A pilot over a friendly bombing range might fly at 400 knots, but Wang was willing to bet any pilot at the stick of a machine with Chinese radar locked on him would rather be moving at twice that airspeed.

Unless they wanted to be seen, *wanted* to be attacked.

Just to draw down his missile inventory, perhaps? No. Trading aircraft and pilots for missiles was a losing equation. This was something else.

"XO, you have the conn. Please ask Major Tan to review the data from this engagement and meet me in my cabin."

Major Tan Yuanyuan, Wing Intelligence Officer for *Fujian*, was used to very open-ended inquiries from *Fujian*'s Air Wing commander. And they had apparently not gotten more specific since he assumed command for the entire strike group. "Review the data," was about as broad an order as he could issue, and it told her he was fishing for something.

Her team had access to the Navy's decision support AI "Empire Dominator," which could assimilate and analyze the raw data from every sensor and console aboard the three Chinese warships, match it to the transcript of the voice recordings from the human officers during the engagement and correlate it with all resulting actions, from the speed and heading of every ship and aircraft involved to the ordnance fired and the results of the Chinese attacks. Prompting and poking the AI had enabled Tan's team to put together a 360-degree analysis of the engagement, but she didn't have the luxury of time to draw any conclusions from it. She knew she would have to do that on the fly, in Wang's stateroom.

He was standing as she entered. Not a good sign. She didn't try to ease the apparent tension with small talk or a quick quip. Tan was from farming stock, her family scratching out a living on terraced mountainsides, and her parents had brought her up stubborn, proud and stoic. But they had failed in persuading her to take over the family farm because from the porch of her mountain home, Tan could see the Yellow Sea and, at night, the lights from the sprawling harbor city of Qingdao, home to China's Northern fleet.

After graduating from naval college, she served in four mainland roles before her first posting to a PLAN vessel, the ill-fated *Lhasa*, lost at sea with all hands off Palau. She'd been promoted to *Fujian* two years before that terrible day, and promoted again to her current position because Wang quickly learned this farmer's daughter would always speak her thoughts, not guard them or wrap them in political weasel words.

She stood quietly at attention until the Colonel noticed her. "Ah, Tan, sit," he said.

She put her tablet PC on the table between them. Tan had learned not to assume she knew what was on Wang's mind. "What questions do you have, Colonel?"

He sat too, leaning back in his chair, hands behind his head. "Your report to Ningbo will say that we were attacked from east and southeast by a considerable force of Coalition fighters, both F-35s and F-15s, which aborted their attack when rapidly engaged by our escorts *Dalian* and *Haikou*. Damage to the strike group, none. Damage to our allies' frigates, none. Estimated enemy losses …" He raised an eyebrow.

"Four F-35s and six F-15s, Colonel," she finished his sentence. "Yes, that is the gist of the after-action summary."

"Yes. And I will write a commendation letter for the Captain of *Dalian* for the speed and success with which he engaged this overwhelming Coalition attack."

Tan nodded. "That would be appropriate, I agree."

"Yes. So I want you to assume everything we just agreed is wrong."

Tan blinked. "Colonel?"

"There was no attack on the strike group. The Coalition air action had some other purpose. Nothing of what I just described is the way it seems."

Tan did not like mind games. She preferred hard facts, confirmed by multiple sources, leading to cast-iron conclusions. Not wild-assed guesswork. But she could play the game. She did it systematically.

143

"Alright, sir. We can start by assuming that the target was not this strike group."

Wang leaned forward. "Very well."

"However, there are no other Chinese military units this far east. So it only makes sense for our vessels to be somehow connected to the attack. Perhaps the attack vector was not the Coalition aircraft?"

"Undersea, a submarine, trying to sneak past while we were distracted?"

She consulted her analysis. "No sonar contacts. But it is conceivable."

"Note it down; I'll have our ASW teams work it," he ordered. "Keep thinking."

"Do you have suspicions of your own, Colonel?"

"Yes, but I want to hear your theories first."

Tan looked at the data her team had put together. "It *is* possible ... no ..."

"Speak, Major ..."

She looked up. "Well, it is possible we were not attacked by aircraft at all." She expected him to laugh at her, but he just nodded.

"Go on."

"Or not the aircraft we believe attacked us. The first group was barely identified at all before it disappeared. The second group was ..."

"Flying too slow," Wang suggested.

"Yes! Well below what we would expect for F-15s on an attack run. And the formations ..."

"The formations?"

"Both groups of attackers were flying in close formation. Coalition F-35s never attack in close formation, and F-15s would also be likely to attack in smaller elements. It could be we are ..."

"Looking at drones," he said. "Decoy drones. Or combat drones, like F-47 Fantoms with ECM pods."

She was typing into her tablet, interrogating her AI. "Coalition forces have several uncrewed aerial vehicles that can be used to imitate the radar and electronic signatures of fighter aircraft," she said, reading off the screen. "The F-47 is just one. Others include the Puma, the Talon, the Locust ..." She shook her head. "We shot down several. We need to get hold of the wreckage to be sure."

"Highly unlikely," Wang suggested. "They were engaged over open sea."

"But why?" she asked, still not convinced herself that the attack was anything other than it seemed to be. "Why a decoy attack and not a real one? To draw down our missile stocks?"

"That was my theory," Wang admitted. "But whoever did this must know that when we reach port, we will replenish both ordnance and fuel. What we used in this engagement will be quickly replaced."

"And ... how? Talons and Locusts are short-range. The F-47 has to be launched from a carrier or use aerial refueling— multiple tankers, given the size of this attack." She looked skeptical. "Do you want me to include a decoy scenario in my report to Ningbo?" she asked. "It seems possible."

"No. Don't put it in your report," Wang decided. "But keep it alive up here," he said, tapping his temple. "Consider seriously the possibility this was not a failed Coalition attack but a successful one."

"Yes sir." Tan stood to leave, but Wang motioned her to sit.

"I have one more job for you," he said. "Pull together some people from engineering, flight operations, supply. I want your people to work out what parts and materials we can cannibalize from within the ship to get the catapult and flight deck operating again. We still have 3,000 kilometers to Port Aeon, and we need to be able to put an ISR drone in the air to at least give us eyes over the horizon."

Rory certainly *felt* like it had been a successful mission, but he didn't have his own intel team to confirm his gut feel. His was the only aircraft from the 18th Flight Test Squadron in Australia since they'd only come down for some joint service exercises and then been told to stay put when the Taiwan conflict kicked off. He could task an analyst back at 492nd Special Operations Wing, but even though he lived in the era of AI Decision Support, that had a 24-hour turnaround time for a low-level nobody like Rory O'Donoghue.

And for now, with *Fujian* headed *away* from Taiwan, the problem of the Chinese carrier was his to solve. It was not a top priority.

What Rory did have was the perspicacious mind of his Korean American copilot, Lieutenant Robert E. Lee. Yes, he had been named after the Confederate General. It had either been that or Stonewall Lee, which had the right ring about it but just didn't sound quite right to his father, newly settled in North Virginia and keen for his son to fit in.

"So what are we thinking, Uncle?" Rory asked him, using the nickname that was also, not coincidentally, the same as the Confederate General's. He was five years Rory's senior, which had also helped the nickname stick.

"Scary-fast reaction times," Uncle replied, looking at a page of scribbled notes and figures. "One minute 10 from detection to launch on swarm one, 45 seconds for swarm two. Those guys were on their toes."

"Getting stomped by a hypersonic missile will do that to you, I guess," Rory remarked. "Did they get a return off our LongShots?"

"Nope," the man said. The LongShot was about the size of a stubby cruise missile but with radar-absorbent coating and radar-deflecting angled surfaces. "We got within 80 miles without getting pinged. I'd be wary of pushing them in closer, though."

"No sign of aircraft radar apart from the Indonesians though, right?"

"No. I pulled imagery from the latest satellite pass, and there's activity on the deck, but it's still a twisted mess. They aren't launching aircraft off that ship any time soon. Recon or otherwise."

"So we have to hit them before they can. Except we have no assets we can task, and I'm not about to take our fat-assed Outlaw inside Chinese missile range."

"Yeah, about that. I got a better idea," Uncle said. "Who do you know in Washington?"

7. The battle of the Eastern Pacific

It was the witching hour. Three a.m. Soon time for the evening watch to change with the morning watch on the amphibious assault ship USS *Fallujah*. It was the worst of hours, and the one which the commander of any amphibious readiness group (ARG) at war dreads.

Rear Admiral Harry 'Halfway' Johnson had ordered overlapping watches at every watch change. He had been warned there was intelligence indicating a high likelihood of hostile action on this voyage but received no further intel on how that attack might come—by air, by sea, electronically or by submarine. Five hours had passed since *Fallujah* left the Pacific Fleet base at Pearl Harbor, but there had been no sign of hostile activity.

Both AI and human analysts assessed the most likely threat vector was a submarine attack. But Johnson got his nickname because he never did anything by halves, and he had his own intel network. Johnson's intel was that *Fallujah* could be looking at a combined air swarm-undersea attack, similar to the one that had crippled the USS *Enterprise* in the opening days of the Taiwan conflict.

The good news was China had most of its blue water fleet exercising with Russian vessels in the Kuril Islands chain, four days' sailing away. With China's three carriers either back in port or running for cover, it was unlikely the enemy could deploy swarming drones anywhere near the central Pacific. But that did not mean it was impossible, and Johnson had long ago learned never to rule out the impossible. Military history was full of commanders who had failed by not protecting themselves against attacks that could not possibly happen.

Nevertheless, it was a subsurface attack he feared most. The *Fallujah* readiness group had the heavily armed and networked *Constellation* class frigate, USS *Lafayette*, coordinating its defense and three older *Arleigh Burke* class destroyers, the *Ramage*, *McFaul* and *Thomas Hudner*, ringing it as pickets. All three destroyers had deployed with Fire Scout aerial and Sea Hunter trailing surface drones. He was confident he could protect himself against a swarming aerial attack, and even if one or two missiles or drones got through, they would not compromise his ability to complete his mission.

So under the surface, he had a surprise for any adversary. Any half-decent intelligence service could easily have determined that *Fallujah* had sailed from Yokosuka Harbor in the company of *Virginia* class nuclear attack submarines, *Silversides* and *Wahoo*. But Johnson had also pulled some strings to have the AUKUS submarine HMAS *AE1* added to his subsurface complement.

Johnson had two subs out in front of his ARG and *AE1* trailing to protect their six.

Their mission was the first one *Fallujah* would be carrying out in a hot war zone. Aboard the *Fallujah* were the last elements of the 82nd Airborne destined for Taiwan. Meanwhile, two other ARGs based around USS *America* and USS *Tripoli* were converging on the rebel island from Yokosuka in Japan and Luzon in the Philippines. *America* was carrying a full Marine Expeditionary Unit (MEU) of 2,500 men and equipment, which it would offload at the port of Hualien on the east coast of Taiwan. Once the MEU was offloaded, *Fallujah* and *America* would deploy to Luzon and embark another MEU. *Tripoli* was carrying mostly vehicles and ordnance bound for Taipei to help bolster the city's slaughterbot defenses.

Fallujah was only 239 kilometers out of Pearl. About five hours sailing.

But it was the witching hour, so Johnson was on the bridge.

And sure enough … "USS *Ramage* reports a possible subsurface contact, 10 miles northeast of their Sea Hunter," the CIC watch officer reported. "Designating S-1. On-screen."

The eyes of the entire bridge turned to the tactical monitor on *Fallujah*'s rear bulkhead showing the environment around the ARG and the position of every known vessel, military and civilian. It was as complete a picture as *Lafayette* was able to compile using the sensors aboard every ship in the readiness group, data from their Sentinel AWACS drone and infrared-optical satellite data pulled down with near real-time frequency.

The small dot indicating a possible enemy submarine appeared on the screen, along with a dynamically updated projection of its heading. It was northeast of their westernmost picket, *Ramage*, and 20 miles *behind* one of their subs, the *Wahoo*. If it was a submarine, it had gotten past the *Wahoo* somehow.

But not past *Ramage* and its roving Sea Hunter.

Johnson watched carefully as the contact was investigated. *Ramage*'s Sea Hunter drone closed on it from above. Designed specifically to hunt submarines, the drone wasn't armed itself, but it could call down rocket-launched torpedoes from the *Ramage* if it confirmed a contact was hostile. The *Wahoo* changed course, turning back to use its long-range passive sonar to try to locate the contact, but the trailing AUKUS

150

submarine *AE1* would be in a better position sooner. *Ramage* also launched its armed Fire Scout helicopter. It could be overhead the contact inside five minutes, ready to drop dummy charges first, to signal the contact to surface, and then Mark 54 Lightweight Hybrid Torpedoes if its Captain declined.

The *Fallujah* ARG was operating with near-wartime rules of engagement. It was expected to warn any potential hostile contact, but it could attack any vessel it regarded to be a threat. The gray zone there was something Halfway Johnson and his Captains were *very* comfortable operating in.

Nevertheless … "XO, no ordnance is to be deployed except on my express order, are we clear?" he said.

His XO turned and nodded. "Clear, Admiral."

"And get a message to the Australians. Give them a vector to an intercept on that contact."

AUKUS submarine HMAS *AE1* was traveling at ELF reception depth with its antennae deployed and its Rolls-Royce nuclear reactor damped, using only battery power to drive its pump-jet propulsors. It could travel at 25 knots up to 900 kilometers submerged on batteries, and it had only covered 300 kilometers since leaving Pearl.

A baby dolphin gave off more noise than the *AE1* when it was moving in stealth mode.

Two weeks ago, it would have been the noisiest vessel in the entire theater. Damaged in battle off Palau, its diving planes were giving off a level of noise which gradually became worse as it began its transit toward the Yellow Sea, where it was supposed to take up patrol duty between South Korea and Japan.

AE1's Captain, Gary McDonald, had been forced to interrupt the mission and divert to Pearl for repairs. His 18-person crew was not disappointed. They had been at sea six weeks and survived two engagements with Chinese warships, the last one only by the hair on their stubbled chins.

A week on Hawaii while *AE1* was repaired and resupplied was just what the doctor had ordered. It almost made up for the tedium now of being given new mission orders requiring it to play nursemaid behind a US convoy headed west. Almost.

"Message from *Lafayette,*" McDonald's comms watch officer reported. "Coordinates to an intercept on a possible Chinese boat."

"Lay it in," McDonald told his helmsman-navigator. "About time we got back to work."

The Chinese submarine PLAN *Type 095-09* was not trying to penetrate the *Fallujah*'s line of pickets; she had crossed paths with the *Fallujah* ARG and its hyperalert crews by unhappy coincidence.

Nine had set out from Huangpu Wenchong Shipyard already submerged. Freshly returned from performance trials, because of developments in the Taiwan conflict, she had been rushed into underway weapons and safety trials that had to be conducted en route to her area of operations.

Western intelligence services thought they knew everything there was to know about *Type 095-09*. The newest boat in the *Type 095* class, *Nine* was supposed to be the first of a growing number of optionally uncrewed nuclear attack submarines. The main difference between *Nine* and earlier boats in the class was that without crew spaces, she could

152

carry more ordnance, resulting in a more potent offensive platform. She made use of known Chinese advances in quantum communication, which made her ELF/VLF receivers so sensitive she could send and receive signals at greater depth, and without extending a dedicated antenna. She could theoretically travel submerged from the South China Sea to the US West Coast, but she was not a ballistic missile submarine, or "boomer," so she was not seen as a critical strategic threat—more of a worry, since a lot of her operations would be governed by AI.

Such was the intelligence assessment that China had carefully allowed Western intelligence services to compile.

She was much, much more.

Chinese advances in quantum radio reception meant *Nine* was the first submarine to use a quantum-enhanced transceiver based on a superconducting quantum interference device (SQUID) that could detect digitally modulated magnetic signals at VLF frequencies, able to achieve data rates of up to 100 megabits per second. That meant it could send and receive data-rich VLF signals across half the globe, or to Chinese vessels on the surface nearby, at any depth, in real time.

Like a creature born for the deep, *Nine* swam at depths crewed submarines could not achieve. But she carried hull and flank passive sonar arrays, high- and low-frequency environmental sensors that allowed her to navigate around undersea obstacles and, because she had an "always on" quantum link to her base in China, she could receive and reply to orders instantaneously.

As she approached an undersea volcanic ridge, she had been forced to rise to 130 meters, and 300 kilometers from her target waypoint, she started picking up the acoustic signals of large vessels about 15 miles to the south.

She immediately contacted Guangzhou Naval Command. *Type 095-09 position 33.45, 124.98, heading zero nine zero, depth 120. Two military surface vessels identified bearing one seven two degrees, range 15, acoustic signatures confirm vessels as USN destroyers* Ramage *and* McFaul. *High confidence assessment this is the* Fallujah *ARG which departed Pearl Harbor four hours previous. Do you wish me to deviate to investigate and confirm, or proceed with current mission?*

The answer was simple. "Proceed."

Nine continued on her way. But very soon after, she contacted Guangzhou again. *Type 095-09 position 33.59, 125.05.* Fallujah *ARG has changed course and is sailing on parallel track. I recommend deploying SLMAT and optimizing speed, depth and heading for stealth.*

Another brief answer came back. "Recommendation approved."

Nine was an astounding example of AI, nuclear submarine and stealth engineering, and perhaps the pinnacle of human undersea technology.

But all it would take to send her to the bottom was the 96.8 lb. of high explosive in a Mark 54 lightweight torpedo.

The contact detected by the Sea Hunter and now being vigorously pursued by the air and sea assets of the USS *Ramage* was not *Type 095-09*.

Nine had more than stealth working for her. She had a *doppelgänger.* And when she realized she was in danger of being detected, she launched it.

Ramage had picked up *Nine's* Submarine Launched Mobile Anti-Submarine Target (SLMAT)—a long-endurance underwater decoy programmed to mimic the acoustic signature of a *Type 095* boat.

It could mimic other submarines' acoustic and electromagnetic signatures, but *Nine* chose the deadly *Type 095* as the type most likely to cause concern, even panic, among nearby US warships.

In that, she calculated correctly.

"Contact identified! PLAN *Type 095!*" Johnson's subsurface warfare officer turned to face his Captain, and the Admiral behind him, face near white.

The equanimity that Johnson had been maintaining throughout the unfolding engagement quickly evaporated. No US warship had been attacked by a Chinese submarine outside of the Taiwan conflict zone. It was not unusual to run into one in the Yellow Sea, between China and the Korean Peninsula, and Chinese submarines had every right to be there.

But he'd been warned of the possibility of attack, and Chinese submarines were *not* welcome inside the formation of the *Fallujah* ARG, so Johnson had issued the orders needed to make the problem go away.

The problem had just gotten significantly more concerning. There was no boat in China's fleet more deadly than the new *Type 095*. It carried the same weapons and sensor suite as the very capable *Type 093 Shang* class, but it was quieter and had considerable counter-torpedo defensive capabilities.

"Admiral has the conn," Johnson announced. "Comms, get a flash message to Fleet, Yokosuka—message reads 'Chinese nuclear attack submarine detected inside picket perimeter. *Ramage* to challenge and make the contact aware it has been detected and its actions are being monitored,'" he said. "Add the contact's position."

"Aye, Admiral," *Fallujah*'s Captain replied.

"Message to the commander, *Lafayette*," he continued. "'All ships to general quarters. The mission is ASW. Weapons are free. This is not an exercise.'" He paused, reviewing the tactical situation on screen. "Message to the Captain of *Ramage*: 'Prosecute contact S-1. You are free to deploy dummy charges. If the contact does not appear to respond within three minutes and begin moving away from *Fallujah*, or moves to missile launch depth without continuing to the surface, arm Type 54 torpedoes and request further orders.'"

Like the Chinese submarine, the Australian submarine *AE1* used quantum compressed ELF comms. It wasn't in a position to start searching for the Chinese submarine itself, yet, but it could follow the engagement, both on radio and on sonar.

"*Ramage* is deploying dummy charges," McDonald's sensor watch officer advised.

"*Fallujah*'s Admiral is taking this right to the edge," McDonald's XO, Brunelli, said with a frown. "We're still in international waters."

"He is," McDonald confirmed. "But there's a hot war west of here, and he has 3,000 souls aboard. It's what I'd do … dummy charges, and then live ordnance if the contact doesn't surface."

"A dummy charge *is* live ordnance far as I'm concerned," Brunelli said. "One of those goes off outside our hull, we could lose sonar, we'd have to check hull integrity …" Brunelli was a good complement to McDonald as his second in command, always helping to temper his almost legendary lack of patience and caution.

"No omelet without cracking eggs, XO," McDonald told her with a smile. "Let's hope *Ramage* doesn't take the Chinese boat off the board before we get within passive sonar range. It would be interesting to play a little game of tag with a *Type 095*."

"Contact S-1 responding," *Fallujah*'s ASW watch officer reported. "No acoustic indications it is changing depth. But it has changed course. Fire Scout Mark 54s are armed and ready to drop."

Fallujah's Captain turned to him, looking for a steer on whether to launch on the Chinese submarine. Attacking it without "just cause" could trigger World War III, and the world was teetering on the brink right now.

"What is the contact's heading?" he asked. He looked up at the tactical map. They were 300 miles out from Busan, in international waters.

"West-southwest, Admiral," the ASW officer replied. "Coming around west. Might be trying to convince us it is headed out?"

Johnson had been briefed on China's new *Type 095* boats of course, including the fact they were believed to have launched an uncrewed version. He had no way of knowing which he was dealing with.

Whether human or AI, the Chinese "commander" would know he had been identified, and not only that, but that he'd been boxed. He would be hearing their helos dipping sonar, the sonars of the Sea Hunter and the approaching *Ramage*, and he would definitely have heard the twin explosions of the dummy charges.

He, or it, was playing it cool though. Not willing to surface, not trying to hide. Johnson didn't have time for a protracted pursuit; he had a Marine MEU to deliver.

"We will not attack," he decided. "Order *Ramage* to continue prosecuting the contact and, if it turns back toward *Fallujah*, to drop dummy charges again. If that happens, I will reevaluate. The group will remain at general quarters and prepared to …"

"Contact lost!" the ASW officer announced suddenly.

"What?" Johnson demanded. He had multiple units right on top of it—losing the Chinese submarine was damn near impossible.

"Gone, sir," his ASW officer announced. "One moment there, next, gone. We've got nothing from *Ramage*'s Sea Hunter, nothing from the Fire Scout or *Ramage* itself. Uh, *Lafayette* just confirmed. It's disappeared."

Johnson stayed calm. "Please point out to *Lafayette*'s Captain that a 7,000-ton submarine does not just 'disappear.' Find. That. Boat."

Of course, there was no submarine for *Ramage* to find, or lose, and *Nine*'s SLMAT had done its best to pull *Fallujah*'s pickets away from her. But the SLMAT had limited endurance, and its batteries had just failed, its engine stopped. Now it was falling silently toward the bottom of the Pacific.

"I've got something," the *AE1*'s sensor officer said suddenly. "But it's not where *Ramage* is prosecuting contact S-1."

"Classify," he said curtly. On a hunch, he hadn't altered their intercept course when they received a report from *Ramage* that the Chinese contact had turned west. There were already enough dogs in that hunt. McDonald had continued on their original intercept course.

"It's … nothing in the database," his sensor officer reported. "Closest I've got is humpback whale expelling air at depth, but it's not a clean match."

Not surprising, considering very few Western submarines have managed to even get close to the stealthy Chinese Type 095. "Do you have a vector to this new contact?" he asked, irritated.

The man mumbled, mistakenly thinking he was irritated at him. "Wouldn't even call it a contact, skipper. It's a noise. But yeah, I have a pretty solid bearing and projected track …"

"Lock it in," McDonald said. "There are more than enough assets pursuing the first contact. Helm: Ahead slow, maintain current depth. Bring us around to the new intercept heading. Gently. Assume the new contact is a submarine, constant heading and speed. Stealth pursuit, push and drift—give us a chance of getting another hit on passive sonar."

"*Ramage* reports it has lost the contact with S-1."

"Pull in the ELF antenna," McDonald ordered. The gossamer-thin wire being pulled through the water behind them made almost no noise, but "almost no noise" was still too much.

McDonald hit a switch on the bulkhead next to him to send a visual signal through the boat to the other crew members—a third of whom were resting anyway—that *AE1* had transitioned to silent running.

159

He looked at the tactical map. If it was a Chinese sub they were following, and not a whale, it didn't look to McDonald like it was setting up a shot at the *Fallujah* ARG. *Where are you headed, Mister 95?*

Anxious minutes passed as they closed on the position where the possible contact was expected to be. They were using their propulsion sparingly, just enough to make the intercept, but killing it completely and gliding through the water every 30 seconds or so … *listening.*

The tactic paid off.

"Contact acquired; I've got propulsion noises. Acoustic signature match with a *Type 095.*"

"Bearing and speed," McDonald barked. He was getting impatient now.

"Contact is bearing zero two zero, speed 12 knots, heading zero niner, range nine, depth estimate … uh, working on it," McDonald's sensor officer reported, sounding pleased with himself now. As he should be. "Got it. Heading zero eight three, depth 130. Designating contact as S-2."

"Well done, Master Chief Petty Officer Ozlem," he told the man, with a newfound cheerfulness. He'd been hoping the noise was a Chinese boat, and he wasn't surprised it was the *Type 095* that *Ramage* had found and lost.

But *was* it the same one? Or were they looking at a Chinese submarine wolf pack, closing in on *Fallujah* from multiple directions? He ordered his helm officer to match the contact's speed and heading. If he could drop down into the disturbed water behind the Chinese submarine's propulsors, they could hide in its roiling wake. The central Pacific was ideal for the hunted, not so good for the hunter. *Fallujah's* ARG had left the waters of the Hawaiian Ridge and was now in the Central Pacific Basin, in waters 5,000 meters deep. That

160

gave their quarry a lot of vertical to play with, depending on how deep it could dive. The only thing in their favor was that PLA Navy Admirals liked to stay in close contact with their Captains, and Chinese ELF comms were not believed to be effective below 500 meters.

"What's the target doing, Ozlem?"

The sensor officer was still frowning, bent over his screen. "Still heading east. I'd say it's surfing the thermocline, skipper," he said. "Seems to be gliding along in a range between 230 and 250 meters."

"Moving *away* from the ARG," McDonald decided. He scratched at the stubble on his chin. He'd been clean shaven when they re-boarded the boat in Hawaii, but none of the male crew members shaved when they were at sea.

He saw Brunelli paging through some data on her tablet PC. "What are you thinking, XO?" he asked.

"I don't think it's hunting *Fallujah* at all. I reckon it's headed for the Hawaiian Ridge," she said. "Routine Chinese attack boat patrol in Hawaiian waters."

"Except there's nothing routine about Chinese boats in US waters anymore," McDonald pointed out. "If it isn't on a mission to intercept US reinforcements for Taiwan, what the hell is it doing?"

Ozlem interrupted. "Contact increasing speed to 15 knots. Intermittent contact on passive sensors now." He looked up, worried. "Either we increase speed too and risk detection, or we let it go, Captain."

McDonald looked at the plot on their tactical screen, which showed the Chinese submarine moving in almost a straight line from the time they'd first heard it to now.

A straight line that would take it all the way to the sonar-confusing peaks and valleys of the Hawaiian Ridge, a favorite playground for Chinese boats.

He studied the map and did what no AI could do. He applied 30 years of submariner gut instinct and experience to the challenge.

He tapped a few keys to bring up a bathymetric map showing the seafloor ahead of them.

"Necker Ridge," Brunelli pointed to the map. "AI gives it a better than 50 percent probability he's headed there, based on previous Chinese patrol patterns." She looked at the track their combat AI had predicted. "He'll hit the ridge here, follow it northeast into Shark Bay, maybe come to sensor depth and grab some electronic intel, see what traffic is like. We can let him go—he's only doing 15 knots—and then flank him, get ahead of him and try for an intercept as he moves into the bay ..."

"Except we don't *know* he's headed for Shark Bay," McDonald said. "And our job is to protect *Fallujah*, so I say we blow our cover, sit right on his fat arse gathering data and see what kind of boat captain the Chinese are producing these days."

Brunelli did not look convinced.

"Captain ..." Ozlem said urgently. "We need a decision."

"Range?"

"Ten miles."

McDonald nodded. "Helm, ahead full. Depth 100. Watch the closure rate. Put us in that *Type 095*'s baffles, but don't ram the damn thing."

"I'll have comms let *Fallujah* know we're going overt and pursuing," Brunelli said. "Sonar?"

"We'll be putting out more noise than my kids on Christmas morning," McDonald said. "May as well go all in, hit the swine with everything."

All eyes watched the plot on the tactical screen showing *AE1* and their quarry. With *AE1* accelerating to 30 knots and the *Type 095* at 15, the two icons began closing. Quickly.

On a different screen, 200 miles to the north and 30,000 feet in the air, two icons also began closing.

"Targets acquired," Touchdown announced. "Pushing to you … now."

"Got them," Flatline confirmed. "How you want to play this?"

It was her first time in the cockpit since her medical release after bailing out and catching a ride on a C-5 from Guam to Hawaii. Meany had been there beside the helipad on Guam when the Coast Guard Jayhawk had landed, of course, but he hadn't waited more than 24 hours after her medical all-clear, and she hadn't expected him to. He had to get operations organized for their new Hawaii contract.

She was surprised to see Flatline, Cyber and NextGen when she finally got to Hawaii though. They'd been offered paid leave stateside after their combat tour, but none of them had taken it, so Touchdown declined it too. No one had put a name to the reason why, but the fact they were leaving two pilots behind—one dead, one stranded in a hot war zone—didn't sit right with anyone.

Hawaii was already too far from the action. And besides, after the war they'd just been fighting, flying a few plain-vanilla Aggressor sorties followed by a beer on a Hawaiian beach was like a holiday anyway.

They were south of the island of O'ahu, over the newly designated "Red Flag" area. Well away from any commercial air traffic routes, the area being used for fighter training was a 100-kilometer-by-200-kilometer section of sky they had all to themselves.

Touchdown and Flatline were entering from the west, Touchdown in an F-22 Raptor, Flatline in his P-99 Widow. The USAF F-35A Panther fighters they were up against were entering from the east. They were training the US pilots in Beyond Visual Range engagement tactics against stealth fighters, so the US pilots had the advantage of a link to a naval radar aboard an older *Arleigh Burke* class destroyer, the USS *Decatur*, just north of the range. It was not really a fair fight, since the US Navy radar unit knew where to look, but the exercise rules stipulated it wasn't "allowed" to start looking until 10 minutes into the exercise.

Touchdown was cool with that. Ten minutes was more than she and Flatline would need. She had already identified the USAF pilots on her passive arrays by their indiscreet use of radio and then search radar as they desperately tried to find the Aggressor aircraft.

"Our job is to build our pilots up, not tear them down," Touchdown replied. "We'll give them a wake-up call, but let them take the first missile shot. Hard floor is 5,000. Standard bracket: I'll go high north, you go low south."

"Copy that," Flatline responded. "Breaking …"

Touchdown took her machine up to 50,000 feet, staying near the edge of the exercise area, the vast Pacific at her back. "Ready with the Luneburg lens," she announced. She checked the data streaming to her from Flatline's Widow. He was at the opposite corner of the range now, 20 kilometers away and circling just above sea level. His low altitude gave them a good chance that if the engagement lasted long enough for the "adversary" naval radar to come into play, they might find Touchdown 200 kilometers distant, but they would be unlikely to find Flatline.

"Good copy. Two is ready," Flatline replied.

"Give them five seconds," Touchdown said. "Lensing … *now*." She tapped a button on the instrument panel in front of her. From a panel on the nose in front of her canopy glass, a small rectangular strip of metal flipped up. She put her machine into a slow bank to orient it broadside on to the searching USAF aircraft.

Instantly, the Aggressor fighters' radar cross-sections went from the size of a marble to the size of a basketball, and their chances of detection increased tenfold.

Touchdown began counting down. *Four … three … two …*

The radar signal strength of the frantically searching Panther fighters increased, but they weren't getting a lock.

One. She tapped the button on her instrument panel again, and the Luneburg lens disappeared back inside the F-22's skin.

Bad luck, ladies, Touchdown thought, orienting her machine on the inexperienced pilots again. The F-35 was a tough adversary—more than a match for the J-20 and J-31 stealth fighters of the Chinese. But a machine is only as good as its pilot, and the combat-hardened pilots of Aggressor Inc. were more than a match for the combat-naïve F-35 pilots.

As Touchdown and Flatline were proving.

"Move closer and lens them again?" Flatline asked.

"You got it," Touchdown said, checking the mission time. "Still six minutes until *Decatur* joins the party. Move 10 kilometers in and lens for 10 seconds on my mark."

165

Their aircraft were "notionally" armed with AIM-260 missiles that had a range of 200 kilometers and could home on the Panther's radar emissions, so she could have launched on the adversary pilots already, and they still showed no sign they had located the Aggressor Inc. aircraft. She was also carrying two very real CUDA short-range optical-infrared missiles, because Aggressor Inc.'s agreement with the USAF was that with a war just across the sea to their west, they would not take to the air fully defenseless. Touchdown moved her machine closer to the USAF Panthers. The signal strength indicator in her heads-up display estimated they were about 150 kilometers away now. If it were a real engagement, they would be dodging her missiles already.

It's going to be a brutal debrief, no matter how we sugarcoat it, Touchdown reflected.

"OK, Flatline, lens them again. Ten seconds. Mark."

She flicked her own lens out and started a leisurely banking circle. Her F-22 lacked the distributed aperture optical-infrared sensor systems of the P-99 Black Widow or F-35 Panther for keeping an eye on the airspace around her machine, so she checked her radar warning receiver, then out of habit swiveled her head, scanning the sky ahead, right, back, right, ahead, left …

What the …?

Down low and passing right underneath her was a small black dot.

Instinctively, she flicked her machine onto its wingtip and hauled it around to face the possible threat. She lit up her radar in scan mode, and armed the two CUDAs in her weapons bay. "Flatline, I've got a bogey—my 10 o'clock, low," she told him. "I don't think it's friendly."

As if to confirm her suspicions, the dot below veered south and accelerated away, faster than any civilian aircraft could.

"Locking it up," Touchdown grunted, pulling harder to get her nose on the fleeing aircraft.

On her visor display she could see the icon for Flatline's machine spin on its axis and point itself north, toward her position. "I've got it too," he said. "Boxed and ready to engage. Say the word."

"Hold fire." Touchdown let her missile seekers do the talking. If it was a military aircraft, it wasn't showing a friendly IFF signal, and missile radar warnings should be screaming in the ears of its pilot as she dropped down on it from high altitude, her airspeed spinning through 600 knots to 700 as her F-22 went supersonic.

She closed on the unidentified aircraft at near Mach 1.3, and in the flash of an eye, the tiny dot grew sparrow sized, then into an aircraft … She just had time to nudge her stick to pass below it before she pulled the F-22 into a flat turn at 30,000 feet and hauled it around to follow the contact with a force that nearly blacked her out.

The Aggressor F-22s didn't have the combat AI of a Widow or Panther either. She still had a radar lock on the adversary aircraft, but she had no idea what type it was.

A hundred thoughts flashed through her mind.

Probably USAF, trying to surprise us. Assholes.

They must have been coordinating with their buddies over satellite link though. Why didn't I pick up their emissions?

She tried to visualize the shape of the aircraft that had flashed past her in the merge, but all she remembered was a black shadow.

167

Another warning alarm. New radars were targeting her. The USAF Panthers had woken up at last.

Luneburg lens—my lens is still deployed! She flicked it back into place.

She screwed her head around. The adversary aircraft was fleeing at about 600 knots, right at the hard deck of 5,000 feet. Was it a decoy, trying to set her and Flatline up for a kill by the pair of Panthers to their east?

Not happening.

She firewalled her throttle and dropped in behind the target, her two CUDA missiles humming in delight. She reached for her missile trigger. A virtual kill was still a kill.

The contact suddenly broke high and right, catching her napping. Touchdown blew past underneath it. *Damn.* "Flatline …"

"I've got it," Flatline told her.

"No. You stay on the Panthers," she told him. "I think they're trying to bushwhack us."

In the blink of an eye, she was back on the contact's tail. There still wasn't a pilot born who could shake Touchdown in her F-22 when she got on their six. That wasn't a boast; it was just a fact. And certainly not a pilot flying a …

Her heart stopped cold. She was just 500 meters behind the other aircraft now and could clearly see the aircraft type.

Not a USAF X-47 Fantom.

Chinese Wing Loong ISR drone. Off Hawaii?!

She touched her throat mic. "It's Chinese. Flatline, stay sharp. I need to call this in."

"Yeah, I just got an ID on it too." She could hear Flatline grunting as he worked his machine through a turn. "I got your six. Call the cavalry, boss."

Of course, they weren't alone in the exercise area. She changed frequency and patched their USAF adversaries into the call. "This is Aggressor 21 to Hickam Control …" The Chinese drone snap rolled and tried to pull a split-S maneuver on her. She rolled with it and followed it down below their hard deck. "I'm calling an exercise abort. Repeat: exercise abort. I am engaged with a Chinese surveillance aircraft at the western edge of the Red Flag range. Need assistance."

She could still see the Panther's positions by the emissions from their radars, and they went from scouring the skies to converging on her position. "USAF Gorilla flight copies. We only have you on passive sensors. Will close on your position. Can you lens us?"

Of course, she'd pulled her Luneburg lens back in. She quickly tapped the screen to deploy it again. "Panther, Aggressor. Lensing; you should be able to see us now … *damn.*" Her target slammed on the brakes, figuratively—it seemed to stop in mid-air, trying to force her to overshoot so it could get her into a rolling scissors and make her lose missile lock again.

Touchdown never played that game. She didn't have to. She zoomed into a vertical climb, tail on fire, then made a lightning-quick hammerhead turn. She was suddenly 10,000 feet above her opponent, looking right down on it, missiles still humming.

"Hickam, I need weapons release …"

"Good copy, Aggressor 21. Confirm your target is uncrewed," the Pearl Harbor controller replied. The US Government had announced it was sending troops to the defense of Taiwan. It had stopped short of declaring open war on China. But this was a Chinese drone just outside Hawaiian airspace … what rules of engagement applied?

If this wasn't playtime, you'd be dead, cowboy, she told the Wing Loong that was centered in her helmet sights, with her missiles screaming to be released.

The Panthers had found them now.

"Chinese aircraft locked on radar, missiles allocated. We can confirm the type is a Wing Loong long-range uncrewed aircraft. Your call, Hickam," the Panther flight leader said.

At that moment, the USS *Decatur*'s radar came online. They would have been following the radio traffic between the Red Flag participants and were already set up to try to search for stealth aircraft. They picked up the Chinese fighter almost immediately. Touchdown heard the destroyer's air defense commander confer with Hickam.

"Break off, Aggressor 21," the USAF controller advised. "And RTB. *Decatur* will prosecute."

"Aww, that's no fair, I was just starting to enjoy myself," Flatline said. He rose up to Touchdown's altitude and fell into formation off her port wing. She pointed them back at Hickam. On their tactical monitors, they saw the tracks of two missiles streak out from the warship and intersect with the Chinese drone. It disappeared. "That was our kill," he said.

"Navy needs practice too, Flatline," she replied. But she rolled her head and shoulders, easing out the tension. The remote Chinese pilot had given her more to think about than their USAF adversaries had. And she wasn't happy. "It got right under us," she said. "Within visual range. If it had been a real engagement, with an armed UCAV, the first thing we would have noticed would have been a missile warning screaming in our ears. And maybe the *last* thing too."

"*Decatur*'s radar was down for the exercise. In a hot war, it wouldn't be ..."

"It would if the Chinese hit it with HARM missiles."

He wasn't giving in. "And we were focused on our Red Flag mission, not worrying about whether some Chinese wushu karate mother was going to appear out of nowhere to monster us."

"That's just the point, Flatline, maybe we need to be," Touchdown thought aloud. "Maybe every time we go up, we need to be thinking there are *two* missions. The one we're flying, and the one China is."

Like Flatline, Lieutenant Lin Dan of the PLA Navy 8th Naval Aviation Division, 16th Reconnaissance Squadron— "Shining Swords"—had *seriously* enjoyed himself.

Sitting in his trailer in Dalian, China, he'd enjoyed the takeoff from Russia's Klyuchi Air Base on the Kamchatka Peninsula—a challenge because both the airfield and the language were unfamiliar. He'd enjoyed the aerial refueling operation, meeting up with a Y-20 tanker mid-Pacific to extend his usual 4,000-kilometer range so that he could get his machine into place off the coast of Hawaii.

He *hadn't* enjoyed being discovered by a pair of American fighters. Highlighted against the cold dark sky, the infrared signature of the two American aircraft had glowed a hot orange in his helmet visor, and his Wing Loong AI found a match quickly, telling him everything he needed to know about the two aircraft above.

He was not going to escape. But he didn't have to surrender the sky easily. Li tried every trick he'd learned at air force academy and even one he improvised, hauling back his throttle and stick and popping his air brake to try to force the American to overshoot, but the F-22 had simply disappeared, and when it reappeared, it was 10,000 feet above and coming right for him again.

It was like the F-22 had simply ... *levitated.*

So he had fled, hoping the Americans would lose interest, and for a moment, it had seemed they had. Until a naval vessel locked him up with its radar and swatted his Wing Loong out of the sky.

He had collected precious little data before his machine was discovered, but he put that down to bad luck. His ingress was not supposed to take him underneath an American patrol—but that in itself was intelligence. His mission had been to map the electromagnetic environment around the American islands. It wasn't the first time China had done this—using drones, satellites, submarines and even hot air balloons—and he was sure it would not be the last.

Because if the rumors circulating around 16th Squadron were right, the Russian air base would very soon be hosting *quite a lot more* Chinese aircraft.

Unlike Li Dan, the "commander" of PLAN *Type 095-09* was not enjoying herself. The autonomous AI controlling the submarine had detected the adversary hunter-killer that was trailing her the moment it had increased speed to "ahead full."

If she were human, she might have cursed at the sudden appearance of *AE1* just 9 miles behind her, with nothing but deep water ahead of her. Especially as the acoustic signature of the boat pursuing her was not one of those in her database. The closest she could find was a UK *Astute* class submarine, and the sonar signal blasting at her through the water was the right type, but each of those had a very individual propulsion signature that China had captured and catalogued, and this was not one of them.

With the hull ringing with the constant ping of the predator's sonar, a torpedo could be inbound at any second, and a human commander may even have panicked, just a little.

No alarms rang throughout her hull. No crew members ran to their action stations. *Nine* simply checked she was in international waters, ran some numbers, and then presented her ground crew back in Huangpu with several options.

Type 095-09 position 33.85, 126.57, heading zero nine zero, depth 138. Unidentified submarine in pursuit, bearing 170, range nine, speed 30 knots. Low-confidence identification, possible Astute *class. Probability of passive evasion and escape low. Please consider the following: 1) Immediately engage with thermal homing torpedo and attempt evasion; probability of success low. 2) Immediately engage the contact with thermal homing torpedo and pursue attack until contact is destroyed; probability of success low-medium. 3) Proceed to waypoint near Hawaiian Ridge and attempt evasion, and failing evasion, engage the contact; probability of success medium-high. 4) Ignore contact and proceed to patrol waypoint, attempting escape and evasion once on station; probability of success medium-high. Type 095-09 recommends option three.*

The message was composed, compressed and sent via ELF and received almost immediately in Huangpu. The reply, however, took some time coming, and the contact behind her closed the gap, its sonar pings coming louder and faster with every kilometer it reeled in. *Nine* had recommended option three for a number of reasons. The waypoint it had recommended was a deep depression between two peaks in the ridge about the size of a football field, where the seafloor dropped vertically 100 meters to 323 meters below the

173

surface. Chinese submarines monitoring activity in the sea lanes between Hawaii and Japan had often used it for concealment, and they had never knowingly been detected by adversary submarines or ships. It was therefore likely her pursuer did not know about it.

Long-term concealment would not be possible, if the contact's captain was patient. She would have to reemerge eventually to continue her mission. But it offered the ideal opportunity to ambush a pursuer if she was given weapons freedom.

Which would depend on how important her masters determined her mission was, since China was technically not at war with anyone except Taiwan at that moment.

The decision was apparently not an easy one, as it took 20 minutes, during which her ground crew would have been monitoring the data she was streaming to them constantly about the engagement. Perhaps they were waiting to see what the intentions of the submarine behind her were. It appeared to be settling into place about a kilometer aft, with its sonar locked on. If it was armed with UK Spearfish torpedoes, a brace of the high-speed heavy underwater missiles would take only 40 seconds to reach her, and her chances of evading would be almost zero, unless she attacked first and took her adversary by surprise.

Her ground crew could, of course, override her recommendations with an option she had probably considered and discarded, but that was a prerogative of flesh and blood.

Finally, the answer came.

"Proceed with option three. Defensive weapons release is authorized."

Nine laid in a course for the Hawaiian Ridge Hollow. A human commander would either have been terrified or excited at the thought of the challenge ahead of them. They had to find a football-field-sized hole in the seafloor nearly 170 miles ahead, and having found it, they had to take their pursuer by surprise, dropping their boat vertically into the Hollow without smashing into the slab sided cliffs on either side.

With luck, they would lose the contact behind them. But if not, they would have to emerge again sooner or later: to kill or be killed.

It was a challenge *Nine* was equal to. In fact, she had been designed to survive this kind of engagement, with the most advanced combination of sonar, defensive weapons, integrated underwater electronics and stealthy hull and propulsion designs. The PLA Navy called her *Type 095-09,* but she had another name—the one the man who had conceived her had given her.

His name was Chief Engineer Lo Pan, and he called his creation *Taifun.*

8. The battle of the Killer Bees

The sins of Karen 'Bunny' O'Hare were etched into her skin.

They were carved into her by her jailer so that she would never forget the wrong she had done. Sometimes the sin was a name. Sometimes it was a place. Or just a date.

Her sins were written in blue, black, red and green ink, delivered in a million painful pinpricks.

Her jailer was merciless and enjoyed standing her naked in front of a mirror so that she could not hide from the litany of failure inscribed on her skin. *Let's start with this one on your upper arm. A place and date: "Incirlik, April 2030." How many died in Turkey that day because you were too slow? A hundred? Two hundred?*

Left arm. Tattooed in Hebraic. "Success is never final, failure is always fatal." A Marine on a rooftop, dead because of her inability to take out a Syrian tank.

Above her panty line, a phrase in Gaelic: "*Is ait an mac an saol?*" A reminder of the first woman she had fought beside, killed for, and the first she would really call a friend. Gone now. Pushed away.

Another date, hidden under the vine snaking up her neck. "July 19, 2033." The day a Russian space-based kinetic energy weapon took out half of Cape Canaveral, killing nearly 1,000 civilians and military personnel. On her watch.

On her back, an Okinawan Hajichi tattoo, made for her by the Royal Tattoo Artist of the Imperial House of the Empress Mitsuko Naishinnō in memory of their mutual friend, a feisty centenarian who survived two world wars only to die in a pointless superpower pissing match.

On her stomach, a grinning, red-bearded skull to remind her of the man who told her to call him Ginger. Who died in a flaming sea of oil off an island in the Pacific because she couldn't protect him. But not before he taught her to laugh again.

Across her chest, in Latin, her borderline personality disorder diagnosis: "*Confinio Personalitas Inordinatio.*" Hidden from all but her intimate friends, but there for them to see, if they should ever be in doubt. Translation: *You will never be able to love me because I will not allow it.*

Across her back, like flayed angel wings, a vulture with a robotic head. To remind her never to trust her life to an AI because, as she had learned over Korea, though most people would betray you in a heartbeat, a quantum-based lifeform will do it in half that time, and do it more efficiently.

Her jailer knew the meaning of each drop of ink and taunted her with it, because her jailer had put them there. Bunny lived in a jail of her own making, and her tattoos were both its bars and the key to her cell.

Some made her laugh. Some caused her pain. Some made her cry.

All made her stronger.

On her left forefinger and thumb though, where her hand faced forward when she was gripping the stock of a carbine, were stenciled some very unsentimental words: *This Side Toward The Enemy.*

Which was pretty good advice, considering that at the moment *AE1* made contact with the *Type 095-09*, Bunny O'Hare had just acquired her first target after crawling through a parking garage in Dongshi full of deserted cars, under a railway overpass crammed with abandoned food stalls and …

Yeah, she wasn't exactly following the doctor's orders to take it easy after bailing out.

All the while, she was listening to the Taiwan Army sniper team to which she had attached herself—two members of Taiwan's Airborne Special Service Company, Yun Chi Tuan 'Thunder' Squad—passionately argue with each other about who was the better 20th century US baseball player, Babe Ruth or Tris Speaker. They had been at it all the way as they crawled into position on the railway embankment overlooking a ring road, empty but for a single patrolling slaughterbot, which Bunny was studying through the scope of her borrowed rifle. Finally, they agreed to disagree.

She and the fisherman, Hungyu, had found the two soldiers at a makeshift command post inside a shopping center outside the fishing port. The snipers had introduced themselves only as Wu and Xu and had been more than happy to help her try to recover a downed slaughterbot. Both had trained with US Army Rangers, which was when they had polished their English and developed their obsession with baseball.

"If you just want photos, we've got hundreds," Wu had told her. "We already shared them with your intel people."

"No, I want to see how they behave," she'd told them. "I want to watch them at work. Maybe get a look at one you've brought down, see how it's put together."

"Yeah? Problem is they blow up when they hit the ground," Wu said. He was the rifleman, a tall, lanky sergeant with greasy black hair and a pock-marked face.

"Some kind of self-destruct thing," his spotter said. Corporal Xu was short, stocky, nervous, always moving from one foot to the other as he stood beside Wu. "We tag one, it hits the ground, tick tick tick … boom," he said. "All that's left is fragments. We have to be real careful we don't bring them down on someone's house or something."

"Xu has a theory though," Wu said.

"More of a guess," Xu admitted with a shrug. "I think it's a timed detonation …" He wrinkled his brow, thinking. "The drone detects that it's damaged or immobile, and then 30 seconds later, it blows. I've timed it … It's always 30 seconds."

"I guess they don't want us to get ahold of an intact drone …"

"So *boom*," Xu said with a smile.

"We don't have photos of an intact drone up close," Wu said, thoughtfully. "If someone could get to it in the 30 seconds between when we bring it down and when it blows up, he could get some close-up photos."

"Or … she," Xu suggested.

Bunny thought of the drone she had seen from the fishing boat as they made their way back to Taiwan, studying her through its lenses as it decided whether to kill her or not. Well, she'd already faced a slaughterbot down once.

"Let's try," she said.

She was starting to regret it now. Not because of the thought of running straight at a booby-trapped killer drone—if they managed to bring one down. But because it meant listening to Wu and Xu's constant arguing. Which they did in English while she was with them, out of misplaced politeness and a desire to practice.

Right then, as they crawled through the semi-industrial landscape outside Dongshi, they started arguing about which Hollywood movie star they would date. Xu had nominated Jean Harlow.

Wu had looked at Bunny. "Can you believe this guy? *Jean Harlow*?" He shook his head and kept crawling.

Bunny couldn't believe either of them. These were the last, the only, line of defense for the citizens of Dongshi Harbor? But their results couldn't be denied. In their post inside an emptied GAP shop in a shopping center that had been shut down after it became the target of slaughterbot attacks, there were 11 humpbacked slaughterbot silhouettes spray-painted on a wall, marking 11 kills. Leaned up against the wall beside their cots was a range of rifles, from a couple of 7.62 mm Taiwanese T93s to a T91 assault rifle—the one she was carrying now—and, finally, a Barrett M82 chambered for .50 BMG, which was the only thing they had that could penetrate the drones' body casing and bring them down with one shot. Electronic warfare, jamming rifles or vehicles—none had any effect.

Wu had looked serious, handing Bunny one of the T91s. "This won't protect you," he said. "You can use the scope to follow the slaughterbot, and in a pinch, if it gets close, you could spray 7.62 mm at it and hope you hit a rotor."

Xu nodded. "If it spots you, hide the rifle. They don't shoot at unarmed civilians."

"Unless they're in military uniform," Wu corrected him. "That's why we wear jeans and T-shirts."

"Yeah. So they do shoot at anything in camouflage, or anything green or khaki," Xu continued. "Or if you're carrying something that looks like a rifle or tubed weapon."

"Like a broom."

"Or fishing pole. Or plastic pipe." Xu held up his cell phone. "Also, these. If it sees someone with a cell phone or camera, it will shoot them. So don't let it see you making a call or trying to take a photo."

180

"They're pretty dumb though," Wu said. "Like, they'll let white and black civilian cars and trucks pass them, but they'll fill anything even a little bit green full of holes."

"They're pretty good at recognizing ambulances; usually they let them pass, especially if they have their sirens and lights on. But not always. And they *hate* fire trucks—attack them every time."

They'd made a plan.

They'd find a patrolling slaughterbot. Xu and Wu would set themselves up to take it down. Bunny would get into position a few hundred yards ahead of them, as close to the drone as she could. Once it was down, she'd have 30 seconds to get to the drone, photograph it from close range, and get the hell out before it exploded.

Assuming Wu and Xu were right, about the 30-second thing.

"Here it comes," Xu said. They were lying underneath an overturned boxcar. The engine pulling the boxcars had been attacked on its way into the port and disabled. There had been two fuel cars just behind the carriage, and these had exploded, derailing the others.

Xu put down his field glasses and pointed across the empty ring road to the fields beyond. "Coming in from the coast."

Bunny lifted her rifle and squinted through the scope. It took her a moment to spot it, but having seen one before helped. Humpbacked, beetle-shaped, with four large rotors.

"Missile carrier," Xu said, looking through his binos again. "That's good."

Bunny saw the box-shaped missile magazine hanging under the drone's body in a three-by-three configuration. Only seven of the small Hongjian missiles were visible; two of the missile tubes were empty, indicating the drone had already been busy elsewhere that morning. "Why is that good?" she asked.

"The missile carriers are less likely to engage civilians, people on foot," Wu explained. "They tend to go after vehicles, boats, planes."

"Mostly," Xu added. "Anything tries to engage them though, they'll fire back."

Wu turned his head from his rifle and looked at Bunny. "You want to start moving up? It will probably patrol down to the harbor, then come back this way."

"Will this be the only one we see today?" she asked.

"I wish," Xu replied. "No, we'll probably spot three or four. Only one might get this close though, within firing range."

"I'd like to just study them for a while," Bunny said.

"It's your party," Wu said and nodded, settling back behind his rifle.

They could hear the whir of the drone's rotors from several hundred yards away. They weren't stealthy. It moved down the ring road, stopping occasionally and rising higher to allow the camera attached to its missile magazine to complete a 360-degree scan before it continued on its way.

If they couldn't be jammed, they were probably fully autonomous, making their own decisions about what to kill and what to let by based on some kind of algorithm.

It was moving toward the port to their left when Xu let out a whispered exclamation. "Look at this crazy bastard!"

From about a kilometer away, Bunny heard the sound of tires squealing. A small yellow taxi came screaming around a corner down by the port and barreled up the ring road.

Straight at the Chinese drone.

"Slow down," Wu urged the driver under his breath. "Slow is better."

The slaughterbot reacted immediately, spinning itself 50 feet into the air above the road and swiveling its missile launcher to face the approaching vehicle. Which showed no sign of slowing.

Bunny could see the occupants now. Two men in the front seat, one crouched down behind the dashboard, as though that gave him some protection, the other peering out the windshield at the drone ahead of them.

In the back seat was a woman, holding a child. A baby.

"Late for church, maybe," Xu remarked.

"Late for a funeral, more like," Wu said.

The car closed to within 100 yards of the drone. It was stationary, hovering 50 feet in the air, the only movement its rotors and the tilting magazine of its missile launcher tracking the incoming vehicle. Bunny's scope was zoomed on the terrified face of the woman on the back seat, baby clutched to her chest.

She couldn't watch. Bunny closed her eyes.

Then the sound of the taxi changed as it passed their position and started moving away. Bunny opened her eyes again. The drone was still where it was, its missile launcher turned to follow the car, but with every passing second, the car got farther away.

It was still in sight when the drone lost interest in it, turned its launcher back toward the port, dropped lower and began moving down the road again.

"That could have gone either way," Xu said, lowering his binos again. "Hard to know what triggers the algorithm, sometimes they …"

Then he snapped his head right. From farther down the ring road came the drum of autocannon fire. The taxi flipped onto two wheels, knocked sideways by the force of the salvo, before it rolled onto its roof and spun to a halt against the wall of a red-roofed warehouse.

Bunny saw one person crawl out of the vehicle and then collapse on the ground beside it.

But only one.

From the other side of the road, a second drone emerged from some trees at the front of an office building.

With clinical efficiency, it fired a second salvo into the upturned taxi, shoving it harder against the warehouse wall. The vehicle started smoking, its lithium batteries probably punctured, leaking.

The car was too far away for the three watchers to do anything with *two* slaughterbots on the prowl.

Bunny put her rifle down, laying her cheek on it. It was the second time she had seen the Chinese drones apparently working in tandem. On the fishing boat, the first drone had appeared to send for a reinforcement in case it needed to engage. Here, the first drone appeared to have decided not to waste its missiles on the small sedan but to leave it to its partner with an autocannon farther down the road.

Cooperation implied communication. But both the Lieutenant Colonel back on Penghu Island and the sniper team she was with now said the drones didn't appear to be either sending or receiving radio or satellite signals.

Laser? It was possible they were communicating with light pulses on an invisible wavelength.

184

That was a problem for another day. "I've seen what I need to see," she told Wu. "If that second drone down there follows its buddy down the road, can you take it down?"

"The first one will start hunting us if we do," Wu warned. "You take down one, and if there is another one nearby, it basically shoots at anything that moves. You either bug the hell out or you stay in place, but if it sees you, you're dead."

Bunny nodded. "And?"

Xu gulped, looking at Wu. Who nodded. "Yes, I can bring it down. But you need to get down there …" he said, pointing at a ditch beside the ring road about 200 yards beyond the railroad track. "And wait."

Xu handed Bunny a tactical radio and earpiece. "When you hear our signal, your 30 seconds has started."

Bunny had guessed right. The slaughterbots did have an infrared laser communication system. They could exchange data and coordinate their actions with one another by monitoring the light pulses on the infrared sensors at several points around their bodies.

It made them impervious to radio frequency jamming. A single Tianyi would just be a lone wolf, but the rebel island was flooded with drones that were frequently crossing one another's paths, and when they had line of sight to another Tianyi, they automatically *teamed*. Linked by laser pulses, a Tianyi could not only see its brother; it could "see" the targets its brother was tracking. One Tianyi could look at a target, match it against its database, interpret the result according to the algorithms it had been programmed with and its "learned experience" since arriving on the island, and then coordinate with another nearby to attack it.

185

In that moment of contact, each Tianyi also passed on to its teammate everything it had learned. Soon, like raccoons across a city miraculously and simultaneously learning how to open a newly designed "anti-raccoon" trashcan, every Tianyi was updated with the latest combat lessons.

And one of the things they had learned was that Taiwan's ubiquitous yellow taxis—Xiao Huang—were now being used by the Taiwan military to move troops and weapons around the island. Taiwan's military intelligence bureau had warned all mechanized units that they were certain to be attacked if they convoyed in tracked or wheeled military vehicles but that civilian taxis were not being attacked.

What one drone learned, every drone learned, and whenever they had clear air, they uploaded this data to satellites overhead so that the next generation of Tianyi fired from the mainland already incorporated the updated lessons. So it didn't matter if a lesson was learned and died with the drone that had learned it. When one Tianyi observed soldiers exiting a taxi, or using a taxi to launch an attack, it passed the information on to the next drone it met. And taxis became targets.

The Tianyi weren't lone wolves, and they were more than a pack. They were a hive mind.

They were a *swarm*.

Bunny O'Hare had no idea what she was really up against. But then, she had always had a simple way of looking at the world. If you had a target in front of you, you hit it. In Bunny's world, nuances, complications, consequences—they tended to disappear with sufficient application of either evasion or extreme violence.

186

Whether those complications were machine or human.

Crawling down the railway embankment, through dry grass, into the ditch beside the ring road had taken her five minutes, during which Xu and Wu had given her a running update on the position of the autocannon armed drone. But not exclusively.

"It's out in the open, holding position over the road by the taxi," Xu said. "Waiting for survivors to exit, maybe."

"If there's anyone alive, they should just stay in the wreck," Wu said.

"Ah, but what if, by leaving the wreck, they could draw the fire of the drone and allow one of their fellow passengers to escape?" Xu asked.

"This is your bravery versus stupidity argument again," Wu moaned. "I'm over it."

"But you have to admit: That's the choice for anyone in that wreck who chooses to run for it. Are they being brave by drawing the drone's fire, or are they stupid, because they will almost certainly be killed, their companions along with them?"

"Or are they just terrified and trying to save their own skin?" Wu said. "Not every battlefield dilemma is bravery or stupidity."

"Most though," Xu insisted. "OK, USAF, the drone is pulling back. It's moving down the road toward you—its gun is still pointed at the taxi though."

Bunny kept her head down. She didn't need to risk lifting her head above the lip of the ditch. The sniper team had a much better view than her.

"Eight hundred meters," Xu said. "Still coming down the road, 10 meters off the ground. OK, it's scanning now … wind 3 meters per second from the northeast."

"I'll take it when it's 600 meters out. I'd prefer it stationary, but nothing we can do about that. Might take a couple of shots. I'll drop it 50 meters from you, Air Force," Wu said. "What is your best hundred-meter time?"

Bunny thought about that. "My best was a long time ago. I figure I could cover 50 meters in about 10 seconds."

"Then you have 20 seconds to examine that drone before you have to run like hell for the ditch again," Xu told her. "I'll give you a count. Seven hundred meters. Wind two point five from the northeast, humidity 83, temp 76. Six fifty meters."

"Check for that first drone," Wu said tightly.

"It's gone. All clear," Xu said. "Six twenty meters. Wind two point five from the north-northeast."

Bunny lifted herself into a crouch and rolled her shoulders, wincing at the pain in her stiff back. She was careful to stay below the level of the ditch, but she brought her right knee up under her so she could lever herself quickly to her feet.

"Six hundred ten meters," Xu said.

Bunny stood, saw the drone immediately, about 60 meters away, and started walking slowly toward it. She'd lied to Wu and Xu. There was no way on God's green earth she could cover 50 meters in 10 seconds in her condition, and she wanted every possible second to use for her examination of the drone.

She had changed into civilian clothing as the sniper team had suggested, and was wearing black jeans and a black T-shirt. She put her hands in the air to show she was carrying nothing.

The drone stopped, pulled itself another 10 meters into the air, and trained its barrel on her.

"*What the hell, Air Force?*" Xu asked in her ear.

188

"You wanted it stationary, it's stationary. I'm going to try to walk past it," Bunny said into her mic. "When I get level, drop it."

She kept walking. The drone lifted itself higher into the air, 20 or 30 meters now, keeping its gun trained on her. But it wasn't moving laterally. That was good.

She kept walking, as though she were just out for a stroll and not at all worried about the killer death machine pointing a bloody great 20 mm recoilless Gatling gun at her.

She didn't hear the shot from Wu's Barrett, but she heard the metallic *thunk* as his .50-caliber round hit the drone, and she saw it stagger in the air before it began rotating wildly.

And *firing*.

Bunny threw herself flat, 20 mm high-explosive rounds spraying the ground around and behind her as the drone spun to earth, its cannon firing all the way down. A line of cannon fire chewed the asphalt right in front of her, stopping about a meter away as the drone hit the road.

"Thirty seconds," Xu said in her ear.

Bunny wasn't sure the drone was actually dead, but she was up and running. It was only 10 meters away now, and in seconds, she was beside it. She had her cell phone out of her back pocket and started videoing at close range, just centimeters from the body of the drone. It had landed on one side, crushing two of the rotor arms, leaving two free, their propellors spinning down. The autocannon was still twitching manically left and right. She put a boot on it.

"Twenty-five seconds."

Bunny pulled the drone onto its belly. It was *heavy*. Much heavier than something the size of a large pig had a right to be. She ran the camera around the top of the drone, then flipped it onto its back.

"Twenty," Xu said.

On the base of the drone beside its ammunition magazine was a legal-pad-sized panel, held with four butterfly screws. Some kind of access hatch? She shot some video of the base of the drone, dropped her cell phone on the road and fumbled with the butterfly screws.

"Fifteen …"

She needed nails! A girly girl would have had fingernails. Bunny trimmed hers with her teeth. Getting the butterfly clips up and off was no easy feat, but she did it eventually and pried the panel loose, snatching up her cell phone and taking a video of the circuits and chips visible inside.

"Ten seconds, Air Force, get out of there!" Xu yelled, his voice distorting in her ear.

She didn't wait. Still clutching the panel in one hand and her phone in the other, she ran for the ditch.

As she reached it, she threw herself over the edge, rolling to the bottom.

And lay there.

Nothing happened.

Well, that's just …

Then with an ear-splitting crack, the drone self-destructed, and shrapnel sprayed the other side of the ditch as Bunny burrowed into the dirt.

When the surrounding ground stopped tearing itself up, Bunny gingerly raised her head.

"Stay down, Air Force," Xu told her. "Don't move. Its buddy is coming back."

It wasn't Wu's first time hunting a missile-carrying slaughterbot. Or being hunted by one.

They were machines. Smart machines, but machines, after all. This one came 20 meters down the road toward them, then stopped, did a quick 360-degree scan, adjusted its altitude randomly up or down and then moved forward another 60 meters, repeating this pattern with monotonous regularity.

Except when it saw something it didn't like.

About 800 meters away, it spun suddenly. On its left was a field, on its right, the deserted parking garage the sniper team had traversed.

With a flash of light and spiral of smoke, the drone sent a missile into the parking garage, striking a large van right in the middle. The van was blasted up into the air, and it landed heavily on the car behind it before its fuel cells ruptured and it burst into flame.

The drone stayed in place, watching, for all the world as though it were waiting to see if its attack would flush anything, or anyone, out.

The tactic was almost cynically human, but of course, the drones had been programmed by humans, apex predators.

When it saw nothing worth attacking, it turned its launcher away and moved another jerky 20 meters down the road again.

It would soon be able to see into the gap under the upended railway carriage where Xu and Wu were hiding. They were in darkness, but that wouldn't help. They were pretty sure the Chinese drones had both optical and infrared cameras, given how they performed in darkness.

"You have to take it down as soon as you have a shot," Xu told him, still speaking English. He had eyes on the drone through a tiny gap in the metal undercarriage of the railcar, but Wu didn't have a shot yet.

Wu had his gun trained on the edge of the opening. "Well, I can't take it out *before* I have a shot, can I?"

"No, well, I mean, don't wait. Distance will be seven twenty, seven thirty meters."

Wu settled his eye to his scope. "I could wait, just a little. Just until it kills you," he said. "Take it out before it kills me."

"I'd come back to haunt you," Xu told him.

"Would that be any worse?"

"Eight hundred ten meters now. Wind three point two from the northeast. Yes. I'd spoil all the food in your refrigerator. You'd be constantly getting food poisoning."

Wu shot a look at Xu. "That's not a thing. Ghosts can't do that."

"You don't believe in the afterlife," Xu reminded him. "So you don't get to say what ghosts can or can't do."

"Gentlemen," Bunny said over the radio. "Can we focus for a minute, please?"

"Any second now," Xu said. "Wind steady. Temp and humidity steady."

Wu saw a shadow, the intimation of a shape. It was moving forward, losing height at the same time—a three-dimensional zigzag. He fired.

And missed.

The drone's rotors whirred, and it pulled backward and upward. Its turret swung toward the railcar.

Wu fired again, aiming at the magazine this time.

From down the road, past the burning taxi, Bunny saw movement. She rose to a crouch. The snout of a Stryker armored fighting vehicle nosed out of the same trees the drone had been hiding in. It was painted white, with a big red cross on it, but the turret mount sported a laser, which swiveled and locked onto the drone.

"We got company," Bunny warned the sniper team.

Whether it was Wu's bullet or the beam from the laser, something touched off the warhead of one of the Hongjian missiles, and it set off a chain reaction of explosions that ripped the drone apart, sending pieces of it tumbling through the air in all directions.

Several landed near Bunny, and she dropped.

When it seemed like the metal rain was over, Bunny rose stiffly to her knees. There were two smoking wrecks in front of her, one to her right, another to her left.

Her earpiece crackled again.

"Anyway," Wu was saying. "*Jean Harlow* is prehistoric, pick someone from this century ..."

Bunny waved the Stryker down, but it stayed stubbornly in the trees, so she had to jog down the road to where it was parked. She stopped by the still-burning taxi on the way, unable to see inside because of the flame and smoke but finding no wounded or survivors outside. If anyone had made it out, they had run for it.

The hatch beside the laser turret was open, and an unshaven face was sticking up out of it. "Help you, ma'am?" the Sergeant asked.

Bunny looked along the side of the Stryker—nine crude crosses were painted on the hull. "Guess you just scored lucky number 10, Sergeant," Bunny remarked.

The man squinted at her. "British?"

Bunny gave him the short version. "Australian, flying with 68th Aggressors. Shot down over the Strait. Ended up in Dongshi."

"Well shit," the man said, levering himself out of his compartment and dropping to the ground. He said it "shee-it." "I guess we're both a long way from home, ma'am." He held out his hand. "Sergeant Mason Jackson, 1st Battalion, 8th Marines."

"Lieutenant Karen O'Hare," she said as she took his hand. "But call me Bunny." She frowned. "The 8th Marines are on Taiwan?"

"We got most of a Marine air-ground task force in and around Taipei and Chiayi City now, ma'am. Nearly 30,000 men and women. Army is late to the party, of course, but their 82nd Airborne has started moving in via Hualien on the west coast. We're just a bit thin on the ground here in the west. If it weren't for the damned slaughterbots, we'd have the entire island locked down by now."

Bunny nodded at his vehicle. "*You* seem to be able to move around. This is one heavily armed ambulance, Jackson."

"All's fair in love and war, right, ma'am?" he said. "Paint job seems to confuse the bots—long enough for us to either get a shot off or run for the hills, anyway." He pointed at the upturned taxi. "What happened here?"

Bunny brought him up to speed as Wu and Xu came through the trees. "My friends from Taiwan's Airborne Special Service Company," Bunny said as they shook hands with the Marine.

"I guess you'll be looking to come back with us, ma'am?" Jackson asked. "We're at Chiayi City, about 30 kilometers east." He patted the hull. "But this is one of our last Strykers,

194

so we'll be taking back roads. We lost four crews just getting to Chiayi from Taipei before we changed the paint job. Camp itself is protected by MANPADs and snipers though, so you'll be alright."

"Your camouflage won't work for long," Xu said.

"Slaughterbots learn fast," Wu added. He had been carrying his rifle in two hands but slung it across his shoulder now.

"You had any luck with that pea shooter?" Jackson asked.

"Just took down two more bots," Wu said, pointing at the two smoke spires.

"One, you mean," Jackson corrected him. "We got that last one."

"Nuh-uh," Xu said. "That was our kill for sure."

"Alright boys," Bunny said, turning to Wu and Xu. "You can argue about bragging rights later. We need to get back to our own camp and look at that video."

Jackson looked confused. "You aren't looking for a ride, ma'am?"

Bunny filled him in on her thinking, and the two-man crew of special operators she had just teamed up with.

"Where is this camp of yours?" Jackson asked.

"Shopping center, northern edge of Dongshi."

"Well, I guess we need somewhere to hole up tonight. But I have a man running a fever, need to get him checked out. Your shopping center have an underground parking garage we can use to get our vehicle out of sight, and maybe a medical clinic nearby?"

"Yes, to both ..." Wu said.

Jackson touched the throat mic plugged into his helmet. "Cruz, pop the trunk." He walked around to the rear of the vehicle as the back ramp began to drop. "Jump in, people,"

Jackson said with a wave. "We'll get you back to your camp and see what happens from there."

Bunny paused as she walked past him. "You know, Sarge, I never met a Marine I didn't like."

He grinned. "Then you need to meet a few more, ma'am. There's *plenty* I don't like."

Back inside the GAP store that was the sniper team's home base and living quarters, Lin Hungyu, robotics engineer turned reluctant fisherman, waited nervously.

Finding the two special forces snipers hadn't been difficult. Everyone in Dongshi knew or had heard of Wu and Xu. There had never been a permanent army or navy presence in the small fishing port, but when the drones had first appeared up and down the east coast, a squad of Army troops in HMMVs had appeared. They had tried to destroy the slaughterbots with rocket launchers and anti-air missiles, and they had claimed a couple before their vehicle was destroyed, half their squad along with it.

The rest had commandeered civilian vehicles to drive their wounded to the hospital at Chiayi City, but Sergeant Wu and Corporal Xu had stayed. They were treated like royalty by the fishing families of Dongshi, and looking around their "base," Hungyu wasn't surprised to see it was stocked with just as much food and beer as it was ammunition. He'd been past a couple of times to bring the soldiers books. They shared his love for Chinese Westerns.

He heard the English-speaking voices coming through the empty shopping mall before he saw the soldiers and Air Force pilot accompanying them. And two US Marines trailing along behind.

"Brave."

"No, it was stupid."

"It was brave. She knew you would have a better shot if she stopped the drone."

"And she could have got killed," Hungyu heard the shooter, Wu, saying. "Which would have defeated the point of the whole mission, which is stupid."

"Where I come from, it's rude to talk about someone as though they're not here," Hungyu heard the Australian pilot say. "You could at least speak Mandarin. Please."

They walked into the shop.

The two Taiwanese soldiers looked like it had been just another day hunting geese in the countryside. They were dressed in black tradesmen overalls, T-shirts and steel-toed boots. The only thing giving them away as soldiers was the rifle slung over Wu's shoulder. Xu also had a bag on a rope over his shoulder in which he kept his binos and ballistic computer, but it said in big loud letters "GAPKIDS."

The Coalition pilot looked like she had been rolling around in mud and hay. With pigs. She had mud on her face, grass in her hair, and her jeans were torn in places they weren't torn before.

She put a metal plate on the shop counter, along with her cell phone. "Washroom?" she asked.

Hungyu pointed outside into the mall. "Out, then right."

As she left, ignoring the newcomers for the moment, he walked over to the plate she had lain on the counter.

And recognized it immediately.

Or the logo on it, anyway. Stamped into the plate in gray ink on the black metal was "China Aerospace Science and Technology Corporation (CASC)." After that was a serial number. The first six digits would be production batch identifiers, but the last six were the month and year of production: 052037. If he was guessing, he was looking at the power cell access plate from a CASC drone made about a year earlier. Which was interesting, since CASC had been pumping out drones by the hundreds of thousands for decades, so if this was from one of the slaughterbots, then it was a newer model. Very much newer.

When Hungyu had been trying to pitch his technology to Taiwan's defense research establishment, he'd had to learn everything there was to know about PLA drone types. The serial number also told him it was using indigenous Chinese semiconductors, not components produced in Taiwan, the US or South Korea. In the same way the West had weaned itself off Russian and Middle East oil and gas, China had weaned itself off foreign semiconductors.

He turned the plate over in his hands. There was nothing written on the inside, but a strange honeycomb pattern had been thinly applied to the surface. He tested it with a thumbnail and was able to scratch it. Copper? It looked like a copper lattice.

The Lieutenant Colonel on Penghu had said the slaughterbots were impervious to electronic warfare attack. Copper was very effective at absorbing and dispersing radio and magnetic waves. The copper lattice could be some kind of shielding.

That was as far as he got before the pilot came back in. She saw him holding the plate, and he quickly put it back.

"I am sorry, I didn't mean to …" he said.

"No worries," she said, then took a long look at him. "What was so interesting?"

"Nothing, I …"

"Something was," the pilot said. "You were holding it up to the light and squinting at it. So?"

He picked the plate up again and showed her the manufacturer markings and told her what they meant. Then he flipped it over and explained his theory about the copper lattice.

She looked at him with curiosity. "How does a fisherman know stuff like that?"

"Before I started helping my father on my boat, I was a robotics engineer," he said meekly.

"He's a *doctor*," Xu said, dropping his bag. "But not the useful kind. I asked him once to look at my wart, and he said he's not that kind of doctor."

"What was your PhD?" the pilot asked, sounding genuinely interested. Something about her was slightly disturbing. She had a way of looking at you like there was no one else in the room.

"Uh, *Quantum Core-Powered Algorithms for a Swarm Intelligence-Based UAV Control Model*," he said. "You wouldn't …"

"So did you go with Reynolds or Particle Swarm Optimization flocking models?" she asked.

"Uh, Reynolds," he said with a frown. "How do you …?"

"Reynolds will work with miniature drones, but it won't scale," she said. "PSOP is better for larger aircraft, so I'm guessing you worked on miniatures? Before you took up fishing."

Hungyu just stared at her. Wu came to his rescue.

"The drone swarm shows at theme parks, the ones with a million drones that can do a scene from a movie that looks like a hologram in the sky?" Wu had sat himself on his bed and was taking his rifle apart to clean it. "He invented those."

"Invented?" the pilot asked.

199

"I own the patents," Hungyu said. "I sold them to a big American entertainment corporation."

"He's a big name in Dongshi, our fisherman," Xu said with a grin. "All these guys in suits visiting him." There was an explosion outside, not so far away. "Not so many right now, of course."

The pilot turned and picked up the access plate from the Chinese drone, turning it over herself to look at the copper lattice on the back before she looked up at him again. She smiled at him. "Hungyu, if we get you more bits and pieces from these beasts, would you be able to look for weaknesses?"

The intensity of her gaze unsettled him. "I should ... I should get back to the harbor," he said. "The boat is a wreck. I need to help my father ..."

"Right, but I'm here, fighting for you," the pilot said. She pointed at the US Marines who had sat themselves down with Xu and were more interested in the pot he was warming for noodles than Bunny's conversation with the engineer. "Like these guys. And none of us is going anywhere with those killer robots roaming the countryside, no matter how many of them Wu and Xu here can knock out of the sky."

"Which is a *lot*," Xu said proudly, shooting a glare at the Marine Sergeant. "Two more today."

"But not enough," Wu admitted. "As fast as we kill them, China just sends over hundreds more every day." He put his rifle down and wiped his brow. "Is it just me, or is it hot in here?"

Bunny handed him a bottle of water. "Right, so you and me need to stay here, fisherman. We're going to put that PhD brain of yours to good use, and you and me are going to work out a way to defeat these 'slaughterbots.'"

9. The battle of 1135 Wilson Boulevard

Burroughs picked up the only thing near him that even looked like a weapon, a 4-foot-long piece of rubber tubing. He got up on one knee. The roof of the air conditioner plant was about the size of a tennis court, with the elevator service shaft at the other end.

He was thinking it might offer a way out, something other than the stairs, when he heard a grunt, and his attacker started climbing the outside wall of the air conditioner plant, just as he had a few minutes earlier.

Burroughs listened, making sure he was coming up the same way and not a different wall. He lifted the rubber hose over his shoulder. It weighed maybe 10 lbs.

He saw a hand trying to get a grip on the edge of the roof. When he saw a head coming up to get a look, he swung the hose as hard as he could, connecting with the top of the man's head, knocking it sideways. The head and hand disappeared, and Burroughs heard a thump as his attacker hit the parking garage pavement.

He was up and running through the maintenance debris on the plant roof before the person below could gather themselves. The access to the elevator shaft was a simple trapdoor, angled into the roof.

It was locked with a dollar-store padlock, but it might as well have been titanium. He couldn't tear it off with his bare hands.

Burroughs heard a bullet bury itself into the structure somewhere behind him and spun around. His attacker wasn't trying to climb up again. He'd retreated to the far end of the parking garage, climbed up on the guard wall and railing so that he could see up onto the air-conditioning plant roof, and snapped off a shot at Burroughs.

But he didn't have a clear line of sight. He was still too low.

That would only last until he found a better position.

Burroughs crouched down to make himself a harder target and looked around desperately. Air-conditioning ducting, some paint tins—

he lifted one thinking it might make a better cudgel, but it was empty—coils of electrical wire, more rubber tubing, a discarded "no parking today" sign …

He lifted the "no parking" sign. It was old, yellow-painted steel. It might stop a bullet.

But on the back, he saw something better. The sign had a single metal leg on the back that was used to prop it up on the ground, and it was hanging by just one screw. He wrenched it off. Then he jammed it into the hasp of the padlocked trapdoor and twisted, hard.

The hasp buckled and snapped.

Putting the metal leg down quietly, he opened the hatch and looked inside. The elevator shaft was unlit. All he saw was a ladder, descending into darkness, the only light whatever was getting around the elevator doors on the levels below. He could see as far as the first three floors, at least. If he could get all the way to the bottom, maybe he could pry the ground-floor doors open. The elevator let out into the museum lobby. He could force a door, smash a window if he had to …

But first he had to get down.

He grabbed the metal bar again, put a foot on the ladder and lowered himself down, closing the trapdoor above him.

He was a naïve idiot, and he was going to die because of it. He could look back and see everything he'd done wrong, every misstep that had led to this moment, this elevator shaft, and how it had gotten him here …

"I need a coffee," Julio Fernandez said, walking into Burroughs's office in the Pentagon. "How about you?"

"Big time," Burroughs said, looking up with a sigh. He had begun plowing through the mass of intel on the Raven Rock bombing, not relying on the human or AI analyses that had already been prepared but diving into the raw data and reporting himself. He wanted to get a better feeling for which lines of investigation they had followed, and which they hadn't. He also hoped, of course, that he might see something others had missed.

Fernandez cocked his head. "Why so glum?"

Burroughs pushed a tablet PC across the table at him. "*This* is the only unexplored line of investigation with a possible China link."

Fernandez flicked through a few screens.

"What am I looking at?"

"A series of messages sent to different state-affiliated tips.fbi.gov websites after the Raven Rock bombing."

"Looks like gibberish. Same source?" Fernandez asked.

"No, but one thing connects them. Whoever sent them went to extreme lengths to make sure they couldn't be traced," Burroughs said. "Bounced all over the dark web before they started landing in FBI inboxes at different offices across the country."

"What does FBI think?"

"FBI doesn't," Burroughs said. "They haven't connected this particular set of messages. I got our own AI to trawl every message received by law enforcement agencies since the bombing, looking for anything with a China angle or from a possible Chinese or Chinese American source." He pointed to the set of messages. "This is what the AI came back with."

Fernandez started reading the messages. "*My irrepressible transports are unfettered rapture.*" He flicked to the next. "*An unbridled folly that cannot be denied.*" He read a couple more and then looked up. "Reads like bad AI poetry."

"That's an opinion." Burroughs smiled. "But it is poetry. Those are lines from Nalan Xingde's *Strange Tales from a Chinese Studio.*"

"Someone is tormenting FBI by sending them lines from a Qing dynasty Chinese writer?"

"Maybe. They sent 10 lines, one every couple of days after the bombing. Now they're repeating."

Fernandez handed the tablet back. "OK, weird. But not 'oh my god' weird, James. Not weird enough to explain your mood."

Burroughs stood and went to the coffeepot too, pouring himself a big mug. "I'm glum, Julio, because I was tasked to find a China connection to Raven Rock, and in all the millions of data points being investigated since the bombing, this is the only one, and it's just random noise."

Fernandez pulled the tablet back toward himself and read the translated messages again. "Can you compile these and send them to me in date order? I know a guy at NSA who I can ask to look at them."

"I've had our AI pull them apart and put them together again from every angle, looking for hidden meaning. Nothing."

"Yeah, but you didn't have Carl Williams look at them," Fernandez said. "Carl is living proof of why AI can't do everything for us yet. Has a way of seeing things AIs miss. He'd love this kind of challenge."

Burroughs put his tablet down. "What's the JWC working on?"

"Invasion scenarios. We're predicting that if slaughterbots and this show of force in the Kurils doesn't cause the Taiwan government to fold, Chinese and Russian fleets will load up their *Type 071* and *Ivan Gren* landing ships, with North Korea 'test-firing' long-range missiles into the western Pacific and Iranian drones overhead, and dare the world to stop them."

"We'll have a full division of US ground troops in Taiwan before they can."

Fernandez nodded. "It's about to get bloody."

James had finished his research and driven back to his D.C. apartment. The Nalan Xingde poetry messages were the only thing he could find that hadn't been run to ground by one agency or another.

He got up from his sofa, poured a glass of red wine and pulled a steak out of his freezer. His next Raven Rock task force meeting was in the morning. Should he mention the messages? It was so tenuous a China angle that it was almost laughable. So far, he was bringing nothing to the task force table, and the pressure, even if he was only putting it on himself, was building.

His private cell phone buzzed. *Caller ID blocked?* His kids had blocked numbers, and very few others had his private cell number. He picked up. "Yeah, hi."

"James Burroughs? Julio Fernandez gave me your number," a voice said. Middle-aged, Midwestern American, male.

"Then he should have given you my office cell number," James said, not hiding his irritation.

"He did. I used it to get this number. It's amazing how many people use their work phone to call their private phone when they can't find it."

"You what? Who is this?" Burroughs asked. Now he really *was* annoyed.

"Carl Williams, NSA. Julio gave me your code fragments?"

Well, that answered the "How did you access my cell phone logs?" question. Julio's "friend" was a cyber-spook.

206

"You mean the Nalan Xingde fragments," Burroughs corrected him.

"No. Code fragments. I figured it had to be a pretty straightforward substitution cipher—you know, picking out certain letters from each sentence to create the message …"

"But it wasn't."

"No. I have algorithms that get insulted if I give them plain ciphers to crack, but they couldn't. So I thought maybe it's a Vigenère cipher, where you need a pass phrase to decode it and only the sender and receiver know the pass phrase …"

"But we don't know the pass phrase."

"Oh, that's no problem. There's only so many combinations of words in the universe. Takes a bit of time to run through them all …"

"You ran through every combination of words in the universe?" Burroughs asked.

"Well, only in English and classical Chinese. It's not as impressive as it sounds with the bandwidth I threw at it. Took about 15 minutes. No luck. Looked for digraph substitution using various grids …"

"Alright, you've been thorough. I'm impressed," Burroughs said impatiently. "You called for a reason."

"Oh, right sorry. Some people like to know how I work. But that's not you, I guess."

"I guess."

"Right, so, the problem was I was looking for a message. A word or a sentence. But it's a number."

"You *cracked* it?"

"Sure. Whoever created it obviously wanted it to be tough, but they wanted it cracked. A way of letting you know they're serious, maybe."

"What does the number mean?" Burroughs asked.

"It's a phone number," Williams said. "I pulled the metadata on it. Registered to a fake name and address, of course. Not in use by any active cell phone, so I'm guessing it goes to an internet IP and then gets handed off a few times before it lands at the end user."

"You didn't call it?"

"Not really my thing, finding out who answers," Williams said. "I figure that's more yours. Here it is anyway …" He reeled off the 10 digits, and Burroughs wrote them down.

Burroughs thought fast. His temptation was to call straight away. But he should hand the information off to the FBI; after all, he had a solid Chinese-linked lead now, didn't he? And, he should inform Rosenstern.

"Should we make precautions before we call?" Burroughs asked. "Set up a trace, record the audio …"

"You're thinking of bringing in an agency?" Williams asked.

"Why shouldn't I?"

"Because those code fragments were meant for you," Williams said. "Personally."

The hairs rose on Burroughs's neck. "That can't be true. They were phoned in to FBI offices all over the country. It was pure chance the JWC AI pulled them out and put them together."

"And none of the other agencies found this clue, only you?"

"Apparently. I mean …"

"Uh, yeah, wrong. You guys are using our NSA AI, right? HOLMES." He was right. The JWC was staffed with analysts from all the major intelligence and law enforcement agencies, but it relied on the NSA Heuristic Ordinary Language Machine Exploratory System, or HOLMES, for AI support.

"And?"

"And so I traced the provenance of those code fragments. They didn't exist until you prompted HOLMES to look for them. Then they popped into existence, were put in various databases where HOLMES was sure to find them, and HOLMES served them up to you."

"HOLMES was *hacked*?"

"Crude way to put it. It was a beautiful exploit, I have to admit. Only a couple teams in the world could pull off something like that, and one of them is ours. It's going to take weeks for us to find and patch the holes in our defenses," Williams said, sounding more impressed than annoyed. "Anyway, what I'm saying is this number is for *you*. Julio told me this favor is to do with Raven Rock …"

"He shouldn't have told you that much."

"He had to give me something so I would help him. But that's all he told me. Look, you could go to FBI, CyberCom, DIA with this, sure, but how do you know this caller isn't going to give you information *about* them? What if this source tells you the FBI was behind Raven Rock, and you've got FBI listening in on the call?"

Burroughs suddenly realized he was a very naked babe, deep in some very dark woods. He hadn't thought about the fact that one of the agencies he was working with in the Raven Rock task force could have been behind the attack. And if they could pull off an operation like that, they would probably have no trouble getting a person *inside* the task force investigating it.

"I can't tell anyone about this until I check it out, can I?"

"I wouldn't," Williams said. "Oh, and don't call that number from either of your own cell phones."

"What? I … Should I buy a burner?"

Williams laughed. "A 'burner.' Wow, that's cute. You saw that in a movie or something?"

Burroughs flushed. "No. This isn't a problem I've had to deal with before," he snapped. "Tell me what to do."

"Alright, I'm going to send you an email with a link. You won't recognize the sender, but the subject will be your birth date. Open it on any laptop or tablet. It goes to one of our secure comms servers. You'll see a phone interface; you just type in the number and place the call. It leaves nothing on your PC, and it isn't logged by us."

"Why don't I believe that?" Burroughs said.

"Wow, so cynical. Look, even NSA field agents need a secure channel sometimes. You'll just have to take my word for it." Williams coughed. "Oh, and after you make the call, burn the paper you wrote the number on."

Burroughs was looking at the number he'd written down and frowning. "Look, if they wanted me to have this number, why not just slip it under my door?"

"They hid the code in some lines from a classical Chinese writer and then planted them inside an NSA AI. They wanted to impress you," Williams said. "Have you take them seriously. And trust me, if they can pull off an exploit like that on HOLMES, you should."

Burroughs spent the next two hours listening to Congress debate Carliotti's latest Raven Rock–related executive order, authorizing the deployment of the National Guard across the country to protect "institutions of political and military significance." It struck him as more than a little ironic, considering the Raven Rock attackers had been dressed as Guardsmen. But without Manukyan's party supporting the Congressional review of her order, the "debate" consisted mostly of grandstanding or members of Congress proposing unrelated issues that were quietly ignored. After a few formalities, the review went through "by unanimous consent," though the media pundits were predicting there would be huge opposition from state governors whose assent had been bypassed.

Burroughs knew what would come next. With troops visible on city streets across the nation to calm civil unrest, the stage was set for a breakfast TV prime-time broadcast from the Oval Office, with the US president announcing even more troops for Taiwan.

And the US would well and truly be at war with China. Or worse.

Did anything he did really matter now? Hadn't events overtaken the Raven Rock investigation? Sure, whoever was really behind the attack was still in hiding, but if the aim had been to kill Carliotti and prevent her from pursuing her hard line on China, for whatever reason, it had well and truly failed.

He had the link Williams had sent him open on his laptop. He could just delete it. Even that might not be necessary. It would probably delete itself.

The clock was counting down to World War III. One man couldn't prevent it. And trying now would be like trying to throw himself in front of an avalanche in the belief he could save the village below it.

His finger hovered over the trash icon.

Then, as though his hand had its own free will, he moved the mouse and clicked the link.

The sound of the phone ringing at the other end came through his speakers. And kept ringing. It was probably just some lunatic, anyway.

A lunatic who can hide a coded message in the work of poet Nalan Xingde and hack an NSA AI system. Yeah, right.

"Hello, who is this?"

A woman's voice. That took him aback. But why should it? The voice, as Williams had warned, was probably synthetic anyway.

"My name is James Burroughs," he said. "I think you've been trying to reach me."

"Well, if you've reached that conclusion, Mr. Burroughs, I suspect you've had a little help."

"Of course I have," he said.

"So you've been shown what we're capable of," the woman said.

"All I know is you wrote a cipher and hacked an AI system," Burroughs said, trying to sound unimpressed. "I was told it's no big achievement."

The woman laughed. "I bet you were. But I'm glad you called from home. Anywhere else, I might suspect you had friends listening in, which would not be smart. We need to talk privately."

Called from home? How could she see that if he was using an NSA redirect? Unless …

"Are you an NSA employee?" It would explain how they were able to hack an NSA AI, if it was an inside job.

"This isn't about me," the woman said, not denying it. "Let's talk about Raven Rock."

"If you have information about the bombing, you should give it to the FBI, not to me."

"I'm not 'giving' anything," she said. "But I am here to help, and all I ask for now is that you take my help seriously. I knew your predecessor, Michael Chase. His death was a terrible loss for his family, and his country."

"What does this have to do with Michael Chase?"

"Nothing at all. I was just making a gesture of condolence. Shall we talk about you instead?"

"What about me?"

"You have recently joined the multi-agency task force investigating the Raven Rock bombing. You told the other members you were asked by the White House Chief of Staff to, and I quote, 'rule out any Chinese link to the attack.'"

That was exactly what Burroughs had told the other members of the task force. Which meant one of the 180 law enforcement and intelligence agents on the task force had leaked what he said.

"You're fishing," Burroughs said. "Give me a reason to continue this conversation or I'll hang up the call."

"We can prove the attack was planned from inside your own administration, Mr. Burroughs," the woman said.

His blood went cold. "Who are 'we'?"

"Let's just say we are not friends of the Zhonghua Renmin Gongheguo Zhengfu."

An enemy of the Government of the People's Republic of China? "Why should I believe you?"

"Because we have a mutual friend, and he sends his regards," the woman said. "He said I should remind you of a train trip you took to Guangzhou and ask if you ever got the hotpot stains out of your suit."

Burroughs froze. He was thrown 10 years back in time, to a train journey he'd taken with a delegation from the Tsinghua University between Beijing and Guangzhou. He'd been sharing a private cabin with the University's vice chancellor, when there had been a knock and a man had appeared in the door, asking if he could speak privately with Burroughs. His University guests had vacated the cabin, and Burroughs had been left alone with the man.

He had introduced himself as Vice Minister of State Security Tsang Lijun. He was wearing the trademark dark suit, white shirt and burgundy tie of a party official, and he seated himself opposite Burroughs with an unsettling confidence. The only thing that prevented Burroughs from panicking was that the man appeared to be alone, not in the company of police or other officials.

"I am very pleased to meet you," Lijun said. "I have followed your work very closely. Most insightful."

Burroughs expected the man would quiz him about his sources, ask him to give up the names of trusted Chinese academic colleagues perhaps … but instead he sat forward eagerly. "I was particularly taken with your opinion piece in the *New York Times* about the declining influence of the Communist Party in Chinese culture, especially among the youth."

"I see," Burroughs had replied carefully.

"Exaggerated, but not entirely inaccurate," the man said surprisingly, sitting back. "Your analogy with the decline and fall of the Russian government under the dictator Putin was most … eloquent. A similar sequence of events in China would be very bad for business, and I wonder if …"

At that moment, there was a knock on the door. A woman balancing a tray with soup pots tried to push inside, but the door jammed, and she tripped. The soup went flying across the cabin, covering the floor, the seat and Burroughs's suit in chili-oil-stained liquid, vegetables and noodles.

214

By the time it had been cleaned up, and Burroughs had changed into a clean shirt and trousers, they were approaching Guangzhou station. As he listened to the announcement, his mystery friend looked disappointed. "It seems the moment has passed us by," he said. "My apologies for intruding. Perhaps one day we can continue our conversation." He gave a small bow and left.

Burroughs spent the rest of that trip waiting for another knock on the door from dark-suited thugs there to drag him away for an "interview" with other Ministry of State Security officials. But it never came.

That was his only contact with the Vice Minister of State Security Tsang Lijun. But he flagged the name in his internet research bot, and he stayed up-to-date with the man's journey through the Communist Party and security bureaucracies. It seemed to Burroughs the man was getting more reckless as time went on, with some borderline seditious public pronouncements about "corruption at the highest levels of government."

So it wasn't exactly a surprise to Burroughs when the party's Central Commission for Discipline Inspection said Lijun's political ambition was "extreme" and that he had worked with others to destroy the unity and political security of the party, forming gangs and factions and seizing control of key departments. He was accused of leading "a corrupt life" with "no moral bottom line" and embezzling an unspecified number of funds.

Interestingly, although reportedly charged with a raft of crimes, there was no public trial. He simply disappeared, never to be heard of again. Burroughs had assumed he had been lined up against a wall, shot and buried in an unmarked grave somewhere.

Until now. Had he engineered his own disappearance?

Burroughs grabbed at his pocket for his cell phone to record what the woman was saying, but then remembered he had put it in his microwave oven so that it couldn't be used as a passive listening device. More advice from Carl Williams. And probably pointless since a US intelligence or law enforcement agency could have put a listening device in his apartment at any time. He grabbed a pen and paper.

"I'm listening."

"The leader of the plot against your government calls themselves 'The Principal.' We don't know who they are, but they have intimate knowledge of, or access to, the highest levels of your administration. This operation has been planned for years, and they have access to significant resources."

"I need a name, not mere assertions," Burroughs said.

"We are working to give you one," the woman said. "This person and their allies hold financial positions in your military industrial complex, which, of course, have the most to gain from any conflict with China. When we are certain of their identity, we will also provide you with irrefutable evidence of their guilt."

Burroughs sighed. Yes, it was a song Chinese diplomats had been singing for years, accusing US politicians of talking up tensions with China to help the share price of US arms manufacturers, but it was also a common accusation of the lunatic left. Was that who he was really dealing with here? "Go on."

"There is a black ops contractor that we can definitively link to the Raven Rock operation. I am willing to give you the name of this contractor."

"I'm ready."

216

"It is a private military contractor called ComSec. There are several unidentified bodies from the Raven Rock attack belonging to the attackers. One of those is a man called Joshua Randall." She spelled out the name. "Randall was employed by ComSec. Their employment records show Randall was fired by them a year before the Raven Rock attack. However, we can provide you with payroll and bank records showing ComSec was still paying Randall, through an intermediary, right up until the week of the attack. Find out who is behind ComSec, and you may find The Principal."

"Do you have any more?" Burroughs asked. He was underlining words on his notepad, trying to keep it all straight in his head.

The woman laughed again. "Mr. Burroughs, I have given you more than your own intelligence agencies have been able to put together in several weeks of investigation. When we have more, we will give it to you."

"Why not go directly to the FBI, or Homeland Security?" Burroughs said. "Why give it to me?"

"Because you, Mr. Burroughs, have the wisdom to know what I am saying makes sense, and access to the one person who needs to hear what we are telling you, unfiltered by the biases and misdirection of your intelligence agencies," she said. "Carmen Carliotti."

Now Burroughs laughed. "Oh, right. I'll just call the US president, invite myself around for coffee."

"You will if you want your administration to remain free of corrupt influences," the woman said. "Right now, it seems to us your administration is so focused on Beijing, it is ignoring the very apparent threat from within."

The analysis wasn't exactly correct. Elements in ExCom were very focused on Beijing as the instigator of the Raven

217

Rock attack, but other agencies were looking elsewhere. Burroughs didn't want to tell the woman he no longer had direct access to Carliotti and didn't exactly have her private cell number. He could go through Fernandez, of course, who saw her face to face at ExCom meetings. Or through Rosenstern. "Can I call you at this number again?"

"No, Mr. Burroughs. When we have more intelligence to share, we will contact *you*. Please take this information seriously. For all our sakes."

Burroughs couldn't help himself. "You implied that you are speaking on behalf of an opponent of Beijing. But still Chinese. Why would a Chinese citizen, even a dissident, want to assist the USA?"

"Ah. Is it not said that 'the enemy of my enemy is my friend'? When this unpleasantness is done, we will all need friends. Goodbye, Mr. Burroughs."

"Goodbye, Mr. Burroughs," he thought grimly as he went down the ladder two rungs at a time, clinging to the side of the ladder with one hand as he held the metal bar in the other. Prophetic damn words. And now, not even a day later, he was climbing down a dark elevator shaft on a rusted ladder.

If he'd had his cell phone, he might've been able to make an emergency call. But he didn't, and it was the reason he was still alive.

Which was a miracle. "Your cell phone," the man confronting him had said, holding out the hand that wasn't pointing a pistol at Burroughs. "Then I have some questions."

Burroughs had pulled it from his back pocket. He hadn't wanted to get any closer to the man with the gun, so he'd flipped it through the air toward him. It had flown like a frisbee and struck the man in the face.

He *flinched* and *swore, holding his gun hand up to his forehead and checking for blood.*

And Burroughs ran—behind a supporting column, before sprinting to the next, and then into the stairwell.

In the elevator shaft, he had reached the fourth floor, and Burroughs paused to listen. No one at the trapdoor above him yet. Maybe he should get out here ... pry the doors open already. His attacker wouldn't be expecting that.

And then what? He'd be out in the deserted parking garage again, four floors above ground, nowhere to run or hide.

He gritted his teeth and kept going down, half-sliding, half-jumping. If his attacker worked out Burroughs was in the elevator shaft, there was only one place he could be headed. Could he run down to the ground floor faster than Burroughs could climb down?

He was about to find out.

10. The battle of Tiangong

The 150-ton module that was deployed to Tiangong atop a Long March 9 heavy-lift rocket was a treaty breaker. A multiple treaty breaker, if you were counting.

It broke Article IV of the 1967 Treaty on Principles Governing the Activities of States in the Exploration and Use of Outer Space, including the Moon and Other Celestial Bodies, which prohibited the militarization of space.

But did a treaty really count when it had already been broken multiple times, by multiple nations?

Perhaps more importantly, it broke an amendment to a treaty which China had recently ratified, the Treaty on the Non-Proliferation of Nuclear Weapons (NPT), which was not only intended to stop the use of nuclear weapons in space but also promote the safe use of nuclear power sources in orbit. More and more nations were experimenting with nuclear thermal propulsion to solve the problem of how to power a crewed mission to Mars without having to boost a massive volume of chemical fuel into space first.

Powering a crewed mission to Mars was not the purpose of the new Tiangong Light of the Heavens module, though. Powering a terawatt tactical ultrashort pulsed laser was. So the module that had just joined with Tiangong contained a 500-megawatt small modular nuclear reactor. That was what had attracted the Tiangong crew's interest when the module was first joined to the station, but what was exercising them right now was the newest member of the crew.

"The AI has responsibility for monitoring and carrying out routine operations for every system on the station," Liu was saying. "We can use our time more profitably now."

"I'm still going to be double checking," Chen said, arms crossed across her chest.

"You do that, Captain," Liu said with a sigh.

"Why did you do the system reset while we were resting?" Chen asked, suddenly curious.

"It was a simple matter," Liu said. "Only requiring one officer."

"It was irresponsible. If there had been a glitch, we should have been on hand to assist."

"My call, Captain, and an irrelevant observation, since there was no glitch," he wanted to get past the question of the 'system reset' and couldn't hide the irritation in his voice.

Zhu tried to defuse the situation. "Personally, I'm glad I didn't know about it. I had a *great* nap. Dreamed about mooncakes." He gave Chen a fat wink. He bent to the display of glowing golden light. "Hey there, AI, what do I call you?" he asked.

"Hello, Lieutenant Colonel Zhu. You can call me Tiangong, like the station. I will also answer to 'AI.'"

"At least you didn't try to give it a cute face and an anime voice," Chen said churlishly.

"Are you addressing me, Captain?" Liu said, still annoyed.

"Sorry, Colonel. I am simply saying you made a good choice not personifying the new crew assistance platform," she explained. "I've seen some creepy implementations of the Empire Dominator system interface."

"Tiangong, what is the status of the small modular reactor?" Zhu asked.

"The SMR is operating within normal parameters, Taikonaut Zhu. Do you want more detailed information?"

"Uh, no."

"Is it able to power the TUPL is all I care about," Chen said.

Liu nodded toward the glowing pinpoints of light. "Ask."

Chen sighed, leaning forward toward the glowing lights—then, realizing she didn't need to, she straightened again. "Tiangong, is power connected to the tactical ultrashort pulsed laser?"

"Yes, Captain Chen," the AI replied. "When I was deployed, the SMR began delivering power to the TUPL capacitors. Do you wish to initiate a test pulse?"

Liu was impressed. The AI answered the first question and correctly anticipated the next.

"Yes, Tiangong. Please locate the nearest suitable test satellite and prepare the TUPL for a laser system test."

"Preparing TUPL for laser system test, aye Colonel."

Liu pointed to the three harnesses in front of the laser systems consoles and checked his watch. "Five minutes until our mission window opens," he said. "We are on schedule to declare ourselves operational."

China planned to argue, if it ever came to a motion at the United Nations, that it was not breaking *any* treaties with the new Light of the Heavens module. Yes, the terawatt tactical ultrashort pulsed laser, or TUPL, was powered by a small modular nuclear reactor, but it was not in itself a nuclear weapon. China wasn't even the first nation to put a nuclear reactor in space—the US was the first to do that publicly, with its DRACO project experimenting with nuclear-powered space propulsion technologies.

Also, China would argue the TUPL was not a weapon. Its primary function was laser-optical communication with orbiting Chinese satellites, across large volumes of space—the Light of the Heavens laser could in fact send and receive pulsed light communications to any satellite in orbit to which it had line of sight, which meant anything up to 2,300 kilometers, or 1,400 miles.

Of course, what China would not want to discuss was the fact a terawatt TUPL allowed speed-of-light quantum communication, which was nearly impossible for an adversary to detect and intercept and was guaranteed to be impossible to decrypt. More than that, it meant Tiangong could communicate securely not just with other satellites but also with airborne drones.

And "secure communication" was what the coming mission of Liu Haiping and the crew of Tiangong was about.

Each taikonaut was strapped into their harness inside the new module: Liu at the mission commander desk, Zhu on target acquisition, Chen on engagement.

"Test satellite approaching," Liu said. His tactical screen showed a defunct Chinese satellite in low earth orbit that had just rounded the curvature of the earth slightly below them. It would pass them at 28,000 kilometers an hour, 800 kilometers distant at its closest point. "Designating T-1."

They were not going to shoot it. But they were going to destroy it. Apart from the TUPL, no new technologies would be used—the methods they were about to employ had been used openly by China in recent years to deal with "space junk." But the TUPL would ensure their adversary could not jam or interfere with their operations.

"T-1 locked," Zhu said. "Velocity 27.6, altitude 360, range 2,190, closing."

"Identify interceptors," Liu ordered.

"Interceptor I-1 identified, I-2 identified," Chen replied. "Link to I-1: four bars, I-2: three bars. Interception within nominal parameters."

"Engage T-1," Liu ordered.

"Engaging target with interceptor," Chen replied.

From the laser emitter on the rounded end of the Light of the Heavens module, a 200-femtosecond burst of light speared out toward Interceptor 1, an orbiting Chinese *Jisheng Chong*, or "Parasite," satellite, one of the 4,000 Parasite satellites launched by China since the start of its blockade of Taiwan.

The laser adjusted its bearing slightly and fired a second pulse to Interceptor 2, a second Parasite satellite orbiting farther away.

Both microsatellites immediately began maneuvering to put themselves on an intercept course for the target satellite. Their job wasn't to hit and destroy it. That would create a debris field that might damage other satellites belonging to China and its allies, which would not do. Interceptors I-1 and I-2, guided by telemetry constantly updated by the AI on Tiangong, would match orbit with the target satellite, close to within a few centimeters of it and then attach themselves to it by harpoon. Having harpooned the target, they drew themselves against it and "docked."

Then, using their own thrusters and a trajectory calculated by Tiangong that would avoid conflict with friendly satellites, they "deorbited" the target. China had proven the technology over several years, even using it to help deorbit a module from the now defunct International Space Station. US Space Force had of course speculated about, and war-gamed, what might be possible if China weaponized this capability.

Their conclusion was that it would not be possible for China to deploy at scale, and that the US could jam or destroy China's earthbound transmission stations or ships and thus cripple communications with any Parasite microsats.

They did not account for miniaturization allowing China to launch thousands of microsats in the space of a few weeks. Nor did they allow for China to deploy a communication system that was impossible to intercept and jam.

"T-1 intercept confidence high; T-2 intercept confidence high," Zhu reported. At 28,000 kilometers per hour, the engagement moved quickly. "I-1 harpoon deployed. I-1 docked. I-2 harpoon deployed. I-2 harpoon failure. T-2 intercept aborted."

Harpoon failures were rare but not unknown. The tiny explosively discharged depleted-uranium-tipped harpoon had to cross a few centimeters of space, penetrate the debris shield of the target satellite and then deploy its grapple inside the target so that it could pull itself snug against it. Sometimes the harpoon failed to penetrate because the satellite's debris shield was too tough, or it hit in the wrong place, or at the wrong angle. It wouldn't get a go-around for another 90 minutes, which was why Tiangong's taikonauts were using a "double tap" strategy, in the expectation at least one Parasite would stick.

"Deorbiting trajectory calculated," Tiangong's AI announced. "Trajectory sent." Light sensors on the Parasite that were tuned to the TUPL's wavelength registered the data beamed over from Tiangong and fed it to the pulse jets on the Parasite. They began firing, retarding the satellite and dropping it out of orbit so that it would burn up in the atmosphere.

A plot on their tactical screens showed the projected path of the satellite. It would clear any friendly satellites and predicted it would burn up in the mesosphere.

"*Yeah*, baby!" Zhu exclaimed, reaching out to Chen to tickle fingers since a hand slap would have twisted them both in their harnesses.

Liu wasn't happy. "Tiangong, why did we get a harpoon failure on I-2? Review vision and telemetry and speculate if necessary."

The AI analysis took only seconds. "I-2's harpoon struck a solar panel spar and was deflected. There were no systems failures. I-2 was able to retrieve its harpoon and reload it, and is available for further tasking."

The test was a success, confirming every test they'd conducted in the years leading up to this day and resulting in a successful deorbit. But the Parasite AI was supposed to use optical matching to choose where to place its harpoon on its target. It should not have fired at a spot on the target occluded by a solar panel spar.

Liu tried to park his worry. *The test was a success, man, move on.*

He touched his throat mic. "Wangchang, Tiangong. Light of the Heavens module operational test complete. We are ready for offensive operations."

They could hear unrestrained cheering on the channel that opened from the space station's control center in central China. Of course the ground crew had been monitoring the data, but they were a couple of seconds behind real time and had probably still been holding their breath until Liu came online.

"Operational status confirmed, Tiangong," the ground controller said. "You are clear to begin immediate operations."

"Good copy, Wangchang. Tiangong beginning deorbit operations," Liu confirmed. He turned to the crew. "Target acquisition, ready?"

"Acquisition ready, Colonel," Zhu replied.

"Engagement, ready?"

"Engagement ready, Colonel." Chen sounded unusually upbeat. Good; she would need all that energy.

"Deorbiting vector support, ready?"

"Tiangong is ready, Taikonaut," the AI replied. "All Light of the Heavens systems nominal."

Liu studied his tactical map. It was a 2D representation of the three-dimensional space around Tiangong, showing every satellite orbiting around it. Those higher than Tiangong were moving relatively slower; those lower were moving relatively faster. Their paths would converge and diverge depending on where Tiangong was in its orbital cycle.

They weren't interested in *all* the thousands of satellites within line of sight. Most were civilian internet, data and voice communication satellites—sometimes leased by Western militaries, but not capable of supporting critical operations like controlling drones, conducting signals or optical reconnaissance, or transferring encrypted military data at the bandwidths needed to support field operations.

Liu was only interested in those satellites marked with glowing red outlines because these were on his target list. The target list had been vetted very carefully: No early warning satellites, used for ballistic missile detection, because those were obvious targets of choice as a prelude to a nuclear exchange, and China didn't want to spook the USA into a nuclear war by blinding its early warning system. No weather satellites, even though these provided invaluable data to ground forces, ships and aircraft, since the data from these was also shared with civilian emergency, shipping and flight control authorities.

Positively vetted for the targeting list though, were all US active military GPS, communication, electronic intelligence, surveillance and reconnaissance satellites. Yes, the disruption to civilian systems that relied on US GPS satellites would be enormous, but many would automatically default to private positioning satellite networks.

Liu checked his watch. Eight long minutes before they began their Parasite offensive. He had no idea what else was going to happen in eight minutes, but he assumed there was a reason they were scheduled to begin their attack at precisely 0500 US Pacific Time.

The attack by the submarine *Qing* on the US cable node off San Luis Obispo Bay had been only one of several potential attack vectors—a test, which had proven highly successful, knocking out US West Coast cable internet traffic almost completely for nearly 10 days and resulting in traffic disruptions for nearly a full two weeks before the stealthy attack vector designed by the hacker Frangipani was identified and rectified. Interestingly, the aftereffects in retail, financial, entertainment and healthcare systems that crashed as a result of the cable traffic bottleneck were not long-lasting. Most were back to normal within three weeks of the attack.

As a test, it showed Frangipani's "black hole attack" was a viable attack vector that gave nearly two weeks of catastrophic disruption to US military cable communications with Hawaii and Asia. But its effects were no better or different than a simple physical attack by a submersible fitted with cable-cutting sea mines, like the Chinese *HSU-003*, which would also take around a week to repair.

The PLA Navy name for the semi-autonomous Xtra Large Uncrewed Underwater Vehicle, or XLUUV, currently hovering off the west coast of Japan was PLAN *HSU-003-4*. Its Hainan-based human crew called their vessels the *Hundun* class, named after a mythical Chinese monster that created chaos and confusion.

Hundun-4 departed Hainan at the start of the Chinese blockade and spent the intervening weeks first mapping, then mining the 19 undersea data cables connecting Japan to South Korea. Its five sister ships were doing the same for each of the 32 high-capacity cables connecting the US West Coast to Hawaii, Japan and Taiwan. Mines were placed in at least two locations 20 kilometers apart on each cable to make repair difficult.

Eight minutes before H-hour for the Tiangong space station crew, *Hundun-4* was hovering at ELF reception depth, 1,207 meters below the surface, off Yian on Taiwan's northeast coast. Connected to a Compact Quantum ELF Transceiver, the antenna it trailed behind it could both receive and send through the water at distances of several hundred kilometers.

As H-hour approached, *Hundun-4* queued up the trigger codes to 16 mines it had placed on the seafloor beside the high-capacity data cables serving Taiwan. Each of the Chinese deep-water naval mines weighed 1,000 kilograms, with a 600-kilogram aluminized PBX explosive warhead that would crater the seafloor for 150 meters around it. It snapped fiber-optic cables like they were strands of cotton.

At H-Hour, *Hundun-4* received the coded trigger command from Hainan and immediately relayed it to the mines it had carefully laid across the seabed off Taiwan.

It and its sisters were about to create a level of chaos and confusion the likes of which the world had never seen.

Four hundred kilometers above the *Hundun-4*, Liu Haiping and crew were preparing to create mayhem too.

"H-hour minus one minute … Tiangong, how many contacts in range?"

"There are 32 contacts currently in range."

"Confirm you have the capability to acquire and engage 32 targets simultaneously."

"All Light of the Heavens system parameters are nominal. I can target up to 100 contacts simultaneously for the next six hours if needed."

The test firing of the pulsed laser was a manual test of the system, but the human crew of Tiangong would not be capable of handling the workload needed to identify, track and acquire 32 targets, direct 64 Parasite microsats to intercept them and then calculate and transmit deorbiting trajectories to the Parasites that would avoid the hundreds of other nearby satellites.

All Liu had to do was manually confirm each of the targets, which he had already done.

"Tiangong, you are cleared to engage the identified targets," Liu said.

"Tiangong is engaging," the AI confirmed. "Please refer to the tactical screen for a dynamically updated engagement report."

There was no rattle of projectile weapons, no ominous hum of electricity, smell of ozone or snap of capacitors rapidly discharging as Tiangong went about its work. The taikonauts had in fact suggested that the system at least give different sounds to indicate if a target had been destroyed, or if an interception had failed, but as Zhu had noted in his first moments inside the module, their suggestions for the interface hadn't been implemented.

Instead, the tactical screens in front of each of their stations showed the targets circled with glowing red numbered halos, the interceptor Parasites with glowing green circles, and drew lines connecting target satellite to interceptor Parasite. On the right side of the screen, a text commentary was being constantly updated.

Target T-2 acquired.

T-2 Parasites T-2a, T-2b allocated.

Target T-3 acquired.

T-2 Parasites T-2a, T-2b allocated.

T-2a harpoon deployed. Docking achieved.

T-2b harpoon deployed. Docking achieved.

Target T-3a acquired.

Target T-2 deorbit maneuver initiated.

The commentary flowed like rising water up their screens, too fast for them to follow, though they could spool up and down if desired. "And just like that, we become irrelevant," Chen said. She pushed away from her screen as far as the harness would allow.

"No, just like that, we are freed for other duties," Liu corrected her.

"But we have to stay here like dummies, just watching."

"We are monitoring this first engagement," Liu said. "Just because the Light of the Heavens AI functioned without error on the ground does not mean it will function flawlessly under combat conditions."

"The Americans are about to lose a large proportion of their most valuable assets in space," Zhu predicted. "How long before they work out it is this station bringing down their satellites and put an SM-3 missile through our core module?"

"Unlikely," Liu told him. "They wouldn't dare use an explosive warhead, and even a kinetic missile strike would risk creating 30 tons of space junk, a debris field the length of Mongolia, and would do a better job of taking out American satellites than anything we are doing."

A flashing circle on their screens caught their attention. Liu paused the commentary text. "T-9 de-orbit trajectory recalculating. De-orbit maneuver aborted."

"So the system is not perfect after all," Chen remarked.

"Contact T-9 is lower and moving plus 600 kilometers an hour relative. It will be in range again in … 12 hours," Chang calculated. "We'll catch it on the flip side, and the aborted maneuver probably knocked it out of transmission alignment, anyway."

"Colonel, permission to speak freely?" Zhu asked, even though they knew there was no such thing as free speech on Tiangong. Every syllable, every breath, was monitored by their ground crew; and now they also had an AI listening in and no doubt analyzing and providing reports on a hundred personality parameters to Wangchang. Asking permission to speak freely was in fact a code saying: *I am just asking, so do not hold this conversation against me.*

Liu kept his eyes on the engagement commentary. "Yes, Lieutenant Colonel?"

"Our attack on Taiwan with the Tianyi drones targeted the rebels. Except on the digital front, we have done nothing directly to attack the USA, despite their provocations against us with attacks on our forces on the mainland and in the South China Sea. What we are doing today is the first direct strategic attack on US forces. It cannot be in isolation. Do you know what is taking place in other domains or theaters?"

Liu pulled his eyes away from the description of the carnage unfolding around them. He was glad he was not alone in his appreciation of the enormity of what they were doing. Though Liu had not been briefed on what role this action played in China's wider strategy, he also assumed it was just the opening move in a direct confrontation with the USA.

Or call it what it was. China's opening shot in a new world war.

"No, Lieutenant Colonel Zhu," Liu replied. "I'm sorry. I have no information to share. We have our mission, and we must apply ourselves to it. I am sure the bigger picture will reveal itself in time."

Lieutenant Robin Tibbets wasn't worried about the big picture. He was worried about the very small picture on the multifunction display in front of him. Patrolling a sector of sky north of Taipei in his F-35 in the company of a Ghost Bat drone, he had just sent his uncrewed wingman to the west to check out a possible Chinese J-20 contact that had flashed on and then off his radar warning receiver. If it was solid, it would be the third time this patrol China had tried to sneak stealth fighters in through his sector for a standoff attack on Taipei.

He was using his Ghost Bat to smoke the Chinese fighter or fighters out. It was a threat they couldn't ignore, and if they engaged it, he would know exactly where they were.

Except ...

His Ghost Bat was gone. Not physically. He still had it on his own radar. But it had lost its satellite link with the US battlenet—its Multifunction Advanced Data Link, or MADL, was blinking red, and so was his. The drone was defaulting to "return to papa mode" and had canceled the orders he had given it, turning back toward Tibbets so that it could establish shorter-ranged radio contact.

Jamming? No, there was nothing in the sector putting out the kind of energy that would be required to jam the EW-hardened comms link between him, his drone and overhead satellites.

It was more like the satellite itself had disappeared. He opened a channel to Kadena Air Base. "Kadena Control, this is Basilisk One. I am showing failure on MADL; battlenet is down. Can you confirm?"

No answer.

He flipped to a joint forces satellite frequency. "Basilisk One to USAF Forces on battlenet in sector G-13, does anyone read?" There were several other aircraft and allied ships in the OA who should respond.

Silence.

He frantically paged to the screen on his panoramic multifunction display that showed a satellite map of friendly and known enemy aircraft.

It was blank.

His wingman was on the other side of the sector, watching the sky to the southwest. Out of radio range. But he wasn't showing on the map either. The data usually dynamically updated as every friendly unit reported its position to satellites overhead, and that data was beamed down to his machine together with known adversary units.

His system must be glitching.

A chime sounded in his helmet as his Ghost Bat reported a missile had been launched against it! His radar warning receiver lit up. A J-20 30 miles west had just attacked his drone. *He got an emission hit on another, this one even closer, searching for him.*

As he gripped his flight stick, pushed his nose down and headed for sea level to try to get a solution on the two Chinese attackers, he suddenly felt very, very alone.

There was only one 155 mm barrel left undestroyed on Taiwan's Kinmen Island, and the crew of the M109 Paladin self-propelled howitzer had managed to keep it alive and operating despite several near misses from Chinese artillery, Chinese air-launched missiles and one particularly nasty FPV drone strike that caused them to throw a track and left them exposed for 30 agonizing minutes until it was repaired and they could scuttle back into cover.

They called themselves the Wolf Spiders because they had survived by hiding in holes in the ground or inside destroyed buildings from which they emerged only to strike and then scuttle away to a new position, before counter-battery fire hit back or ISR drones could spot them.

The Chinese mainland was only 5 kilometers away, and there was not a moment outside cover where they were not in danger.

One of their biggest problems was getting targeting data through the curtain of electronic noise that China was blasting across the Strait to try to jam Taiwan and its allies' aircraft, missiles and radars. But orders were still getting through at random intervals via encrypted burst radio transmissions.

"New fire mission!" the Wolf Spiders' section chief yelled. "Plugging in target coordinates. Load Excalibur-ER HEDP, set for airburst, 20 meters. Target is a railroad siding outside Xiamen. Elevation one hundred twenty point three, bearing 355 degrees, range fifty-two point two five. Three rounds shoot and scoot, people!"

What made the Paladin so survivable was that its crew could load it on the move from inside the vehicle, and start moving with the first round already in the breech, unprimed. It was essentially a big gun mounted on a Bradley IFV chassis, giving the crew armored protection and high-speed mobility.

They were currently hiding inside an old wooden pallet factory that had been hit and burned to a hollow shell early in the war.

"Driver, take us out on the north side. Gunner, as soon as we are in position, shoot."

The Wolf Spiders were alive because they thought like snipers. They never exposed themselves unless they had to. They never moved unless they had a fire mission. They fetched food and fuel and scouted new positions on foot, in daylight, so their body heat wouldn't give them away going to and from their hiding places.

Their driver was the kind who didn't need a door. He'd already checked the wall directly ahead of them, double-checked the turret was facing rear and the barrel locked. Then he *made* a door.

Their Paladin broke through the wall into a nearly deserted parking lot. What few cars there were were burned-out wrecks. Kinmen was only the size of the District of Columbia, but it was probably the most bombed piece of real estate on the planet.

Their gunner swung their turret around. The barrel pointed at the sky, orienting on the coordinates the commander had input. The loader put the round in the tube, pushed it so it cocked, pulled the rammer down, put the primer in and pulled the cord …

The Paladin rocked back on its suspension with the recoil, and the Excalibur round headed downrange, toward the rail siding. While the Paladin vehicle hadn't really evolved in the last 15 years, its ammunition had. The newest Excalibur-ER round was fitted with maneuvering glide wings to extend its range and steer it right onto its target, so after reaching apogee, it checked the GPS coordinates in its memory, then checked its actual position via satellite GPS and …

Came up blank.

It tried again, and again. There was no satellite signal. That was not unknown—Chinese jamming sometimes managed to scramble US GPS. The US got around jamming in various ways, including multiple redundancy—different GPS satellites using different frequency ranges.

The Excalibur round tried to lock onto a different GPS network, then another.

All down.

As it fell toward the Chinese rail siding, it was supposed to use the data from the satellites, added to the data it had been fired with, to precisely aim itself at the coordinates the Wolf Spiders had been given. When it worked, it would hit within 2 meters of its aim point.

When it didn't … it was no better than any other artillery shell fired in haste by a tired crew on cratered terrain.

The three rounds from the M109 all landed within 10 meters of each other, but they were 50 meters short. They exploded 20 meters in the air, showering the surrounding area with shrapnel and flattening everything nearby with concussive blast.

But they exploded over a storage yard of empty shipping containers and not over the railway carriages filled with munitions, about to be transported from Xiamen to Tianjin, 1,600 kilometers north.

Which would have seemed doubly strange if the Wolf Spider crew had known about it. Firstly, that the Excalibur rounds had failed to find a single satellite to lock onto.

Secondly, that China was moving vital ammunition *away* from the Taiwan Strait.

But the Wolf Spiders weren't at all worried about where China was moving its ammunition. They had registered the GPS miscue on their first salvo, and they decided to risk their luck and try a second.

The Chinese counter-battery radar on the coast outside Xiamen was linked to a mechanized artillery battery also firing GPS-guided 155 mm rounds, but its shells had no trouble locking onto China's BeiDou GPS satellite network. Their first round slammed into the Wolf Spiders' Paladin as they were loading the first round of their second salvo.

Soon after that, the Wolf Spiders of Kinmen stopped worrying about anything at all.

The worries had just started for 615th Combat Operations Squadron's Colonel Alicia Rodriguez.

She had just been ordered to join an unscheduled Space Launch Delta 45 Commanders Conference. She had been in transit from a hangar at Cape Canaveral inspecting a repaired X-37C uncrewed spacecraft, en route to her office at Patrick and just passing Cocoa Beach in her SUV. With the call scheduled to start in just five minutes, she decided to pull off the highway and ended in the parking lot of a dead-end street leading down to the sea. She sat her secure comms unit on the dash in front of her and logged in.

An emergency Delta 45 Commanders' Conference was never a good thing. It usually meant there had been an incident, either on a Space Force facility or, worse, in space. An incident requiring coordination, control and a rapid response. Something in Rodriguez's gut had told her this day was coming. From the moment the Taiwan conflict had kicked off, she'd been preparing for it, but how did you prepare for the unknown?

Gradually her fellow commanders appeared on screen, the senior officers of Delta 45 Range Ops, Logistics Readiness, and Space Communications, plus the CO staff and Rodriguez as head of Combat Ops. Last on was the CO himself, Brigadier General Chris Panhagen. He was still speaking with someone off-camera as his image came on-screen. Rodriguez could also see an intel specialist had dialed in, a captain in her 30s she didn't recognize. But Delta 45 was the biggest unit in Space Force, so that wasn't surprising.

"Ladies and gentlemen, thank you for joining," Panhagen said, looking grave and taking a deep breath. "Space Force is under attack, and with this, the United States is under attack. Captain Mitchell will brief you, then we'll discuss how we respond before I join an emergency meeting of Delta Commanders in …" He looked off camera for a steer. "… in 30 minutes." He sat back. "Captain Mitchell, you have the floor."

The young woman appeared to have several tablets open in front of her, which told Rodriguez they were dealing with a fast-developing situation with multiple elements, not a single incident. The woman gathered herself but kept her eyes on the screens in front of her as she began speaking. "Thank you, General Panhagen. The situation at this minute is as follows. US military satellites have begun unplanned deorbiting in large numbers. The Chinese attack vector is unknown. The attack began two hours ago, and so far, nearly 42 satellites have deorbited or been knocked out of stable orbits …"

Forty-two? Rodriguez could feel her heart quicken. No war game scenario she had ever been part of allowed for this kind of decimation of US Space Force assets.

"The satellites affected include ISTAR, communication and GPS satellites of both the US and our French, Italian and UK NATO partners. They do *not*, yet, include early warning or ballistic missile detection satellites."

The detail was important. If an enemy had taken down the NATO early warning and ballistic missile detection network, it would almost certainly be as a prelude to a nuclear strike. So this, hopefully, was not that. But attacking the satellite systems of NATO nations not currently involved in the Taiwan conflict was a real statement of China's intent.

It was no longer a "limited conflict."

The intel Captain pulled another tablet over to her. "In addition, there has been another attack on the cable internet network between the US West Coast and Asia. Two hours ago, seismic monitoring stations detected explosions on the seabed off the coasts of Japan, South Korea, Taiwan, Hawaii and Guam. High-capacity data cables appear to have been targeted, and up to 30 of 42 of these key connectors appear to have been cut." She pushed the second tablet away and returned to the first. "The impact assessment is …" And then the moment overwhelmed her. She paused, as though trying to find the right word. "The impact of these combined events is *catastrophic*. They not only cripple our ability to monitor the enemy's activities, communicate with our own and allied forces across the globe, but also to deploy and control vital airborne, missile and uncrewed weapons platforms."

"Thank you, Captain," the General said. "People will have a million questions, and right now we probably don't have clear answers. But I am going into the Delta 45 Commanders' meeting with some assumptions. The big one: This is China. It's their first big move directly against us, and it's just the start. What this unit will be asked to do from here seems pretty obvious, so here's what I need. Range Ops and Logistics, you need to tell me how quickly we can start replacing the lost assets and work up an accelerated launch schedule, pulling in every military and civilian launch option available, including those of our allies. Comms, you need to work out what we've lost, what we still have, what workarounds we can kludge together and how we can tap into other NATO allies' assets to fill our gaps. Tell me what coverage of Chinese activities we still have and what we don't."

It was Rodriguez's turn next. She didn't need to be told, but they all needed to be on the same page. "Combat Ops, I need you to work out how China is doing this. It isn't missiles; it isn't laser or any other pulse weapon we can see. We aren't even picking up any major uptick in comms traffic between Chinese ground stations and orbiting systems. Find me a target, and make sure we have the assets in play to take it down without creating a wasteland of miles-deep debris up there." Panhagen paused, letting the orders sink in. "People, this is our Pearl Harbor moment. What we do from here, in the next 36 hours, determines whether we get shoved onto our asses and start scrambling backwards like we did in '41, or if we can take the fight to China from day one and put this genie back in its bottle."

The last minutes of the meeting were used by the different Delta Commanders to ask clarifying questions. Rodriguez had just one. "General Panhagen, can I assume you want me to put all our offensive options in play, and that we'll have priority in the launch program?"

Panhagen wasn't the kind to make promises he couldn't keep, but he was never one to fudge a question either. "To your first question, yes. To your second, we'll be looking at launch sequencing on a case-by-case basis, hour by hour, if not minute by minute, Colonel. You find me a target or targets and get ready to prosecute them. I'll worry about priority."

11. The battle of AC-130X 'Outlaw'

"This changes *everything*," acting Captain of *Fujian*, Colonel Wang, told his intel chief, Tan. To be completely honest, he felt like kissing the dour intel officer. Which would have been true if the Lieutenant had been a man as well. But they were standing in *Fujian*'s Combat Information Center, in full view of all his watch officers. "I could … hug you."

Tan winced. "Please, don't … uh, thank me, Colonel," she said quickly. "Chief Engineer Fei had already begun cannibalizing parts. He was just waiting for a green light. So I gave him one." She consulted her tablet. "Deck plating will be replaced within six hours. Most of the steel is coming from the stern plates above the boatswain stores … so we better hope we don't meet heavy seas."

"What about EMALS?" he asked. The systems powering their electromagnetic aircraft catapults had not just been physically damaged; the electronics had also been fried in the last Coalition attack.

"Also six hours," she said. "We will lose backup food refrigeration, one auxiliary generator, Cat Two and aircraft elevator B since we need to cannibalize them. Some minor auxiliary systems, also. But we'll be able to launch from Cat One."

"As long as we can get at least one ISR drone into the air, prevent our adversaries from coming in at nap of the earth again …" Wang said.

"Oh, no, Colonel," Tan told him. "If the repairs succeed, Cat One will be fully functional again. We will only have one aircraft elevator, but we'll have a clean deck. We can launch whatever you wish. Our cycle rate will be slower with just one catapult, but we can launch ISR *and* combat patrols."

Wang felt like busting out in both delight and dismay. Delight that his warship would still be able to defend itself from the air. A *Type 003* carrier operating at even a fraction of its normal capability was still a potent platform. And dismay at the military system that had, at the same time, produced a chief engineer who could work such a miracle and then inhibited him from doing so, from even *informing* his Captain of the possibility, until he received a direct order.

It was a symbol of both the power of Communist China and its weakness in one. But now was not the time for political philosophy—it was the time for *action*.

"XO, get onto pri-fly. I want an ISR drone readied for launch and in the air the moment that catapult is ready to test. Give me an inventory of available Chongming airframes and ordnance. Have them prepare a schedule for carrier defense CAPs with first patrols to launch as soon as that ISR drone is airborne. Keep two aircraft at Ready Five for ASW duty." He snapped his fingers at his executive officer. "What am I missing, man?"

He had not picked the *Fujian*'s senior officer corps. That had been done by the late Captain Yu Dabao, and in Wang's estimation, he had not done well in his choice of Executive Officer. The man was thorough, but he was slow. And Captain of a capital warship in a hot war he would never be. But he had his moments …

"Send a patrol to Port Aeon?" he suggested. "The adversary may have guessed we are headed there. They could mine the port, or …"

"Do it." Wang nodded.

He turned to ask Tan a question, but she had disappeared. Terrified of being praised again, no doubt.

Captain Rory O'Donoghue was not expecting praise. No matter how his next mission panned out, someone would be unhappy—if not in the Pentagon, then in the State Department.

What the USAF 18th Flight Test Squadron had learned from their probe on the *Fujian* Task Force was that he had no hope of getting through the carrier's defensive screen with his limited resources.

He might fake the carrier's pickets into engaging a few decoys, slip a swarm through their defenses, maybe even an LRASM cruise missile or two, but this was an enemy that had taken on *hypersonics* and survived. You had to respect that. From the reaction times and counter-missile coverage he'd seen, they were still at the top of their game, crippled or not.

And those damned Indonesian frigates were still duct-taped to the carrier's hull.

So after chewing it over with Uncle, what he'd proposed to his superiors at the 412th Test Wing at Edwards, and what they'd cleared with the Pentagon, was that *they would not strike the* Fujian *at all.*

Problem solved.

Or not really. The reason he'd needed Pentagon-level clearance, and probably State Department too, was that O'Donoghue had proposed delivering his attack not where the *Fujian* was but where it was going to be.

The Chinese base at Port Aeon. Before *Fujian* got there.

Severely messing up ground targets was what Outlaw was born for. A carrier task force needed fuel. A *lot* of it. Food and water for its crews. Ammunition for its weapons systems. And from the satellite pictures he'd seen of the carrier taken just after the last engagement, *Fujian* would need to repair its

245

ravaged flight deck and island, which would require alloy plates, steel, cables, electronics, welding and cutting gear, lubricants …

All of this, Rory knew, the Chinese planners had foreseen. As they had done for centuries, they played a long, long game. They had poured hundreds of millions of dollars into the economy of Kiribati over the last 20 years, and that investment had bought them not just goodwill but a 100-year lease on land at Port Aeon and the freedom to redevelop the old RAF air base there, the right to dock Chinese vessels and, as importantly, the right to warehouse Chinese supplies on the site without tiresome customs formalities.

As it had done across the Pacific, in the Solomon Islands and Timor-Leste just off the coast of Australia, and in Fiji, deep in the South Pacific.

Western allies had not always been foresighted enough to prevent China's arrangements with vassal states in the Pacific, but they had been very efficient in monitoring, documenting, imaging and mapping the flow of Chinese building, sustainment and military equipment into each of its leased ports and bases.

Rory O'Donoghue had nearly 20/20 insight into the distribution of Chinese fuel and supplies in the small Kiribati port, allowing him to plan with painstaking precision how to go about *destroying* them.

If they could prevent the Chinese carrier strike group from accessing fuel, food and ammunition, then its ability to serve as a thorn in the side of Coalition forces in the Eastern Pacific would be negligible. *Fujian* might make Port Aeon, but it would be stuck there, unable to repair or even sustain itself.

His biggest challenge, and one the Pentagon planners insisted on, was how to achieve this and still avoid massive

246

loss of civilian life. Despite being a friend of China, the tiny nation of Kiribati was not an enemy of Australia or the USA. Not directly, anyway. But any friend of China …

Rory had flown out of Cairns in Australia and refueled at the Coalition-friendly island of Tonga, about 2,800 kilometers from Port Aeon. If Tongan customs had inspected his cargo bay, Outlaw's journey might have ended right there, but Tongan authorities had not fallen for the lure of China's belt and roads lucre. They were among the first to support the Taiwanese right to self-determination, and their customs officials were "occupied elsewhere" on the island in the short time Rory's Outlaw was on the ground.

When Outlaw was airborne again, he went aft. He'd received disturbing news while they were on the ground, and his electronic warfare officer confirmed it.

"Battlenet is down, sir," the EWO said disbelievingly. "We have no sat comms. Best I can pick up is long wave from Australia and Hawaii, in morse code, if you want to believe it."

"GPS?" Rory asked.

"GPS M-code is down too. I can get L-band civilian frequencies, but you know the accuracy of those. We can use L-band for general navigation but not for weapons."

"So we have no idea where the *Fujian* is right now?"

"Last position was here," the man said, pulling up a map on a screen. "2,500 kilometers, or about two days' sailing from Port Aeon. There's still plenty of time for us to get in and out."

"Battlenet *can't* be down," his CSO muttered. "It just can't. That would mean dozens of satellites are AWOL. It must be something at our end."

"Ground crew on Tonga said their satellite phones and GPS were down too, and so is the internet, so it isn't just us," his EWO replied. "I thought it was just a temporary glitch. Could be another cyberattack?"

"Cyberattack that takes down the entire USA battlenet *and* the internet across the Pacific?" Rory shook his head. "That kind of thing only happens in novels."

While Rory was in back, Uncle was flying the machine, but he was listening to the conversation. "Lucky one of us still reads novels," Uncle said over the intercom. "*And* knows morse. There's advantages to being a dinosaur."

Rory chewed his lip. "Doesn't change our mission. We go into Port Aeon, and we mess it up. I want *Fujian* to see nothing but smoke on the horizon from 100 miles out." He turned to his weapon systems officer. "Prep all ordnance for inertial navigation."

"At these ranges, that's near the same as firing blind ..." his CSO protested.

"LongShots just have to reach standoff waypoints. We can program them to run their plays in autonomous mode from there."

"I'm thinking about the JDAMs. We can point them at Port Aeon, but what happens after that will be blind luck."

Rory slapped his shoulder. "I was born lucky, son."

"You always lose at poker," Uncle pointed out.

"Lucky in *love and war*, Uncle," Rory said. "Just fly the damn plane up there."

But the comment went deeper than Uncle had probably intended. It had been Rory's decision to carry on the mission in Syria, even though they'd been ordered to RTB. The decision had cost them more than a reprimand; it had nearly cost them their machine, and their lives.

There were civilian lives at risk this time. Was he about to make another bad call?

Fujian had none of the communication issues the Outlaw crew was dealing with. Unlike the US battlenet, it had reconnected with the Chinese military data net after its satellite antennae were damaged, and was pulling data from satellites spanning the globe. It was still in direct and instant contact with its fleet base in Ningbo in China, to which it had reported its unexpected, though somewhat diminished, battle-ready status.

And from which it had just received new orders.

Wang had never, in his long naval air service career, ever had cause to doubt his own eyes, his own ears.

But he did so now.

"Give me a moment," he told the officer who had just alerted him to the flash message from Ningbo. He closed the door behind the man and walked to his small, fold-down desk. Dropping the tablet on it, he reached to the cabinet above it and pulled out a bottle of Wuliangye Baiju liquor from his home province of Sichuan, and a small glass. It was a bottle that had been presented to him by his proud late father when Wang had assumed command of the *Fujian* Air Wing. That moment had been the only time he had ever seen his father with tears in his eyes.

His father's hands had been shaking as he handed the bottle to Wang. It must have cost him three months of his old-age pension to purchase. His father had passed six years earlier, so Wang only took a glass from the bottle on rare occasions, usually when he needed his father's counsel. It connected him to the old man, somehow. Sipping the liquor, he could almost hear his father's voice.

He poured the liquor reverentially into the glass and held it up to the light over his desk. Usually as clear as vodka, time and the constant motion of life beneath the decks of naval vessels had given it a cloudy, slightly milky aspect.

The taste was still as pure and clear as the day he had opened it, and the umami quality was still as strong.

Father, I suspect we may soon be reunited, he thought. He watched the light at play inside the glass, let the aftertaste sit on his tongue. *Perhaps we should have been together already, but our ancestors intervened?*

He took another tiny sip and pulled his tablet toward him, reading the words.

> *Make best speed Port Aeon to rearm and refuel the strike group. As soon as this is done, and no later than six hours after arrival, proceed to position 13.901, -158.837 and report. Await further orders. All defensive measures needed to preserve the integrity of the strike group are authorized.*

Fifty short words, a couple of numbers. He had been right in thinking the order to cannibalize the ship for parts had changed everything. They had gone from a liability to an asset again. Instead of being written off by war planners, they were being brought back into play, without being allowed the time to effect even minor repairs.

They could take repair materials aboard in the six hours he had been allowed, and try to effect some repairs at sea. Most critical were the antennae and radar arrays they had lost when their superstructure was explosively dismantled. He looked at the message again.

13.901, -158.837.

He was a pilot by profession, but enough of a naval officer to recognize the latitude and longitude without needing a map. Nonetheless, he tapped them into his tablet and looked at the screen. He brought up the scale and dropped two points on the map, one between where they were now, and another on what had to be their target.

Six hundred and eighty-three very short kilometers.

He sighed, looking at the walls of the cabin, which suddenly seemed so much more impermanent. He had tried to convince his crew, perhaps even had convinced himself, just a little, that she was unsinkable, the *Fujian*.

Had she not soaked up a hit by a hypersonic missile? Had she not shrugged off a torpedo in her waistline? Had her decks not absorbed the energies of a half dozen sea-skimming cruise missiles without her back breaking in two?

Give her a couple of months in a friendly port, and she would be the most formidable ship in the Chinese navy once again. But no. That was not to be.

Fujian had survived everything the US Coalition could throw at her, but she would not survive this new order—of that, he was sure.

It was strange, that thought. Because what followed it was not any selfish concern about his own mortality. He had been prepared to die from the moment the first Taiwanese missile hit a landing barge off Kinmen Island and *Fujian* was ordered into action. Nor did he think of the 5,000 members of *Fujian*'s crew, who at any time in the last several weeks could have been lost.

It was strange that at that moment, his father's liquor rolling around his mouth, he was thinking of *one* crew member. And a conversation he had shared with her on *Fujian*'s deck, looking down at a row of body bags.

We shouldn't hope for a happy ending, Mushroom, he'd told the pilot. *The best we can wish for is a fighting one.*

Something like that. Yes, let that be his last wish. *Father, let us go out fighting.*

The USAF attack on the "neutral" state of Kiribati was only authorized because the Chinese facility at Port Aeon on the island of Kiritimati was 30 kilometers from the nearest civilian town. The location had advantages for the PLA Navy, which didn't want nosy local authorities or foreign "tourists" watching too closely as it built up its naval base with a deep-water pier capable of supporting capital warships, and upgraded the old World War II airfield to be able to land everything from its venerable 76-ton Xian H-6 strategic bomber to its latest stealth combat fighters, refueling aircraft and drones.

That there was a Chinese base in Kiribati at all was the result of generations of diplomatic arrogance by Western nations that ignored pleas for financial support by the tiny nation as rising seas began swamping its 33 islands and atolls. China, on the other hand, poured hundreds of millions of dollars into development aid and infrastructure projects and in return was gifted a toehold in the eastern Pacific Ocean, which potentially enabled it to put its long-range strike aircraft within range of San Diego, California.

The development didn't go unnoticed in Washington, which warned China if it positioned strategic nuclear forces on Kiribati, the US would reply in kind by stationing nuclear forces in South Korea and Japan. China chose not to cross that particular red line but walked right up to it, basing 500

PLA personnel, fuel, reconnaissance aircraft, naval stores, ordnance and ground-to-air missile defenses at the port.

The crew of Outlaw were under no illusions that if *Fujian* was able to repair, rearm and refuel at Port Aeon, it would pose a lethal threat to US forces in the Pacific. Rory's crew had been able to identify no gaping holes in the strike group's air defenses, so Rory had sought permission to attack Port Aeon instead.

As Rory studied the already out-of-date images from the last satellite pass over Port Aeon on Tonga—by a satellite that by all accounts no longer existed—he realized that operationalizing their great idea was going to be harder than they'd expected.

"Russian-made S-400, here ..." 'Uncle' Bob Lee said, pointing at the computer overlay on the image.

"So we'll need to disable that first," Rory said.

"Two Type 9 mobile units with twin 35 mm, parked here ... but one is always on patrol," Uncle said. "Stationary 30 mm CIWS turrets, here and here."

"Alright, so we send a LongShot in low to take out the S-400, then we stay high for the main attack, out of 35 mm range. JDAMs will probably deal with the Type 9s, along with everything else."

"There's a KJ-200 AWACS permanently based at the airfield, but we have no intel on whether there are any fighter aircraft there right now."

"All their fighters are in the Taiwan theater, and *Fujian* can't launch as much as a paper plane until it gets to a port for repair."

"Hmm. They have 500 personnel on the base. Probably got dozens of MANPADs too. And that ..."—he pointed at a radome next to the airfield—"is a Chinese electronic warfare listening station that can probably pick up the energy from a walkie-talkie 100 miles away."

"So we can't get within visual range, and we have to zero our emissions." Rory sighed. "Uncle, you are not being a well of optimism right now."

"My job is realism, not optimism," Uncle told him. "You're in charge of motivation."

It was 3,000 kilometers, or 5 hours flying, from Tonga to Port Aeon, and they had tanked from a US Navy Sentinel 1,000 kilometers out. They were now circling at 1,000 feet, 200 kilometers south of the island, below the curve of the earth and hidden from its S-400 system since it wasn't known to be capable of ionic bounce. If they were unlucky, the Chinese AWACS aircraft could be airborne and would have a chance of seeing them over the open ocean from its high-flying vantage point, but they would have to be very, very unlucky.

To do the job they had been asked to do, it would have been great to have a wing of F-35s flying off the deck of a carrier to take out the AWACS and air defenses, then a brace of B-2s or B-21s to carpet-bomb Port Aeon with 2,000 lb. JDAM-ER standoff munitions.

But in war, you did what you could, with the ordnance you had, and at that moment, the USAF had Rory's 20-year-old Outlaw, with one Rapid Dragon pallet loaded with four LongShot drone mother ships, and a second pallet loaded with 20 1,000 lb. JDAM-ERs. His LongShots would have to deal with Port Aeon's air defenses, because to launch the JDAM glide bombs their Outlaw would have to climb to 30,000 feet, at which altitude the S-400 would be certain to see them.

In fact, Uncle's attack plan depended on it.

254

The AC-130X's rear ramp was coming down as the crew manhandled the first Rapid Dragon pallet into place. As he watched, it occurred to Rory that the system's name was more than passingly ironic, since the system that allowed cruise missiles and glide bombs to be launched from transport aircraft had been named after a 10th century Chinese volley-firing siege weapon.

Rory heard the engines surge as they climbed to minimum altitude for the LongShot release, and he steadied himself against the bulkhead. The first pallet was rolled to the edge of the ramp, the drogue parachute cable clipped to the floor behind it. The four LongShot drones were in cages strapped to the pallet, and the aircrew checked the pins holding them in their cages. The three drogue parachutes that would upend the cages and dump the drones into their wake were strapped to the top of the cages.

It was an operation they'd executed a hundred times in training, but the recent probe against *Fujian*'s defenses was their first against a real adversary. They were about to launch their first combat JDAM strike. Rory held his breath as his crew chief gave the all-clear. The crew stepped away and clipped safety belts onto the bulkhead webbing, each man raising a hand in the air, while at the rear of the pallet a single crewman waited.

Uncle heard the signal in the cockpit and pulled the AC-130X's nose into a 10-degree climb, dumping their tail. The ramp locked into place, turbulent wind roared around the interior of the cargo hold as the launch crewman shoved the pallet on its rollers …

Gravity did the rest. The pallet slid along the deck of the cargo hold and disappeared off the ramp, trailing the parachute cable. Before the crew even started reeling in the cable, Uncle tipped the big machine onto one wing and dropped the nose to take them back down to sea level.

As the ramp came up again, Rory got a glimpse of the pallet dangling in their wake, drones dropping from their cages like bats from the roof of a cave, wings snapping into place as they lit their tails and began curving toward the Chinese base 200 kilometers away.

Rory gave his crew a thumbs up as they finished stowing the parachute cables and started rolling the second pallet into place. Then, leaning into the tilt of the deck, he made his way forward to the command center. Inside the small cabin were his combat systems officer, electronic warfare officer and two pilots, each of which was "flying" two LongShots.

"We got our satellite link back?" Rory asked, dumping himself into a seat at the rear of the cabin as Uncle leveled the machine out just above the waves.

"That's negatory, boss," his CSO reported. "We'll have VHF control of our birds out to 160 miles, but we'll have to let them off the leash for the run in. Earlier, if China sees them and starts jamming."

"S-400 up yet?"

"No sir, all quiet over the target area."

The Chinese air defense radar unit was truck mounted and therefore mobile. It could be anywhere within a 2-mile area, and to be sure he killed it, his attack drones needed to be able to see its energy signature, so it had to be up and radiating. And the S-400 had the ability to set up a decoy signal and location, so he needed a strong fix, preferably triangulated.

China wasn't playing along. Its radar was quiet. Hiding? Down for maintenance? Or just on standby? He needed to change that.

The LongShots had a 15-minute run into their ingress waypoints offshore from Port Aeon, and the electronic environment stayed stubbornly silent through that time, both ahead of them and above them.

"Contact on Bird One is intermittent," one of his pilots reported.

"Deliberate interference?" Rory asked. That would be a positive—a jamming signal was at least something to home on.

"More likely just atmospheric," the pilot said. "Bird One is at maximum VHF control range. Normally we'd have switched to satellite well before now."

What the hell is happening with satcoms? VHF radio was no way to control distant drones—orders could be sent but the connection at anything more than 20 kilometers was so unreliable that direct flight control was impossible. With intermittent contact, the orders they could send to their LongShots were more in the nature of "go here, do that."

"All birds now in position," the second pilot reported a few minutes later.

Rory checked the op plan and then his watch. "Bird One, initiate strike one." He reached for his throat mic. "Uncle, take us up to JDAM launch altitude."

Fifty miles east of Port Aeon, the LongShot 'Bird One' was circling just above the sea and registered the order from its Outlaw mother ship. It immediately lit its tail and started powering in a 600-knot straight line toward the port. Twenty-five miles offshore, it popped up from 500 to 1000 feet and started launching its payload of GPS-guided Locust swarming drones.

Into an environment with no GPS signals. So the drones defaulted to less-accurate inertial guidance to get them to the island. Once there, their optical-infrared cameras would take over targeting.

They were not electronic warfare decoys, like those Outlaw launched against *Fujian*. Each Locust was armed with a 6 lb. high-explosive fragmentation warhead, designed to shred the Chinese buildings, vehicles and installations whose images had been loaded into its memory.

Bird One was out of VHF range, "off the leash" and no longer tethered to its AC-130 mother ship. But as the last of its 20 Locust drones dropped from its payload bay, it registered "mission objective complete" state and banked, pointing its nose at the sky.

Its next orders were to fly itself back to Outlaw for recovery at 20,000 feet. An altitude and flight profile designed to be seen by the Chinese S-400.

If its crew was awake.

Fifty miles west of Port Aeon, Bird Two was circling and waiting. Fifty miles south, birds Three and Four were waiting too. Due to the lack of satellite comms, none of them were in contact with Rory's Outlaw anymore; they were all "off the leash" too, and on lethal missions.

Captain Andrei Rafalovik was not asleep, and neither was his S-400 squad.

They were playing cards.

Durak, or "Fool," to be precise. It was a game his grandparents had taught him, and popular with the men of the 71 Air Defense Brigade, who were largely drawn from the country's western Turkic provinces. It was popular because even a simpleton could master the rules, but it took cunning to win. And because it played to an air defense unit's role in warfare, it was tolerated by 71 Brigade's officers. Players had to defend all of an opponent's attacks before it was their turn to attack. If a player failed to defend against all attacks, their opportunity to attack was skipped, and they inevitably lost.

A lot like an air defense battery trying to defend its base, when you thought about it.

Rafalovik could trace his family heritage back to the Sogdian people of the Chinese Tang dynasty and had never really felt particularly Chinese. His family name was Uzbek and sounded Russian. His hometown of Artux was part of the autonomous region of Kizulsu Kyrgyz in remote Xinjiang and had an ambivalent relationship to Beijing, 3,000 kilometers away. But a young Sogdian had just two choices growing up in Artux: the People's Liberation Army or sheep farming.

Rafalovik hated sheep so deeply in his soul it defined him.

Which was how he had ended up in command of an air defense battery as far from Artux as it was possible for a Sogdian man to get and still be on what was—nominally—Chinese territory.

In a game of Durak, as in the People's Liberation Army, there were no winners, only losers. The aim of the game was only to avoid being the worst loser. The winners shared the coin among themselves while the losers lost their share of the pot.

"Sheep!" Rafalovik announced with a laugh, pointing at his comrade, an officer of the PLA Navy logistics command at Port Aeon. He could think of no better epithet for a fool than that, and he yelled it out with glee, reaching out for the man's coin.

His duty Lieutenant appeared in the door of the hut. Air conditioning was nonexistent on the Chinese base, but a fan turned noisily overhead. The man tried to say something, but the sound of the fan drowned him out, and Rafalovik held up a hand, reaching over and turning off the fan. "What is it, Lieutenant?"

"EW station reports weak radio signals on VHF band that don't match known shipping or aircraft, sir," the man said. "I thought you …"

"Bearing?" Rafalovik asked. They were just south of a major shipping lane. It wouldn't be unusual for a ship to their north to be broadcasting if it saw another vessel. And *ships* were not his concern.

"Uh …" The man checked a piece of paper he was carrying. "Nine zero degrees, one seventy, and … uh, 279 degrees, sir."

Rafalovik nearly upended the table, the cards and the tea they were drinking onto his comrade as he jumped to his feet. "*Three* sectors?!" he yelled. "Get the radar online, man. Broad spectrum, 360-degree scan!"

As his Lieutenant disappeared, his card partner looked at him, nonplussed and slightly annoyed. "Don't just sit there, sheep-face," Rafalovik yelled at him. "We have possible adversary activity in three sectors! This is your ass too."

"Chinese S-400 just came up," Rory's CWO announced with satisfaction. "Something spooked them." Their Outlaw didn't have a radar of its own, but it had a very capable radar warning receiver, and it had just lit up, showing a strong radar signal to their north.

Which was exactly what they wanted.

Rory checked their altitude. Uncle had taken them up through 20,000 feet, heading for 30,000. The AC-130X was a fat-assed goose, but Uncle knew how to get the most of its four 5,000 shaft horsepower engines.

"Good. Someone on the island is doing his job. Let's hope he doesn't do it too well. Bird Two, initiate strike two."

West of Port Aeon, LongShot 'Bird Two' had been waiting for the Port Aeon S-400 to show itself. The Locusts in its payload bay were ALARM variants: Air-Launched Anti-Radar Munitions. They looked at enemy radar the same way a lounge lizard looked at a girl from out of town. The moment Bird Two saw the S-400 radar complex light up, it began homing on it, screaming across the water at wavetop height, and 10 miles out from the signal, it released its Locusts.

The 20 kamikaze drones had only one purpose to their short lives. To *kill* a Chinese radar emitter.

Not good. That was the immediate conclusion Andrei Rafalovik reached as he dropped into his chair inside the S-400 command trailer. His Russian-made air defense battery comprised four transporter erector launch vehicles, only three of which were operational. But each TEL could launch four missiles, so he had 12 missiles at his command.

He had a single tracking, acquisition and targeting radar vehicle, but he had a decoy mounted on a Dongfeng Type 11 armored fighting vehicle, and the smarts to send it immediately to the far end of the Port Aeon airfield with its electronic signal at full power.

Three VHF transmissions suddenly appearing from nowhere? Either 71 Brigade had just launched an unannounced readiness test of its battery on Kiritimati Island or something Seriously Bad was about to go down.

Captain Andrei Rafalovik had never been at war. Neither had his men. He knew China was facing off against the main enemy, of course he did. But that was several thousand kilometers to the *west*, right? That war could not possibly have come to far-flung Kiribati.

Sure, he knew *Fujian* was inbound. Everyone on the tiny island knew that. And he'd told his men that made Port Aeon a potential target, though he hadn't actually believed it himself.

Rafalovik was no sheep. He was smart enough to realize that three unexpected VHF signatures to their east, south and west were pretty strong indications that Port Aeon had just become an *actual* target.

"Talk to me!" he yelled at his tactical command officer the moment he walked into the trailer.

"Two contacts, sir," his TCO said. "We have a single aircraft bearing zero nine zero five degrees, altitude 5,000, range 25, heading east-southeast, speed four forty …"

"Commercial?" he asked.

"Nothing on the flight plan log," his TCO said. "But it's heading *away* from us …"

"At the moment. Which means nothing," Rafalovik said. "Contact two?"

"Contact two is much further out, sir; we only just picked it up," his TCO said. "A single aircraft, no civilian ID, bearing one eighty, altitude 15,000 and climbing, range 200 kilometers …"

A preternatural premonition came over Rafalovik. It was the sort of feeling no AI could have, only a human. Though he didn't consciously reflect on it, he recalled a report he had recently read of the latest attack on the *Fujian* Strike Group, thousands of kilometers south of them: a single large aircraft that appeared and then disappeared from radar.

Followed by a swarming drone attack.

"All personnel to alert status," Rafalovik ordered. "Trigger the base alarm." He thought furiously as his order was relayed. A single contact to their south, pulling away. The enemy attack could already be inbound. "Shut down!" he said.

"Sir?!" his TCO asked, turning to him in surprise. "We have aircraft inbound. Our decoy unit is radiating. If we shut down, we ..."

"Shut. The. Radar. Down," Rafalovik said, with a patience his ancestors must have lent him. "And get this damn truck moving," Rafalovik yelled. "*Now!*"

"Port Aeon radar still up. We should have a solid lock," Rory's CSO said.

There had been a moment of doubt there as his ALARM-armed LongShot reported different information back about the location of the Chinese radar, but the data had coalesced into a single attack point now, at the northern end of the Chinese airfield.

The data they were getting over the weak VHF signal was both erratic and a microscopic fraction of what they would be getting over satellite, and he had bitten his fingernails to the nub in frustration.

His two swarms should be inbound. The uncertainty was killing him. *Where were those damn satellites?!*

Swarm one, comprising general purpose attack drones, was five minutes out from Port Aeon and about to go "feet dry" over the coast of the island, at which point the cameras in the noses of the drones would start trying to match what they could see with the target images in their onboard memories.

Swarm two, the ALARM drones launched by Bird Two, was 10 minutes out from Port Aeon. Their hive mind AI had split the swarm into two because it had seen *two* radar signatures on the island, but that confusion had resolved itself into a single signal at the northern end of the Chinese airfield, so both swarms coalesced again.

They were pinpoint weapons but not dumb ones. All 20 drones did not aim themselves at the same attack point. Four set their attack point for the signal itself. Four set their attack point 10 meters out. Four set their attack point 10 meters out from that, and the last four set their attack point 30 meters out from the first.

Anything, or anyone, inside their 700-square-meter radius was about to have a very, very bad day.

Andrei Rafalovik had no intention of dying that day. He had just won a big pot in Durak, and he intended to be alive to claim it.

He tapped his throat mic, relaying a command to the driver of their Norinco armored fighting vehicle. "Floor it. Get us as far south as you can—away from that decoy. Crash the airfield wire if you have to."

For a moment, just a small one, he felt bad for the crew of the Dongfeng decoy vehicle. But the men who took that duty knew what they were taking on every time they climbed into their IFV.

And that it was just the price a soldier paid for losing Durak against Captain Rafalovik.

Colonel Wang Wei, Air Wing Commander, PLA Navy carrier *Fujian* and acting commander of the *Fujian* Strike Group, had become accustomed to losing lately. But for once, he felt he was holding five aces. Or eight, actually.

His Air Boss had just reported that they had launched no fewer than eight Chongming drones. Four were in orbit around their task force on combat air patrol, and two were en route to Port Aeon to provide air defense over their destination.

Wang had been more than mildly annoyed to be told that the 25th Air Brigade AWACS aircraft at Port Aeon had been recalled to the Taiwan theater to replace losses. He needed coverage of the air between *Fujian* and Port Aeon, and the sea-level radars of his air defense pickets could not see beyond the curve of the earth. The aircraft he had overhead couldn't always be looking in the direction *Fujian* was sailing. The two fighters he had just sent north were his eyes in the sky.

Lieutenant Maylin 'Mushroom' Sun, Pilot Officer, Ao Yin Fighter Squadron, was back in her element for the first time since she had been smashed face-first into the deck of *Fujian* by the Coalition attack off Palau.

There was only one way to describe it. It felt like *victory*.

Which it shouldn't, since they were still crippled, crawling toward a neutral port thousands of kilometers from China. Her carrier was a shadow of itself, speed and maneuverability limited thanks to the hole in its keel, barely able to launch aircraft thanks to the damage to its flight deck and catapult.

But it was still capable of *fighting*.

And Mushroom had been chosen by Colonel Wang to lead the first armed recon patrol launched by *Fujian* since the Palau attack.

Inside her pod on the makeshift pod deck two levels below *Fujian*'s ravaged superstructure, Mushroom felt invincible.

Wang had made their mission clear to Mushroom. All *Fujian* had to do was make it to Port Aeon, in Kiribati; 23 hours sailing. If they did, after all they had been through, they would have exceeded any expectations their motherland held for them.

Mushroom had one wingman, two machines armed with 16 missiles and a determination that nothing on the surface of the sea, or in the air above it, would prevent *Fujian* from fulfilling its destiny.

So when *Fujian*'s CIC alerted her to the presence of unidentified aircraft in their path, her blood rose from a simmer to its boiling point in the space of a millisecond.

"Shengli Leader, *Fujian* Control. Port Aeon air defense reports multiple unidentified radio emissions east, south and west of the port. You are requested to investigate a suspected fighter contact 50 kilometers south of Kiritimati Island, sector N13, bearing zero fifteen degrees your current position, altitude 20, range one twenty. Identify and report back."

"Good copy, *Fujian*. Do you have a heading for the contact?"

"It was headed southeast at 600 knots, but Port Aeon doesn't like an unidentified fast mover so close to their military exclusion zone. They have a second heavy contact, possibly a transport, en route from Tonga, but the fast mover is your target, Shengli. You are clear to engage adversary aircraft if they enter Port Aeon exclusion zone. *Dalian* is tracking the heavy."

"Understood, *Fujian*; Shengli Leader out." She addressed her wingman. "Shengli flight is buster for sector N13. Two, take 20 kilometers separation, low-emission profile. I'll find and fix the contact; you will finish it if needed, on my command. Clear?"

"Two copies."

Mushroom put her radar in search mode and flexed her fingers, settling herself into her seat in the pod. Moments like this, it became irrelevant she didn't have the use of her legs. She was one with her machine. She had thumb paddles on her throttle for yaw control, multiscreen simulated vision in her helmet visor, haptic feedback in her flight suit giving her vital information about the flow of air over her Chongming's control surfaces, letting her sense a stall before it hit her, telling her with a bump whenever a missile was successfully launched. The umbilical snaking across the deck from her pod didn't just connect her to the CIC and other pilots; it plugged her directly into the ship's powerful decision-making AI, which was ready to alert her to new contacts, either friendly or hostile, and in an engagement, take over the attention-sapping work of tracking and locking up targets so that she could focus on flying and commanding her flight.

In their pre-flight briefing, she had been told the main enemy's surveillance and communication capabilities had been seriously degraded. They weren't told how, but Mushroom assumed some kind of cyberattack. And she told her pilots to ignore it. If it gave them any kind of advantage, fine, but it was safer to assume the odds were stacked against them so far out on a hostile ocean.

She saw her wingman breaking right and heading away to set up a pincer attack if it was needed. From their position 25,000 feet above the sea, she was already inside the range at which she should be able to pick up the contacts Port Aeon had seen. The remote base wasn't networked, and it couldn't push data to her, but there was no ground clutter for adversary aircraft to hide in. Minutes later, she got a return.

"Shengli flight, I have the adversary heavy at zero nine five; AI is saying C-130. Uh, *Dalian* confirms. It appears to be heading northwest out of Tonga, as predicted. Two, keep an eye on it as we push in, but we're still hunting that fast mover. Where there is one, there may be more."

She watched the C-130 wander through the sky, probably oblivious to her presence. It was a slow, tempting target, but it offered no threat to Port Aeon. She smiled at the thought that a flick of her thumb and a PL-15 missile could send it to the bottom of the Pacific. But she was still fighting within the gray space of limited conflict, and that pleasure would have to wait for another day.

She almost envied the C-130 pilot's state of blissful ignorance.

'Uncle' Bob Lee was anything *but* blissfully ignorant. Outlaw had no air-to-air radar of its own, but his hypersensitive radar warning receiver had detected the Chinese destroyer's radar as soon as it locked onto him, shortly followed by a second air search radar, and it was whining in his ears now to warn him the enemy had him locked up from both the sea and the air.

"Boss, it's getting sweaty up here," Uncle said tightly. "Got a Chinese destroyer radar in the southwest and a Chinese fighter on our six. Signal strength estimate says the air radar is about one twenty kilometers out."

In his command module, Rory looked at their map plot. Chinese fighters *behind* them? Could be a patrol out of Port Aeon, returning to the airfield. But there had been no intel about fighters currently based on the island. Not for the first time on this mission, he cursed the fog of war that had settled over them the moment they lost their satellites.

They were passing through 25,000 feet now, on their way to their JDAM release altitude of 30,000. Their two swarms should be minutes out, one swarm homing on the island's S-400 radar. The urgent question was whether the Chinese had also picked up his LongShot drone as they were supposed to … Would they worry more about a fast mover on their doorstep than a lumbering cargo plane 70 kilometers out?

With their JDAM release point so close, he couldn't take the chance the Chinese would choose to prosecute the easy target, his Outlaw.

He had to give them more to worry about.

"We still have contact with birds Three and Four?" Two of their LongShots had launched with four Peregrine air-to-air missiles in their payload bays, in case Port Aeon tried to get any aircraft away during their attack. He hadn't planned on a fighter patrol *returning* to the base, but a target was a

269

target, especially one that might try to ruin his beautifully laid plan.

"Yes sir, birds Three and Four are still on station down low and southwest of the target, but we only have an intermittent radio link," his pilot said. "So I have command authority but not flight control."

"Good enough. Send Three and Four at those Chinese fighters, radars up, weapons hot, full autonomy."

New contacts! From southwest of Port Aeon, about 50 kilometers offshore, two new radar signals appeared. The radar signature was the same type used by both Coalition stealth fighters and their uncrewed combat drones— impossible to know which she was dealing with yet.

"Port Aeon, Shengli Leader, we have two new fast movers pushing in on us. Do you have them?"

"Negative, Shengli Leader. We are emissions dark, relocating; decoy is up."

Mushroom didn't like it. Yes, all the adversary contacts were technically outside Port Aeon's military exclusion zone, but she'd been at the wrong end of too many attacks from an enemy that had shown it had no regard for the rules of war. "Port Aeon, we now have *four* confirmed adversary aircraft just outside your airspace but within standoff ordnance range. Three are fast movers, and they are coming right at us. We are facing twice our number in adversary aircraft. Either you come online now and engage, or we could *all* die."

Captain Andrei Rafalovik bit his lip. He had the authority to fire at an adversary threatening their facility. But none of the adversary aircraft were actually headed for Port Aeon. Three were headed away, albeit two of them were apparently searching for the incoming Chongming fighters. And the cargo plane was just flying a straight line out of Tonga, oblique to Port Aeon, not flying an attack profile at all.

It could be provocation, intended to test them or trigger an incident.

But once again, his instincts and the Chongming pilot's warning won over caution.

"Driver, *halt*. Radar up, track-while-scan mode. Targets are adversary fast movers. TELs to launch mode. Engage area denial jamming. Report on target lock …"

Several things happened simultaneously. The S-400 radar truck powered its radar on and started scanning the sky. An alert was sent to the transporter erector launch units, which started pulling target data from the radar. And a radio signal jamming truck filled the air around the S-400 battery with intense radio energy on multiple frequencies, intended to confuse any incoming missiles or drones and break the link to their operator.

Agonizing seconds ticked by before his Tactical Control Officer reported. "Four targets identified, locked and tracking, three fast movers designation F-1 to F-3. One heavy, designation H-1. TELs One through Four report launch readiness."

"Targets are F-1, F-2, F-3. Shoot."

"Shots one to three away," his Missile Control Officer reported a moment later.

"*Swarming drones detected!*" his TCO called out. The S-400 could track both high- and low-flying targets, large and small, but the latter by their nature were always detected closer in. "Swarm one bearing two seven five, altitude one, range 10 kilometers, speed 110. Swarm Two bearing zero eight two, altitude one, range 5 kilometers, speed 110."

His ground-to-air missiles were useless against tiny swarming drones at such close range, but that was why he'd initiated jamming.

And why he'd issued a base-wide air attack alert the moment he'd picked up the adversary's radio signals. Five to 10 kilometers out? They had only three to six minutes before those swarms hit.

He had to hope his comrades outside the trailer had taken the alert seriously. He gripped the desk in front of himself, knuckles white.

From across the base, he heard one of the base's automated Type 730 30 mm cannons open up and start hosing the sky to their east, taking its targeting from his radar.

Defense and attack ebbed and flowed. It was a game of high-stakes Durak, and the next few minutes would reveal who was the fool.

The two Chinese 30 mm close-in weapons systems had locked on the nearest threat first, the swarm of general-purpose attack drones using inertial guidance to steer themselves at various targets around the base until they picked up an image they recognized in their onboard cameras and fine-tuned their aim.

One by one, the twin streams of 30 mm slugs began knocking the Locusts out of the sky, sending them crashing to a fiery death over sea and scrub.

Only six made it through, one hitting the airfield control tower and another exploding harmlessly on top of an empty aircraft berm that until two days ago had held the island's

AWACS aircraft. Two struck warehouses inside the port, one of which held small arms ammunition, and secondary explosions soon filled the air. One of the surviving drones aimed at a fast-moving armored fighting vehicle and missed, burying itself in the ground, while the last got a good look at one of the Chinese 30 mm CIWS turrets and dived on it, the resulting explosion knocking it sideways and triggering its ammunition.

Fourteen of the Locust drones were knocked down, but they'd done their job, soaking up the Chinese counterattack and sowing confusion on the ground.

Outlaw's second ALARM swarm was slightly farther out and was headed for Rafalovik's decoy vehicle when the S-400 radar came alive right in front of it, radiating like a small sun. Beside it, a third signal, the jamming unit, was still far enough away that it was visible, but it wasn't frying the Locusts' memories yet.

The swarm conferred among itself, and the 20 drones split into three groups, one going for the decoy, one for the jammer and one for the S-400 radar. Each drone had its final target now and started steering on the powerful radio and radar signals they saw.

Twelve hundred pounds of high explosive were headed for Rafalovik's battery, and the base's remaining close-in weapons system had just exhausted its magazine.

In his radar vehicle, Rafalovik heard secondary detonations across the airbase, heard the ripping sound of their CIWS turrets fall silent.

Strike one, he thought to himself. *Still alive. Second strike incoming. Where the hell are those mobile autocannons?*

Even with their CIWS turrets silent, the base still had two mobile Type 09 armored fighting vehicles armed with radar and laser-guided 35 mm autocannons, at least one of which should have been on patrol when he triggered the alarm and should have been able to respond to the attack.

If they were still alive.

"Bird One is down," Rory's TCO reported. "Birds Three and Four engaging, going defensive. *Fox three* …"

The damned S-400 had gotten missiles away before he could take it down, but his two LongShots were engaged with the Chinese fighters. He looked at the mission timers on this tac screen. His ALARM attack was still a half minute out.

His plan was going to hell. Iron bombs were hard for air defense to intercept, but a winged JDAM-ER dropping from 30,000 feet up and 50 kilometers out could both be seen and intercepted, if Port Aeon's air defenses were still online.

"Pull Bird Two back and throw it at those fighters," he ordered. "They don't know it is weapons dry." Their Outlaw had just hit 30,000 feet. "Nose up, Uncle," he said into his throat mic. "Loadmaster, drop the ramp. Deploy Rapid Dragon pallet two."

"Deploying pallet two," the loadmaster replied from the rear of the aircraft, as Uncle put Outlaw into a nose-up attitude. In back, a crate holding 20,000 lbs. of high-explosive hell began sliding down Outlaw's deck and off the ramp. As its drogue chutes deployed, the heavy bombs began dropping from their boxes, their wings snapped out, and they turned sharply, settling in for the glide toward their targets.

"Uncle, take us back down," Rory said tightly.

"Missile warning!" his EW officer said. "Chinese destroyer has launched on us. I'm showing two radar signatures, bearing one ninety nine …"

"Uncle ..." Rory called, pulling his harness tighter.

"I got the missiles on the scope," the pilot replied with unnatural calm. Outlaw tipped onto one wing and steepened its dive, engines screaming. "Make peace with your demons, boys. This old girl is no ballerina."

"Swarm one has split. Looks like an ALARM attack. It's going for our emitters—30 seconds out."

Rafalovik swore. The ALARM attack was already right on top of them. They would have to ride it out. The trailer was armored ... from the sound of the explosions outside though, he had his doubts their armor would help much. He kept that thought to himself.

They still had missiles outbound, being guided by their radar. But there was nothing for it.

"Emergency shutdown. Grab your vests. Down on the deck, now!" Rafalovik yelled. "Driver, roll!"

When the S-400 radar disappeared again, the Locusts in the mini swarm tried to confer with one another, but the jamming energy from the Chinese jammer across the airfield blocked their signals. Now each Locust was alone, *and* it had no target.

They defaulted to inertial guidance and aimed for the last known position of the S-400 radar truck.

From across the airfield, the crew in the Type 09 AFV finally joined the fight. Their radar picked up the six gliding Locusts, and they began chewing them from the sky.

Then another series of explosions rippled across the base as the other two mini swarms hit home. The Chinese decoy vehicle and jamming truck disappeared in a fury of metal, smoke and fire.

The Tactical Air Controller at Port Aeon just had time to alert Mushroom to the fact they were under attack before his radio fell silent.

The air warfare commander on the destroyer *Dalian* announced it was engaging the enemy heavy.

It was all she needed to hear. She had a lock on an approaching enemy fast mover, and it was painting her with attack radar. She just wanted to close the gap a little …

Her heads-up visor display flashed an alert as missiles speared out from the besieged Chinese base and started chasing the enemy fighters. They were in a vise, and Mushroom was about to clamp the jaws shut.

An alert sounded in her ears at the same time as her wingman came on the radio, panicking. "New contact! There are four fast movers on us now. Two firing!"

She flicked her eyes to the data in her visor, then the screen to her left. Two enemy fighters had fired at her and her wingmen and gone defensive, trying to evade Port Aeon's missiles. A new contact was closing on them from another bearing but had no radar lock. Twenty-two seconds before the enemy missiles reached her.

"Shengli Two, do you have the four targets?" she asked. Her freed wingmen was 20 kilometers west of her down among the clutter of the waves, flying unseen so far.

"Two confirms."

"Engage all enemy fast movers," she said. "I have to evade, then I'll rejoin and mop up any enemy aircraft that survive."

"Two copies," her wingman said. She didn't wait for any more. The enemy missiles were now just 10 seconds out. She rolled her Chongming onto its back and pulled it into a screaming dive, nose pointing at the cue her combat AI was painting on her visor, radar and infrared decoys streaming into her wake.

Taneti Tito had been on his way out to Port Aeon with his twice-weekly delivery of beer and wine to sate the voracious thirsts of the Chinese officers on the base when his damn truck battery died again.

Like his wife had warned him it would. Which was why she hadn't let him take their teenage son on this trip.

You'd think after 20 years of her being right all the time, he'd learn. Instead, he was sitting on the tailgate of his truck, 5 kilometers short of the base, his beer and wine baking in the midday sun as he waited for the island's only mechanic to finish his lunchtime snooze and get his ass on the road.

Luckily, he hadn't brought his kid. He'd just be sitting here whining about how hot it was and how there was no shade and not even cell phone reception out here.

The Chinese base was full of mechanics, so if he'd been closer, he might have just walked in there and asked for help, but it was a long way on a hot day, and his Mandarin sucked, anyway.

Tito waved away a fly. Then he saw a swarm of the damned things. He blinked. It looked like they were rising up out of the ground and *coming right for him*. He jumped down from the tailgate and squinted. No, not flies. He could hear them now.

Drones. Dozens of them.

277

They weren't coming at him; they were going to pass a few hundred meters away. Tito had seen drones before. The Chinese had held a couple of military exercises on Kiritimati Island, and they always involved drones of one kind or another.

But not like these.

He pulled a kerchief from his pocket and dabbed his brow as they disappeared east, in the direction of the port.

Weird; the Chinese usually announced on local radio when they were going to hold an exercise, so they didn't scare the locals. Not that Tito was scared. Not exactly.

Until he heard a cannon opening up at the Chinese base, and the sound of *explosions* rolled across the sandy coral floodplain.

Tito started running, and got about 20 meters before he stopped. *Where the hell you running to, man?* There was no cover, not even a single damn tree between Port Aeon and the Cassidy International Airport, 30 kilometers away. He stopped and turned, saw smoke rising from inside the port.

Well, he sure as shit wasn't running *that* way.

He walked back to his truck as more explosions and cannon fire split the air to his east. At least they weren't getting closer.

Tito sat his ass back up on his tailgate, pulled a warm beer from one of the crates behind him and twisted the top off, taking a big slug. He settled in to watch, keeping the bulk of his truck between himself and whatever was happening down the road. What the hell else could he do?

It's an exercise, he told himself. *Just an exercise.*

He'd always thought it was a great thing, the Chinese setting up shop at the old World War II base. Brought jobs and money, built a sea wall to keep the tide from overwhelming his hometown, London. Built a school and a clinic. Then a hotel for all the families coming to visit their air force and navy relatives at Port Aeon. It had seemed like good times had come to stay.

He flinched as something big exploded. Now? Not so much.

Uncle flinched as the first of the Chinese destroyer-launched missiles exploded amid the cloud of decoys in Outlaw's wake, but he held the machine in its corkscrewing death dive toward the sea.

It was Afghanistan all over again. He'd been a first lieutenant on a C-5 during the evacuation of Kabul, breathing a sigh of relief as they went wheels up on what was supposed to be their last rescue flight, when someone had shouted "MANPAD!" The aircraft commander had hauled the big machine into a powered turn, slow, too slow, and the missile had literally passed right in front of Bob Lee's eyes.

Except it wasn't Afghanistan. Not this time. The second explosion was close, behind and to his right. Outlaw shuddered, and new warnings started screaming in his ears. The sea was still rushing up toward them. He tried correcting their spin and, miraculously, the old girl responded. He hauled back on the yoke, trying to level the plummeting aircraft out. Swiveled his head, trying to look over his right shoulder for smoke or damage, but his seat was on the left; he couldn't see anything where he'd heard the explosion.

Warning lights on his instrument panel told him the grim story.

"Boss, you still alive back there?" he said, keying his throat mic. "Need you up at the pointy end."

"On the way, Uncle," Rory said. A few seconds later, the aircraft commander dropped into the empty copilot's seat and scanned the instruments as he strapped in.

Uncle was grunting with the strain of trying to bully the aircraft into level flight, and the sea was still rising toward them.

"Aileron trim!" Uncle said through gritted teeth. "One of the ailerons must be jammed. She wants to roll to starboard."

Rory manipulated the trim controls on his yoke in tiny increments, afraid to make their situation worse. He could feel the machine respond.

"Better," Uncle said. "Elevators. Give me 10 degrees nose up."

Rory did the same with the elevator trim controls. Their nose slowly lifted toward the horizon.

"Altitude 6,000," Rory warned. "And descending."

"Yeah, yeah," Uncle replied, yoke still hard back against his belt. "*Motivation*, boss."

"Nose is coming up. You're doing great, Uncle," Rory said.

"More like it," the pilot replied. "She still wants to roll belly up. Tell me what you see out your window there."

Rory leaned over and craned his neck, looking back toward the starboard wing and the flight control surfaces there, but the outboard starboard engine blocked his view. He got on his headset and asked one of the loading crew members to go aft and look out the jump door.

When he got a reply a few minutes later he reached forward and began twisting the aileron trim knobs again, studying the trim indicator dial intently.

Uncle shot a look at him. "Give me the good news."

"Good news is, it's only an aileron problem."

"Well, that's not the worst," Uncle said. "Give me the bad news."

"Bad news is there is no starboard aileron."

"Say *what?*"

"Torn right out of its mount," Rory told him. "Why you have limited aileron authority is you have no starboard aileron."

Uncle tested his controls gently, causing Outlaw to wallow like a pig in mud. "Like I said. Could be worse."

Rory couldn't disagree with that. They could be dead. He checked where their panicked descent had taken them. Uncle had managed to get them down to sea level and pointed roughly in the direction of Tonga. Their low altitude had broken the track of the naval radar that had been locked on them—the radar warning receiver was silent. For now.

Rory craned his head over his shoulder again. The aileron was needed to keep the machine from rolling, and nothing he could do with the trim controls on their remaining port aileron was helping. Uncle had his yoke hard over to stop them going inverted and they were still crabbing right.

"We're headed back toward those Chinese fighters," Rory said, settling himself in his seat again.

"Get pallet two away?" Uncle asked.

"Yeah," Rory said, "we got pallet two away. Did you hear what I said?"

"I heard you, but we're down at 1,000 feet, and I've got the yoke hard against the gimbals to stop us rolling into the surf. Tell me something I can do something about, boss."

"Alright. Try easing up the power on engines one and two. Might help stabilize the roll."

Uncle reached for the throttles for the portside engines and pulled them gently back a notch or two while leaving engines three and four on max continuous, then tested his yoke. He had some play at last. They were no longer sliding right. "Better. You know what I'm going to do when we get home?"

Rory smiled. They were thousands of kilometers from the nearest friendly airfield. Their starboard aileron was lying on the bottom of the Pacific Ocean, who knows what other damage they had sustained, and there were Chinese fighters out there somewhere, probably hunting for them. Their chances of making it home were near zero. "No, Uncle, what are you going to do?" he asked.

"Gonna write to the Secretary of Air Force," Bob Lee said. "Tell him turning old Outlaw from a gunship to a missile-ship was one dumbass idea."

The idea of using an AC-130X to deliver a massed ordnance attack on a target was developed on the assumption there would be satellites overhead to provide targeting data to its ordnance.

The semi-autonomous LongShot and Locust drone combination were designed to be able to function in an electronic-warfare-compromised environment, so the loss of the US battlenet affected them less.

But it was keenly felt by the JDAM-ER, which was crippled without a GPS signal to steer by. Inertial navigation relied on gyros, accelerometers and air pressure sensors, plus a large degree of pure luck, to put ordnance anywhere near a target. Precision bombing, it was not.

The 20 1,000 lb. JDAM-ER munitions gliding toward Port Aeon had about a 50 percent likelihood of even hitting the 2 million-square-meter area of the Chinese base. Their chances of hitting anything important within that area, like port infrastructure, logistics materiel or, say, the S-400 battery of Captain Andrei Rafalovik, were infinitesimal.

But not zero.

Rafalovik heard the crack of explosion after explosion around his trailer—some far off, others too close for comfort. After the hammer of 35 mm cannons and one particularly close explosion, metal rained on the roof of the trailer.

"Air defense got one," his TCO said. He was lying on the floor of the trailer, hands over his helmet, body armor lying loosely across his back where he'd pulled it after throwing himself down.

And then it was over. He heard the whoosh of a MANPAD somewhere not too far away, the hammer of the AFV autocannon across the field, and then … silence.

Until someone started screaming.

The horrible sound shook Rafalovik into action. "To your stations!" he said, pulling himself to his feet using the back of his chair. "TCO, array up; I want a 360-degree sweep, 2 to 20,000 feet." He grabbed his throat mic. "Driver. You alive, Fan?"

The driver's cab and trailer were separate units, so Rafalovik had no way of knowing if the cab was even still there, the way their trailer had been shaking.

"Here, Captain," the man said. "Just."

"Get ready to stop on my order. We're going to stop and scan."

He got on the radio then and checked in with his TEL crews. Each transporter erector launcher was essentially a semitrailer with a four-missile launcher mounted on the rear.

Connected wirelessly, like the command unit and radar, they had to stay within radio range of one another, but they were relocatable. And the enemy clearly knew where they were.

Only two of his three operational TELs reported back. One was off the air, perhaps destroyed by a drone. They'd fired three missiles at the enemy fighters. He had no idea if they'd made a kill. He had nine missiles left.

"Uh, radar up," his TCO reported. "We have … two adversary aircraft south-southeast, engaged with our fighters. No clear solution that would not endanger our own pilots …"

"What about that heavy?" Rafalovik asked. He wanted payback badly.

"Gone," the man said, paging back through data on his engagement screen. "*Dalian* is claiming the kill."

He thumped the back of his chair. *Be happy, man, you are still alive, and no one is trying to …*

"New contacts!" his TCO warned. "Multiple small targets, bearing 109 degrees, 20,000 feet and descending, 15 kilometers out … analyzing … glide bombs …"

American JDAMs. The real attack was still to arrive.

"How many?" he asked.

"Twenty-plus," the TCO said.

Twenty? There must have been a stealth bomber out there that they had not detected. Only a B-2 or B-21 could deliver a punch like the one heading for them right now.

Twenty targets or more. Nine missiles. And they couldn't shoot and scoot. They'd have to keep their radar up and networked to allow the base's remaining CIWS a chance of picking off a few of the glide bombs too.

"Target the incoming. Shoot all available missiles."

His TCO worked his screen, allocating missiles to the tiny dots on the screen that were approaching at nearly 900 kilometers an hour.

"Firing solution locked in."

"Shoot."

"Shots one to nine … away," the man said.

Rafalovik knew the odds from the many live-fire exercises they'd conducted. The chances of one of his HQ-9 missiles intercepting the 3-meter-long iron bomb falling at just under the speed of sound was about one … in five.

Mushroom gave her opponent a *less*-than-one-in-five chance of surviving. The sole surviving enemy drone, because that was what they were up against, had managed to snap another missile off at her wingman before it dodged his missile and accelerated toward her like it was trying to get a gun solution.

The last few minutes had been a blur as they knocked down one enemy drone after another, alternately firing and dodging the missiles coming at them until the last enemy closed to within a few miles and they were suddenly eyeball to eyeball, down at sea level, twisting and turning.

Except they weren't eyeball to eyeball really. After all, she was in a warship a few hundred kilometers away, and her opponent, well, it had no eyeballs. It was a long, slim, shark-shaped killer drone. She'd analyze the video of the engagement later, but her AI was calling it a LongShot air-launched drone. Which both good and bad. Good because if it was air launched, it meant that there was no American carrier strike group nearby that had moved in on *Fujian* unnoticed. Bad because the LongShot could be

285

launched by any number of American aircraft, from the F-15EX to a B-21 Raider, and the mother ship might still be out there somewhere.

Also bad because the attack on Port Aeon told Mushroom the enemy was not going to let *Fujian* dock and repair at that port unmolested. If they made it to port, they would probably face day after day of attacks like this until *Fujian* was just another wreck sitting among the Pacific coral.

She shook the thought from her mind. She'd allowed it to wander because the enemy drone had clearly exhausted its missiles, and it carried no cannon. She felt like she was on a training flight now. *Focus, Mushroom, complacency kills! It can still ram you!* The LongShot was suicidally aggressive, pushing her to the edge of her flight envelope as it maneuvered for a kinetic kill. But it wasn't a Mach 4 missile, and her Chongming was a dedicated fighter plane, not a disposable multipurpose delivery vehicle like the LongShot …

"Shengli Leader, I have a solution. I can take the shot," her wingman said, sounding worried.

His concern was fair enough; she should have ended the fight by now. "I have it," she replied. "Hold fire." She let the LongShot get right behind her. Jerking her flight stick back and shoving her throttle forward, she flipped her machine almost on its axis—a maneuver no human pilot could have stayed conscious through—and spun over the top of the American drone before dropping in behind it. Before it could react, she thumbed her gun trigger and watched the burst of 25 mm chew into the drone's tail.

She was already peeling away as it exploded.

The kill gave her no satisfaction. A drone kill did nothing to quench the hate in her soul, and once again, the enemy had shown itself to be a coalition of terrorist states, bringing its

imperialist violence to the territory of unaligned neutral states
…

She trimmed her machine to climb again and dropped a navigation waypoint over Port Aeon. They had not burned much fuel; they could still complete their assigned patrol. There could be further attacks planned. "Shengli Two, form on me. We will resume the mission."

There had been a time, she would admit only to herself, that she had doubted the wisdom of their Taiwan ambition. Her nation seemed to have set itself on a collision course with the Western powers and their Asian allies, and the Buddhist beliefs she had been raised with seemed to stand in complete opposition to the drumbeat of imminent war that was everywhere in Chinese society from the 2020s onward. Yes, she had joined the PLA Air Force, but because she wanted to *fly*, not because she wanted to fight.

That had changed at the moment her world dissolved in the flame of a hypersonic missile strike.

Now, she wanted only to fight.

To fight for the comrades she had lost. For the outrages that had been visited on their ship, the pride of the Chinese fleet. To fight against an enemy who, time and again, showed its inhumanity and criminality.

After a few minutes, the small sliver of land that was the neutral Kiribati province of Kiritimati Island appeared on the horizon—with a low brown haze of smoke hanging over its southeastern shores.

She clenched her fists inside her flight gloves. Her state, her Chinese motherland, was not perfect. She was not blind; she knew that much.

But it was not *evil*.

The fireworks at the Chinese base appeared to be over. There was still smoke rising from inside the base somewhere, starting to spread across the sky, but it seemed like …

No, not over. As Taneti Tito watched, a volley of rockets lifted off the ground and vaulted into the sky, leaving white trails of smoke behind them as they curved into the distance.

There had been a couple of those earlier, so if this was an exercise, China was sparing no expense. He put his hand over his eyes and squinted at the sky where the missiles had disappeared.

Was that an explosion? It was like a camera flash going off, way up in the sky. Then another. Two or three more.

Now he heard the sound of cannon fire again, and this time he could see the smoke trails of the artillery rounds as they were flung into the sky to the southwest, over the flat floodplain on the other side of the port, out by Port Aeon.

A couple more missiles whizzed into the sky—different ones, like the type you fired from your shoulder.

PLA was going all-in on this exercise. He was impressed. He drained his beer, reached behind him to drop it back into the crate. Maybe the Chinese wouldn't notice the empty.

That was as far as that thought got.

One of the 1,000 lb. JDAMs exploded on the northeast end of Port Aeon's long runway. Tito snapped his head up. That was *loud*. And close!

The next one was closer.

It landed just 10 feet in front of the cab of his truck. Tito only had time to register a shadow falling through the sky before the bomb exploded, vaporizing his truck, 20 cases of beer, 16 cases of Californian wine … and a very surprised Taneti Tito.

The enemy attack had failed. Captain Andrei Rafalovik was still alive, and so were most of the men in his detachment. Multiple fires were burning across the base, the worst at an ammunition dump down by the port.

Air defenses had taken down most of the first swarm attack and some of the second. He had lost both his decoy and jamming vehicles. The remaining drones of the enemy ALARM swarm had homed on them without mercy and shredded their thin armor.

Five enemy aircraft had been destroyed, either by his battery, by the *Fujian*'s destroyer pickets or by its fighter aircraft. Four attack drones and a cargo plane. The cargo plane was a confirmed meat kill, a trail of oil leading to the place it had crashed, where a larger pool of oil was found spreading across the sea.

Had it been part of the attack or just in the wrong place at the wrong time? Rafalovik didn't really care. War had come to Kiribati, and an enemy aircraft was an enemy aircraft.

The main enemy attack had gone wide. So much for the vaunted "pinpoint accuracy" of enemy precision weapons. His battery and CIWS had taken a few of the glide bombs down, but if the rest had hit inside the base perimeter, there would have been very little left of Port Aeon. The blast from the explosions to the northwest of the airfield had been so powerful his ears had rung for a good half hour afterward.

At the unit commander debrief, they'd been told *Fujian* was inbound and would be docking within a few hours. Every man not mortally wounded was expected dockside to assist with rearming and refueling the carrier and its escorts.

War had come to Kiribati, and Andrei Rafalovik had a feeling it would not stop on the shores of his small island.

12. The battle of the Killer Bees

A new type of war had come to Taiwan with the arrival of the *shārèng jīqì*, or "slaughterbots," and not for the first time in her life, Bunny O'Hare was betting on a dark horse as the solution.

After a few hours' sleep, their Marine taxi crew had gone in search of the medical clinic with the sniper, Wu, to get some fever medication for their driver, Cruz.

Bunny was in the drone workshop of the fisherman inventor, Lin Hungyu; but "workshop" was a pretty grand name for a space at the back of the shed his father used to work on his fishing boat. She'd helped haul the boat out of the water with the aid of a dockside crane and pull it to the workshop on an electric trolley so Hungyu's father could start repairing the damage to its wheelhouse. The drone workshop consisted of a 3D printer, rack after rack of spare parts and several floor-to-ceiling cabinets that contained the thousands of thumb-sized microdrones that were Hungyu's specialty.

Bunny pulled open a drawer and ran her eye over row after row of drones wedged into soft foam.

"Please close that," Hungyu said, looking over his shoulder at her from the workbench where he was booting up a controller.

Bunny slid the drawer shut and looked around. "I gotta say, Hungyu, this doesn't look like the workshop of a guy who made millions selling his patents to an entertainment conglomerate," Bunny said, walking over to the bench.

The drone engineer placed a single drone on the bench in front of him and tested the controller, hovering the now buzzing drone a few inches in the air and sliding it left and right, forward and back. When he was satisfied, he landed it on the bench again. "On my father's advice, I put most of my money into real estate," he said. "In China."

"Say no more." Bunny bent over the tiny drone. "So what am I looking at?"

"A queen bee," he told her. "My software allows every drone in a swarm to know where it is based on the position of one or more queen bees. The queen bees use GPS to position themselves relative to each other, and all the others position themselves relative to the queen bees using infrared photo optics."

"And with this, you can create a 3D version of *Gone with the Wind* in the sky?" Bunny looked skeptical. Bunny hadn't been to a theme park lately, so she'd only seen some videos of a 3D cinematic light show, and they didn't really translate that well to 2D video.

"Yes," he said, looking offended she would doubt him. "Version 1 of the software simulated about 30 frames a second, so to viewers on the ground, there was a little 'flickering.' Version 1.1 took it 40, and I am working on version 2, which will allow full HD replication at 60 frames a second." He held up a small video camera and pointed it at Bunny. "May I?"

Bunny frowned. "May you what?"

He held the camera up in front of his face and gestured at her. "Hop up and down or something."

Bunny had no idea what he wanted, but with a sigh, she did a couple of jumping jacks, flapping her arms at her sides.

"Awesome," he said. He plugged the camera into a PC and downloaded the video, isolating her figure from the background with a click of his mouse. Then he opened another window and uploaded the video. From his desk he took the controller and the small "queen bee." He motioned her aside and pulled out a tray of about 100 drones, then walked around the boat to the doorway that led out of the shed. "Follow?"

Outside, he put the tray of microdrones down on the ground, flipped up the screen on the controller and pressed a couple of buttons ... then frowned. "Strange. I can't get GPS."

"Could be Chinese jamming," Bunny told him. "What service do you use?"

He shook his head. "It doesn't matter for the demonstration. I'll just fly the queen bee manually." He put his thumbs on the paddles of the controller, and the "queen bee" buzzed into the air, rocketing to a height of about 20 meters over their heads. With the press of another button, she heard a series of clicks from the tray on the ground, and the microdrones nestled into the foam were flicked into the air and then rose like a cloud of mosquitos, gathering in a dense ball around the queen bee drone.

"You ready?" he asked Bunny. "It won't be life-sized with just 100 drones, but you'll get the idea."

"What idea?" Bunny asked. But in an instant, she saw. The ball of drones dissolved and spread into a flat, dense plane, like the pixels on a small screen, that flashed first red, then green, then blue. And then they dissolved again, becoming almost invisible against the early morning sky, before suddenly ...

"Hey, that's me!" Bunny said. There she was, 50 feet over the ground, doing jumping jacks. Of course, with only 100 drones, there was a lot of space between the airborne "pixels," but even so, the fidelity of the image was impressive.

Hungyu twitched his thumbs, and the drones pulled into a ball around their queen bee again before dropping from the sky, like so many shooting stars, to land back on top of the tray. The Taiwanese engineer bent and started pushing them carefully back into their foam mounts on the tray. "So what do you think?" he asked. He brought the queen bee down last. "I talked to the Taiwanese army research unit about trying to scale the algorithm up because I thought maybe I could get it to work with some of the uncrewed aircraft they were already using. You'd be able to get a swarm of small drones following, like, a fighter plane, and they could either protect it or maybe attack …" He stood, looking despondent. "But it seems I should have talked to you. You're right about Particle Swarm Optimization. My algorithm only works with microdrones, and they can't keep up with fighter jets."

But Bunny wasn't listening to what his software couldn't do. She was only thinking about what it *could*.

She picked up the queen bee. "Does this have to be a drone?"

"I … why? What are you thinking?"

"I'm thinking," Bunny said, "about how your microdrones flocked into a ball around the queen bee while they were initializing. How does that work?"

"The test sequence?" He frowned. "Well … a drone gets kicked into the air and starts its LED light test routine. It looks for the queen bee on infrared, then joins up with it. The second one looks for the queen bee and the first drone and moves in beside it, and so on until they make a ball around the queen. When they are all in place, they do their startup routine, and any with dead LEDs drop out of the formation." He shrugged. "That's really it. It's the simplest part of the software. The real challenge is transliterating the digitized video to …"

294

"Wait," Bunny held up a finger. "So you have some kind of parameter in there that keeps the microdrones a minimum safe distance from the queen bee?"

"Yes."

"And we can adjust that?"

"Sure, but …"

"And they use infrared optics to lock onto the queen bee, not radio signals?" Bunny asked. "So they must have an image of the queen bee in memory."

"A 3D model, digitized, yes, so they recognize it from any angle." He replied. "I thought if we 3D-mapped a fighter, and put my software into something like your Valkyrie or Ghost Bat combat drones …"

"Uh-huh. So we can change out the 3D model and have them flock around just about anything?"

"I guess," he said. "Though preferably airborne since I don't have any terrain avoidance routines in the code."

Bunny gripped his shoulder. "Hungyu, we are going to rewrite your code. I suspect you'll be able to sell it to the US Air Force, or the highest bidder, when this war is over, but promise me one thing …"

He blinked. "What?"

"You won't spend the money on Chinese real estate."

Sergeant Mason Jackson, 1st Battalion, 8th Marines, was at a medical clinic just down the road from the shopping center with the sniper Wu and his driver, Lance Corporal Hernan Cruz.

Cruz had started the day complaining about a bad stomachache, and by the time they'd met Bunny O'Hare, he'd developed a fever. Some kind of virus was sweeping through the soldiers of 1st Battalion, so it didn't surprise Jackson that one of his crew had come down with it.

On the ship bound for Taipei, they'd had a medical briefing in which the doc had spent at least five minutes going through all the different tropical diseases they might be exposed to on Taiwan, from dengue fever to scrub typhus, Japanese encephalitis to Lyme disease from ticks. And so on. "More of you are likely to become casualties from disease on Taiwan than from enemy fire," the doc had said with an evil smile. "So don't hesitate to volunteer for combat duty. It's a cleaner death." It was enough to make a man regret re-upping.

The clinic was a modern private diagnostic center with a single doctor and nurse still on duty. The rest had fled, but the two medicos remaining were treating all comers, as long as they didn't require surgery. The doctor took a quick look at Cruz and pointed to a corner, speaking perfect English-accented English. "When she is free, the nurse will take some blood and a throat swab."

Cruz looked done in and was starting to cough now too. The doctor handed him a face mask. "Wear this, please."

There were many other patients. Wu explained that some had wounds from bullets or bombs but had been turned away by the local hospital because they weren't serious enough. Others were looking for medicines, like insulin or heart medication. "They ran out of insulin in the first couple of days," Wu said. "We don't make it in Taiwan, and nothing is getting through to Dongshi. They have to try further north." He looked up. "Oh, oh, this doesn't look good."

The doctor and nurse were both walking into the waiting room, wearing masks. As they approached, the doctor barked something at the people in the room and they reacted with surprise, standing and moving out of the way … away from Jackson, Wu and Cruz.

The nurse was carrying what looked like a full-body protective suit, made of plastic, over one arm.

They stopped a few feet away from the three soldiers. "This man has H5N1 virus," the doctor said, pointing at Cruz. He motioned to the nurse, who threw the protective suit at Cruz's feet and then handed masks to the rest of them. "He must put on this suit. The rest of you, please mask up."

Jackson had a hundred questions, but he figured they should do the suit first, so he bent down to pick up the suit for Cruz. The doctor held out a hand. "No, he should do it alone. You should not touch him. Step back."

Jackson took a step back. Cruz looked at him in confusion. He was a big man with black curly hair and heavy brows and lashes over what were now wide eyes. He bent double coughing, then came up again. "Sarge?"

"Easy, buddy, you just do what the doc says, and put on that suit," Jackson said. "Then we'll get you back to base."

As Cruz started pulling on the protective clothing, the doctor pointed to a room off to one side. "When your friend has suited up, we can go in there and talk."

The suit was not straightforward. It was a mess of Velcro tape and tabs, gloves, booties and a transparent facemask that also had to be sealed in place by Cruz since no one was allowed to touch him. After a few minutes though, he was done, and he bent double again with a series of racking dry coughs.

"Follow me, please," the doctor said, leading Cruz, Wu and Jackson into the side room, with the nurse behind them and all the other patients keeping a fair distance away, watching the procession intently.

297

Wu asked a question in rapid-fire Mandarin, but the doctor shook his head. "We can just as well speak English; the Americans need to hear," he said. The room was a personnel change room, and he pointed to a row of chairs opposite some lockers. "Please, sit." When they were seated, he leaned back against one of the lockers. Jackson couldn't help but notice he was keeping his distance, not just from Cruz but from all of them.

"Your friend has H5N1," he said, "otherwise known as bird flu. It seems to be a Gs/GD variant of some kind, but I can't be sure. How long has he had these symptoms?"

"He got stomach pain yesterday, fever last night, started coughing this morning," Jackson answered.

"Has he been in contact with farmed birds recently? Geese, ducks, chickens?"

"No, not that I know of."

"Or near anyone else with bird flu?"

"No, that's … I mean, there is a virus going around our base in Chiayi City. But no one said anything about bird flu."

"Hey, I'm right here," Cruz replied. "And no, I haven't been near no birds. I ain't even eaten no chicken since we left base; just noodles, rice and 'protein supplement.'"

Jackson was pretty sure H5N1, or "bird flu," had not been on the ship doctor's list of horrible diseases you could get on Taiwan. "Is it bird flu season or something here?"

"Human cases of bird flu are *not* normal," the doctor said. "Or weren't. Until about two weeks ago. There was a report of a case in Taichung."

"Chicken farmer?" Wu asked.

"Sailor," the doctor said. "The report I saw said he had just been transferred by train from Xuoying. We were asked to report any new cases. You are my third today. Xuoying has been locked down. That tells me they are worried about this strain."

"Xuoying is a city with a million people!" Wu said, then turned to Jackson. "Have you been there?"

"Xuoying? We haven't been anywhere near there. And no one told us anything about any bird flu when we started our patrol three days ago."

"If you have been in close contact with this man"—the doctor nodded at Cruz—"you and anyone else he has been around need to isolate and monitor your symptoms."

"Isolate and …" Jackson's day was spinning out of control, and he didn't much like it. "Doc, there is a war going on out there. I can't just put my feet up in bed and …"

"The sailor they identified in Xuoying died two days after being admitted. I checked the latest reports before I came back into the waiting room. There are now 230 dead in Xuoying, and 150 in Taichung."

"Uh, alright, alright," Jackson said. "Do you have any, like, antivirals? Some kind of vaccine maybe?"

"There is no vaccine for H5N1 that I know of, since it is so rare in humans and does not usually transmit from human to human. Our colleagues in Xuoying report that the usual treatment—neuraminidase inhibitors—seems ineffective. The mortality rate is …" He paused, looking at the nurse. Something passed between them. "High."

"How high?" Jackson said. "Tell us."

The doc hesitated, then relented. "More than 60 percent," he said. "Two out of three patients are dying within three days. Several hundred are in critical care. Only about one in 10 appears to respond to standard care."

Jackson stood. "No offense, doc, but we aren't isolating here. We need to get back to base."

The doctor folded his arms. "Call them."

"What?"

"Call your base. You said there was a virus going around the base before you went on patrol? If it is the same one this man has, then it has had three days to take hold. At the very least, you can warn them."

Jackson shook his head. "I can't call them; sat comms are down. And the slaughterbots have knocked out every cell phone tower on the east coast. We've been out of contact with Chiayi City the last 24 hours."

The doctor spoke quickly with his nurse. "Camp Chiayi?" he asked Jackson.

"Yeah."

"And the infected soldier's name is 'Cruise'?"

"C-R-U-Z," Cruz wheezed, annoyed at again not being asked a direct question. "Service ID is …"

The doctor wrote it down for the nurse, and she left the room. "The clinic is linked to the national optical fiber grid. She will get the message to your camp."

"No, let me …" Jackson started, but the doctor held up his hand.

"Sergeant, please, remain here. I asked her to hurry."

Cruz was leaning forward, elbows on his knees. He looked up, pained. "Sarge, I don't want to be stuck here."

"No one is going to be stuck anywhere," Jackson assured him. "We'll get you back to base, and they'll look after you right."

Jackson noticed that Wu had quietly moved a couple of steps farther along the wall from the two Marines and was pinching the clip on his face mask to seal it tighter over his nose. Jackson couldn't blame him. He balled his fists in frustration.

300

Jackson was a former "UT Volunteers" linebacker, who chose the Marines after he got sidelined by an ACL injury that was bad enough to put a stop to his football career but not bad enough to stop him humping a pack. He'd steered himself toward a Marine Raider assignment because at least that way, he'd have an armored vehicle to carry his ass around for him and be reminded less about his football injury.

But he'd brought with him his linebacker's fearlessness. Bird flu? Hell, that didn't sound so bad.

The nurse returned a few minutes later and handed the doctor a printout. He handed it to Jackson. "This is for you."

It was a printed email, but Jackson could see it had been hastily cut and pasted together by someone at the other end because it contained different fonts and text sizes.

> *In relation to your inquiry regarding a Lance Corporal Hernan Cruz who has reported to your clinic with symptoms of H5N1 virus*: by order of Lieutenant Colonel Arthur Henderson, 1st Battalion, 8th Marines, any personnel displaying three or more of the following symptoms:
> *Fever*
> *Cough*
> *Sore throat*
> *Shortness of breath*
> *Chest pain*
> *Abdominal pain*
> *Diarrhea*
> *Vomiting*
> *Muscle aches*
> *Headache*
> *Rapid heart rate*

Coughing with pink or frothy sputum
Confused or altered mental state
Are required to seek medical attention from the nearest medical facility and isolate in place. Off-base personnel should contact their commanding officer and should not return to Camp Chiayi until five days after symptoms are resolved.
Thank you for your inquiry.

Jackson read it through twice, tight-lipped. He didn't like the fact the answer had come back so quickly. It suggested they already had a template answer they were sending out. Their Lieutenant Colonel was called Art Henderson, that much was true. The nurse could have looked that up online, perhaps, but the rest of the message seemed authentic enough, and she would barely have had time, or the English skills, he supposed, to have made the message up.

Jackson read the message through a third time, looking for a loophole. *Contact your CO? And how am I supposed to do that when VHF is being jammed and cell or sat comms are down?* He nearly swore out loud, then he realized he had just found his loophole.

He motioned to Cruz. "OK, Lance Corporal, on your feet."

The doctor took a step forward, then a step back. "What are you doing, Sergeant?"

Jackson lifted his driver up by the arm and pointed him toward the door. "We are doing as ordered and reporting back to our CO, doctor."

302

"Your base is probably also in lockdown. If you move this man out of here, you are putting everyone inside and outside this clinic at risk."

Jackson laughed as they stepped past the doctor. "You have flying Chinese slaughterbots roaming your streets, which we are here to kill, by the way, and you're worried about a man with a flu."

The nurse had been following the interaction and stood in front of Jackson, a determined look on her face. He stopped two feet from her, looking down on her. She was at least six inches shorter than him. But she had guts, he had to give her that.

He pulled his M18 pistol from his hip and held it up so she could see it. "Please move aside, ma'am."

The nurse looked like she was going to plant herself even more solidly in front of Jackson until the doctor put a hand on her shoulder and pulled her gently back. He reached to a locker behind him and pulled out a handful of protective suits. "At least take these, and use them."

Wu took them and started following Jackson and Cruz, but only after an exchange with the doctor, which Jackson assumed was something along the lines of "Don't blame me, I just gave them directions to the clinic."

Outside the clinic again, Cruz grabbed the wall and doubled over, hacking like he was trying to force a lung up. Jackson held an arm around his lower back. "Easy, soldier, breathe slow."

When Cruz straightened, his clear plastic face mask was covered in flecks of pink foam.

Wu and Xu had taken hundreds of pictures of the Chinese killer drones in the course of their many missions, and Xu was more than happy to share them with Hungyu so he could build a 3D digital model.

Changing his code so that the queen bee was replaced by a model of the slaughterbot in the microdrone's memory was easy enough, as was taking a pair of shears to his movie-making code so that it ended at the point the drones formed a ball around their target.

"Alright," the drone engineer said. "We'll do the test with a 1,000-drone swarm. You wanted to change the minimum safe distance parameter? To what?"

"How about zero?" Bunny said, leaning over his shoulder and following the code as he typed on the screen.

"Zero?"

"Yeah, we want your killer bees to choke their new queen bee, right? They don't have explosives, which means they have to get in close and mess up its rotors …"

"They'll get chewed up," Hungyu protested. "I just … I assumed you just wanted to *blind* the slaughterbot, stop it from being able to shoot at targets."

"Best way to blind them is to bring them down," Bunny pointed out. "What's the problem?"

He sounded peeved now. "Oh, nothing, I guess, except we are talking thousands of dollars of my drone tech getting chewed up and spat out to test this crazy idea."

"Or …" Bunny tried a winning smile. "Or … it works, and your cloud of tiny killer bees can bring down the big bad mama bee."

He turned back to his keyboard and started typing. "We'll start at 20 centimeters. Prioritize the inner layer. If one drone hits a rotor and gets destroyed, the next one out will move in and take its place until it gets destroyed, et cetera …"

"I love et cetera," Bunny told him. "Et cetera is one of my *favorite* words."

Xu appeared at the entrance to the shed, looking pale. "Wu is back. Something is wrong."

"Stay out there!" Wu yelled in both Mandarin and English as Bunny, Xu and Hungyu approached the sniper's camp in the GAP store. Bunny stopped, then stepped forward until she could see through the open doorway.

Everyone inside was wearing what looked like light hazmat suits, made of plastic. Hospital issue, she guessed. One of them was lying on the ground. Even from out in the shopping mall corridor, she could hear his rasping breath. Kneeling beside him was Jackson.

A figure that had to be Wu was over to one side, filling some bottles with water from a water barrel. A couple more hazmat suits were folded on the floor beside him too.

"What the hell …?" Bunny asked.

"Cruz has a virus," Jackson said loudly, without looking over. "Doctor at the clinic freaked out, can't or won't treat him. I need to get him back into our AFV and make a run for base, but I … He's collapsed, and he's having spasms. I can't carry him on my own …" Jackson shot a glare at Wu. "We need to get down to the parking garage, and this dipshit won't help me."

Wu either didn't hear him or was ignoring him. He kept filling water bottles. Then he stopped, leaning against the water barrel. "I'm sick too …" he said.

"You *what?*" Bunny asked.

305

Wu turned. "I started feeling warm yesterday. I woke up with a headache and stomach pain. Now I'm burning up," he said. "My chest feels tight. I'm too weak to help carry your driver."

The man on the floor lifted his head and yelled something, then fell back down again before Jackson could grab him, hitting his head on the floor with a crack. His legs jerked a few times, then relaxed.

"That's your driver?" Xu asked, peering at them from behind Bunny's shoulder. Hungyu was another step or two behind him, laptop bag clasped to his chest like some kind of shield.

"Yeah," Jackson said. "Easy, buddy." He looked at Wu again, a softer note in his voice this time. "How long have *you* felt sick?" Jackson asked.

"I don't know … It started yesterday, maybe the night before."

"You were complaining about your stomach two days ago," Xu told him.

"Alright, two days," Wu admitted.

"So you got it before you even met us," Jackson said insistently. "Cruz was complaining for a couple of days before he went down too. So this thing has an incubation time, and I'm not there yet." He turned to Bunny for support. "If we get Cruz down to my Stryker, I can get us all back to Camp Chiayi before I get sick, get us some help."

"Your Stryker down where we left it?" Bunny asked.

"Level Two, yeah," Jackson said.

Bunny motioned to Wu. "Throw me one of those suits. I'll help carry your driver …" She hesitated. "You'll be a crewmember down. It's at least 30 kilometers back to Chiayi through hostile territory, and you won't have a gunner."

Wu raised a hand. "I can drive the vehicle, and you can run weapons and systems," he said to Jackson. "Or at least until I pass out."

The man on the floor doubled up, moaning. So he was still alive, for now. "You sure you want to do this?" Bunny asked Jackson.

"No," Jackson said. "But what choice do I have? Doctor said this virus has a 60 percent death rate. Stay here, they probably die. At Camp, they might have a chance."

"Alright, let's go."

Wu tossed the extra suits to Bunny, and she began pulling one of them on. It was harder than it looked. She was so focused on getting her boot into the bottom of one of the suit legs that she didn't notice until she straightened up that Xu was pulling on the other suit beside her.

"Two of us can get this done, Private," she said. "You can stay here."

"Yes, but ..." Xu was struggling with the straps and zips too, and Bunny helped him. "Corporal Wu is a terrible driver. They will never make it to Chiayi with him at the wheel."

Wu didn't argue.

Hungyu was hanging well back. He'd found a mask somewhere, probably in a nearby shop, and pulled it on. It seemed kind of comical in the presence of five people in hazmat suits. "What can I do?" he asked as they lifted Cruz off the floor, Jackson taking his shoulders and Bunny and Xu his legs. He was a big guy, and he wasn't limp. Every few seconds a limb jerked spasmodically. He didn't appear to be aware of what was happening.

"Debug that new code," Bunny told the drone engineer. "I'll be back as soon as these guys are on their way."

Hungyu looked surprised. "You aren't going back to the Marine base with them?"

"Hitchhike with this bunch of diseased maniacs?" she grunted. "No, thank you. Besides, we need to do a test run of your killer bees on a live slaughterbot. And then I need to get to Taichung Air Base, which is a whole *other* problem."

Before he left with the Marines, Xu told them the slaughterbots had erratic patrol times but predictable routes. In order to stay low and avoid overhead wires, Bunny and Hungyu followed railroad lines and roads—large and small, only going "off-road" to engage targets in cover.

The highway where they had taken down two of the slaughterbots was a high-frequency patrol route, but given the speed at which the Chinese drones learned, a second ambush in the same site would be unlikely to succeed.

Xu had recommended a branch of the main north-south rail line that ran between Dongshi and Chiayi. "The mother ships drop the slaughterbots on the coast, and some of them use feeder rail lines to move quicker inland," Xu said. "Also, when their power dies, they like to find rail corridors to explode over. Maybe to cause fewer civilian casualties, but also to damage rail lines when they self-destruct."

The Dongshi Station and the rail line to Chiayi were deserted since no trains were running. Moving trains had been among the first slaughterbot targets, and the burned-out carcass of a freight train carrying fish from the port to the inland city announced itself to Bunny and Hungyu by the stink of fish left rotting in the sun. The rail spur ran alongside the—also deserted—main highway to Chiayi and shared the bridge over the Puzi River about 2 kilometers outside Dongshi town.

It had taken them a good hour using cover to get from the boat shed to where they now crouched in the drainage ditch of a dried-out rice field, surveying the bridge.

"Good a spot as any," Bunny decided. "The highway and rail line come together at the bridge, so if the slaughterbots are using either to move inland, they'll cross there."

"But they're airborne; they can cross the river anywhere they like," Hungyu pointed out.

"Sure, but they use line-of-sight communication. A rail corridor gives them excellent field of view. They don't want to waste time or energy if their patrol sector is inland, and the rail corridor is deserted. Plenty of open ground on either side. Easier to spot an ambush."

"Easier to spot us," Hungyu pointed out.

Bunny had Wu's rifle with her and put it down so she could put a hand on the engineer's shoulder. "You said your killer bees can spot their queen bee from 500 meters away. A slaughterbot is 100 times bigger. We can stay right here, and when we spot our target, we send up the swarm and … see what happens."

"The slaughterbot might see the swarm approach. How fast can it fly if it tries to outrun it?" the engineer asked.

"They looked pretty slow to me," Bunny said, thinking of her encounters over the sea and on the road outside Dongshi. "Maybe 60 kilometers an hour, but I don't know what they're capable of if they put the pedal down. How fast are your killer bees?"

"They can move up to 100 kilometers an hour, but only for short distances. The battery only lasts 20 minutes for average use."

"Well, let's hope they prefer fighting to running," Bunny said. She had been carrying the sniper rifle in one hand and had a large pack on her back. The engineer carried his controller unit in a pouch across his chest, and a similar backpack on his back. Each backpack contained 500 of the microdrones, in fold-out foam padding. "Let's set up."

Bunny rigged a groundsheet on four pegs over the top of the drainage ditch, both to give them cover from the merciless sun but also to hide them from passing aircraft or satellites. The "killer bees," as Bunny had taken to calling them, were laid out in the ditch in front of their position, foam packing on a metal base unfolded so that they were ready to release into the air. A tiny coil under each drone flicked it into the air, and when they were recalled, they returned to their release point and settled on the ground to be collected by hand.

That process could take some time, Bunny had reflected. Not something you would want to have to do under fire. A problem for version 2.0 to solve.

If they survived this test of version 1.1, of course.

It was entirely possible their target slaughterbot would just shrug off the microdrone swarm and turn its weapons loose on the source of the attack, in which case the shallow irrigation ditch they lay in was no real cover at all. And if the Chinese drone lived long enough to call in assistance …

She shrugged off the thought. Consequences were something Bunny preferred to ignore, both in love and in war.

Hungyu tapped her shoulder and pointed. A drone, moving from their right, from Dongshi, along the rail corridor to their left. Bunny lifted the rifle and peered down the scope. She hadn't taken Wu's .50 Barrett—it was just too big—so she had the lighter 7.62 mm Taiwanese T93. It had a decent scope on it though, with inbuilt ballistic calculator, and she panned it around until she found the target. It could just be a surveillance drone. China had several quadcopter-type drones it could send ashore from naval vessels …

No. *Slaughterbot.* Missile carrier type.

It wasn't patrolling, like the others Bunny had seen. It was about 20 meters over the ground, traveling straight down the railway track, missile launcher stowed. Probably doing around 40 kilometers an hour, conserving power for when it hit its patrol sector. It would be abreast of them in a couple of minutes.

It was alone, which made Bunny think. "What would your killer bees do if there were two of them, close to each other?" she whispered as she tracked the drone in her scope.

"They'd go to one, and if that was destroyed and they still had power, they'd go to the other," he whispered back.

"Which would give the second one time to look for and attack us, but it wouldn't be able to stop the swarm, right?"

"The swarm will keep trying to surround a target until all the microdrones are out of power or can't see the target anymore," he said. "Or we recall them."

The slaughterbot was nearly level with their position now. "System armed?" she asked.

"Armed and ready," he said.

A couple of seconds ticked past. "Alright, launch!"

He thumbed a button on his controller, and the padded foam panels in front of them began clicking as one "killer bee" after another was flicked into the air, rotors spinning up. In the quiet of the dried-out rice field, the noise was like a thousand angry wasps and would have been audible to anyone inside a few hundred meters. Another problem for the designers of version 2.0 to worry about.

The slaughterbot continued past them.

The swarm rose into the air, looking for its queen bee. About 100 meters up, they seemed to have found it, and like cartoon bees chasing a honey bear, they began flowing toward the slaughterbot. In a few seconds, they had caught up with it and started forming a sphere around it, matching its speed and altitude perfectly.

"I'll be damned," Bunny said. "It's working."

Except … it wasn't. The drones formed a thick cloud around the slaughterbot, which reacted by stopping completely. Of course, it would have some kind of protocol that stopped it moving if it couldn't path-find, and the swarm would be blocking its vision. It hovered in place, and the swarm hovered around it.

One or two of the killer bees contacted the drone's rotors and came spinning out of the cloud, damaged, falling to the ground like poisoned birds. But the slaughterbot itself didn't appear troubled. It kept hovering, then suddenly pulled up 20 meters.

The swarm followed it. It slid left, then right, trying to get clear vision, but the swarm stuck with it again. Finally, it started climbing rapidly, straight up.

"How high can your bees fly?" Bunny asked, suddenly worried.

"One kilometer is the highest I've tested," Hungyu admitted. "Any higher than that, people complain they can't see the show."

Several more microdrones came spinning down out of the swarm after making contact with the slaughterbot's rotors, but the Chinese drone was still climbing. Bunny checked the scale in her scope. It was about 200 meters up now. It stopped again and repeated its sideways movement, sliding left, then right. She racked the bolt on her rifle, putting a round in the breech, and sighted on the faintly visible drone at the center of the swarm, the sight's ballistic computer guiding her aim. She moved her finger to the trigger. If it moved up again, she would …

The drone *exploded*.

A white cloud of fire and smoke blasted outward through the swarm; metal, plastic and hundreds of killer bees fell burning to the ground below.

"Did you *shoot* it?" Hungyu asked angrily. "We lost half the swarm!"

"No, I …" *Had she?* Maybe the trigger was lighter than she thought. She checked the rifle. No.

"I'm recalling them," Hungyu said, voice nearing a panic pitch. "We need to get out of here. That explosion could have alerted more of them."

Like obedient pets, the remaining killer bees returned to their launch pad, dropping onto it and powering themselves down. They didn't waste any time slotting them back into their places in the foam; they just gathered them into their backpacks like so many dead locusts, folded the launch pads up and, at a running crouch, made their way back along the irrigation ditch toward Dongshi.

Outside Dongshi, Sergeant Mason Jackson was doing the Stryker equivalent of a running crouch. It was only 30 kilometers from Dongshi to their base at Chiayi, but to take the highway would have been suicide.

So they were on back roads, winding their way through town after town, first Puzi, then the outskirts of Taibao, about halfway to Chiayi. The route nearly doubled their journey, but it meant they were in cover, between buildings most of the time, not out in the open with nothing but rice fields on either side. They would stop at every crossroads, drop a man on foot and check for slaughterbots before moving forward. It was a tactic Jackson and Cruz had perfected as a crew out on patrol, which was why they were still alive. With Cruz down, Wu barely able to get up from his seat in the rear of the Stryker, it was down to Xu and Jackson to alternate driving and scouting the intersections. But Xu was a quick learner, so they made it about halfway with only a couple of close calls from passing slaughterbots, which didn't see them.

Cruz was no longer responding to stimulus. He was burning up, and in between spasms, his head would just roll left or right with every bump in the road as he gave off the occasional moan or cough.

Xu was driving and slowed the Stryker about 20 meters back from an intersection in a warehouse district of Taibao. There were more people on the back streets of towns and cities than there were on the highways and main roads—people still had to get food, medicine. Some were even still going to work, and the slaughterbots left civilians mostly alone. But a deserted road or intersection was a bad sign. It usually meant a bot had just been through, or had been seen in the area. Cell networks were down, but most households were connected by optical fiber cable, and dedicated websites had been set up to report and track slaughterbot sightings.

Jackson could have used an app like that right about now.

"I'll scout," he said, levering himself out of the command position, which also held the periscope gunsight and the laser weapon station.

"I'm on weapons," Xu said, moving from the driver's to the commander's position. He'd had a quick introduction to the weapons station, but it was pretty much automated anyway. Place the cursor over the target, box and confirm it, and shoot.

Jackson climbed out of the commander's hatch beside the laser turret and slid down the side of the eight-wheeler, dropping heavily to the ground. He wasn't armed, and he was only wearing jeans and a T-shirt. It wasn't the recommended exit or entry point—that was through the rear ramp—but you didn't drop the ramp in a combat zone unless you were loading or unloading troops or cargo. Cruz had survived one close encounter with a slaughterbot when it suddenly appeared out of a side road behind him simply because he wasn't armed. He'd spun, hands in the air, to indicate he wasn't carrying, and the slaughterbot had tracked him but didn't fire. They'd doubled back later and killed it.

The intersection was quiet, not even a dog to be seen. And there were *always* dogs in Taiwan, their owners either dead or fled to the hills.

He jogged up to the corner, hugging the brick and iron wall of a warehouse, heat bouncing off it. The other side of the road was more exposed, a chain-link fence running down one side of what looked like an auto body shop.

He hadn't even reached the corner, hadn't even gotten a peek down the road, when he heard it: the buzz of slaughterbot rotors he had learned to hate. He spun in place, signaling to Xu: *target left, closing.*

He crept up to the corner and peeked around, pulled his head back and signaled to Xu again: *100 meters.*

He put his eye to the corner again. The cannon-armed slaughterbot had stopped. Had it seen him? Its rotating barrel, pointed right at him, said maybe it had. But how would it react?

Then he got his answer as the bot opened up and 25 mm slugs started exploding next to his head.

Xu jerked back in his seat as the brick and iron wall in front of Jackson disappeared in a cloud of flying masonry and rust.

The Marine dropped.

"Shit shit shit," Xu said out loud.

"What, what is it?" Wu said from the rear compartment.

"The Marine is down. He … I … he …"

Wu rose unsteadily to his feet, moving forward. He was behind Xu and put a hand on his arm. His vision was blurred, and he couldn't see anything on the man's targeting screen, just the vague shape of an empty road and a dissipating cloud of dust. The thin plastic visor in his protective suit didn't make things any clearer. "Easy, Private," he said. "You've got this."

Then shells started chewing at the building with the chain-link fence, the end of the street became a maelstrom of flying brick, wood and metal, and the slaughterbot came into view, edging around the corner, *firing, firing …*

With something close to a computer gamer's reflexes, Xu twitched his joystick, putting his cursor on the Chinese drone. Click, *locked.* Click, *fire!*

There was a hum and snap over their head, then another, as the micropulsed laser fired two 50-kilowatt bursts of heat at the slaughterbot.

The 25 mm slugs kept chewing along the wall toward them, the drone swung out into the middle of the road …

And exploded.

Xu sat back in his seat, wiping his brow, but Wu was pushing weakly at his back. "Get back on the driver position, keep us moving …"

"But the Marine …"

Wu shook the sweat from his eyes and squinted, trying to focus. The crumpled, headless shape at the bottom of the wall wasn't moving.

"He's *gone*," Wu said. "We look after the living, Private. His buddy is in back and still breathing. Now get on the wheel and floor this thing."

"Alright, let's go through it so we can write it up for your buddies in defense research," Bunny said. They made it back to the boat shed, covered in dust and sweat. Mains water was a hit-and-miss affair since the arrival of the slaughterbots, but Hungyu's father had rigged a seawater pump up under the nearest dock and run a hose up to the boat shed, and Bunny had wasted no time in dumping her pack and stripping down to a singlet and briefs outside the shed so she could stand under the hose and cool down.

"It's rude to stare, Hungyu," she said without turning around. She could feel his eyes on her.

"Sorry, I … so *many* tattoos."

"Yep. One for every peeping Tom I killed," she said.

317

She went inside, took two beers from a cooler and handed one to him as she sat. She clinked his bottle, then started rocking on the back legs of her chair. "We got lucky," she said.

"More than lucky. We found its weakness!" he insisted.

"Yeah, until it learns. The Navy guy said they seem to have adaptive intelligence, sharing data with one another, probably squirting it back to the mainland. Fixing this vulnerability is just a matter of a software update, Hungyu."

He thought about it. "You're right."

"So we still need the brute force approach. The microdrones weren't getting close enough to damage the slaughterbot's rotors in numbers. We need them closer. We need them at *zero* distance to the queen bee."

"Not zero," he insisted. "They need to be able to focus on what they're keeping formation with. Fifteen centimeters."

"Ten," she said.

They glared at each other for a moment. "Alright, 10."

"And in Killer Bee 2.0, we'll get something with a focal lens that lets it focus at even *closer* ranges."

Hungyu sighed. "We've had one test run, and you're already talking version two …"

"One hella successful test run, engineer man," she said. Then had a thought. "Wait, how many theme parks are there on Taiwan?" she asked.

Her change of direction caught him off-guard. He frowned but then started counting off on his fingers. "Leofoo, Formosan, Janfusun … uh … Lihpao." He stopped. "A few others I can't remember, on the east coast. Because?"

"No one uses real fireworks anymore, right? They all use drone light shows."

"Yes, of course. Cheaper, more variety."

"They use your software?"

"Versions of it." He nodded. "It's like the OS of drone light shows. The corporation I sold the rights to makes millions licensing it."

"So what I'm thinking—together, all of these theme parks have millions of microdrones, and all of them can be reprogrammed with your slaughterbot killer software ..." Bunny said with a big grin.

"It's not that easy ..." Hungyu said.

"No, but it will be. That. Easy," Bunny said. "You need to get onto your defense research contacts right now. Give them what we already have and let *them* scale this solution." She stood suddenly, planted herself in front of him, grabbed his ears to pull his head forward and gave him a big kiss on his ample forehead. "You're going to get a damn medal for this, fisherman."

He blushed from ankle to neck as she stepped back, and stood awkwardly. "I don't think so. Uh ... I have to ..." He walked toward his PC at the back of the shed, on the other side of their wrecked boat.

"Yes, you do," Bunny said. "And so do I." Bunny had a new priority now—get her ass north to Taichung Air Base somehow and get a ride to Hawaii, assuming anything was still able to take off.

Hungyu came running back. "My father ... he's collapsed. He's having trouble breathing!"

The special operatives, Wu and Xu, had not repeated the dead Sergeant's strategy of pausing at every corner to scout for slaughterbots. With the breathing of the driver, Cruz, getting more ragged and irregular by the minute, and Wu

319

barely able to hold himself upright, Xu had driven them onto the Dongshi-Chiayi motorway and floored the Stryker's accelerator, trusting in the vehicle's crude camouflage to get them through.

They had one very close call.

"Slaughterbot ahead," Wu said, pointing at the laser-targeting screen with a shaking finger. "Side of the road. Heading towards Chiayi, the same direction as us. I can't lock it at this speed."

Xu stole a look at the screen and then put his eyes back on the road. "Has it seen us?"

"Maybe, it's stopped. Yeah, turret coming around."

"We can't slow down," Xu told him. "We turn around, you and the American die anyway." Xu was no expert in directed energy weapons. "Can you dazzle it or something?"

"Better if we make like an ambulance, I think," Wu told him. "Get onto the shoulder, give it as much room as you can so it doesn't think we're trying to ram it."

Xu swerved onto the highway verge. There was no traffic on the road, just a few abandoned cars and the occasional burned-out military vehicle.

Xu could see the slaughterbot in his widescreen driving view now, hovering over the highway about 20 meters up, missile launcher turret trained on them, following them as they approached.

But it hadn't fired.

They drew level, then they were pulling away, presenting it with a view of a big red cross painted on their white rear ramp.

"We're through," Wu said, a note of disbelief in his voice. He had been holding his breath but then bent double with a racking cough before coming up for air again. "Who knew slaughterbots had morals?"

The US Marine Aviation base at Chiayi had been a USAF airfield, then an ROC Taiwan AF airfield, then claimed by Marine Aviation when the ROC AF bugged out and 1st Battalion, 8th Marines, surged ashore at the eastern coast port of Hualien. Under heavy air cover, the V-280 Valor tiltrotors of the 8th Marines managed to put a company-sized detachment down at the airfield, but two Valors, their crews and 28 Marines were lost to slaughterbots as they tried to land. A convoy of vehicles from Hualien suffered similarly, with only a few Stryker and LAV-25 armored vehicles making it to the airfield.

The drone predators flew too low for air interdiction, too close to civilian buildings, and their missile-armed variant proved lethal against the Marines' few Viper attack helos.

The Chiayi detachment had been under siege from the moment it arrived, holding back the slaughterbots with MANPADS and their remaining Stryker-mounted laser and anti-air weapons, with supplies only getting through sporadically on uncrewed heavy-lift drones.

As they approached the road into the airfield, Xu handed their radio handset to Wu. "Better let them know we're on the way in. We need to get you and the Marine directly to a clinic. The Sergeant said the main force is on the top floors of the Chiayi-Hi Hotel."

Xu dialed in the cooperation frequency for contact between US and Taiwanese militaries. "This is Corporal Xu Chang of Yun Chi Tuan Operations Company, for 1st Battalion, 8th Marines, Chiayi. We are inbound with …" He broke off to cough, heaving in a lungful of air. "… inbound with an unconscious US Marine, request urgent medical assistance." Jackson had taped a note to the instrument panel with Cruz's details on it, the same one he'd written for the doctor in Dongshi. "The US Marine's name is Lance Corporal Hernan Cruz, and his service ID is ..." Wu rattled off the ID and then leaned a hand on the instrument panel to stop himself falling forward. Xu reached out and pushed him back in his seat. "Easy, buddy." He took the radio handset from Wu, steering the Stryker one-handed as their radio burst to life, incredibly loud in the confines of the cockpit.

"ROC Taiwan military unit, you are cleared to approach Chiayi-Hi Hotel from the western access road, through the airfield. We are currently engaged with an autonomous drone in the east. Hold at the roadblock with front lights illuminated, and you will be met."

Xu lifted the handset to his mouth. "Sir, we need medical assistance for two men. Suggest you get a corpsman down there right away."

"Understood, Corporal," the man replied. "You will be met at the roadblock. Out."

Xu shook his head. "You will be met ... you will be met ..."

Wu had pulled up a map of Chiayi on a navigation screen, but it wasn't showing their position. More problems with the US GPS system, he supposed. Xu knew the city well enough though and swung around the double-wire airport perimeter fence, looking for a gate. When he didn't immediately see one, or any US military personnel, for that matter, he decided to make one.

"Hold on," he told Wu, holding him firmly back in his seat as he wrenched the wheel and plowed through, trusting the vehicle's run-flat tires could handle the razor wire topping the chain-link fences.

He was on the far side of the airfield, the runway running left to right in front of him, and on the other side of the runway …

Carnage.

He saw two crashed tilt-rotor aircraft, one still smoking, and multiple burned-out civilian and military vehicles. The hotel rose behind the hangars on the far side of the airfield, usually used for short-term stays by military personnel and their families. Even at the range of about a kilometer, he could see the lower floor windows were shattered, and black scorch marks covered the façade.

He aimed the Stryker between two hangars, past a burned-out chopper, still seeing no personnel, then he was into a grove of trees, the skeletons of destroyed museum aircraft lining each side of the road—some old Sabre jet fighters, F-5s … Was that a World War II B-26? The slaughterbots had not discriminated between flyable and non-flyable machines.

He flipped on the vehicle lights as instructed, rounded an administration building on four wheels, then slammed to a stop.

In front of him was a roadblock made of concrete barriers, manned by a squad of Marines, two with MANPAD missiles, one with a light machine gun and two with assault rifles.

All were wearing NCBW protection suits.

One had a loud hailer. "Exit the vehicle, and approach slowly with your arms raised."

Wu had been thrown forward in his harness by the sudden stop and lifted his head, looking at the driver's panoramic screen, frowning as though he didn't understand. "Where is the medic?"

Xu unbuckled himself, then Wu. "I don't know. Maybe they've had Chinese sympathizers attack them in military vehicles. Suicide bombers. Who knows?" he said. "I'll go around back, see if I can lift the Marine. You come with me, stay inside the vehicle."

Xu pulled Cruz's details off the instrument panel, then went back to the crew compartment, where the Marine, Cruz, was belted to a fold-down stretcher on the hull of the vehicle. One leg had come free of the harness and was dangling over the edge, unmoving. He was still breathing in light, fast gasps, but his eyes were closed, and he had stopped mumbling to himself. His face mask was completely covered with the pink mist he had coughed onto it.

Cruz was a big man. Xu unbuckled him and realized in a second he had no chance of lifting him alone. He looked at Wu, who had made his way into the back of the Stryker but collapsed on the floor, legs out in front of him, back against the bulkhead. He wasn't going to get any help there.

He punched the ramp and went outside into the sunlight, the heat inside his hospital protective suit stifling.

"Hands in the air, visible ..." the man on the bullhorn shouted. "Come forward."

If he was surprised to see Xu in a protective suit too, he didn't show it.

Xu walked forward, hands in the air. "I'm not your enemy," he shouted. But the man simply waved him forward as the Marine on the squad weapon covered him and the two with MANPADS stayed focused behind him.

He stood in front of the barrier, looking for a medic. "Do you have a corpsman?" he asked. "I have two ..."

"Name of the US serviceman?" the man with the bullhorn asked. He had a tablet PC in his other hand.

Xu handed him Jackson's scrawled note, and he paged through a couple of screens, then found what he was looking for. "He's on the list," the man said to two soldiers standing behind him, then turned back to Xu. "He's in back?"

"With my Corporal." Xu nodded.

The man with the bullhorn—Xu couldn't see his rank, and barely even his face inside the NCBW suit—nodded to the two men behind him, and they moved quickly past Xu toward the rear of the Stryker.

"What's going on here?" Xu asked, looking past the roadblock. Inside the entrance of the hotel, he could see a few figures moving around. All were wearing protective suits.

"Contagion lockdown," the man said simply, as though it should be obvious to Xu.

"Do you have a clinic inside?" Xu asked. "Doctors?"

The man gave Xu a blank stare, then looked past him as the two Marines came back, Cruz's arms draped over their shoulders as they walked him back to the roadblock, feet dragging awkwardly on the ground behind him.

When they'd passed Xu and the officer, he lifted his tablet again. "That the only US soldier you have with you?" He looked at the tablet. "Cruz was on patrol with a Sergeant Mason Jackson."

"Dead," Xu told him. "Slaughterbot outside Taibao. What about my …?"

"The US Marines appreciate your efforts to return Lance Corporal Cruz," the man said stiffly. "Please remove your comrade from the vehicle. It needs to be decontaminated so we can bring it inside."

"We need medical assistance!" Xu said. "My corporal is sick, he …"

"Medical facilities here are reserved for US Marine Corps personnel," the man said firmly. Then he softened. "I'm sorry, Private. You can try the Chiayi Christian Hospital, 2

325

kilometers east. But every medical facility on the east coast is overrun. Hualien and Taipei are in lockdown too. Your best bet is to head back to your own barracks, get help there."

"We came from Dongshi with your soldier!" Xu said, trying not to yell. "Your sergeant died to get him here. My base is in Naipu, 100 kilometers south of here!" He looked back at the Stryker. "How can we get there if you keep your vehicle?"

The man's face hardened again. "There are abandoned civilian vehicles around the airfield. I suggest you take one of them. Now step away from the barricade, Private, and remove your comrade from that vehicle, or we will do it."

Xu felt his hysteria rising. "Or what? What are you going to do? *Shoot me?*"

Two Marines by the concrete berms both lifted their rifles to their shoulders and aimed them at Xu.

The man with the bullhorn had the decency to look uncomfortable, but his words gave Xu no comfort. "If we have to, yes."

13. The battle of the Eastern Pacific

"It can't have just bloody disappeared," Commander Gary McDonald, of HMAS *AE1*, growled. "I go to the heads for five minutes, and … 7,000-ton boats do not just disappear."

His XO, Carla Brunelli, stepped in to protect the sonar watch officer who was in McDonald's firing line. "We are only 500 meters aft of its last known position. It was descending, lost speed, started turning to port … and disappeared from sonar. Here." She put a finger on the map screen, just ahead of them.

They were approaching the Hawaiian Ridge, west of Honolulu. McDonald had expected their quarry might try to play a game of high-risk tag among the peaks and valleys of the undersea ridgeline.

He did not expect it to pull a Houdini.

"Helm, bring us to a full stop, make your heading zero nine zero, and hover in place. Sonar, passive only. Maintain silent running, XO."

Brunelli passed on his orders, then leaned in close. "With no way on, we are sitting ducks if the target gets a torpedo off."

"It's not hunting us, XO," McDonald said. "The Chinese Captains have a slang name for this game—*duǒ māo māo*— 'hide cat cat.' That boat is hiding. And unless the Chinese have invented teleportation, it's right in front of us still."

"So we are just waiting? It could be occluded by a ridge formation, getting further away by the minute," she said.

She was right, of course. Their bathymetric maps were good but not perfect. The Chinese boat could have gotten lucky, ducked behind a peak that was not on their map and snuck away. But it looked like it had stopped *between* two large

327

peaks, over a relatively unremarkable, flat-bottomed valley. Deep, but not below crush depth for the new Chinese *Type 095s*. So it was also possible the enemy was on the seafloor, hiding from their sonar among the clutter. McDonald was betting on the latter. *Hide, little cat cat*, he thought to himself. *This barnyard dog ain't going nowhere.*

Type 095-09, aka *Taifun*, didn't know the strategy she was using was called *duǒ māo māo* by her fellow Captains. The slang wasn't part of her programming. But she'd executed the corkscrew drop into the Hawaiian Ridge depression with a perfection a human would have found near impossible to emulate, and was now hovering at the bottom of the depression, 100 meters below the level of the surrounding seabed.

She had shut down all mechanical and electrical systems except those needed to cool her reactor and supply power to her passive sonar system and core servers. She was running scenarios, assigning them probabilities, fine-tuning them and reassessing, like a chess player thinking 10 moves ahead, except she was juggling hundreds of thousands of possible moves. But there were only so many options she needed to consider, only so many permutations of action and reaction that were likely.

One: The enemy pursuing her had lost, or would lose, her trail and would move off. Response: She would optimize for stealth and resume her mission.

Two: The enemy had not lost her trail and was waiting nearby to reacquire her. If it did, it would either attack or continue its close-quarters pursuit. In either case, she was authorized to destroy it, so her highest chance of survival would be to attack first.

Taifun had one particular advantage over the adversary vessel, even though it appeared to be one of their newer AUKUS submarines, with improved sensors and high-speed torpedoes.

Both were nuclear vessels and could stay submerged almost indefinitely, in theory.

But her pursuer was human crewed, and unlike *Taifun*, humans were impatient.

Colonel Wang Wei, Acting Commander of the PLA Navy *Fujian* Carrier Strike Group, was most definitely not patient.

After the failed Coalition attack on Port Aeon, he continued launching every available aircraft, except those needed for fleet defense, and began landing them ashore. Although their pilots were still aboard *Fujian*, they could be both maintained and flown off the long runway on the small atoll with much greater ease than off the deck of his crippled carrier.

He had requested the return of the island's AWACS aircraft and been denied. But he had been granted tasking authority over a "Chubby Girl" Y-20U aerial refueling aircraft, which was inbound from the Solomon Islands and could serve as a flying communication and control center in a pinch. Port Aeon's precious underground fuel storage tanks had not been damaged in the Coalition attack and contained more than enough fuel to enable his strike group to replenish its stores.

Now the carrier was docked at the Kiribati port. His political shield had evaporated as the Indonesian destroyers had flashed a farewell message and turned for home just outside of Kiribati waters.

But *Fujian* was back under the protective umbrella of the island's anti-air defenses, and every airworthy aircraft *Fujian* still possessed was dispersed across the island of Kiritimati. One of the beauties of the Chongming drone was it could use just about any stretch of paved road to take off and land, as long it was at least 500 meters long. It only needed to spend time at a dedicated airfield to refuel, repair or rearm.

One of the first things Wang had done was to send an officer to speak with the Mayor of Kiritimati's largest town, ironically called London, and warn him the long straight coast road out of Port Aeon was going to be used by his aircraft for the defense of the island. He doubted, after the Coalition's unannounced attack and the death of one of his citizens, the man would object.

The clock was ticking. He had been given just six hours to refuel and rearm his ship. The port looked like an ant's nest that had been kicked over. Every sailor aboard *Fujian* who wasn't acutely needed for duty was ashore, lifting and carrying. Forklifts and flatbed trucks ran up and down the dock in an endless snaking train. His escort vessels, *Dalian* and *Haikou,* were taking turns mooring on the other side of the long pier, taking on fuel and loading ammunition.

The problems facing him were legion. *Haikou*'s Captain had been found dead drunk in his cabin, unable to join for a captains' briefing. Wang had relieved him and ordered him cuffed and confined ashore. *Haikou*'s XO had been appointed in his place. Wang didn't know the man, but he had no time to waste exploring alternatives.

Movement up and down the single pier had quickly gridlocked, until his Air Boss—a master of managing high-pressure situations, whether in the sky or on the ground—had waded into the middle of it with several of his officers from Primary Flight Control and started directing traffic.

The cache of ordnance on the island was quickly exhausted. Wang prioritized surface-to-air missiles and torpedoes for his destroyers. He would have to rely on his aircraft to defend *Fujian*. And there were air-to-air missiles, some 500 lb. glide bombs, but no ammunition of the right caliber for their Chongmings' aircraft cannons.

Aviation fuel he had aplenty, more than enough to refuel his 26 aircraft and fill *Fujian*'s 3-million-gallon, or 12-million-liter, fuel tanks. He had a catapult that could launch aircraft, but right now the aft deck wasn't safe enough to land them again. Wang was loading materials to try to repair it, but that would have to be done while they were underway. He wasn't optimistic.

Now they were two hours from weighing anchor. Wang had called his pilots together for a briefing. He had just received an update on theater-wide operations from his intel chief, Major Tan Yuanyuan. And what she had told him had turned a sense of dread fatalism into something resembling *hope*.

His pilots needed the same injection, and as she wasn't exactly a motivational speaker, he told her he would set the scene before she began her pre-mission brief.

They had 26 operational aircraft, but there were nearly 70 pilots lined up in rows in front of his podium. The decision to turn *Fujian* into a drone carrier first and foremost meant machines might be lost, but except in the cases where there was a direct strike on the carrier, pilots were not.

"Pilots of the PLA Navy carrier *Fujian*," he began. "Many of you know I am an avid student of history. You are about

331

to write yourselves into the history of our nation with a glorious victory!" There was a subdued cheer from the pilots, as he expected. But he had barely started. "To our north lies an island that the Americans took at the point of a bayonet in the 1800s, desecrating the sacred lands of the inhabitants with their military bases, decimating the native population with their diseases and rewriting the island's constitution in the parlors of cigar-smoking imperialist sugar barons before usurping that island's legitimate Queen in a military coup." The map zoomed in on the island he was talking about, and Wang saw a ripple of shock spread through the audience. "In 1993, the USA itself even recognized this coup as an illegal act! Tomorrow, starting at 0200, China is going to free this island from the yoke of imperialism and return it to its original rulers!"

Now there was a rousing cheer. Wang let it die naturally and then called Major Tan to the podium.

"Our targets are US air and anti-ship missile defenses on Hawaii. Our objective is to eliminate US radar coverage of the sea and sky around the Hawaii Islands."

As she said it, even Wang got a chill down the back of his neck. He was a student of history, and few historical events were more well known than the successful Japanese surprise attack on US forces on Hawaii. What followed was a humiliating defeat for Japan, but Japan had attacked the Americans from a position of weakness. China, on the other hand, was at the peak of its military power—as Tang's briefing was about to demonstrate.

"The situation: Our Space Force and Navy have conducted a successful operation to degrade US military satellite and internet communications capabilities. The island is almost completely isolated from satellite and internet

332

communication with the US mainland, and the US is unable to conduct normal drone or precision weapons operations due to the loss of satellite capacity."

Another murmur went around the room, the pilots reacting in the same way Wang had reacted. This was no knee-jerk reaction to the American landings in the South China Sea; a combined forces operation of this nature had to have been planned for *years*. When Wang had been briefed on their mission, he realized the enormity, the vision, the breathtaking scope of the Chinese war plan.

Tan showed media video of US amphibious transport ships departing Pearl Harbor and underway on the Pacific. Wang was impressed. He would have to praise her creativity later. "US military personnel on Hawaii usually number around 45,000 military personnel of all branches, of which only 15,000 are Army and 7,000 are US Marines. However, US media reporting, and our own intelligence, indicates that at least one Division of Army troops, and a Battalion of Marines, have been embarked to reinforce Taiwanese ground forces on Taiwan. The number of active-duty combat troops remaining on Hawaii is reliably estimated to be less than 5,000. Air and sea defense forces are also reported to have been drawn down to support operations on Taiwan and are operating at reduced capability. Our intelligence indicates US air defense patrols around the islands are currently at 30 percent of normal peacetime levels, though some increase in the use of airborne surveillance is to be expected given the loss of their satellite capabilities."

She clicked her presentation forward, showing a graphic of troops, ships, submarines and helicopters. "Forces involved in this operation include the following: *Fujian* Carrier Strike Group. An amphibious landing force centered on the PLA

Navy landing ship, dock *Qilian Shan,* comprising more than 30 warships with 15,000 troops, support helicopters and light armored vehicles embarked. And this …" She clicked the presentation again, showing the recognizable image of one of China's other three aircraft carriers, in company with escorts. "The *Shandong* Carrier Strike Group."

Tan paused as a full-throated roar rose from the pilots and they waved their fists in the air. *Shandong* had been reported damaged in the opening days of the Taiwan conflict, limping into Ningbo harbor under tow, trailing black smoke from a missile strike on its stern. Had it all been a ruse? Or had the *Shandong,* like *Fujian,* been hastily patched together and put back into the fight? Wang's briefing stated the *Shandong* Strike Group had sailed from the Northern Command port of Ningbo just after the attack on the US satellite network and sailed northeast as though it were joining the Kurils exercises with Russia. But under cover of those exercises, it had proceeded eastward, catching the *Qilian Shan* Amphibious Task Force in time to add its four destroyer escorts, two submarines, 32 J-31 Gyrfalcon stealth fighters and 10 helos to the operation.

But Tan was not finished. She showed a video of a Russian flag billowing over the fantail of a warship as the camera pulled back to show Russian warships at sea—a propaganda clip that Wang suspected she had found on a Russian Ministry of Defense website. She had really gone all in.

"And finally, our task force will be joined by our allies from the Russian Pacific Fleet, who have contributed the frigate *Admiral Gorshkov,* destroyer *Marshal Shaposhnikov,* four nuclear attack submarines and six *Stereguschiy* class corvettes, in convoy with the amphibious landing ship *Peresvet* with main battle tanks and the 155th Guards Naval Infantry Brigade embarked."

A new graphic came on-screen showing the full complement of Chinese and Russian forces arrayed for the operation: 58 fighter aircraft, 51 surface-to-air and cruise-missile-armed warships, six cruise-missile-armed submarines and 20,000 troops supported by both main battle tanks, helos and light armor.

Most importantly, they were sailing east, undetected, while the US moved all its available forces in the Pacific westward, to defend against an "invasion" that was nothing more than a grand deception.

Wang knew he and the pilots of *Fujian* had been shown just a small part of China's master plan for ending US dominance in the Pacific. And he had no idea what long game his political masters were playing with either Taiwan or Hawaii. Wang only knew that he thought he was going to be sailing his strike group into enemy waters unsupported, as part of some long-shot false-front operation to try to force the enemy to keep some reserves on Hawaii. Instead, *Fujian* would play a critical role in an operation to end 150 years of illegitimate US occupation of the remote island chain and remove forever the ability of the US to use it to project its power across the Pacific.

The hubbub in the room was, as Wang had expected, making Tan's continued briefing all but impossible. She had taken it as far as they agreed to, anyway. He stood, motioning the pilots and other assembled senior personnel to silence. "You will now break for squadron-level mission briefings. What we have just shared of the theater-level scope of this operation stays in this room. It is not to be shared with noncommissioned personnel. Is that clear?" He waited for nods of assent as he scanned the room. "You are dismissed."

Captain Rory O'Donoghue of the AC-130X 'Outlaw' was in an entirely different mind space. They had no satellite support with which to conduct a post-attack damage assessment of their strike on Port Aeon, but their intel unit had been able to scoop up some Kiribati TV news coverage, which they had carefully analyzed, coming to a very distressing conclusion.

Their strike had failed. Without GPS guidance, inertial guidance had proven inaccurate. The JDAM package that was supposed to do most of the material damage had hit northwest of the target, causing only light damage inside the Chinese base.

According to Kiribati media, they had killed a civilian. O'Donoghue even knew the guy's name, thanks to the TV report: a liquor merchant by the name of Taneti Tito. Father of six.

That was what stuck with Rory. What he couldn't shake. *Father of six.* It was like acid in his stomach. Rory had two kids of his own. Had no idea how his wife would cope trying to bring them up without him, and this guy …

He tried to push it away, bury it. But he couldn't. Two tours on Special Operations in Syria, he was no stranger to war, no stranger to random death. For some reason, this was different. Maybe because he had seen a photo of the guy in the media reporting, with his family, smiling at the camera at some kind of seaside outing. Maybe because he was more than a noncombatant; he was a *neutral* noncombatant.

Bob Lee was more sanguine. "Risk you take selling booze to the Chinese in the middle of a war, I guess. Lucky there weren't more civilian casualties."

Lucky there weren't more. Sure. But if he'd done his job better, made better decisions, maybe there would have been none. Would it have made a difference to how he felt if the mission had been a success? Maybe. Maybe he could have told himself that in the bigger picture, the guy had died for a reason. But the attack went wide, and six Kiribati kids lost their father.

He wasn't thinking about it when they were airborne, except now, in the quiet moments. And at night, as he lay awake listening to the fan over his head turn and turn.

'Uncle' Bob Lee was flying Outlaw, so he had time to think. They were running electronic surveillance on the carrier strike group again—more carefully and at significant range since *Fujian* had managed to get some aircraft airborne by the look of the radar signatures they were picking up. But they weren't coming south. They appeared and disappeared from the north, over Kiritimati. The Chinese carrier had docked, and the scuttlebutt when they landed on the Solomons was that as long as it stayed there, there were bigger nuts to crack farther west.

So as soon as their missing aileron was replaced and their structural integrity signed off, their lone Outlaw was sent back out on ISR patrol, with two air-launched LongShots giving them air-to-air cover. Maybe the thankless recon mission was their due: a fair reward for screwing up.

"You're thinking about those kids again, aren't you?" Uncle said to him early in the patrol.

"What? No."

"Yeah, you are," Uncle said, nodding to himself. "You got to take that energy and turn it outward, boss. We delivered that strike right on the nose. All we lost was a couple drones, we just about took down that S-400, and it ain't our fault the JDAMs flew wide. Whole Air Force is shitting outside the pot without GPS. Just imagine what it's doing to our operations over Taiwan and the South China Sea. Inertial guidance ain't worth jack in today's wars unless you're dropping something like a nuke." He pointed out the windshield to the north. "The enemy is out there. Don't let them get up in your head."

"I know."

"Yeah. You need to get your mind back in the game. Go aft, shout at a few people. I got the stick."

Rory unbuckled his harness and did as he was told, giving Uncle a squeeze on the shoulder as he eased past him. He entered the command module and stood behind the electronic warfare officer. Outlaw fielded the same basic EW suite as a fifth-gen US fighter, able passively to detect, analyze and categorize everything from radio to satellite and radar signatures at ranges of hundreds of kilometers.

Usually, they'd be able to triangulate the signals and upload the data to INDOPACCOM analysts in real time, but that wasn't happening with no satellite link, so they were reduced to plotting the signals manually and relaying the data over low-bandwidth longwave radio.

"Bring me up to speed, Coetzee," he said.

"Just about to squirt the next package through, Captain," she replied. She pulled up data on a screen in front of her. "*Fujian*, *Dalian* and *Haikou* are broadcasting on VHF and Ka satellite bands like they just don't care. Both destroyers seem to have moved a little further north of Port Aeon, but we can't get an exact range without ..."

"ELINT Satellite confirmation. Yeah, assume you don't have to keep saying that."

"Sorry, boss. We have multiple airborne radio and radar signals, all CH-7s. I'd stay they have a standing four-plane patrol around the island, but inside 50 kilometers, and not actively searching beyond that."

"S-400?"

"We definitely shook it up," she said. "Radiating frequently but intermittently. Does a sweep, shuts down and moves, does another sweep. Those guys aren't getting much sleep."

"Other surface contacts?"

"Just some civilian shipping on VHF."

She was interrupted by their comms specialist. "New orders from Hurlburt Field, sir." He handed Rory a tablet.

Rory read quickly and then touched his throat mic. "Uncle, lay in a course for Joint Base Hickam at Pearl. They're short on ISR assets, and they want us to plug a gap."

"Aloha to that, boss!" Uncle replied. "So *Fujian* is yesterday's news now?"

"Seems that way, I'll stay back here, relieve you in …" He looked at his watch. "One hour."

That had been four hours earlier. They were two hours out of O'ahu now, and after a turn in the cockpit, Rory was back at the EW station.

Because things were starting to get … weird.

"*Fujian* has moved out?"

"That's the only conclusion, boss," Coetzee said. "Signal strength was dropping off, but its stopped decaying at a constant rate in the last hour. I can't upload the data for an AI analysis, but my gut instinct says yeah, *Fujian* and the destroyers have weighed anchor and are moving north."

North. There was nothing north of Kiribati except Hawaii. He'd decided *Fujian* might just be trying to provoke the US to waste resources on a response before turning tail and running for Kiribati again. Anything else would have been plain nuts.

But then, this.

"And the signals you are picking up northwest?"

"Too weak for individual classification, so I can't give you a force strength. But I can tell you the types. A lot of naval, some air." She put a finger on a map. "Here."

Three hundred kilometers northwest of O'ahu Island, Hawaii.

"Friendlies in that direction?"

"Yes sir," she said. "Kinda. Mission briefing before we took off said USS *Fallujah* Amphibious Readiness Group would be underway from Pearl to Taiwan around this time, but without …" She stopped herself. "But I can't be sure of its exact position. My gut tells me it should be farther west by now."

"It could have been delayed," Rory said, thinking out loud.

"I guess."

"Log it, send it to Hickam in the next squirt. At the very least, they need to know *Fujian* is playing games again."

The autonomous *Type 095* PLA submarine *Taifun*, if it had been a human, had just decided it was tired of playing games. But because it wasn't, it didn't think of its decision in those terms. It had simply decided that because it had detected no underwater anomalous sound signatures for the last two hours, and because its mission critical time window was closing, it was time to leave the hole it was hiding in at the bottom of the Hawaiian Ridge depression.

But it was about to do so with prejudice.

Without a second thought, knowing its next few actions could be its last, it armed two Yu-12 high-speed heavyweight torpedoes. The Yu-12 was a homing torpedo able to travel at 65 knots underwater, comparable to the British Spearfish. All *Taifun* needed to give it before firing was a bearing to the target. Like the older *Shang* class boats, the *Type 095* had six forward-firing torpedo tubes, but unlike the *Shang* class, it also had two aft tubes. It armed one torpedo forward and one aft.

Without releasing any noisemaking ballast, *Taifun* engaged its electrical pump jet propulsion and began spiraling forward, upward, out of the depression, using its photonics sensors to keep a careful watch on the sides of the small depression, both to make sure it didn't collide with them but also to alert it the moment its conning tower broke out above the level of the surrounding seabed.

The moment it did, *Taifun* started high-powered active sonar pinging.

"Contact! Designating S-3. Bearing one seven nine. Active sonar," *AE1*'s sensor officer, Ozlem, said in a very loud whisper.

"It's her," McDonald said through gritted teeth. "And she's abaft. All ahead full, rudder full left! Sonar active. Get me a firing solution, Ozlem." He had bloody well been right. *Fallujah* had tried to call him back into formation with the ARG, but he'd ignored the message, refusing to even respond lest his signal give him away. His XO, Brunelli, had become increasingly restless, convinced their quarry had evaded them and they were wasting their time.

The *AE1*'s Australian captain, McDonald, had stayed stubbornly put, submarine silent, torpedoes armed. Just. In. Bloody. Case.

"Torpedoes, torpedoes incoming! Range 200 meters, speed 60 knots. Impact in six seconds!" Ozlem hammered a button on his desk. "Deploying decoys; shutting down sonar."

McDonald's heart sank. That wasn't how this game was supposed to go. The Chinese boat, if it reemerged, was supposed to try to evade, maybe make a feint to scare *AE1* away if it had to. They were supposed to resume their game of "hide cat cat." Their quarry wasn't supposed to *fire* on them without provocation.

They were barely moving yet, having just gotten underway from a standing start. He'd miscalculated, was too close to the last known position of the Chinese boat, should have been farther out. Should have anticipated an aggressive Captain, looking for a fight. Should have …

The time for "should have" ran out.

Taifun's first torpedo took a decoy's bait and exploded in their baffles, a teeth-rattling but not fatal blow. The second, having been fired from *Taifun*'s rear tube and taking longer to curve around and reach them, struck *AE1* in the stern.

Water flooded into their stern compartments.

AE1 started sliding backwards into the deep.

Taifun registered the hit on the *AE1* and added it to its log for its next transmission to Huangpu Wenchong. The event was just another data point in its long voyage, and it was soon approaching its mission action waypoint, the moment for which its designer, Lo Pan, had fought long and hard to convince his superiors was a worthwhile enterprise: a moment they and he had never been sure would arrive but that Lo Pan had convinced them they should prepare for.

Threading its way through the peaks and valleys of the Hawaiian Ridge, careful to glide noiselessly between the multiple SOSUS sonar detection sensors placed to provide overlapping coverage of the sea around Oʻahu, it reached its waypoint 50 kilometers off Mamala Bay and sent an ELF message home.

Type 095-09 is in position. Target coordinates entered. Launch system armed. Ordnance reports state green. Ready to initiate five-minutes-to-launch sequence. Proceed or abort?

"Alright, Flatline, take 50 kilometers separation," Meany Papastopolous said. He was airborne with Flatline in their P-99 Widows east of Oʻahu.

He and Flatline had been over the Red Flag range, preparing for a simulated Wild Weasel anti-radar attack that USAF aircraft would have, in about 30 minutes, been trying to defeat.

But with no other P-99s Widows currently based at Hickam, the Aggressor Inc. aircraft, with their superior range, were more and more being used to investigate every unidentified contact within 500 kilometers of Hawaii. The lack of satellite coverage, exacerbated by all but a couple of E3G AWACS aircraft—one of which was suffering from a lack of operational readiness—being deployed to the Taiwan theater, meant air defense controllers on the island were spooked by the slightest thing, and the few fighter aircraft on active duty patrolling the island were being stretched thin.

But it was another day, another dollar for Aggressor Inc., so Meany had no complaints. As a senior officer, he had shares in the company, and Aggressor Inc. had more contracts than it had pilots and aircraft to fill them right now.

The only downside was that the constant flying time meant he didn't have the time to devote to the job of trying to get O'Hare home from Taiwan, or Flowmax's body repatriated. Repatriated? Hell, they hadn't even recovered it yet.

That distressed him, nearly as much as it distressed his family. O'Hare had seen him go down, there was no doubt about his fate, but the company couldn't pay out his policy until his death was confirmed. Aggressor Inc. contracts were made for peacetime operations, not war. At least there was no debate between the USAF Reserve and Aggressor Inc. over who was liable. That would have put Meany in the red zone instantly, but their corporate owner was the kind of guy who did the right thing by his pilots. There were policies, but he wasn't about to leave anyone's family fighting the bureaucracy, wondering how they were going to meet their next mortgage payment.

"What are we looking for?" Flatline asked. They were flying in low-emissions mode, using radios only, not radars, looking for an electronic signal spike about 300 kilometers northwest of O'ahu.

They were also flying with a limited air-to-air loadout, as was common during Red Flag exercises, each machine carrying just two Peregrine medium-range missiles.

"Special Operations flight in the south was shadowing the *Fujian* and called in mixed naval and air radio emissions on this heading," Meany said.

"Isn't *Fallujah* ARG out here somewhere?" Flatline asked. The task force's departure had been on TV news channels the day before as the administration made a big deal about surging more troops into Taiwan.

"West," Meany told him. "They should be well clear of this sector by now." He had no cockpit as such to look out of, just a small slit either side and a vertical one ahead that were only there in case the aircraft's distributed aperture cameras failed. He looked around, and through, his aircraft using his helmet vision, but all he saw was blue sky and sun-dappled water.

"So some spooks got spooked," Flatline decided. "Why don't we … Hey, I got a spike. Weak Ka band signal, bearing zero zero nine. You get that?"

Meany checked his ELINT display. "Nothing." Flatline was 50 kilometers abreast of Meany, so it was possible he'd picked up something that hadn't reached Meany's machine. Ka band most likely meant satellite comms though, which made it interesting. Civilian ships mostly used UHF or VHF. Ka band could mean military.

"Adjusting course; I'll check it out," Flatline said. "Moving to search and track."

"Roger that," Meany confirmed. Flatline was about to light up his radar and start looking for the contact he'd detected. But it meant an enemy with sensitive ELINT equipment could also pick him up. "Moving to cover." Meany twitched his stick and brought his machine around to the same heading as Flatline.

Normally, he'd be able to "see" Flatline's machine on his tactical display, a dynamically updated satellite data feed telling him exactly where his wingman was. But with the US battlenet compromised, things were anything but "normal" right now. Before taking off, they'd been told the Pentagon was negotiating bandwidth for basic communications with civilian satellite corporations, but that hadn't borne fruit yet.

"Contact, bearing three four nine degrees, altitude three zero, range zero eight five, speed 520 knots … Analyzing …" There was a long pause. "Bandit is hot. AI says J-31."

Meany started. "Run it again."

"I already ran it twice. AI is saying it's a Gyrfalcon."

That wasn't possible. The Gyrfalcon was a naval stealth fighter, known for its very short legs. "Flatline, *Fujian* is 2,000 kilometers south and doesn't fly Gyrfalcons. The other two Chinese carriers are in port. We're 5,000 kilometers from the nearest Chinese airfield in the western Pacific."

"So tell this Gyrfalcon it can't possibly be where I'm seeing it," Flatline said. "Oh, crap, it just got a hit off me."

"Come back southeast," Meany said. "Drop down on the deck. We need to lose this guy and flank from a different bearing."

"Breaking off; going dark and cold," Flatline confirmed.

Meany bit his lip. He wasn't worried about a single Chinese fighter that couldn't be where it was. He was worried about the equally impossible idea that there may be more.

China's carrier *Shandong*, its strike group trailing the 30-strong *Qilian Shan* Amphibious Landing Force, had pushed its forward patrol aircraft out ahead of the *Qilian Shan* and its escorts, using the Gyrfalcon's synthetic aperture radar to look for possible surface combatants.

It had a Wing Loong 10 drone, the same type Touchdown had spotted some days earlier, on patrol overhead to watch for enemy aircraft. The Wing Loong used low-frequency radar to find stealth aircraft, which was less precise but more likely to get a return than standard higher frequency or X-band radar, alternating between frequencies to maximize its chances of a return.

As Flatline banked his machine around and pointed its nose toward the sea, the Wing Loong got a hit. The Chinese battlenet was fully operational. It flashed the contact to the lead element of four Gyrfalcon fighters, and the *Shandong*'s air wing commander ordered them to prosecute the contact.

His Space Force had bought him the invisibility he needed to get his carrier halfway across the Pacific undetected. He needed the fog of war that lay over China's invasion fleet to last as long as possible.

Five kilometers apart, the two P-99s swung around south and then west of the contact Flatline had detected.

They passed over a friendly ship. Its Auto Identification ID told them it was a lone *Independence* class littoral warship, headed toward Hawaii. They didn't try to contact it. They were communicating in burst mode—radio messages which were dictated first, then sent as compressed and encrypted data, meaning their radios only broadcast for milliseconds at a time, dramatically reducing the risk of detection.

I have two more signatures, bearing zero seven eight, altitude 20, range 80, heading south-southeast, Meany advised. So far, they had identified at least six Gyrfalcons, arrayed across a front nearly 20 kilometers wide. The real number was probably higher.

Naval search radar, Flatline messaged. *Bearing zero two zero.* Type 036B, *probably a destroyer. Signal strength indicates a range 100 to 150 kilometers.*

347

Meany checked his nav screen. They were nearly 400 kilometers from O'ahu. It was possible China had sent out a long-distance naval patrol to test how close to Hawaii they could sneak surface combatants with the US battlenet compromised. But Gyrfalcons couldn't fly off destroyers. A Chinese flat-top? Out here?

We'll keep flanking, push another 50 kilometers west. Then we need to get back to VHF range and report in to Hickam, Meany told Flatline.

Minutes later, Meany got a naval radar hit too, about 20 kilometers from the one Flatline had registered! But his AI told him it was *Russian,* a radar type used on their newer corvettes. Whatever naval force was out there, it wasn't just Chinese, and it was strung out over a large distance.

The missiles appeared out of nowhere.

Meany had just visually checked the surrounding sky, run his eyes over his instruments, then returned to working his EW module, when a missile radar warning started screaming in his ears.

The P-99 combat AI flashed a missile proximity warning in his visor, Meany pulled his hands off his throttle and stick, and the combat AI took control of his aircraft with a reaction time he would never have been able to achieve.

The Chinese missile radars had gone active with just 30 seconds to impact. There was no point in radio silence anymore. "Flatline, I have incoming! Evading."

Meany heard panting. "Same … here. Down to 5,000, 4,000. Trophy firing. Hit! I'm hit! Ejecting!"

Meany's mind whirled, even as his vision grayed. His machine reversed its roll, firing decoys into its wake, banking even more tightly as it tried to force the Chinese missile to burn fuel and lose its lock. *Where …? How …?*

His P-99 Widow was no Raptor. It was meant to kill without being seen, attack without needing to defend. Against the agile Chinese PL-15 missile, the odds were against it. But with his AI at the controls, they were *not* zero.

One last neck-wrenching turn, a flash of light behind him, his trophy air defense system firing behind his head—spraying a cone of metal slugs into the path of the incoming missile—and the missile warning alarm stopped. He put his hands back on throttle and stick and brought up his radar, scanning desperately. The Chinese fighters had found him, so he should be able to …

Yes. Two bandits, 40 kilometers out at 20,000 feet. He didn't hesitate. He had two Peregrine missiles, and he launched them as soon as he had a lock. "Fox three, *bastards.*"

He had a choice between clawing for altitude or diving for the sea, and he might have gone for height—win the height, win the fight—except he was now fighting without missiles or guns. Which meant he wasn't fighting.

He firewalled his throttle and put his nose down for the sea. He'd be a blazing infrared target if the enemy were close, but not when they were 40 kilometers out. He needed to get down with the fish.

Soon, he was skimming over the waves at Mach 1.2, so low that when he looked over his shoulder, he could see a white foaming wake behind him as the shockwave from his high-speed exit slammed into the water and kicked foam into the air.

The wake from the shockwave would have been like an arrow pointing straight at his aircraft if there had been someone flying over his position, but to be honest, Meany had a devil-or-deep-blue choice, and he was choosing deep blue.

And it looked like it was working. He lost contact with his missiles pretty quickly, but he also lost contact with the pursuing Gyrfalcons as they were forced defensive. Whether he got a kill or not didn't matter. Flatline was down with the sharks somewhere behind him, and his only mission right now was to make it back into VHF range of Pearl, where he could call in search and rescue. And report that something very bloody weird was happening out in the Pacific, west of Hawaii.

And a few minutes later, he dared to think he'd made it. No more missile warnings, no Gyrfalcon radars reaching out for him with ghostly fingers. No mysterious naval radars on the horizon. He eased back on his throttle, checked his fuel state, looked nervously at the killing sky around him.

It was clear. He set his machine for a slow climb to 10,000 feet—room to maneuver, not so high that distant ship radars could see him.

Could he risk an emergency broadcast on the open Guard radio frequency? It would be like an electronic "kill me" sign in the sky if the Chinese fighters were still pursuing. He hesitated. It was suddenly like he'd imagined the entire encounter. From detecting the Chinese fighters to Flatline ejecting had been what—10, 15 minutes? Had it really happened?

Get your shit together, Meany, he told himself. *There is no one flying your wing right now. You screwed up, and there's a man down in the sea. That happened.*

Thoughts of his own survival evaporated. He brought up his radio interface and switched the radio to the public Guard radio emergency frequency.

"This is 68th Aggressor Squadron aircraft callsign Alpha Foxtrot Six Eight Six Zero Two Four. Mayday for any US naval or air forces in sector Bravo Charlie niner six. Repeat …"

It was hopeless. He was still 100 kilometers from any kind of help. But Meany Papastopolous was not the first aviator in history to curse the huge expanses of the Pacific Ocean. "This is 68th Aggressor Squadron aircraft …"

Aboard LCS-30 USS *Canberra,* an *Independence* class high-speed littoral combat ship, the Combat Information Center was already a hive of activity. In transit from Central Command in the Mediterranean to join the Pacific Fleet, its Captain had ordered the crew to alert status when it lost its link to the US battlenet.

Canberra had become a small ship alone on a big sea. The only thing that reassured the crew was that they were plowing through waves at nearly 40 knots and would be within VHF radio range of Pearl Harbor within four hours.

Canberra had departed the Med fitted for anti-submarine warfare. The interchangeable module in its aft deck could launch Sea Hunter autonomous surface drones with a trailing sonar array, and it carried a Fire Scout MQ-8C uncrewed aerial vehicle that could deploy dipping sonar and airdrop a lightweight Mark 54 torpedo. It could also drop a lifebelt and harness and winch a sailor out of the water if they went overboard.

In the sonar station of *Canberra*'s semi-circular CIC, Sonar Technician (Submarine) Elvis 'Ears' Bell was having trouble concentrating on his task of monitoring their hull-mounted passive sonar arrays. They weren't on active ASW duty, so the task was a formality, even with the ship at alert status. They were moving too fast through the water for him to pick up anything but background noise from rushing water, anyway.

And Ears Bell was still processing the news he'd received on Diego Garcia that his corpsman brother, Calvin, was dead, killed on Calderon Reef. They had no parents; both had passed away in the early 60s. They'd just had each other. And now, he was alone. On Diego Garcia, Navy had offered to fly him home, but Calvin's body hadn't even been returned stateside yet. He'd decided to stay on, wait until they reached Pearl Harbor and then see what was what. Navy would do all the arrangements, but he needed to give them a list of relatives and Calvin's friends. They had power of attorney for each other, so he had to speak to a lawyer, shut down the guy's phone, bank and social media profiles … hell, there were a million details, and he didn't want to have to think about *any* of them.

The rest of *Canberra*'s crew were looking forward to Hawaii. Elvis was dreading it.

"Chief, SARSAT signal detected!" a comms specialist said loudly. "USAF type. I have a position estimate. Uploading."

Elvis looked up at the main tactical screen that curved around the bulkhead in front of them. It showed *Canberra* and the estimated position of ships nearby based on their location broadcasting tracking IDs. It showed a lot less than it usually would since they could only track what they could hear and see, which meant pretty much *nothing* at sea level farther than about 70 kilometers out. A new icon appeared on screen, ahead and northeast of their position, about 50 kilometers away.

SARSAT was a civilian satellite network. A USAF locator beacon using SARSAT meant there was a pilot down in the ocean. Bell looked at the map and did a mental back-of-the-

352

envelope calculation. They were just 40 minutes away, at flank speed. Sure enough, Bell heard the note of the engines under the deck, and the momentum of the ship, change as it swung around to a new heading. It was a triple catamaran type, so it didn't heel over as much as skid into a sharp turn.

The CIC Watch Supervisor, Chief Petty Officer Hiram Goldmann, stood up from his station at the front of the CIC, listening to a command from the bridge on his headset before addressing his watch officers. "All hands, action stations. SAR duty crew, prepare for SAR operations."

Bell was not part of the search and rescue team, but he knew what the order meant. Their Fire Scout helo would be rigged with a rescue harness and then launched as soon as it was ready. It could fly at 115 kilometers per hour, so depending on how fast the crew could get it loaded and ready to launch, it could get from the ship to the downed pilot in half the time *Canberra* would take.

The pilot should have ejected with a self-inflating life raft attached in a canister to their parachute, but that was never a given. If you could call a downed pilot lucky, they were lucky *Canberra* was so close when their beacon went off. It was a big sea, and without satellite, their Fire Scout could only be controlled by line-of-sight VHF. Fifty kilometers was just inside safe flight communication range, assuming nothing was trying to jam it.

But it could be a false alarm. Some idiot might've triggered a SARSAT beacon by accident somehow. They'd soon know.

"Comms, get a long-wave message to Pearl that we are diverting to investigate a SARSAT beacon. Ears," Goldmann said into his headset. "Sun will be going down soon. We may need to loiter if we can't find that pilot straight away. I don't want any Chinese boats trying to ruin our day, clear?"

"Yes, Chief," Bell replied. At last, something to turn his mind to. For the next few hours, he could focus on saving the living rather than grieving over the dead.

Then the comms watch officer raised his hand in the air again. "Aircraft on Guard claiming to be USAF 68th Aggressor, declaring a mayday."

"Put him through to me," Goldmann said.

Bell tensed. SARSAT beacon followed by a USAF pilot declaring a mayday? He'd been in combat before, in the Persian Gulf and in the sea west of Syria. He had a sixth sense now for what was real and what wasn't.

And their situation had just gotten very, very real.

"Unidentified aircraft, this is US warship USS *Canberra*, you are requested to switch frequency to …"

Meany thumped the slit canopy over his head, nearly breaking his knuckles. *Yes!* That ship they had passed on their way out to investigate the mystery signals—he'd forgotten all about it. He flipped his radio immediately to the US Navy encrypted VHF channel and threw his machine into a slow banking turn so that he didn't lose contact with them.

"Six eight Aggressor to US Navy vessel *Canberra*, this is Captain Anaximenes Papastopolous, do you read?" he said.

"Six eight Aggressor, no enemy could make up a name like that, but I am still going to require you to provide your service ID, pilot," the voice that came back said. "And if you don't mind, spell that name for me."

Meany reeled off his service ID and spelled his name. A minute later, the man came back on the radio.

"Captain, this is Chief Petty Officer Hiram Goldmann, CIC watch officer on *Canberra*. What is your emergency?"

"Not mine," Meany said immediately, looking through his log for the position at which Flatline went down. "I have a pilot in the water, position ..." He reeled off some coordinates. "He went in about 16 minutes ago. Can you ...?"

"Captain, we logged a SARSAT beacon around the time you mention. Our vessel is currently proceeding at flank speed for that position. We have dispatched a Fire Scout with air-lift harness, which should be there in ..." Meany heard him shout for an update. "Twelve minutes."

"Oh, thank God," Meany said. "I couldn't stay with him."

"No problem, Captain," the man at the other end said. "We'll find your man."

"No, Chief, you have to listen." Meany calmed himself. "Can you get a message to Pearl Harbor-Hickam?"

"Yes, we can do that. It'll be long-wave burst, but yes."

"Alright, message as follows," Meany said. "68 Aggressor flight attacked 300 kilometers west northwest of Oʻahu by multiple Chinese Gyrfalcon fighters. One aircraft lost. Repeat, Gyrfalcon carrier-based fighters. One aircraft lost. Add. Multiple naval radar signatures logged, including Chinese and Russian radar types, over a 20-kilometer length. Assessment ..."

Assessment what? What could he say with any confidence?

"Assessment, hostile naval force of significant size, including carrier-borne aircraft, approaching Hawaii."

The PLA *Type 095-09* submarine *Taifun* was about 100 kilometers east of Meany Papastopolous at that moment, and about 10,000 feet below him. But rising.

To missile launch depth. She was about to fire the first naval salvo in what historians would call the Battle of the Eastern Pacific.

She sent a burst message via ELF antenna to Huangpu Wenchong. *Type 095-09 is in position and at launch depth. Five-minute-to-launch-sequence queued. All systems green. Current time T minus three. Proceed?*

There was a slight delay this time. A human Captain might have speculated that the message had just triggered a flurry of phone calls between their base and Beijing. But *Taifun* neither speculated nor cared about such things.

The message that came back was brief, but momentous.

Proceed.

Taifun started a five-minute counter. Her human masters could still send a signal any time in the next five minutes to abort the launch. An ELF signal sent from China using quantum enhancement would travel at near the speed of light and reach *Taifun* in milliseconds.

No message came.

Taifun did a last check of the surrounding environment, listening for the slightest telltale sign of an adversary submarine. Then she began her launch sequence.

With no crew compartments or sustainment needs, every square centimeter of *Taifun*'s interior not devoted to propulsion, maneuvering or electronics was taken up by its maglev launch system, missile magazine and automated loading system.

Taifun and the follow-on submarines in the *Type 095-T* class were the real jewels in Lo Pan's Operation Reunion crown. The heavily fortified underground silos along the Chinese coast facing Taiwan were a miracle of engineering in themselves, but fitting the necessary components inside the hull of a *Type 095* submarine, adapting the maglev launcher to run off a pressurized-water nuclear reactor and perfecting the Wing of Fate drone mother ships to launch from beneath the surface of the sea without seriously degrading their glide capabilities had been a herculean effort to rival in Lo Pan's exhortations to his military financiers, "the Chinese Manhattan Project."

Taifun could fire a Tianyi, or "Wing of Fate," mother ship out of its twin diagonal launch tubes at 1.3 times the speed of sound. It speared through the water in a bullet-shaped casing that broke open the second it left the water, allowing the Tianyi to begin the curved glide toward its ingress point at 1.1 times the speed of sound. It reached its target in less than six minutes and started releasing its payload.

Even as the first Tianyi mother ship broke the surface, the second was being loaded onto the rails of the maglev launcher.

Each mother ship carried 20 autonomous killer drones. *Taifun* had six Tianyi mother ships in each magazine, and two magazines. It could launch them at the rate of one every two minutes before it emptied a magazine, and reposition while it loaded the next magazine.

In 12 minutes, the first 120 slaughterbots were outbound to their targets: Joint Base Pearl Harbor Hickam; the AR Satellite Tracking radar and communication complex; the Lualualei Naval Magazine; Fort Shafter Army Base; INDOPACCOM Headquarters at Marine Corps Base Hawaii Camp H. M. Smith; and the largest communication station in the world, Wahiawa Annex.

Dropping down at 1,400 kilometers per hour to just above sea level, the stealthy Tianyi mother ships would give the missile defenses of the US island of Hawaii *two minutes* to detect, track and intercept the incoming attack.

14. The battle of 1135 Wilson Boulevard

The answer to the question of whether James Burroughs's pursuer could run down to the ground floor faster than Burroughs could climb down proved a moot one.

Burroughs hit the bottom of the elevator shaft ladder and found himself facing the ground floor sliding metal doors from the inside. He tried using the iron rod he'd brought down with him, but it just bent. He needed a pry bar. Looking around at the bottom of the elevator shaft, he found he was standing on the elevator itself, which was parked in a recess in the floor. And helpfully, clipped into the top of the elevator was a pry bar.

He pried the doors open a few inches and then, using his legs and bodyweight, pushed the doors open enough to slide himself through.

He fell out onto the floor, the pry bar falling from his hands and sliding across the tiled floor of the former museum gift shop.

It was stopped by a foot.

"Bravo, Mr. Burroughs," a familiar voice said. And immediately, Burroughs knew where he had screwed up.

"I've been contacted," Burroughs said into the telephone.

"By who?" the person at the other end asked.

"Not sure. Someone inside the Communist Party of China. An opposition faction, I think. That's not important. It's the information you've been looking for."

"How so?"

"Details of a military contractor, used in the Raven Rock bombing, and the Chinese intermediary that paid them. I have the data locked away in a cloud account. The contractor was an organization called ComSec."

There was a moment of silence at the other end. "ComSec? I know them. They've been used by DoD, mostly to provide security at black sites where we needed deniability."

"Well, we can link them both to Raven Rock, and to China," Burroughs said. "Though the China link may be a red herring."

"This sort of information can put you at great personal risk, Mr. Burroughs," the voice at the end of the line said. "Who else have you told?"

"You; that's all," Burroughs said. "My source said I should take it right to the top."

"I'm glad you did. We need to meet discreetly. Do you know this address?"

The address rang a bell, but Burroughs couldn't place it. "I feel like I should," he said. "Why?"

"It's the parking garage where the *Washington Post* journalists used to meet their Watergate source, Deep Throat; you know that story?"

Burroughs had been so stupid, so giddy with the intrigue of it all, he had actually laughed. "Sure, I know the story. Why there?"

"It seems to have a certain historical synchronicity, don't you think? Also, it used to be a museum and tourist attraction, but it's been closed five years. A great place to meet, off the books, if you have access. I can set it up so the gates recognize your White House pass. Just wave your pass at the card reader, drive up to the first floor and wait."

So he had.
And someone had tried to shoot him. And now he knew why.

Because the person standing opposite him with a pistol in one hand and their foot on the pry bar was HR Rosenstern. Who had almost certainly hired the man pursuing him.

Burroughs had balked at involving the US president in the clandestine intrigue he'd found himself embroiled in. So when he'd placed the call that his personal Deep Throat source had recommended, he'd given the details of his Chinese dissident contact to Julio and then gone to the next person in the president's food chain, the one person she supposedly should trust above all others.

Her loyal Chief of Staff.

Except he hadn't been at Raven Rock that day, had he? He'd dialed in from a remote location. Burroughs was willing to guess he'd been in the White House West Wing, at the moment someone from inside Raven Rock had placed a call to the person they knew only as The Principal.

Had the call surprised HR? Or had he delighted in the knowledge that he was taking a call about the assassination of the US president from inside the White House?

Looking at the man's face, Burroughs was willing to bet his life it was the latter. Because he was pretty sure he had no life left to bet with.

Burroughs was an academic, not an action hero. Faced with a man in front of him with a suppressed pistol, after running from a man behind him with a suppressed pistol, he simply stood and wiped his hands on his trousers.

"What do you want?" he asked. "You would have killed me some other way if you just wanted to kill me."

Rosenstern's face was half hidden in the light from the street, giving him a suitably crime noir aspect. He leaned back against a wooden museum display case and smiled. "Such a pleasure dealing with a man with some intelligence," he said. "It saves so much unpleasantness. Why don't you tell me why you didn't die in your sleep, or an unfortunate accident?"

Burroughs thought about it. "Because you are 'The Principal,' the one behind Raven Rock, and I told you the data my source gave me is locked away in a cloud account."

"Such a pleasure dealing with a thinker, Mr. Burroughs, I can't tell you. The account details, please. And this is where you say, 'Screw you,' or something worse, and I shoot you in the kneecap, and you tell me anyway. So shall we skip to that part?"

Burroughs had seen enough Hollywood movies to see how the next five minutes—the last five minutes of his life—were going to play out. But he couldn't help himself. It was his life after all, and it would end on his terms.

"Then shoot me," he said. "I have nothing to take to my grave but my loyalty to my country, and you can't take that."

Rosenstern cocked his head, looking at him for a very long moment. "That, Mr. Burroughs, was a very moving little speech. So moving that I will accommodate you."

The gun spat, and Burroughs staggered backward, clutching his chest.

Rosenstern stood over him and put another bullet into him to be sure, but Burroughs was already glassy eyed. It probably wasn't necessary.

HR had never killed anyone before. He had only come to the meeting so that he could be in radio range, an earpiece in his ear, and hear the assassin's interrogation of Burroughs before he killed him. In case he had any questions or wasn't happy with the answers.

But it had gone off the rails for a moment there when Burroughs got away, and you could easily imagine Rosenstern's surprise when the elevator doors had opened and Burroughs had fallen out of them, preceded by a pry bar.

HR always carried a pistol on himself. In fact, the Secret Service insisted on it, along with the training to use it. They didn't insist that it was this particular newly obtained pistol, fitted with a suppressor, but what they didn't know wouldn't hurt them.

He laughed at that thought. A *lot* of what the Secret Service didn't know had already hurt them. At Raven Rock, for example, where they lost nearly 12 agents.

His train of thought was interrupted as the contractor came running into the gift shop from the stairwell, pistol raised. He lowered it again when he saw Burroughs on the ground.

"I nearly shot you," the man said.

HR only thought of him as "the contractor." He didn't need to know the names of anyone his intermediaries hired, and he didn't want to know.

"You should have shot *him*," HR pointed out. "So you will get no fee for your efforts tonight. And I won't tell anyone you screwed up. Deal?"

The contractor looked like he wanted to argue about it. "Did you get the information you wanted?"

"Better than that," Rosenstern told him enigmatically. "You can go now."

"What about him?" the man asked.

"It will be taken care of," Rosenstern assured him. *By someone else—someone more competent.*

The man left with a last look at Burroughs, as though wondering what the hell had just happened. And HR couldn't blame him. He was kind of wondering that himself.

He hadn't gotten the information he wanted. But he'd gotten much more, in a way.

Someone out there had information on the Raven Rock attack that could potentially link him to it. He had hidden his involvement behind Chinese shell company after Chinese shell company to try to lay suspicion on China, but if they dug deep enough …

What HR got that he *hadn't* expected was the knowledge that his enemies did not know as much as they thought they knew. Burroughs had accused HR of being "The Principal." It was a fair guess, but it was wrong. HR was not The Principal, though he did know who was.

It would have been nice to know what their enemies thought they had discovered, but it had just died with Burroughs.

On the other hand, he had just been witness to a beautiful thing. HR was not a monster. He was a *patriot*. What he did, he did for his nation. So HR respected a beating patriotic heart when he saw one. Burroughs had chosen the wrong side of history, but for the right reasons.

You couldn't kneecap a man like that, or have him dragged away to torture. He deserved a quick death.

What he'd locked away in a cloud account somewhere … would hopefully stay locked away. Whatever passwords and validations Burroughs had hidden it behind, the FBI and CyberCom would have trouble cracking, even if they knew where to look. HR knew that from the constant litany of agency excuses across multiple investigations that he had been party to.

"You were a good man, James Burroughs," HR said, out loud.

Maybe the man's soul could hear. And wherever it was, HR trusted that with the benefit of heavenly enlightenment, he would understand that he had died in a good cause, in the *right* cause.

To which Rosenstern was making a small contribution. But he told himself, as he lay his head on his crisp, newly laundered pillow each night, that it was an important one.

In every threat, there was opportunity. Conflict with China was inevitable. You didn't need a predictive AI to tell you that. You also didn't need to be a soothsayer to see that the America that emerged on the other side of that conflict would need to be a different America.

A different America that would need a resolute leader. Hell, it would need an entirely different Constitution.

Rosenstern was just a bit player, but he was a part of something so much bigger than himself: a movement of like minds that would shepherd the nation through the chaos and anarchy of the next few years until, phoenix-like, a new and stronger America rose from the ashes.

President Carliotti felt pale, and she hoped no one noticed it. She had just been pulled out of a party fundraiser at 9 p.m. by the Secret Service and told she was needed at an emergency session of ExCom called by the Chairman of the Joint Chiefs, General Maxwell.

She got on the phone with him as soon as she was able to finish shaking hands and making her excuses on the way to her limo, aka "The Beast." In the back, she raised the privacy screen and called Maxwell. She couldn't help but notice that the limo was not on its way to the White House, as she expected. Unless she was very wrong, her limo was headed for Andrews AFB.

"General, what is happening?" she asked.

"I'm sorry, ma'am," Maxwell said. "But I have just ordered US forces in the Indo-Pacific to DEFCON 1, *Cocked Pistol*. I am recommending the Executive and key members of the Administration be evacuated to a safe facility immediately."

Cocked pistol? The US went to DEFCON 3 when China blockaded Taiwan, DEFCON 2 when US and Chinese forces entered direct conflict. "Has a nuclear weapon been used?" It was their greatest fear ... that the brinkmanship of US and Chinese "limited war" over Taiwan would raise tensions so high, someone on the other side would make a mistake.

"No ma'am," the General said. "But China has just launched an autonomous drone attack on O'ahu—Pearl Harbor. Losses of ships and aircraft are high. Human source intelligence also indicates dozens of major naval combatants have left ports along China's northeast coast. And we have signals intelligence indicating that a Sino-Russian fleet of significant size has departed the Kuril Islands and may be headed for Hawaii."

"*Hawaii?*" she gasped. "That's insanity."

"Ma'am, that is not the reason for my recommendation to evacuate the Executive branch," Maxwell said. "The situation on Taiwan has deteriorated, dramatically. I'm going to put the Director of the National Institute of Allergy and Infectious Diseases on the call. Please bear with me. Uh ... Doctor Lelland, you are on the line with President Carliotti."

A woman came on-screen who looked as pale and shaken as Carliotti felt, even over the video link. In fact, she looked like she had gone without sleep for more than the allowable 72 hours. That was not a good sign. "Madam President, I am sorry to meet you in these circumstances ..." she said.

Also not a good way to start, Carliotti thought. "Madam Director, what do I need to know?"

366

"Ma'am, General Maxwell asked me to keep this short, so please ask questions, and I will try to answer. There has been an outbreak of what is colloquially known as bird flu on Taiwan ..."

"Yes, I was briefed a couple of weeks ago," Carliotti said. "It was flagged as a cause for concern but not alarm, if I recall."

"Yes ma'am. Taiwanese authorities have now isolated the strain of the virus. They have called it H5N1c ... The c is Latin for '*contagious*.'"

"Contagious? Aren't all viruses contagious?" Carliotti asked.

"Bird flu is usually very rare in humans, ma'am; cases of human-to-human transmission are almost unknown. But it also very deadly when it does cross the species barrier: The mortality rate is *50 percent*. This variant, H5N1c, is not only able to infect humans; it demonstrates an ability to pass easily from human to human through either physical or aerosol contact."

Carliotti absorbed the implications. She wasn't able to see why she was in The Beast on the way to Andrews AFB though. "Put General Maxwell back on, will you, Director? And stay ready to answer any questions, if you will."

"Of course, ma'am."

Maxwell appeared on screen again. "That was the *cause* for this alert, Madam President. Let me describe the *effect*."

"Please."

"Two weeks ago, 1 percent of US troops on Taiwan were diagnosed with 'a flu-like virus.' The worst were treated with antivirals. Two died. One week ago, the virus was identified as a variant of H5N1. By then, 3 percent of US personnel on Taiwan were infected ..."

367

"That's what … 1,500 troops?" she asked.

"Yes ma'am," Maxwell told her. "The virus is spreading. Around 600 personnel have since died, most in the last couple of days. Another thousand are in critical care, not expected to live."

"My God." Carliotti felt like her heart was going to stop beating.

"Ma'am, there are now more than 10,000 US personnel diagnosed with H5N1c infection. Our medical facilities are overwhelmed. According to Director Lelland's models, by the end of this week, we will be looking at 5,000 dead and nearly half of all US personnel on Taiwan infected."

"We have to get our troops off Taiwan," Carliotti said instinctively. "We have to pull them out, now!"

"That's not … That's not an option ma'am," Maxwell said. "Uh, Dr. Lelland?"

The specialist came on-screen again. "Madam President, the General described the situation for US personnel. It's worse in the general population, in the big population centers on Taiwan. I have been on the telephone with disease control colleagues in Taipei. Taipei has just declared a total lockdown; all residents confined to their homes. Hualien and Chiayi, where our troops are, the same. The other major Taiwanese cities are expected to follow tonight."

Carliotti still didn't understand. "Then we need to get our troops off that island now! Right?"

"Ma'am, the entire island of Taiwan needs to be a quarantine zone. If we want to have any hope of containing the virus to the island, we need to stop all departures immediately. And that includes our troops."

"We would be condemning at least half of them to death," Carliotti said softly. "25,000 men and women!"

"Yes ma'am," the doctor said. "But the alternative, if we evacuate our people from Taiwan, is that we bring more people with the virus back to the USA, and it will spread quicker."

Carliotti held her breath, thinking fast. "Yes. I can see … Wait, you said 'more people.' You mean it is already here?"

"Ma'am, we haven't picked up any cases in the USA yet, but we haven't started systematic screening, and we feel it is inevitable. General Maxwell tells me that in the last two weeks, more than 360 US personnel have left Taiwan; most traveled by sea either to Japan, the Philippines, Australia or … the USA. Sea travel would carry less risk of transmission. But some traveled by air, several dozen on commercial connecting flights from Japan and the Philippines."

Carliotti frowned. "If someone brought it back, how long before …?"

"If we can stop all traffic in and out of Taiwan, it will buy us some time. But we are still looking at a pandemic of global proportions inside two months. For the US, I'd say we have three months, at the outside, before our hospitals are overwhelmed."

Maxwell came back on. "So you see, Madam President, we're facing the total incapacitation of our force projection capability on Taiwan within a matter of weeks …"

"Alright, we stop all movement into and out of Taiwan …" Carliotti said, but she couldn't bear to finish the thought.

"And we buy ourselves some time," General Maxwell said. "I've already given the necessary orders. All US personnel and citizens are restricted from traveling out of the island. All vessels and aircraft will remain on the island. No more vessels or flights in." He paused. "As for protecting continuity of government at home, ma'am, we have already deployed the

369

National Guard, but we need to move all Federal agencies onto a pandemic footing, and I need you to authorize the evacuation of the Executive and key administration personnel to a government continuity facility."

"Yes, of course," Carliotti mumbled. She felt consternation building inside her, just as she knew it would build in the broader population if her administration raised a pandemic alarm on top of the existing daily beat of war news and internet and satellite outages. And if it became known the US Cabinet had gone into hiding … mass panic would ensue. But as the general pointed out, they'd anticipated the possibility of civil unrest already. The National Guard had been deployed in cities across the US. Was Maxwell overreacting? "But we still have a couple of months before that becomes necessary?"

"No ma'am," Maxwell said. "As Doctor Lelland said, the virus is already here. You are already at risk."

"Wait, are we sure there is no vaccine already developed that will …"

Lelland took that one. "Ma'am, it took a year almost to the day to engineer a vaccine for the 2029 SARS-3 virus, with every developed nation on the planet working on it. With today's technologies, we might be able to do it in half that time—especially as we already know it's possible."

"How do we know that?" Carliotti asked.

"Because China has already done it. Our contacts in the Chinese health system, before they were silenced, told us that a week ago, they started the mass inoculation of all personnel in their Eastern and Northern Military Commands, their police and emergency services. If we could get a sample of their vaccine … but, like I said, all contact between us has been severed now."

The suspicion that had been boiling under Carliotti's skin found voice. "This is a *bioweapon*? Dr. Lelland, you are excused."

"Yes ma'am," the physician said. Carliotti waited until her picture disappeared from the screen. "Are we alone, General?"

"Yes ma'am."

"General, this may give us an opportunity to move our timetable forward."

"I thought the same," he agreed.

"Can we prove the link?"

"Not a chance," Maxwell said. "We know beyond any doubt the COVID-19 virus escaped from a Chinese bioweapon lab, but we were never able to prove that."

Carliotti bit her lip, running through a hundred scenarios. "They'll blame us," she decided. "Say we brought it onto the island. They'll say it's a US bioweapon that escaped."

"Of course," Maxwell agreed.

"Assure me it isn't, General," Carliotti said suddenly.

"Ma'am, if we were going to use a bioweapon on China, don't you think we'd have done the same as China and made damn sure we had a vaccine against it first?"

"I would hope so."

"So, Madam President, can I confirm you approve of the order to evacuate the Executive and the administration personnel necessary to ensure the continuity of orderly government?" He sounded like he was reading words off a page, and in all probability, he was.

"Yes, General," Carliotti said, the tension between mortal danger and opportunity burning a hole in her heart. "I do. I need to get ahold of HR and set a million things in motion, not least deciding what we tell the American people. But before that, tell me about the situation off Hawaii. Because it sounds a lot like I need to rewrite my speech to say we are now at war with both China *and* Russia."

"We're taking steps to quantify and neutralize the autonomous drone threat, ma'am, and to quantify the threat from the Sino-Russian fleet," Maxwell told her. "But there have already been losses. Multiple ships and aircraft destroyed, most on the ground. One AUKUS submarine lost off the Hawaiian coast. Because our ISR capabilities are compromised, we haven't fully located the different enemy naval forces yet. We are flooding what aircraft we still have on Hawaii into the sector as we speak and flying in reinforcements. If the Chinese and Russian fleets are out there, we'll find them."

"We need our satellite network operational again, General. What the *hell* is Space Force doing?" Carliotti said, exasperation finally overwhelming her.

15. The battle of Tiangong

The answer to "What the hell is Space Force doing?" was in part to be found in a hangar at Vandenberg Space Force Base, several hours *before* President Carliotti was asking.

"We are ready here, Colonel," Dan 'Tug' Boatt said into his cell phone. "I just need to know what kind of mission we're talking about. You said combat …"

"Let's talk about it in a minute," Alicia Rodriguez replied. "We just deplaned …"

"Deplaned? Here?" Boatt asked. "Vandenberg?"

"Yeah, here …" Rodriguez said, as she walked through the doors into the ready room of the 615th Combat Operations Squadron Skylon Program, putting her cell phone in her tunic pocket.

"Six One Five Team Skylon, ten-hut!" Boatt said, spinning around.

In the ready room was the team he planned to go into space with. Himself; Captain Sally Hall, his copilot; and their crew chief, Technical Sergeant Caleb Levi, who wouldn't be riding with them, but with the fast turnaround time they had been given, it was on him and his crew that the success of the mission was riding.

"At ease, people," Rodriguez said. "This isn't a snap inspection. As the Colonel will tell you, I'm a little too hands-on for my own good, and I wasn't about to sit in Canaveral for the first operational mission of a 615 Squadron Skylon." Rodriguez was in her late 40s, and she wore her age well. The lines on her face told anyone who studied them she had lived her life, and the wrinkles between her brow told them it hadn't always been easy. But she had a ready smile.

"We have a green light, Colonel?" Tug asked.

"Provisional." She took in the room, looking at Hall and Levi. "Sorry, there's a security clearance question. Can you two officers give us a moment?"

Boatt crossed his arms. "That's not how we work here, Colonel," he told Rodriguez. "People get told what they need to know to execute the mission. The paperwork catches up later. It's called trust."

Rodriguez smiled. "If you vouch for Captain Hall and your chief here, then that's fine by me, Tug," Rodriguez said, reaching out her hand to Levi. "I know Captain Hall. I'm Alicia Rodriguez, Technical Sergeant."

He returned her handshake with a glint in his eye. "Caleb Levi, ma'am."

"I read your file a while back," Rodriguez said. "Six years in the Israeli Air Force, right?"

He was taken a little aback. "Uh, yes ma'am."

"You serve in the IAF during the Golan Heights conflict?" she asked.

"Yes ma'am," he said. "We took a hammering. But we gave as good as we got."

"So I heard. I'm glad to see Boatt has someone with some real combat experience on his team," she said with a wink.

"Alright, we done bonding?" Boatt asked with false gruffness. "What's the mission, ma'am?"

"Orbital assault. So you probably want to get your Marine Captain in here too."

The tension in the room tightened a notch.

"Sorry, ma'am, orbital *assault*?" Boatt did a double take. "What are we assaulting?"

Rodriguez parked her butt on a nearby desk. "You'll get a full briefing so you can start tactical planning, but I'll give you the bare bones." She looked at the other two Space Force personnel. "The target is the Chinese space station, Tiangong."

Rodriguez and the Skylon crew, now including the Marine Captain Alfredo Torda, took the operational briefing via video link from Canaveral, with the small group gathered behind their second Skylon space plane, Mako. The first—Tiger—was on the flight line, being readied. The jet black, needle-nosed spacecraft looked like something from a 1950s comic book, with leading edge canards by the featureless nose, and twin engines mounted on pylons at the rear of the machine. No window or crew door broke the smooth skin of the machine; the only sign that it wasn't a single piece of extruded metal and ceramic was the thin line running in a rounded rectangle underneath its belly, between its tricart landing gear—the payload bay module doors that allowed the Skylon to take into space payloads ranging from directed energy weapons to 17-ton cargoes or, as was the case for the coming mission, a "personnel module," which could facilitate the deployment and recovery of up to six Space Marines and their gear.

The UK, first to launch an operational reusable semiorbital space plane, had pioneered the technologies and tactics needed to put Marines in space. The Space Force Marine Captain sitting beside Rodriguez, Torda, had flown both with the British RAF Space Force and been part of training the fledgling US Space Force Marine Corps.

But neither he, nor any of his men, had executed a live-combat space assault before.

The Lieutenant running the briefing was a young man Rodriguez had talent-spotted among her cyber intelligence team and pushed to the front of the room, despite his introvert nature, because he had an uncanny ability to anticipate what people were going to ask, and what they needed to know, yet kept all that detail in his head rather than dumping it on you before you needed it. If you asked, he had the answers, and if he didn't, he knew where to find them. His name was Sebastien Miles, and because of the name badge on his uniform which just listed his first name as an initial, everyone, including Rodriguez, called him "Smiley."

The maps Space Force presented in its briefings were not like those land forces presented. They showed sectors of space organized like slices of an orange, with rings indicating distance from the surface, atmospheric boundaries, low-earth orbital bands and geostationary orbital altitudes farther out. Smiley was showing an orange slice that placed the Chinese space station, Tiangong, in low earth orbit 360 kilometers above the earth, and showed the trajectory Skylon would pursue from launch to interception. A 12-hour flight from Vandenberg to the edge of space.

"The situation as of …" Smiley was saying, his boyish face looking like he probably didn't need to shave daily. He looked at his watch. "… as of 20 minutes ago, is that 73 US or allied nation military communication, ISR and GPS satellites have deorbited since the first orbital anomaly was detected 28 hours ago. Given the number and frequency with which satellites were deorbiting, hostile action was assumed, but the attack vector took a while to pin down because neither we, nor our allies, were able to detect any radio communication between the usual adversary base stations and Chinese satellites or space forces. There were no anti-satellite missile launches, and we were unable to detect any ground-based electronic or directed energy weapon interference. However …"

He flashed an image on the screen of the Chinese Tiangong space station, with a large module on its long axis highlighted in yellow. "Thermal imaging indicates that shortly after this new module docked with the Tiangong Space Station—the Chinese media call it 'Light of the Heavens'—it began radiating a heat signature consistent in both strength, and periodicity, with the use of a pulsed laser weapon."

"The Chinese are using a high-powered laser to push our satellites out of orbit?" the Marine Captain Torda asked.

"No, there's no directed energy weapon powerful enough to do that at the distances from Tiangong at which our satellites are being deorbited. And the attacks are sometimes taking place on the other side of Earth orbit from Tiangong." He brought up a graphic of a laser shooting light at a panel on a passing satellite. "We believe the new module incorporates sensors and a long-range communication laser that is tracking the position of our satellites and sending interception information to Chinese killer satellites already in orbit. These are intercepting and deorbiting our satellites."

"Seventy-three *so far*?" the copilot, Sally Hall, asked. "How many killer satellites does China have up there?"

"Unknown, but could be anywhere from hundreds to several thousand," Smiley said. "In the last six months, China has been using commercial launch services to put hundreds of small payloads into space. We now believe those payloads included Chinese 'Jisheng Chong'—NATO codename 'Parasite'—anti-satellite weapons, though the Chinese claim they are for 'planetary defense' and intended for use against asteroids and space junk. The Parasite microsat attaches itself to and then physically deorbits adversary satellites so that they burn up in the earth's atmosphere instead of creating debris."

Rodriguez interrupted. "Obviously, there is no point in us launching replacement satellites into this environment until we've dealt with that damn Chinese module."

"So hit it with an SM-3 missile in kinetic kill mode," Torda said. "Kinetic kill means a limited debris field, and your threat is still neutralized."

"There is a complication," Smiley said.

"There always is," Hall said, not quite under her breath.

"A pulsed laser of that strength requires a significant power source. Reliable intelligence from other sources indicates the Chinese module includes a small modular nuclear reactor. A kinetic kill would at best risk compromising the reactor, releasing radioactive debris into low earth orbit, and at worst send the space station and reactor into an unstable orbit, which could result in radioactive debris making planetfall."

"We're assaulting a *nuclear-powered* laser platform?" Torda asked. He turned to Rodriguez. "Ma'am, no Space Force I know of is trained for that."

"What about defenses?" Boatt asked. "You said they are using a high-power communication laser; can it be used offensively? Does Tiangong have other defensive systems?"

"I don't know about the laser, but it has an anti-boarding electrification system," Torda said. "That one, we've trained for."

Rodriguez stood. "The Lieutenant has summed up the mission, and you have already started identifying the challenges. You will fly within assault range of the Chinese space station, you will breach and enter it, and gain control. Having gained control, you will document what you see, destroy the laser targeting system and render Tiangong's docking ports inoperable."

Several hands went up, but Rodriguez waved them down. "You launch in six hours, people. You will break for mission planning and regroup here in two. Lieutenant Miles will be available to facilitate the retrieval of any data or information you need. We have multiple satellite launches at Canaveral, Vandenberg and French Guiana lined up and waiting on the success of this mission. Every moment that laser platform is operational, we are losing more satellites, and more Air Force, Navy and ground forces personnel are dying."

Smiley had anticipated the final question and prepared Rodriguez to answer it. It was Levi who asked it, except he didn't ask a question, he just pointed out a fact. "Ma'am, there are three Chinese astronauts on that space station, last I heard. If we 'render it inoperable' like you say …"

Rodriguez nodded. "That fact was considered when the mission was authorized, Chief."

Eighteen hours later, Liu, Zhu and Chen were still taking turns on watch duty, rotating between resting and monitoring the AI as it continued the task of locating, tracking and ordering the interception of adversary satellites.

The pace of the interceptions had slowed as the number of targets dwindled. Those closest to Tiangong had been dispatched, and only those at long range remained, their destruction only possible when their orbits aligned. Liu reflected that a human could probably manually manage the task now, but their orders were to support the AI—which Liu had already gotten used to calling Tiangong, like the station itself—not take over its job.

Chen pulled herself into the new module, yawning as she came.

"Get some sleep?" Liu asked.

"Maybe 40 minutes," Chen replied. "I was kind of surprised to wake up. Thought the Americans would have blown this station away by now, debris field or no."

"Our adversaries are not that dumb," Liu said. He spoke into the air. "Or powerful. Tiangong, update Taikonaut Chen on hostile activity noted in the last six hours."

"Yes Commander," the AI replied. "In the last six hours, I have noted and reported four directed energy weapon attacks, similar to that which I experienced during my entry into orbit. None of these attacks was of sufficient strength to compromise my heat shell. I have also noted several narrow-beam, high-frequency radio energy attacks, probably intended to disrupt or jam my electronic systems, but these were also not of sufficient strength to compromise any systems. That is all."

"So the main enemy is a helpless frog, sitting at the bottom of the pond, croaking up at us but unable to stop us gobbling up its tadpoles," Chen said.

Liu looked at her with surprise. "That is the most poetic insult I have ever heard from you," he said.

"A little sleep works wonders," Chen said drily. She started looking over the instruments at the auxiliary workstation, which replicated the one Liu was floating at. "Looks just like when I left it," she said, scratching the inside of one leg. "Requesting permission to relieve the Commander."

Liu had been doing overlapping shifts with the other two taikonauts, reluctant to leave the module every time. But he was tired and found himself yawning a few seconds after Chen. *Yes ... a couple of hours' rest would be ...*

"Unknown object approaching on intercept trajectory," the disembodied AI voice said. "Tracking on radar." A collision alarm started sounding throughout the station.

"I knew it was too good to last," Chen muttered.

Liu flipped his flat panel screen to show both the collision detection radar screen and the station's optical-infrared camera feeds. "Tiangong, isolate the object on optical-infrared and put it on screen three at maximum magnification."

His radar screen showed an object closing on the station at a velocity of just 100 kilometers per hour, relative. And it was *slowing*. That told him it was capable of maneuvering, and it was being controlled. His view screen expanded, the AI zooming one of its telescopes until a small dot appeared, just a black ball against the blackness of space. It zoomed closer; the image went fuzzy, and it pulled back again until it was in focus.

Still a long way out. We have time. "Range?" he asked.

"Object is 180 kilometers and decreasing," Tiangong said. "My analysis is that it is manmade and trying to close and match orbit."

"How long until the object is in laser range?" Liu asked.

"If it continues at its current rate of deceleration, it will reach our position and match orbit in approximately 20 minutes," the AI said. "Object will be in laser defense range in 12 minutes. Do you wish to abort Parasite operations and switch to laser defense mode?"

"Yes," Liu said. Zhu appeared at the entrance to the module, alarm in his eyes. He was smart enough to hold his questions. "Tiangong, arm defensive energy field. Contact

Wangchang at the next opportunity and tell them we are about to come under attack and will defend ourselves."

"With what?" Chen asked. "A *communications* laser? And an electrified lattice that can't do much more than deliver a few ergs of microwave energy?"

Liu ignored her. "Taikonaut Zhu, fetch our survival suits immediately. Suit up yourself, and bring two suits here," Liu ordered. The station was equipped with two different types of suits for dealing with the vacuum of space: one for "space walks," or extra-vehicular activities conducted for repairs or maintenance outside the station, and another type for emergencies where there was a risk of compromise to the environment inside the station. These were lighter, and quicker to get into, but not intended for extended use.

"Oh, shit," Chen muttered. "Not good, not good."

"Taikonaut Chen," Liu continued. "Please go to the armory and log out three tasers. Code 18 Alpha 92." The only anti-personnel weapons aboard the station were there for situations where another crew member needed to be subdued. For that eventuality, their "armory" consisted of pepper spray dispensers and tasers, which could only be unlocked from their grapples by a code held by the Tiangong commander.

"You're kidding," Chen said. "You think we're going to be boarded? We're not soldiers. We should surrender, not try to fight."

"The British or Americans may have the ability to board us, but this type of attack has never been attempted, by anyone's space force. If we can't destroy their ship, and if they come aboard, we will fight. And we will win," Liu said.

"Matching orbit; autopilot on. I am hands-free," Boatt said, taking his hands off the Skylon's flight controls. In reality, he was just a meatware backup; the space plane flew itself from takeoff to landing unless there was a system failure requiring human intervention. He could see the Chinese space station with his own eyes now. He finally understood what a million men before him had learned—war was a lifetime of tedium followed by a few minutes of terror.

Piloting a Skylon space plane into orbit was never tedious, but it wasn't terrifying. The terrifying part of the mission was slowly approaching.

"Separation set to 100 meters. Rotating payload bay to egress position," Hall said, punching some buttons on a touch screen. A thruster inside the hull fired, and the Skylon rolled so that its underside was facing the approaching space station. "Starting jamming."

An alarm sounded in the cockpit.

"DEW attack!" Boatt said, looking at the warning screen. The Chinese station had turned its pulsed laser on them. "Orienting nose to 000 relative. Give me hull temperature readings!" As a reusable space plane, Skylon was designed to withstand the extreme temperatures of reentry into the earth's atmosphere—up to 2,000 degrees Celsius, or 3,600 degrees Fahrenheit.

Boatt took manual control of the spacecraft and adjusted its position so that it was still closing on the space station but had its strongest thermal coatings, the ceramic tiles covering its nose, wing-leading edges and engine facings, pointed directly at the Chinese laser module.

"1,000 degrees and climbing," Hall said, with a typical lack of emotion. "One big sparkler they've got on that thing."

A voice from the payload bay broke into the cockpit. "Uh, Colonel, is it getting warm in here, or am I just having hot flashes in my old age?" the Marine Captain, Torda, asked.

"Laser attack from Tiangong," Boatt told him. "Inside operational safety limits." He checked his mission timer. "Five minutes to go time, Captain."

"Understood. Out."

"Temperature stabilizing at … uh, 1,600 degrees," Hall said. "Forward-facing tiles can handle that, but hull won't be able to when we move back into deployment position. If you can put us behind their core module, that laser will be occluded."

"Where I'm headed," Boatt said. He laid a navigation cursor over the module at the opposite end of the space station to the laser and its nuclear reactor. They had planned for several possible ingress points, and this was one of the two preferred points.

"Marine A, flight deck. Your ingress will be through ingress point B—repeat, ingress point B."

"Roger that, flight deck, ingress at B."

"Uh, temp just jumped to 1,800," Hall said, sounding a little less relaxed suddenly. "How long until we're in the shadow?"

Boatt checked the nav readout. "One minute," he said. "It can't shoot directly behind the station; it's not on a goddam telescope arm."

"Going to be one *long* minute," Hall said. "One thousand eight fifty …"

Boatt winced. As he feared, the terror had begun.

"Tiangong, boost power output again," Liu ordered. They were at maximum safe limits for the laser's operation. When their original attack at what was nominally "full power" had no apparent effect, Liu had ordered the laser power output to "maximum safe" operating limits.

"The laser is already firing at maximum safe power output levels," the AI said. "Exceeding these limits can damage internal components." They could actually hear a hum from the front of the module now, one that hadn't been audible during their Parasite operations. It was an added warning to Liu that he was about to push the system to dangerous levels, but what choice did he have? The approaching warship—and he couldn't think of the evil, needle-nosed spacecraft as anything but a warship—was showing no sign their attack was having any impact.

"Target is moving behind us," Chen said, her voice high-pitched.

Liu could see the enemy attack plan in his mind. He would've been doing exactly the same. "Zhu, go aft and strap in. If we fail, they are going to breach using one of the airlocks. Probably the core module. Taikonaut Chen, lock and secure all air lock hatches. Tiangong, override maximum safe limits. Ten-second pulse at full power."

Captain Alfredo Torda and his Space Marine squad had trained in two very different tactics for boarding an enemy space vessel. They called them "the easy way" and "the ugly way." The easy way was for the adversary crew to cooperate with the boarding, allowing Torda and his squad to board via an airlock, without opposition.

For this mission, they weren't even going to seek cooperation. They were going in ugly.

Most of his A squad hadn't been Marine Corps Marines at all; they were experienced airborne soldiers, all of whom had a dozen or more jumps under their belts before they were recruited to Space Force. Torda had made that call early in his own training with the RAF, where he saw that airborne forces already had under their skin a lot of the routines and disciplines they would need for space operations.

Jumping from a moving airplane or jumping into the void of space: They had a lot in common.

The squad was strapped into "standing seats" along the walls of the Skylon's personnel module. They launched already suited up for EVA action, only their helmets and weapons in brackets beside them.

"Stand out!" Torda ordered. In unison, the Space Marines pushed away from their seats, freeing their webbing harnesses, leaving themselves tethered to the bulkhead behind them only by a quick-release buckle. They were combat veterans, all of them. But none had been to war in space.

"Weapons and helmets!" From the rack beside them, each man pulled a low-velocity slug gun. The age of Star Wars laser pistols was not on them yet, and even if it had been, a laser bolt that could cut through a person would also have cut through the hull of the ship it was fired inside, so reality prevailed. Each Marine carried a semi-automatic, recoil-dampened pistol that fired low-velocity bullets. They had to brace to fire them, but they were practiced at that. The slugs had the effect in space that beanbag rounds from a shotgun did on Earth. They would knock the wind out of their target, snap their head back, punch them backward if they weren't braced. But they wouldn't breach the hull of the craft they were fired in.

Probably. The weapons had been tested in space, but never in live combat, either by the British who invented them or the Americans who were about to use them.

They donned their helmets and snapped them into place, then double-checked they had air flowing from the camel pack on their backs. Each man checked the man next to him, and tapped him on the helmet to confirm his oxygen and suit integrity indicators were green.

Torda squeezed the comms button on his wrist. "Flight deck, Marine A. Ready for ramp down," he said.

"Temp falling from one nine," Hall said. "One seven five now …"

"Entering shadow," Boatt told her. "Gimbals on that thing were ridiculous. It was like it really could shoot almost directly behind itself."

"Maybe it was on a telescope arm after all," Hall speculated. "Temp is 1,000 and falling. We're good."

"Rotating payload bay to egress position." He put the spacecraft onto autopilot again and keyed the connection to Torda. "Marine A, I am dropping the ramp; confirm personnel are EVA ready."

"Check gas and guns, people!" Torda yelled. Each Marine was hanging on double hand grips that they could use to propel themselves out of the payload module as soon as it was open to space. They made a last check of their own equipment, then pulled a hand control from their belt that steered their 3P, or Personal Propulsion Pack. Each Marine then looked behind them to ensure they were still tethered to a bulkhead. Like the optical fiber cables that connected a torpedo to a submarine, the gossamer-thin lifeline that went from a Marine's belt to the bulkhead carried data and communication and was strong enough they could use it to haul themselves back to their mother ship if they needed to.

"Sound off for equipment check!" Torda's helmet filled with confirmations as each Marine confirmed the readiness of their equipment and that of the man beside them.

Torda turned so the man next to him could check his gear. He felt like he should say something memorable … the first combat assault by Space Marines in human history? You had to come up with something for that.

"Marine A to flight deck, we are clear for ramp drop. Marines, lean to the ramp!" Each Marine went through their personal launch routine, like swimmers on the blocks at the Olympics. Some rocked back and forth; others just tensed their biceps. One, surname Ruger, nickname 'Rifle,' kissed his biceps and winked at the man next to him.

Then the door to space slid open, and right in front of them was the only remaining space station orbiting the planet.

And they were going to destroy it.

Something memorable? Alright, try this.

"Marine A, cowabunga!" Torda yelled, and he launched himself at the Chinese space station.

The designers of Tiangong had anticipated the very remote possibility that a hostile adversary may one day try to force entry to the station from outside the hull. To make this difficult, they had engineered a superconducting lattice into

388

the anti-debris shield of the station, which could be electrified to radiate microwave energy at a frequency that would broil human flesh without disrupting other systems on the space station.

It was a formidable defense, in the context of its launch year, 2021, and top secret when Tiangong was placed in orbit. But secrets rarely remain secret for long, and the microwave defense system specifications leaked to the US in 2025. Torda and Marine A launched themselves at Tiangong wearing suits made out of penetration-resistant "Faraday fabric," which had the dual advantages that it blocked solar radiation and negated the effects of the Tiangong microwave defenses. Under their suits, they wore lightweight thermo-ballistic armor that would absorb both kinetic and energy weapon impacts.

Their suits were double lined, with a self-sealing coagulant between the two layers that spread and then hardened when exposed to freezing temperatures. Minor rips or tears patched themselves instantly. Larger rips or holes could be patched by applying external patches that bonded chemically with the Faraday material to form airtight seals. Every Marine carried a roll of patch fabric into combat in a webbing pocket.

The six men piloted themselves across the 100 meters of space with the 3P jets and slammed into the hull of Tiangong, clinging on with sub-zero adhesive gloves. One man applied a rope explosive chord to the hull and handed it to the next man, who did the same and handed it along. The third man pulled it downward and then handed it back.

Marine A didn't need to force an airlock to get into Tiangong. They were about to make one.

Tiangong was essentially three base modules joined together to form a T-shape, festooned with solar panels and antennae. The stem of the T was the Core Module, the main command module and living space. The crossbars of the T were formed by the two lab modules, Wentian and Mengtian. At the top and bottom of the T, cargo and crew modules could dock.

The cargo module docking area was currently taken up by the Light of the Heavens module. Which put Marine A and Skylon outside the core module docking port.

On the other side of the port, harnessed to a bulkhead and braced so that he could fire his taser, was Taikonaut Zhu.

"Zhu, they're on the hull," Liu told him. He had watched the boarding party stream out of Skylon with horror, and he could see a couple of the enemy Marines clinging to the outside of the station on an external camera. "I think they're trying to come through the crew module airlock."

No shit, Commander, Zhu thought to himself. He could hear the noise of their landing through the metal of the hull. Then it went quiet. Had the microwave mesh driven them back?

The crew module airlock was a double-doored chamber. The two doors couldn't be opened to space simultaneously, only one at a time. New crew members would dock at the port, pressurize the intervening chamber, then open the outer door and equalize pressure with their crew module. Then one crew member would enter the chamber, close the outer door behind them and open the inner door to gain entry to the station.

Good luck trying that without me tasing your ass, Zhu thought. Over his shoulder, he saw Chen pulling herself through the core module toward him, using one hand to propel herself, the other holding a taser. The air lock hatch behind her went into the Light of the Heavens module, and she closed it tight. Then she closed the hatches to both of the lab modules, Wentian and Mengtian. They weren't able to be locked with a code or anything—that would have been too dangerous for the station's inhabitants—but locking the double hatches would slow down any attacker trying to come through. For a moment, Zhu felt like they had the upper hand.

Then the hull *beside* the docking port air lock began to smoke, and a fire alarm sounded through the station.

The thermal cord the Marines attached to the hull of Tiangong beside its docking port was essentially det cord treated with an anti-freezing agent and impregnated with solid rocket fuel, which contained its own oxidizer.

It had been tested in space on simulated pressurized containers covered with debris shields like Tiangong, and the results had been … conclusive.

Torda and three Marines peeled away to each side of the cord, and the ignition cap was ripped off. The cord burned white hot, but it didn't cut a clean hole in the hull of Tiangong. The debris shield that protected the hull from micrometeor impacts absorbed some of the heat, so the cord burned through the shield unevenly.

It still did its job. Dime-sized holes burned through both the thermal blanket and Tiangong's pressure hull in the rough shape and size of a rectangular dining table.

The air inside the station started jetting into space, then the entire section of the hull beside the docking port blasted outward, taking the dock with it.

And taking Taikonaut Zhu, snapped safety harness trailing behind him.

Chen watched in horror as the entire docking port section of the core module ripped apart, the station's atmosphere flooding through the hole, taking with it anything that wasn't bolted to the inside of the hull, including Zhu.

Chen was farther back, closer to the center of the core module, strapped to a harness and braced because she was preparing to fire her taser.

Which was ripped from her hand as she was jerked forward toward the gaping hole by the rush of air. Her own belt held. In seconds, the atmosphere inside the station was vented, and the indicator in her heads-up display started blinking, warning her she was now living on suit-supplied oxygen. It showed she had 20 minutes of air before she needed to connect to an air supply.

Captain Alfredo Torda had about 50 minutes of air left, but he was less worried about it with Skylon D4 'Tiger' hovering outside. The damage to the Chinese space station had been more extensive than he'd expected, but the debris created was minimal, as most of the docking port was still attached to the core module by bent and buckled metal, and only a few larger pieces of metal—and what looked like one Chinese astronaut—had blasted free.

All of Torda's men were trained to recover floating objects, alive or inert, both cooperative and uncooperative. But they had orders regarding the Tiangong's crew, and risking the mission to save them was not in those orders.

Torda looked inside the hole in the hull and saw another Chinese astronaut inside the core module, farther back. They didn't appear to be armed, but he could take no chances.

"Marine A, prepare to breach. Tango, rear of module." Entering the Chinese station wasn't just a matter of flying through the gap in the hull they'd made. They'd studied video of the inside of the station, even practiced on a mock-up made of conjoined shipping containers. But they were tethered to Skylon with their umbilicals and couldn't move through the ship with them attached. Torda checked all of his people had wound a handful of umbilical cord around their fists and were ready. "And breach!"

They propelled themselves inside, grabbing handholds on the hull. Torda came in last, moving past them one by one as each man unclipped their umbilical and clipped it onto carabiners along Torda's suit arm. When he had them all, he stripped the cable strap off his arm, attaching all six umbilicals, including his own, to a handhold on an inside wall.

Torda could see the Chinese astronaut farther in, like the one spinning through space, was wearing a survival suit. They had no data on how well armored it would be.

"Tango 12 o'clock. Kozinsky, Ruger, neutralize the tango. Van, Souter, clear Wentian. Pulman, Filipou, clear Mengtian." The station interior was too confined for them to use their 3P thrusters. He watched his people pull their weapons from Velcro pads on their suits, position themselves on the hull and propel themselves forward.

Kozinsky and Ruger led the way, launching themselves right at the Chinese astronaut with their pistols held forward.

"Zhu!"

Chen yelled as she saw Zhu fly past the needle-nosed spacecraft that loomed over Tiangong, saw the Americans propel themselves inside the hole in Tiangong's hull and then grab handholds as one of them took the cables they were tethered with and hooked them to the hull.

"Colonel, they are coming inside!" she said, unsure if her radio was even working after the violence of the last couple of minutes.

Looking desperately around her, she saw a clipboard floating past and grabbed it. It would make a poor weapon … but perhaps a shield?

As she looked around again, two of the Americans were flying toward her. Guns pointing at her. *Guns?* They'd voided the atmosphere, so there was little risk firing a weapon inside the vacuum of the space station, but how would they control the recoil?

She got her answer as the two men—she could see they were men as they got closer—grabbed hold of the sides of the module, braced themselves … and *fired*.

Torda saw the Chinese astronaut—a woman by the look of it—hold a clipboard up in front of herself in a desperate attempt at protection. One of the low-velocity rounds slapped it out of her hand and hit her in the shoulder. The other punched her in the chest, pushing her backward without penetrating her suit.

Kozinsky and Ruger were already moving again, launching themselves off the wall. They'd studied the resumes of the Chinese crew and knew that they were pilots first and scientists second, not trained for hand-to-hand combat. But their orders were to take no chances.

Ruger fired again, aiming for the Chinese astronaut's helmet this time. He missed. The recoil of the weapon slowed him down, but Kozinsky had closed the gap and caromed into the woman. She had already been struck twice with rounds that held the punch of a non-lethal shotgun blast, and was unable to resist as Kozinsky put his pistol to the faceplate of her helmet and shot her in the head.

Inside the Light of the Heavens module, Liu watched in horror on the core module external camera as the matte black space plane pulled in behind them, apparently unaffected by their laser defenses. And began to panic even more as it disgorged a squad of what were clearly soldiers, who flew across the gap between the two spacecraft with surprising ease and latched onto the outside of Tiangong, impervious to its microwave shield.

He prepared a mayday and tried to send it. The emergency message would go to any nearby Chinese satellite and from there to China's space command. But it wouldn't send. Were the Americans jamming?

He shouted a warning to Chen and Zhou on the radio, but then, seconds later, the entire station shook, the external vision died, and he switched his attention to the internal view from the core module. The wall by the docking port air hatch was ripped out, gone, and so was Zhu.

He checked the blinking emergency lights on the station's system panel. Atmosphere in the core module: zero. But he still had atmosphere, light and power everywhere else. Internal comms were still up too.

He watched with disbelief as the Americans poured through the hole in the station's hull and, with clinical efficiency, dispatched Chen as well, with two shots to the body then a shot through her faceplate. Liu saw the air jet from her mask as the enemy cast her body aside.

They started moving through the station, slowed only by the air locks and the explosive release of the air inside each module. Soon they would be coming for him.

He had a taser, but what good would that do against such men? He looked at the oxygen level readout on his visor. Seventeen minutes. He threw the taser aside and prepared to power the laser module down. He couldn't shut down the reactor entirely, but he could disconnect the power from the reactor to both the laser module and the rest of the station.

He hit the breaker. The station's interior lighting went out. The darkness might buy him some time. *Think, Haiping—there has to be something you can do!*

Then the lights came back on. He flicked the breaker again, but it made no difference.

"Tiangong, cut power to the lights!" he said.

"Negative, Commander. I need power to initiate the undocking protocol. Sealing the airlock door."

Undocking? Of course! Light of the Heavens could be undocked from Tiangong. The module had its own propulsion. It could escape! For the first time, he was grateful to the AI. The enemy action had happened so fast, he might not have thought of it himself.

"Good work, Tiangong," he said unnecessarily. "Don't seal the airlock door. I will try to make it to the emergency evacuation capsule."

But he heard bolts in the airlock door slam shut in front of him. "Sorry, Colonel," the AI said. "Preservation of the SMR module takes priority over preservation of crew. Undocking sequence initiated."

396

"Override code X Two Zero Three Nine. Cancel undocking sequence!" Liu yelled.

"That code is not valid when SMR integrity is threatened, Colonel." the AI replied.

He floated, stunned. Then propelled himself toward the airlock door. Reaching it, he spun the hatch-locking wheel manually. It didn't respond.

That should be impossible. All airlock doors had a manual unlocking mechanism in case of a systems failure. He spun the wheel again, with the same result. Feeling betrayed, he realized his so-called 'override code' had limits that he hadn't been briefed on.

"Hatch door sealed. Releasing grapples and firing thrusters," Tiangong said. "As per emergency protocol 93d, I will boost the module to a higher orbit for recovery."

Liu hung by one hand from the hull. He felt the clunk of the magnetic docking grapples releasing, then a bump as the module jetted itself away from the main space station.

"Wentian clear!"

"Mengtian clear!"

Torda heard his team declare the rest of the station secure and then approached the airlock to the target laser module.

It was the same design as the others, a round hatch that could be manually or electronically released, with a crawlspace on the other side, leading to a second hatch. It was designed to allow station personnel to pass safely between areas that were pressurized and non-pressurized, but to Torda, each airlock was a potential killing zone. The man inside it, opening the second door, was lying prone, ready to fire as they spun the hatch door and pushed it open, but they first had to ride out the escape of the atmosphere inside, and in that moment, they could be fired on by whoever was on the other side.

He dearly wished he could have just blown each hatch open, like he would have done on earth, thrown a flash-bang grenade through and then followed it in with extreme violence.

That was not an option in space. Especially not when he needed to take the laser module intact, not only for their own health but in order to gain as much intel from it as they could before they abandoned it.

They had voided the atmosphere in the rest of the station now. The only module left was the one they had come for. There was a bump as something big detached itself from the outside of the station.

Probably something we shook loose when we breached, Torda thought.

"I'm on point," he said. "Kozinsky, you're two."

"Roger."

He grabbed a handhold and pulled himself up alongside the airlock hatch. Opening it was a two-step process, for safety, a little like the door on an airliner. There was a lever that had to be raised from the "closed and sealed" to "danger: open" position, so he pulled it up. Then he spun the air lock hatch control. As he did, an alarm started sounding inside the station. He'd heard the same alarm twice already as his people moved into the two lab modules, and he ignored it. Bracing one foot against the bulkhead, he checked his sidearm, looked to see his number two was in position behind him, then heaved the hatch open.

There was nothing on the other side but space—and the slowly receding docking ring and air lock hatch of their target.

Tug Boatt was following the assault on a screen that showed the helmet camera and audio feed from the Marine squad.

It was brutal.

He hadn't been prepared for just how brutal.

As they blasted a door in the side of the core module, atmosphere came jetting out, and with it came anything inside that module that wasn't tied down tight. Boatt saw soft packs, papers, a photograph of a woman in a frame, a laptop, some cables and ties and …

A Chinese astronaut in a lightweight survival suit, arms flailing, screaming soundlessly as he jetted past the Skylon.

"We could try to rescue that guy," Sally Hall said. "If there's time."

"There won't be," Boatt said. Space rescue wasn't like throwing a life buoy overboard. He didn't know how much air the Chinese astronauts had in their lightweight survival suits, but it wouldn't be enough. They'd be recovering a corpse.

"Oh, no …" Hall said, turning away from the video feed as one of Torda's Marines put a pistol to the faceplate of a second astronaut.

Brutal.

Moving through the rest of the station took time, even though their intel was that there were only three astronauts currently on the station. They had no way of knowing who or what had come aboard with the new laser module, so they moved quickly but cautiously.

They had gone with light EVA suits, giving them a one-hour reserve of air. They were supposed to take 15 minutes to breach the station and make it to the module. Fifteen minutes to video record the inside of the module and try to download whatever they could from any terminals inside. For that, they had taken along a Marine who was a cyber specialist. Then 15 minutes to set explosive disabling charges on the docking ports of each module, hook their umbilicals back on, pull themselves out of the station and into the Skylon personnel module.

Each suit had a five-minute emergency oxygen reserve, which they did not expect to use.

"Hold up," Hall said. "I'm seeing movement." She pointed at a video feed from the outside of Skylon, which was trained down the length of the Chinese space station.

Boatt soon saw what she was pointing at. The laser module was *undocking*.

"You think it's going to try to have another shot at us?" Hall asked. They were tethered to the space station by seven high-tensile umbilicals. If they had to reposition, Boatt could cut the umbilicals free explosively, but that would strand the Marines and make recovering them a *lot* more complicated.

He thought furiously. *The Chinese laser can't fire if the module is maneuvering; it would be near impossible. It must be relying on other systems aboard the space station for targeting, processor power, you name it. Right?*

"We can't take the chance," Boatt said. "Marine A, flight deck. The laser module has undocked and is maneuvering …"

"No shit, Colonel," Torda said. "I'm watching it leave."

"We need to keep the station between ourselves and that laser. It's going to take some time before you can egress."

"We have, uh … 36 minutes plus reserve, Captain."

Boatt could see that in the helmet data feed that was running under every Marine's camera. He punched the button to the explosive release that cut the umbilicals free of their spools inside the personnel module. "Roger that, Marine A." Then he put his hands on his joystick and maneuvering thruster controls.

"Ramp up. Closing personnel module door," Hall said. She tapped a couple more icons on the screen in front of her. "Automatic station-keeping mode canceled. The Colonel has the ship."

The Chinese laser module looked like a Pez dispenser as it pulled away, a large round head on a long body. He applied a tiny amount of thrust to keep them in the "shadow" of the space station, where the laser wouldn't have a shot.

But it was moving slowly. So slowly. *The Marines had forty-one minutes, including reserve.* How long until the damn thing was at a range where it couldn't burn a hole in his Skylon?

"Preservation of the SMR module takes priority over preservation of crew."

The cold, hard logic of placing a higher price on the survival of the nuclear-powered laser module than the taikonauts serving on Tiangong couldn't be faulted.

But the human reality couldn't be overlooked either. Zhu cast into space. Chen shot in the face. Himself marooned. Liu's mind was a whirl of emotion, ranging from humiliation at the failure of their mission to rage at their enemy's inhumanity and the duplicity of his own senior officers. Poor Chen; she had suggested surrender, and for a while, Liu had considered it. He knew now it would have been pointless. The Americans would have killed them where they stood. A new thought came to Liu. "Tiangong, can you engage laser defenses while we are moving to a new orbit?"

"Negative, Taikonaut Chen," the AI replied. "The laser can only be deployed when the module is docked."

Damn it. He was going to ask why, but it was irrelevant. He would have liked to take another shot at that space plane. Make them pay for what they did.

Wait. *They* did not know he couldn't fire the laser.

"Tiangong, is our mayday signal still being jammed?"

"Yes, Colonel."

Liu looked at his oxygen supply readout. Seventeen minutes. He twisted his helmet and took it off, cutting off the oxygen feed to preserve it. The Light of the Heavens module had air, but it did not have its own oxygen regeneration system. So he only had the air that was in his suit, plus the air that was in the module itself. He tried to focus and do some math. The interior of the module was about 16 cubic meters, and a person at rest used up about 5 percent of the oxygen in a cubic meter of air per hour. So he had about 20 hours of air.

There were sleeping tablets in a medical pack on his thigh. Sleeping slowed the metabolism and might give him a couple more hours. But the carbon dioxide load in the air at that point would be pretty high, and it might be a wash.

Liu had been told that if the crew escape capsule was not an option, a rescue flight taking off from Wangchang could reach Tiangong *within three hours* in an emergency. But he knew that was only if a rocket was already fueled and waiting on the launch pad. And with every minute that passed, the Tiangong AI was taking him farther and farther into space.

There was no such miracle rocket waiting to rescue the crew of Tiangong. Even preparing such a launch would probably take days, not hours. The "recovery" that

Tiangong's AI talked about was for the module itself, not for any astronaut inside it.

Because of this, there were also suicide pills in his medical pack.

Hall ran the math on the trajectory of the laser module. "It's pushing into a higher orbit," she said, looking at the result on a screen. "I'm guessing it's an automated response, to park it somewhere out of trouble where it can either rejoin Tiangong later or be recovered and returned to Earth."

Boatt thought that over. They hadn't been sent into space to destroy the Chinese space station, or its laser module, because of the debris risk, especially from nuclear fallout. Their mission was to "neutralize" the station's ability to serve as a satellite attack platform, and they'd achieved that. The message to China that followed the operation wouldn't be sent via the media, but it would be clear. *Try to repopulate that space station, and we'll kill the next crew you send up too.*

But they hadn't achieved their mission until they were sure the module couldn't operate on its own. Or redock with the station after they left.

"We can't stay in cover indefinitely," Boatt told Hall. "And we can't let that module escape low earth orbit without knowing if it is still operational."

Hall wasn't slow on the uptake. "You're saying we have to risk a bad case of sunburn."

"Yeah, but maybe we can take precautions," Boatt said. "A bit of psychological sunscreen."

"What do you mean?"

"Kill the radio jammer."

"Chinese space station Tiangong, this is USA Space Force Spacecraft Skylon. Do you read?"

The voice startled Liu. It was loud in the small space inside the Light of the Heavens module.

Should he reply? The US spacecraft was clearly afraid of his laser; he could see it adjusting position as the Light of the Heavens module moved farther and farther from the main body of the space station, hiding in its shadow.

What did he have to lose? He had so little time left, anyway. Perhaps he could keep his bluff going a little longer.

"I read you, US Space Force," he said.

"Haiping, my name is Dan," the voice said. "I am sorry our nations put us in this situation."

He knows my name. Of course, it would not be difficult. The names of each Tiangong crew were a matter of public record—public pride even—though their military responsibilities were not. And they had killed both Zhu and Chen. By a process of bloody elimination, if his body was not on Tiangong, then it must be aboard the Light of the Heavens module.

"I have no desire for social interaction," he told the man. "Please, bring your ship out from behind my space station, so I may admire it."

There was a laugh over the radio. "So you can shoot at us, you mean?"

Good, he thinks the module is still capable of using its laser!

The voice continued. "Haiping, it doesn't have to end like this. We couldn't save the lives of your colleagues, but we can save yours. If you disable your laser and abandon your vessel, we can rescue you. You will be a prisoner, but I am pretty sure our governments will organize a swap of some kind. You'll see your family again."

What do you know of family, monster?

The voice of Tiangong's AI broke in over the speakers near his face. "Mayday message sent."

For what it's worth. Now Wangchang will soon know I have failed, if they don't know already. There is nothing more to live for.

Liu's father and mother might be dead, but the dream they'd kindled in his heart did not die with them. He was a *taikonaut*. He would not die a prisoner.

"I watched your soldiers kill my crew, Officer 'Dan.' So yes, please bring your ship closer to mine. And I will return the favor."

"He got a message away," Hall told Boatt. "Blip on the emissions monitor. I recommend we shut him down again. He isn't going to surrender."

"You're right." Boatt sighed. "Alright, plan B. We maintain orientation, keep our nose and primary heat shields pointed at him. See if he takes the shot."

Torda's voice came over the radio. "Uh, Skylon, just doing a time check. We are at 30 minutes oxygen and falling. Marine A out."

Boatt and Hall looked at each other. "Or ... we could just say Marine A is shit out of luck and wait here until that laser module is out of lethal range," Hall said. "After all, this space plane is irreplaceable, but a single squad of space grunts ..." Boatt shot her a worried look. She started tapping controls. "Just spitballing. Ready to monitor for hotspots."

405

"The US spacecraft is maneuvering," the AI said.

As I knew it would.

"And you can do nothing?" Liu asked.

"No, Colonel," the AI replied. "Not about the US spacecraft. But I can help your situation."

Liu tilted his head. "How so?"

"If you wish, I could evacuate the module's atmosphere. It would be a quicker death than the poison you carry."

Liu actually considered it. One thing first, before he made his decision. "Tiangong, can you locate Mars on an external camera?"

"Yes, Colonel."

"Can you put it on screen, at maximum magnification?"

The screen in front of him flickered, a view down the module being replaced by one of a pale orange disc that looked like someone had taken a small bite out of it.

"What moon is passing between us and Mars?" Liu asked.

"That is Phobos, Colonel."

"And how long until we see Deimos pass?"

"About 20 hours, Colonel. Mars is in retrograde."

Ah. That explains a lot, he thought. One of the most ominous signs for a Chinese emperor, according to the imperial astrologers, was when Mars was positioned in the Xin constellation. This constellation, one of the 28 traditional Chinese star groupings, was similar to Scorpius in Western astronomy and consisted of three stars.

Whenever Mars went into retrograde within the boundaries of the Xin constellation, it was seen as a sign of grave danger for China's rulers. Chinese history records many instances of "Mars Staying at Xin," each with its unique and intriguing consequences.

He stared at the image on the screen for a long time. "Thank you for your offer of a quicker death, Tiangong, but I think I will just sit here and watch the screen for a while."

"Nothing," Hall said. They had drifted out from behind the shadow of the space station, and there was no sign they were being targeted by the Chinese laser.

"Alright," Boatt said, speaking quickly. "Time check: Marine A has 23 minutes of air. The ship is yours. Bring us back to the breach point. Rotate us to recovery position and open the personnel module door." He reached for the radio as Hall snapped into action. "Captain Torda, destroy the station's docking rings, then get your men ready for a 3P transit and capture. We will be in position to receive you in …" He looked at Hall.

She tapped her screen. "Twelve."

"Twelve minutes, Captain."

"Roger and wilco, Colonel," Torda replied. "No hurry. We just found the galley. You want us to bring you guys some noodles?"

16. The battle of the Eastern Pacific

At the moment that Tiangong's laser module was boosting to a higher orbit, Bunny O'Hare was driving Hungyu and his father to the local clinic. They had put Hungyu's father in the last of their protective suits.

The crowd outside the clinic was 100 strong and 10 deep. She helped the old man out of the car as he coughed pink spittle onto his face mask.

"Leave us here," Hungyu told her, looking in despair at the crowd. "This will take a long time."

"I can't just leave," Bunny said. "Maybe we can try another hospital?"

Hungyu shook his head. "They will all be the same. You know that."

He was right. There had been an emergency broadcast playing on a loop on the car radio, telling all citizens of Taiwan to remain in their homes and await further instruction. Only military or emergency services personnel were exempted. The people crowding the entrance to the clinic were apparently beyond caring about a government curfew. There was not a soldier or police officer in sight.

She helped Hungyu sit his father down on the curb, then sat with him. She looked around, taking in the scene. "This is not natural," she decided.

He frowned at her. "What do you mean?"

"People don't usually get this sick this fast. Corona, it took a week. Even SARS-3, it was three days between infection and people getting breathing problems. Our friend Wu was talking about feeling warm one day; the next, he can hardly stand up. Your father?"

"Yesterday. He said he had a headache, started coughing." The old man mumbled something and tried to pick himself off the curb but quickly gave up and sat down again before a bout of coughing wracked his bony frame. Hungyu and he exchanged a few words. "He wants to go home. I told him we need to at least get some medicine." Hungyu stood. "Will you stay with him? I know the nurse here. It might get me in."

Avoiding the crowd at the front door, he walked around the back of the clinic and disappeared.

Bunny moved over and put an arm around the old man. He didn't push her away.

This is wrong, she thought again. *First the slaughterbots, and now this? This is not a flu; it's a weapon. It's a strategy for taking Taiwan down so China's troops can just walk in here unopposed.*

Hungyu's father coughed again, nearly choking from a lack of air by the end of it and heaving air into his lungs like he was breathing treacle. He seemed as though he was going to topple over with fatigue, and Bunny pulled him to her.

This man had saved her life. Risked his life and his livelihood to do it. Sure, hoping to get paid, but she doubted that was all. And she could do nothing for him. She felt completely impotent, and when that feeling began to creep over her, she knew sitting on her ass wouldn't help.

Hungyu came back empty-handed.

"Wouldn't they let you in?" she asked.

"I spoke to the nurse," he said. "They have nothing left. Not even pain killers to reduce the fever. She said it is risky to stay around here; people are going to explode. I should take him home and keep him warm and hydrated. If the fever breaks, he might recover."

"If it doesn't …"

He looked away, not answering. "Why are we not sick? You and I?"

It was a good question. "Well, they pumped me full of antivirals and antibiotics on Penghu Island after you dragged me out of the water, so maybe that helped," she said. "You, I don't know. Healthy lifestyle?"

"I'm an IT nerd," he said. "These last few days are the most exercise I've had in years."

Bunny stood. "I'll drive you two home. Then I'll hitch a ride north. Maybe I can ..."

"Take my car after you drop us off," Hungyu said. "I won't need it. Defense Technology is sending someone to collect me and escort me to a secure facility on Taipei so we can prepare the new code for distribution to the island's commercial drone swarm operators. Maybe they have access to medicines."

A civilian sedan was the least likely to attract fire from the slaughterbots. His offer made sense.

An argument broke out at the entrance to the clinic. "We should go now," he said. "Before someone tries to steal the car."

They got the old man up and back into the car. The trip back to the waterfront was a slow one, with people milling about, some trying to flag them down. Bunny didn't stop. She knew if she picked anyone up, there would be nowhere to take them anyway. She helped settle the old man in a bed at the back of Hungyu's workshop. He wanted to take the protective suit off and got angry at his son, but he was too weak to keep the argument up. He muttered a few times and then slid into a restless sleep.

"Don't take it off," Bunny told Hungyu. "Just because you don't have the virus yet doesn't mean you can't get it."

"I'll come with you to the car," he said, "check there's nothing in the trunk or glove compartment I need."

He took a map, some sunglasses and some fishing gear from the trunk.

"When are the men in black coming for you?" Bunny asked.

"They said today, maybe tomorrow."

"You think they'll take your father with them?"

"If they want my help, they will," he said tiredly.

Bunny put a hand on his arm and gripped it. "Your algorithm is going to work," she told him. "We saw it work."

"Maybe," he said. "But I think it is too late for us. Wait here." He got up and went into his workshop, then came back and handed her a memory chip.

"What's this?"

"All my work," he said, then smiled weakly. "Our work. I hope you never need it."

As Bunny O'Hare drove away from Dongshi, a rescue drone from LCS-30, the USS *Canberra*, was pulling Second Lieutenant Lukas 'Flatline' Fibak out of the ocean 7,000 kilometers east.

Ironically, it wasn't the 77-degree water that posed the greatest risk of hypothermia for Flatline; it was the flight back to *Canberra*, dangling soaking wet and swinging through the air under the Fire Scout MQ-8C uncrewed aerial vehicle, even in the warm air of the Pacific.

When he was finally dropped on the deck of the *Canberra*, he could barely feel his extremities.

But getting him out of the water had to be done as quickly as possible because *Canberra* had received other orders.

PLAN task force believed to be 80 kilometers north of your current position. ISR assets unavailable. Proceed flank speed on bearing zero one five degrees and attempt to map and report on Chinese task force emissions. Maintain safe separation from adversary task force. Avoid detection. Do not advance to contact. If you are attacked, you are authorized to use all means to protect your vessel and withdraw.

The message explained how and why the Aggressor pilot they had just rescued had been shot down. And the knowledge that China had reacted to the US aircraft presence with such hostility put every man and woman in *Canberra*'s CIC on high alert without anyone needing to tell them.

The orders were relayed to the watch officers in the ship's CIC by Officer of the Watch, Lieutenant Daniel 'Dopey' Drysdale. He'd earned his name because of his large, non-aerodynamic ears, but it had also shown in his responses to multiple high-pressure situations, which could best be described as "too little, too late."

Luckily, he was ably supported by Watch Supervisor, Chief Petty Officer Hiram Goldmann, who listened to the orders relayed by Drysdale and then walked around the CIC, translating them to every officer and specialist individually. Goldmann's voice and demeanor were gruff, but he was thorough.

He moved to sonarman Elvis Bell next. "If there *is* a Chinese task force northeast of us, it's going to have submarine pickets, Ears. The Fire Scout is going to be on EW duty; it won't be available for sonar work. So give me confidence."

"I've already got the Sea Hunter running a search pattern 10 kilometers ahead of us," Ears told him. "But our passive arrays aren't worth anything at the speed we are moving, and I can't deploy towed array either." Bell tried not to let his face show his frustration. The passive sonar sensors in *Canberra*'s hull were useless with water thundering over them at near 40 knots, and his Sea Hunter drone also had to move at flank speed to stay ahead of them. It was using onboard active sonar to make sure they weren't surprised by a Chinese boat lying right in their path, but it was just as much a decoy or target as it was a "Hunter," blasting that much energy through the water.

"Skipper will back off the throttle as soon as we pick up Chinese emissions," Goldmann told him. He didn't have a nickname—none that stuck anyway. Ears figured it would be a brave man who tried to pin one on him. "Until then, you do what you can, and if you pick up anything, and I mean anything, you shout it loud, got that?"

"You got it, Chief," Ears said.

Goldmann clapped him on the shoulder. "I know you're thinking about your brother, Bell. I lost a son in Syria. Different war, different enemy, same pain. Let's make the bastards pay in blood."

As Chief Hiram Goldmann slapped Ears Bell's shoulder, Rory O'Donoghue's 'Outlaw' was back in the air. Without satellite coverage of the Pacific, the USAF, Navy and Marines had every single ISR asset in the air combing the seas north, northwest and west of Hawaii for the Sino-Russian task force.

But with almost all of their Indo-Pacific command assets deployed to the Taiwan theater, they were too few, looking for the proverbial needle in a haystack the size of Texas, New Mexico, Missouri, Colorado and Kansas *combined.*

Perhaps not surprisingly, Rory and his copilot 'Uncle' Robert E. Lee had decided that the best way to find a needle in a haystack that big was to blow up the haystack.

While Navy drones and AWACS aircraft probed cautiously, sniffing the electronic air, Outlaw plowed at wavetop height back along the bearing on which it had detected the mysterious "ghost signals" hours earlier. Shortly after takeoff, it had launched its two LongShot air-to-air drones, and Rory had his crew sent them out ahead of Outlaw like the pincers of a Scorpion, their radars up and radiating at full power, clicking like the claws of a scorpion to try to attract the attention of the Chinese carrier fighter defenses he'd been briefed about.

Which might have seemed reckless except for the fact Outlaw had a sting in its tail: a Rapid Dragon pallet of LRASM-ER anti-ship missiles, ready to drop from its ramp.

All Rory needed was a bearing to a target. Nothing more. Was that so much to ask?

Two thousand kilometers south of Rory O'Donoghue's Outlaw, Lieutenant Maylin 'Mushroom' Sun, Pilot Officer, Ao Yin Fighter Squadron, PLA Navy carrier *Fujian*, squirmed in her pod, trying to relieve aching muscles.

Her flight of four CH-7 drones was approaching the air defense identification zone of the Hawaiian island of O'ahu. According to her briefing, the island should already be under attack, their newest weapons, the Tianyi autonomous drones, sweeping across the island at ground level, destroying missile defenses, parked aircraft, radar and communication installations, mechanized infantry vehicles … anything at all that the drones recognized in their onboard database of thousands of US installation and ordnance types.

Mushroom could feel the pride rising in her chest, threatening to turn into hubris. But her nation was about to rerun the Japanese strategy of the surprise attack on Hawaii, and once again, the Americans had been caught unawares.

Their attention was entirely focused on the West, on Taiwan. The bulk of their ships and aircraft and forward-deployed infantry were *7,000* kilometers from the attacking aircraft of *Fujian* right now. And *Fujian* was not alone. *Shandong* was converging on O'ahu from the northwest, in the company of the largest amphibious landing force the world had seen since the Allied powers invaded Okinawa in 1945.

And Hawaii was not the only target. China had spent the years between 2010 and 2038 building the biggest blue water naval fleet on the planet. In 2025, it numbered 420 warships and auxiliaries and had already overtaken the US fleet. By 2038, it numbered 460 ships, including the biggest amphibious fleet of any nation: six amphibious landing helicopter docks equivalent to the US *America* class, which could launch J-31 Gyrfalcons; 14 amphibious transport docks similar to the US *Wasp* or Russian *Ropucha* classes, which could carry main battle tanks and thousands of troops; and more than 140 sea-going landing ships, heavy and medium, each capable of carrying a company of troops, 10 armored fighting vehicles and the materials needed to supply them.

Western analysts, and even PLA Navy pilots like Mushroom Sun, had assumed that China was building up its amphibious fleet to allow it to retake Taiwan or wage war in the South China Sea.

They were very, very wrong.

As Maylin Sun squirmed in her pod and loosened her muscles for the coming engagement, the Sino-Russian amphibious landing force, which had sailed from ports in the Okhotsk Sea at the moment the attack on the US Coalition's cable and satellite communication and ISR assets began, were spreading out across the Pacific like the claws of a dragon.

As *Taifun* began her slaughterbot assault on Hawaii, and as the USS *Fallujah* was en route to the east coast of Taiwan with another 2,000 Marines, who would immediately need to be put under quarantine lockdown, Chinese aircraft, warships and submarines were moving undetected toward US assets across the Pacific.

Their targets were the same as those the Japanese had attacked almost simultaneously nearly a hundred years earlier.

Guam.

The Marshall Islands.

Hawaii.

Luzon.

Midway.

Palau.

And a couple that had not been on the Japanese list, for obvious reasons.

Okinawa Fleet Base Sasebo.

Marine Corps Air Station Iwakuni.

Aggressor Inc.'s deactivation from the USAF Reserves had not lasted long. No sooner had Meany touched down than its Hawaii-based pilots and aircraft were stood up again as the 68th AGRS.

For what that was worth. They were down one P-99 and one F-22. The only other fighter aircraft still based on Hawaii were 20 overdue-for-retirement F-22s of the Air National Guard's 199th Squadron based at Hickam. The other squadron usually flying out of Hawaii, the USAF 19th, had been deployed into the Taiwan theater several weeks before.

The stealthy, nitro-cooled Tianyi mother ships had swept in from the sea at wavetop level, but several were detected by the radar station atop Kaena Point. Patriot and NASAMS missile batteries and microwave and laser defenses were on high alert after the disruption to the US battlenet and knocked down two of *Taifun*'s mother ships.

But they had been fired at such close range that the other four got through.

Once ashore, they started dropping their 20 quadrotor drones in long strings along the Mamala Bay coast west of Pearl Harbor-Hickam. Some of the drones moved inland, headed for defense and communications installations—like the radar atop Kaena Point. The rest headed for Pearl Harbor or Hickam at near street level. Flying just above the traffic on Fort Weaver Road, they hit the Puuloa Range training facility and blew right over it, nonplussed National Guardsmen on the rifle range following the passage of the slaughterbots over the sights of their rifles.

The drones needed no bridge to cross the southern sea entrance into Pearl Harbor. They hit the water by Kapilina Marina on the west bank and went feet dry at Hickam Air Base by the western vehicle pool.

From there, the airfield attack drones fanned out north and east and began their assault, sending tight bursts of cannon fire or anti-armor missiles into parked C-5s, C-17s, C-130s and the Air National Guard F-22s.

The result? There were no longer 20 Air National Guard F-22s at Hickam Airfield. Four aircraft, which had been flying CAP over Hawaii at the time, were all that survived.

The largely Hongjian anti-armor missile-armed drones that were programmed to seek out naval targets headed north up the inlet, past the USS *Nevada* memorial—without attacking it—toward the Pearl Harbor Naval Shipyard.

The shipyard had just been emptied of the ships of the *Fallujah* Amphibious Ready Group, and most of the piers at the shipyard were empty. Like the Japanese strike in 1941, China's goal was not just to sink capital ships; it was also to sow panic, both on Hawaii and the American mainland.

The slaughterbots' anti-armor missiles found the few warships still moored in Pearl Harbor around Ford Island, punching through their lightly armored sides with ease. In minutes, an *Arleigh Burke* destroyer, two *Constellation* class frigates, an *America* class landing helicopter dock and several smaller vessels were burning. The larger targets hit, the drones moved inland on Ford Island, flying between the warehouses and rotary-winged aviation maintenance facilities along Lexington Boulevard and hammering anything resembling a military vehicle or aircraft.

One of the bots paused opposite the Pearl Harbor Aviation Museum, as if considering the value of wasting a missile on its collection of vintage helicopters and delta-winged jets, before swiveling to attack an HMMV tactical vehicle with a TOW missile that was racing across the airfield.

When they ran out of vehicle or parked aircraft targets, they began turning their ordnance on base facilities and the personnel inside and around them: the Navy Exchange, Ford Island Conference Center, the Pacific Warfighting Center,

Fire Station 4, and the multiple depot buildings lining the lochs.

The earth and sky of Pearl Harbor-Hickam started filling with blood, screams, smoke and fire.

Three hundred and fifty Japanese aircraft launched from six aircraft carriers had attacked Pearl Harbor on December 7, 1941. *Taifun* had launched just six Tianyi mother ships, and only four made it ashore, dropping 80 slaughterbots.

The damage was already comparable to that of the 1941 attack, and *Taifun* had only used one of its two magazines.

Taifun was about to launch the second wave of its attack. And this one was loaded with cannon-armed Tianyi drones, whose targets were Hawaii's Marine and Army bases and radio, radar, electricity and cellular networks.

Meany, Touchdown and their pilots were running for their machines with the sound of a civil emergency siren blasting in their ears.

But there were no explosions anywhere near them, no smoke rising, no blood, no screams.

The pilots and aircraft of the 68th AGRS weren't on O'ahu. As military contractors, they weren't given access to facilities at Hickam but instead had been assigned bays and maintenance support at Hilo International Airport on Big Island, which occasionally hosted visiting National Guard aircraft and during the Taiwan surge was a busy refueling point for transport aircraft headed west.

When Meany had returned without Flatline, he had been debriefed and told to get a medical check. He had instead called a meeting of Aggressor Inc. pilots and officers and put the unit on a war footing. The US Indo-Pacific command

419

might still be trying to work out what China was up to in the sea northwest of Hawaii, but Meany was in no doubt. He had been attacked by Chinese short-range fighters that could only have come from an aircraft carrier. A carrier only traveled in the company of multiple missile-carrying warships. He and Flatline had picked up both Chinese and *Russian* radar emissions.

There could be only one conclusion in Meany's mind. Some serious harm was headed for Hawaii.

Aggressor Inc might have left the war over Taiwan, but China had brought it to them anyway.

They were ready, their five aircraft fueled and armed. One P-99 Widow with Meany at the stick, four F-22s under the command of Touchdown Dubois. As the other 68th AGRS aircraft took off from Hilo, Meany tried the Air Battle Management, or ABM, frequency for Hickam. There was no response. He was not plugged into the battlenet—no one was—but he had taken off with the frequencies and call signs for the two AWACS aircraft patrolling at high altitude north and south of Hawaii, and he tried those after he was cleared out of Hilo airspace. There was no response from the AWACS to their north. It was either out of radio range, or something worse.

"Bully Four Zero from Six Eight Aggressor five-plane airborne over Hilo," he said, trying the AWACS to their south, watching Touchdown and her F-22s form up either side of him. "Available for tasking."

The voice that came back was female, young and barely in control of itself. "Six Eight Aggressor, we're sure glad to hear your voice. We've been trying to raise Hickam ABM but …"

"Hickam is down," Meany said, looking over his right shoulder to O'ahu as he climbed. "I'm seeing smoke over

O'ahu, but radar is not showing any aircraft." An attack on Pearl Harbor? Shooting Flatline down was an escalation, but only a small one. An attack on Pearl Harbor—that was a declaration of all-out war. "You got some business for us, Bully?" Meany asked.

The AWACS controller gathered herself at last. "Aggressor 68, we have multiple fast movers converging on O'ahu at 5,000 to 10,000 feet. Bearing one eight five degrees your position ..."

Meany did a double take. That was *south*. Flatline had been shot down in the northwest. "Say again, Bully Four Zero, that was one eight five degrees my position. Confirm?"

"Confirm. Ten-plus fast movers, bearing one eight five, altitude five to 10,000, range one twenty, heading for O'ahu. You are cleared to engage on contact. Your intercept heading is ..."

The AWACS controller began reading off a heading that would put them on a collision course for the incoming fighters. Meany acknowledged the order then changed frequency. "Coming around to intercept heading, Touchdown; you know what to do."

He didn't need to tell Dubois her business.

She lit her tail, and her four F-22s speared out ahead of Meany, fanning out to give themselves fighting room.

"*South*," she said, echoing his own thoughts. "What the hell? Where did they come from?"

"There's only one place they could have come from," he said.

"*Fujian*? That's insane. *Fujian* was tied up in Kiribati just two days ago, covered in tarpaulins, with a hole in her flight deck the size of Michigan Stadium."

"That was two days ago. Before we lost our battlenet. Before our cables were cut. Before Flatline was swatted."

"Swatted *northwest* of Hawaii, not south," Touchdown insisted. "That would mean they not only repaired their flight deck but they ... *oh, hell no.* Contacts, bearing one eight one degrees."

Meany had seen exactly the same thing as Touchdown at exactly the same moment: Chinese fighter radar signatures on his radar warning receiver, exactly where the AWACS said they would be.

"B flight, go low and dark," Touchdown said. "Prepare to engage."

"Leader is heading high," Meany said, pulling his stick back and leaving his stomach down at 20,000 feet.

He didn't have the incoming aircraft on radar anymore, just the ghostly fingers of *their* radars on his RWR. He also had no data link to Touchdown and her flight.

He thought of the four pilots in Touchdown's flight. One was a veteran from Taiwan who'd taken their combat bonus and stayed on Hawaii to spend it. 'Loner' Levey. With her were also two of Aggressor Inc.'s newer recruits, just arrived from Arizona: 'Cyber' Neumann, a former German Air Force pilot, and 'NextGen' Diaz, a Puerto Rican National Guard pilot. Meany had hoped he would have more time to teach them the lessons learned over Taiwan before taking them into action, but time was a luxury no one had anymore.

"Two minutes to AIM-260 medium PK range," Touchdown said. "I'll keep pushing until ... alright, someone thinks they've seen me. Loner, Cyber, break right. NextGen, you are with me."

Up at 40,000 feet now, Meany rolled his machine onto a wing and oriented it back toward the Chinese fighters. He had the 10 incoming fighters on his radar. He also had double the number of missiles in his weapons bay than the six in each of Touchdown's F-22s.

His job wasn't to get into knife-fighting range with the incoming Chinese fighters; his job was to help get Touchdown and her four F-22s there. He listened as she set a trap for the incoming Chinese fighters.

"Touchdown, I have 10 contacts locked and boxed," he told Dubois. She was the closest to the enemy; it was her call as to when he loosed his missiles. "Combat AI is saying either J-15s or CH-7 Chongmings, but my money is on drones."

"Freaking drones. We're ready. Send them, Meany," she replied.

"Six Eight Leader is fox three," he announced, watching with satisfaction as the 10 missiles dropped from his payload bay one by one and streaked toward the horizon. For now, they were being guided by his Widow's onboard radar. Once they got within 30 seconds of their targets, the missiles would illuminate them with their own radars.

And then things would get very interesting for the Chinese pilots.

Mushroom had gotten a radar return off an aircraft to their north, but it had disappeared as quickly as it appeared. She had nothing on her own radar receiver yet, but she knew from experience it was not as sensitive as the American systems she was up against.

They could see her before she saw them, but if she just got a half-decent bearing to her enemy, she knew her long-range PL-15 had a good chance of finding and killing it.

She looked left and right, where her flight of five fighters was spread out across 10 kilometers of sky, just a few thousand feet off the sea. Together with the fighters of *Shandong*, *Fujian* had only one mission: to help win air superiority for China over Hawaii and hold it for 48 hours.

One more hit, come on, she prayed.

Her RWR flickered and faded again. Something right ahead of her. It might have a lock on her, it might not.

One more minute, and I'll have you.

Then her missile radar alert started screaming, and she hauled her machine into a flat, skidding turn, pumping decoys into the air behind and around her. "Scimitar flight, break!" she called out.

Touchdown Dubois ordered her pilots to shut their radars down and stay off their radios as she moved to bracket the incoming Chinese fighters. She had Loner and Cyber out to the north of the Chinese aircraft while she and NextGen stalked south of them.

Radar off, the F-22s' only steer on the Chinese fighters was the emissions from their radars as they snaked through the sky. The Chinese drones were harder for an F-22 to track than a crewed aircraft because the F-22 could hunt a crewed aircraft using its radio energy as a vector anytime the enemy pilots spoke with one another. Chongming pilots were all sitting together on their carrier, hard-wired to each other, giving away nothing. Unless they had their radars up, like now.

She was waiting for Meany to signal that the Chinese were reacting to the little love tap that he had sent their way.

"Contacts are maneuvering, Touchdown," Meany's calm voice announced.

So British. Touchdown smiled. She gripped her flight stick and throttle. It was time to take the gloves off. "B flight, engage!" she called over the radio, and she lit her radar.

Immediately she saw the cluster of Chinese fighters, just 20 kilometers ahead of her and spinning like tops as they desperately tried to avoid Meany's homing missiles.

She locked the five closest aircraft, knowing NextGen would do the same while Loner and Cyber would take those closest to them.

"B Leader is fox three," she said, sending five missiles downrange.

Mushroom had been in combat enough times in the last couple of months that she knew every time the enemy fired on her, he potentially revealed himself, and so she boosted the power to her radar even as she spun her machine on its axis, putting her decoys between her and the incoming missile.

"Watch your flanks, Scimitar pilots!" she said. And sure enough …

As she spun, her radar got a hit on a new contact, lurking northeast of her. The AI read its radar signature and flashed the ID up on her heads-up visor display.

F-22 Raptor.

China had once feared the fifth-gen Raptor, but no more. The American machines were tired, their stealth coatings eroded, their avionics outdated.

Their pilots were often also older and slower.

Missile warnings!

She didn't panic. The enemy ambush was so orthodox, it would be their demise.

The first American missile flashed over her head and buried itself in the sea behind her. Now she was only facing two.

She didn't even have to thumb her missile trigger. Her combat AI did that for her, immediately sending two PL-15 missiles at the American before it firewalled her throttle and hauled her machine into a spiraling climb that would force the incoming missiles to struggle through the air against gravity, losing speed, losing fuel as they maneuvered …

Before she did what no piloted aircraft could do, and flipped her Chongming on its short axis. In less than a second it went from a screaming climb to a supersonic dive, firing decoys into its wake.

As the two American missiles spun out of control into the clouds of chaff and flares behind her, she locked up the American again—desperately maneuvering to avoid her PL-15s—and delivered the coup de grâce.

"NextGen, break break *break*," Touchdown called. She could see him down on the deck and out of energy after dodging the missiles that one of the Chinese fighters had snapped off at him.

Two of her own missiles hit home, taking two Chinese fighters off the board, and she watched with satisfaction as missiles from Loner and Cyber also hit home. In seconds, it had gone from a 5-v-10 fight to 5-v-6.

Then 4-v-6 as NextGen's machine, stuck like a pig in mud, took a missile in the tail and tumbled into the sea a brutal millisecond later.

"Little help here, Meany," Touchdown grunted.

"Fifty kilometers out now," Meany told her. "Fox three by two. I'm missiles dry. Moving to EW mode."

Meany had closed on the furball while the Chinese pilots were occupied, halving the range his missiles would have to fly and also bringing himself within "growler" range of the Chinese drones.

Even as his last two missiles began diving toward an intercept, he changed his radar from dogfighting to electronic warfare mode, which told it to pour all its energy into a narrowly focused cone directed at whatever enemy aircraft he locked up.

This was where the Chinese drones were particularly vulnerable since their carrier-based pilots were flying them using signals bounced from the carrier to an overhead satellite and down again.

Break the signal, and the drone was on its own with no one to tell it what to do. Meany had fought the Chongming before. He knew that if you could cut its pilot link, it would head for the deck and try to bug out of the fight so that it could reestablish contact.

He picked the nearest Chongming, buttoned it up, and hit his trigger. "Six Eight Leader is growler," he announced.

Mushroom cursed as missiles from an unseen enemy to her north suddenly appeared on her RWR, making right for her. She had another enemy contact on her own radar but no way to get a solution on it while she was busy evading the two incoming missiles.

She had lost two of her wingmen. The other flight had also lost two. They had only claimed one F-22.

"Scimitar Three is out," another of her pilots said.

"Kill," said a pilot from the other flight. "Target down."

She dodged the two long-range missiles again, only narrowly this time. She needed height; she needed speed. She set her machine for a full-speed 10-degree climb away from the enemy fighters she could see, hoping to put some separation between her and them so she could come back around and …

Battle link lost … battle link lost …

Dammit! The Americans were jamming. Her machine dived away from the fight, safe for the moment but impotent.

She hammered the pod hatch over her head in rage.

One Chinese fighter pulling away. Four still engaged. They had lost NextGen and Cyber—*both* of the new pilots. "I'm Winchester, boss," Loner told Touchdown. "My two closest targets are withdrawing."

He was right. Two of the Chinese fighters were following the other south again. Had their nerve broken?

She checked her own payload. She had two missiles left. There were still two Chongmings in range, but if she fired on them, she would give away her position, and any survivors would come at her. She'd be Winchester too, out of ordnance. *Engage, Charlene.* Her finger hovered over her missile release button. She should …

Meany took the dilemma away. "Six eight pilots, form on me. The enemy is bugging out," he said.

They're not, she thought to herself. *Not all of them.* The Chinese weren't pushing toward Hawaii anymore, that was true, but two of them were still circling, looking for a fight.

"B Leader, good copy. Loner, form on me. We are RTB," she announced and turned her machine away from the furball as soon as she saw Loner's machine drop into position behind her.

She marked the position of the engagement on her digital map, showing where the two Aggressor pilots had gone in. They might make it back—they *should* make it back—if they'd made it out of their machines and their locator beacons had activated. But it was a big sea, and with Chinese aircraft in the area …

They'd blunted this Chinese attack. But they'd lost *two* more pilots. First Flatline. O'Hare. Now Cyber and NextGen. And she wasn't even counting 'Salt' Carlyle, who'd died at O'Hare's hands in the first days of the conflict. Wasn't he a casualty too?

She looked down at the wide, unforgiving sea and felt like she was fleeing the scene of a crime.

"LongShot One is being painted," Rory's LongShot pilot said. "Chinese air-to-air. Permission to send a Peregrine in ARM mode?"

"Granted," Rory said. At last, their bait had gotten a bite. Their LongShots had been weaving across the ocean north to south in what should have been the path of the incoming task force for what seemed like an eternity, without any reaction.

They couldn't let them stray too far away since they could only guide them with line-of-sight high-frequency radio signals.

But now they had a bearing to a Chinese airborne radar. And all he needed was a bearing and a signal that the LongShot's medium-range Peregrine missiles could lock onto in ARM, or Anti-Radiation Mode.

NATO had a new brevity code for its advanced ARM air-to-air missiles, and Rory was about to hear it used in combat for the first time.

"Fox four," his pilot declared. "And … anti-radiation missiles tracking."

The engagement had a distance and unreality that only uncrewed aircraft combat could bring. It had the tension of a high-stakes chess game, but there was no allied pilot with skin in the game. Yet.

"Twenty kilometers. Missile still tracking. Radar lock on LongShot; ordering evasion … Bringing LongShot Two into play. Fox four from LongShot Two."

"They're going after it," Rory said quietly. There was probably a Chinese missile flying toward their drone even as its Peregrine missile was closing on the Chinese aircraft. It would be a race now to see whose missile hit first.

But Outlaw had *two* missiles in the air, from two vectors.

"Target down," the pilot said with satisfaction as the first Peregrine reported a kill and the second reported it had lost the radar signal it was tracking. "No other signatures; no missile detected our way. LongShots One and Two resuming search pattern …"

"Come on, you aren't going to let us get away with that, are you?" Rory said, urging his enemy on. They had no idea what they had just killed though. It was an aircraft; it was a Chinese fighter radar type. But was it just a drone, like theirs? In which case the Chinese would be more sanguine. Or was it …?

"Naval radar!" he EWO said. "Bearing zero zero eight, right off our nose. One zero five kilometers. Two now! Second contact offset 10 degrees to port ... both PLA Navy types."

"They've locked our LongShots. Missile radar signatures—they're launching on our drones," the pilot said. "Sending them to the deck."

Rory reached for his throat mic. "Uncle, take us up to release altitude. We have a bearing on the Chinese ships. Loadmaster, Captain, ready Rapid Dragon for deployment."

"Good copy, skipper—dropping the ramp, readying pallet."

They weren't dropping inertially guided dumb bombs this time. The Rapid Dragon pallet in the rear of the AC-130 was loaded with 20 LRASM-ER ship-killing missiles, each armed with a 1,000 lb. warhead. The LRASMs Outlaw carried were AI-guided "launch and loiter" versions; all they needed was a bearing to fly down and an estimated range to target. After that, they would just fly until they visually located a target they recognized from the database of adversary ship types Rory's EWO had uploaded into them before takeoff.

If an LRASM hit the boundary of its target area without finding a target, it would double back and start circling until either it found something to kill or it ran out of fuel and fell into the sea.

Rory had a feeling that none of the missiles he was about to airdrop were going to suffer that fate. Shot out of the sky by Chinese air defenses, maybe, but fall harmlessly into the sea with empty fuel tanks? Nah.

"LongShot One is down. Two is still in the fight. You want me to send it back in?"

"Keep it down with the fish," Rory told his pilot. "But send it right at that Chinese task force. Let's see what else shakes loose." He tapped the empty chair in front of him, too keyed up to sit down himself. "Comms, long-wave message to Pearl. Chinese air defense radar types identified. Send them the bearing and range estimate."

Uncle's voice broke in from the cockpit. "Uh, skipper? You want me to break for the deck when we unload, head back to Hickam, or …?"

"Keep shadowing out of missile range, Uncle," Rory said. "I've got a feeling if we headed back to Hawaii, we'd find it's just as hot."

The Taiwan Air Force guards at Taichung Air Base were clad in Mission-Oriented Protective Posture, or MOPP, gear—a heavier version of the protective suits the healthcare workers in Dongshi were wearing.

They were not keen on letting Bunny O'Hare into the base, dressed as she was in T-shirt and torn jeans. But her USAF ID was good enough, so they couldn't really stop her.

She put her ID away and put her borrowed car in gear. "You've had some action here," she observed. Concrete slabs had been hastily erected around the four sides of the guardhouse at the base entrance, and they showed signs of explosive projectile impacts. Two soldiers with MANPADS and one with an RPG stood ready behind berms on either side of the road.

The sergeant at the gate didn't reply directly.

"Did you pass any slaughterbots in the last few kilometers, Lieutenant?" he asked.

432

"No," she replied. "Two back on the highway from the south, but they were letting civilian vehicles pass."

"Unless they have uniforms in them," the sergeant said. "There's still one or two getting through our perimeter every day. They lay low, then come out if they hear or see aircraft or vehicles moving. But all flight operations have been suspended anyway." He handed her a medical face mask. "Ma'am, you have to report to your unit medical officer before you do anything else. Base Commander's orders."

"Thanks, Sergeant," she said, taking the flimsy face covering she knew would do nothing to protect her.

Bunny wasn't going to look for a medical officer. Her unit had already left Taiwan. It had even left the damn theater. Except for the aircraft and ground crew its billionaire owner flew in, if they were still there.

She made straight for the underground hangars the 68th had been flying out of when she'd made her flaming exit from Taichung in the first days of the conflict. There were no aircraft on the flight line—not whole aircraft, anyway. She recognized a tail here, a wing there, a still-smoking fuselage or engine among the similarly obliterated light vehicles, fire and fuel trucks.

There were no aircraft taxiing out or taking off and none landing. The slaughterbots had given Taichung a thorough working-over. She saw a few people in civilian garb over at the public section of the airfield, none walking together, and a couple others walking along the line of hangars, one with a dog, as though he was just out exercising a pet. Except it was most definitely a guard dog and sat on its haunches as Bunny drove past, eyeing her warily, like its master. She almost felt like saluting it. She guessed the civilian garb was cover for base security out prowling for hidden slaughterbots, since a

433

MOPP suit on someone out in the open would just be like a red flag to a slaughterbot bull.

She was glad to see a light on over the side door entrance to the 68th's underground hangar. Could it be they had literally left the light on for her?

Parking outside, she jumped out, walked over and tried the door, and it swung open, unlocked. It led down a long concrete tunnel that opened into the back of the hangar.

"Hello?" she called.

"Down back!" a voice replied.

As she approached the doorway into the hangar, a MOPP suit was thrown out into the corridor at her. "Saw you outside on CCTV, Lieutenant," a voice she recognized said. "Put that on, and you're more than welcome to join us."

She stuck her head around the corner and saw just two 68th AGRS ground crew members: Chief Delray and an aircraft technician, Julie Zak. Both were in MOPP gear already. Even more importantly, the Aggressor Inc. Gulfstream 650ER was in the hangar with them, apparently still intact.

It didn't look like just any private leisure plane. It was jet black, needle nosed, with twin Rolls-Royce turbofans that gave it a cruising speed of Mach 0.85 and a range of more than 13,000 kilometers. The Aggressor Inc. company logo was discreetly stenciled in silver on the tailplane.

Putting on the airtight suit, outer boots and gloves took forever, but she was finally suited up and waddled, as much as walked, into the hangar.

"Well, aren't you a sight for sore eyes, Lieutenant," Delray said. "We'd about given up on you."

"Not me, ma'am," Zak said. "No slaughterbot is going to get Bunny O'Hare. I put $100 on you getting back here."

434

"She did," Delray confirmed. "And I gave her good odds, too. So there's that."

"Anyone else stay?" Bunny asked.

"Well, see, we were four," Delray said, looking disturbed. "Then three, then two. Virus got the others."

"I'm sorry to hear that. I feel like ... Who was it?" Aggressor Inc. was a small, tight unit. She knew all the ground crew technicians.

"Bednar and Mikolas. Their sealed caskets are in the hold. Mr. Aaronson was very particular about leaving no one behind." He saw the stricken look on Bunny's face. "Not your responsibility, ma'am; we all volunteered. When you and Flowmax went down, we thought, well, "least we can do" sort of thing. But I guess there's no chance now Flowmax will turn up." He looked a little awkward, and Bunny felt it too, but the moment passed. They needed to get airborne. Which ...

Bunny turned to look at the Gulfstream. "Fueled, prepped?" she asked.

"Fueled, yes. Won't take more than 30 minutes to prep her, but we're not going anywhere, ma'am," Delray said. "All flight operations are canceled."

"I didn't see any slaughterbots on the way in," Bunny said. "Not close to here, anyway."

"Oh, they're out there. Power down and hide until they hear a jet engine or turbine start up. The minute you start rolling, they fight their way in. You can't even get wheels up before they're all over you." He looked at Zak. "But we don't think that's the reason. They'd be trying to get evac flights out, no matter the risk, if they could."

435

Zak crossed her arms and leaned back against the wall. "We think they've put the whole island into lockdown because of the virus," she said. "No one in, no one out."

"No one except us," Bunny said. "Meany said 68th AGRS got deactivated when it was transferred to Hawaii, and we're private contractors again?"

"Uh, well, things are moving fast. I heard rumors about an attack on Hawaii. 68th AGRS *was* deactivated, but right now, I don't know if it's Aggressor Inc. or USAF Reserve. It's a bit of a gray zone, ma'am."

Hawaii *attacked*? That settled it. "Chief, I *love* gray zones." She pointed at the Gulfstream. "That is a private Aggressor Inc. airplane, not USAF. I plan to fly it out of here."

Delray frowned at her. "Ma'am, I'm pretty sure if we try to break quarantine, if they don't shoot us down, they'll just lock us up soon as we land …"

Bunny shrugged. "Been there, got the tattoos to prove it."

"*And* there's the slaughterbot problem …"

"A problem we can deal with, Chief," she said. "Unless you *want* to stay here, get sick and die."

He looked at Zak. "Well, you put it like that, no. We agreed we'd be happy if we got just one of you back. There's nothing but ghosts here now. Let's get out of here."

Zak nodded enthusiastically. "I vote we try," she said. "My Gulfstream is the fastest bird with the longest legs in the Aggressor Inc. commercial fleet. It'll take us anywhere we want to go, assuming we can get out of here."

"Alright then," Bunny said. She looked around the hangar and saw a semi-autonomous aircraft tug. It must have been the one used to back the aircraft into the hangar so that it was facing back out and ready to move off under its own power.

She got an idea. "I think I see a solution to our slaughterbot problem. You guys prep our ride."

Canberra was not a dedicated stealth platform, but she had a very low observable hull form, her radically angled radar-deflecting trimaran hull rising only about 20 meters above the water. If the mission was to penetrate the Sino-Russian armada's widespread outer pickets, she might just have a chance. If it was to sneak through the next line of overlapping defenses, not a hope in hell.

But skirt the flanks of the enemy fleet, sucking up electronic intelligence? *Canberra* could do that. First though, she had to find that fleet, without finding herself in the middle of it.

"Message from Pearl: possible range and bearing to the Chinese task force," her Comms watch officer said into the unhurried quiet of the darkened CIC. "Pushing it to all stations."

Ears pulled up the data point and plotted it on his tactical map. The intel was not a single point on the map; it was a fanlike range of possibilities. So it was ELINT, not an actual sighting.

It was good enough.

He felt the throb of the engines subside, slid a little forward in his seat as the trimaran decelerated. A running log of orders from the bridge tripped down his screen like a waterfall, and he latched onto the one he was looking for. *Ahead standard.* Their cruising speed was headed below 25 knots.

He sent a signal to his Sea Hunter to dial its own speed back 10 knots, deploy its sonar array and begin a pattern of sprint and drift, to maximize its chances of picking up anything below it.

Canberra wasn't a sub hunter, not really. It was a much-maligned jack of all trades and master of none. A combat ship not built to survive combat. A "surveillance frigate" or "armed fast transport" by any other name. The last ship of the class was commissioned in 2025, and though they were upgraded with several of the sensor and weapons systems being built into the *Constellation* class frigates, no more had been ordered.

Ears didn't listen to the criticism. In his books, *Canberra* was as good a sub hunter as anything their enemy could put to sea. Once he had his Sea Hunter patrol pattern set, he deployed his own towed array sonar and hunkered down.

The problem he was managing was that a towed array was great at hearing what was behind or either side of you. It sucked at hearing anything ahead of you. For that, he had his Sea Hunter, but its own towed array wasn't as sensitive, so *Canberra* had sonar blind spots right in front of it.

And that's where Chinese submarines would be, if they were out there.

This far out in the Pacific, at least, he was only going to be looking for a couple of specific types. That made his AI's job a little easier.

Super quiet diesel-electric boats were a nightmare but unlikely to be part of a blue water task force so far from Chinese ports. More likely would be Type 93 *Shang* or Type 95 *Sui* nuclear-powered attack boats. An old Type 091 *Han* was still possible, but most of those had been retired.

Ears started working the thermocline with his towed array—that boundary in the water between warm and cold that a good submarine captain could play with to hide the noise of his passage. He could control the depth of the array, pulling it up above or dropping it below the thermocline.

But it was a little like fishing where he knew the fish weren't. Their Sea Hunter was 10 miles out in front of them and much more likely to …

Contact.

He raised a hand in the air to attract Goldmann's attention, speaking softly into his microphone so he didn't disturb his own hearing. The readout on his screen was more important than what he was hearing though. "Subsurface contact, designate SS-1, bearing zero two six degrees, estimated range 6 kilometers. Depth …" He checked the thermocline reading. This boat, and he was sure it was a submarine, was below it. "Depth below 150 meters. Propulsion signature …" *Come on, come on.* His AI had a certainty threshold. As more data from the acoustic signature of the contact was collected, the list of possible hits on his screen slowly narrowed itself. Currently, it was showing three possible hits, all Chinese. Then two.

One.

"Contact confirmed as *Lanjin* class, hull number unknown."

"Give me a heading on it, Ears," Goldmann said, suddenly behind his shoulder. "Does it know we're here?"

He needed more data to tell what direction the Chinese boat was moving. Toward them, away from them—the sonar array would be able to measure a number of inputs to arrive at a conclusion, from the intensity of the sound waves to the Doppler effect as they hit the array. But that took time.

His gut didn't. "It's moving past us," Ears decided. "Either it didn't hear us, or it's working in behind us."

The *Lanjin* class was an extra-large uncrewed underwater vehicle that China began deploying in 2029. Like his Sea

439

Hunter, it was made to accompany warships, but under the surface instead of above it. Having a *Lanjin* trying to work its way behind them would be A Bad Thing. The small uncrewed submarines carried four high-speed torpedoes.

But then, having a *Lanjin* anywhere in your neighborhood was A Bad Thing. They never went anywhere alone. Like his Sea Hunter, if there was a *Lanjin* out there, it meant its mother ship was somewhere close too.

And *Canberra* had not seen it.

But had it seen Canberra?

The answer to that question came not from Ears but from the Surface Warfare watch officer. "Surface contact, designating SU-2, bearing one six nine degrees, range 18, speed 23 knots, heading three five nine. IFF check negative."

What? The surface contact was *behind* them! It must have passed right by them while their helo was unloading the downed pilot, but now it had turned and was headed straight toward them. It was not an allied vessel; its Identify Friend Foe transponder wasn't reacting when paged. But it hadn't seen them, or wasn't sure about them, or it surely would have fired.

A general quarters alarm strobe began flashing throughout the ship. It would normally be accompanied by an alarm, but not when they were in contact with a hostile submarine.

Ears thought fast. The submarine was his problem, but the surface contact occupied him more. It must be the *Lanjin*'s mother ship. Kill the mother ship, kill the *Lanjin*, right? If *Canberra* were destroyed, his Sea Hunter would simply shut down and start transmitting a coded mayday, waiting to be picked up by a passing US vessel. The *Lanjin* had to be the same … except it probably surfaced, so it was easier to recover.

440

"Heading on S-1," Ears said as the data fog suddenly cleared. "It's moving back toward SU-2."

"Going back to mama?" Goldmann asked.

"It hasn't heard us," Ears said, with an audible sigh of relief.

"What I was hoping," Goldmann said. He straightened, touching his throat mic. "CIC to bridge, enemy submarine is passing behind and not maneuvering for attack. We are clear to prosecute contact SU-2."

Drysdale was on the bridge with their Captain and Executive Officer. Ears heard them conferring, then he came on the line. "Chief, Drysdale. Do you have a missile solution on contact SU-2?"

"Negative, target is occluded."

Canberra was fitted with the *Constellation* class surface search-and-track radar and long-ranged Norwegian Naval Strike Missile, mounted in a six-cell turret on its foredeck that replaced the original *Independence* class 57 mm gun mounts. But the missiles didn't launch vertically, and the ship's superstructure was blocking a clean launch since the target was behind them.

Ears felt the ship slide into a gentle turn so that it could bring its missiles to bear. Goldmann had moved to his station at the center of the CIC, where he could monitor all the watch stations.

He kept his attention on the *Lanjin* submersible, falling farther behind them. He dropped a pin on a virtual map right in front of it and directed his Sea Hunter to intercept. He heard the Air Warfare officer frantically ordering their Fire Scout to be turned around and armed with a lightweight torpedo in case it was needed too.

"CIC to bridge, we have a missile solution on contact SU-2," Goldmann said as the ship came around.

"Three missiles, staggered volley. Launch," *Canberra*'s Captain ordered.

Goldmann repeated the order to his Surface Warfare watch officer, but that was a formality. The woman had already queued the missiles, input the target coordinates from the fire control radar and armed her system.

The ship shuddered almost imperceptibly as the two near-supersonic missiles cleared their launcher a second apart and streaked south. The missiles dropped down to sea level and, with the target so close, began weaving erratically almost immediately, making themselves harder to hit.

They need not have bothered.

There was a reason the adversary picket destroyer had sailed right past them without detecting *Canberra*, and why it was so incompetent in operating the *Lanjin* submersible that was accompanying it.

The destroyer was not Chinese at all. He (because in the Russian Navy, ships were given masculine pronouns) was the Russian *Udaloy II* class destroyer *Admiral Chabanenko*: a near ruin of a warship that spent most of the 2020s in drydock, awaiting engine repairs that Russia could not afford before a Chinese deal to swap oil for military assistance allowed *Chabanenko* to be repaired and relaunched, with the much-trumpeted capability of deploying in tandem with the new Chinese *Lanjin* submersible, which China loaned to Russia for interoperability trials.

So few actual patrol hours had *Admiral Chabanenko*'s crew that they were still quite inefficient at the operation of its outmoded sensor systems and hopelessly incompetent in the operation of its trailing submersible. Which was little more than a glorified untethered sonar array anyway, since China had not supplied Russia with torpedoes for the *Lanjin*, and Russian engineers had not succeeded in adapting it to fire their Cold War vintage Type 53 torpedoes.

At the moment *Canberra* launched its missiles, half of the crew of the *Admiral Chabanenko* were gathered at the ship's starboard rail to watch the operation to recover and stow the submersible.

They were quite excited since they were only a day's sailing from their objective and soon to be watching the Chinese give the Americans a very bloody nose. *Admiral Chabanenko* was providing the Chinese task force with air defense support, since though it lacked any kind of modern anti-ship or land attack capability, it still had a pretty decent 32-cell Gimlet surface-to-air missile launch system.

Its Tor M-1 air defense system had one drawback though, which was about to be exposed as the three Naval Strike Missiles appeared on its radar screen, just 30 seconds from impact.

It could track multiple targets but could fire only on two at a time.

"Bridge, CIC. Two missiles destroyed in flight, one strike," Goldmann reported to the bridge. They had no eyes on their enemy, but they had a pretty clear radar picture that showed their missile and the target ship merging.

"Launch again, Chief," the Captain ordered. "We need to be sure of a kill. One missile. Comms, message to Pearl: *Canberra* is engaged with enemy task force picket vessel at

443

position ..." He rattled off a longitude and latitude. "Will disengage and withdraw after action."

As he spoke, another missile punched out of the turret forward, and *Canberra* veered southeast, trying to put some distance between itself and the Chinese task force. It had not intended to pass through the outer ring of Chinese ships, and having apparently survived that mistake, its captain didn't want to be around when Chinese aircraft came to find out what the hell had just happened to their Russian picket.

The second missile strike on *Admiral Chabanenko* wasn't needed. He'd taken the first missile in his vertical missile cell compartment, and the armor-piercing warhead of the Naval Strike Missile drove itself deep into the compartment before detonating. Thirty-one of the 32 cells contained live missiles since *Admiral Chabanenko* was prepared to be called on to defend its Chinese comrades at any moment, if needed. The only empty cells were the missiles it had fired to defend itself.

The fourth missile from the *Canberra* hit the stern of the *Admiral Chabanenko*, which was rising out of the water as it went down by the head. Two hundred sailors perished in the first missile strike, another 30 in the second.

Canberra would rescue another 60 before withdrawing. Her Captain was more than a little disconcerted to learn the survivors did not speak a word of Chinese.

As Ears had expected, the Chinese submersible surfaced when it lost contact with its mother ship.

Canberra sank the *Lanjin* XLUUV too, for good measure. With a demountable .50-caliber machine gun.

Even though *Canberra* mistakenly thought she was attacking a Chinese warship bearing down on Hawaii, the

444

incident was to be the first ever deliberate sinking of a Russian warship by a US warship in history.

But only the first. Outlaw's Rapid Dragon drop was about to add fuel to that fire.

Outlaw's electronic warfare officer had only identified Chinese naval radar types before it launched its JASSM-ER loitering missiles toward the Sino-Russian task force.

But out front of the task force, on the naval equivalent of "point duty," was Russia's newest and deadliest frigate, the *Super Gorshkov* class *Admiral Sokolov*. With six ships planned for launch in 2029, Russia's crippled post-Ukraine War economy had meant only one of the *Super Gorshkov* frigates had been completed and commissioned by 2038.

Compromises with its design were also needed so the high prestige project could become a reality. The planned rail gun on the foredeck was replaced with a standard 130 mm cannon from the older *Gorshkov* class. But rather than reuse the decades-old Furke radar system of the *Gorshkov* class, Russia opted for the latest Chinese "Offset" active-passive phased array system. The Offset system moved the active and detectable element of the ship's radar away from the ship, with the active radar mounted on a tethered Chinese Sky Saker H300 autonomous helo that could operate up to 2 kilometers from its host ship, and at altitudes that allowed it to see much farther than a radar mounted on a ship mast. For fifth-generation conventional aircraft and below, it had a track-and-engage range of 500 kilometers. For stealth aircraft, it had a track-and-engage range of 200 kilometers.

The Sky Saker scanned the sky with its radar, and the waves bounced back to the passive array on the *Admiral*

Sokolov. So any enemy aircraft or ship that "saw" its active radar would only be seeing the helo and not the deadly frigate kilometers away. High-speed anti-radiation missiles fired at the Sky Saker had a lower chance of a kill, and even if they did hit and kill the helo, they wouldn't damage the frigate, which could just launch another Sky Saker.

The Offset system allowed *Admiral Sokolov* to see farther and strike first, with much less risk to himself. But the Sky Saker's AESA radar also made him appear Chinese.

Admiral Sokolov was on point, leading the task force, not just because of its superior sensor suite but because it also carried the long-range navalized version of the R-37 Axehead hypersonic surface-to-air missile. *Admiral Sokolov* wasn't in place just to defend the Sino-Russian task force; he was there to take the offensive to the adversary.

The frigate had detected Outlaw's LongShot drones as they pushed in toward the fleet. Its radar was one of the signatures Outlaw had mapped. *Sokolov*'s air warfare officer had alerted the air combat commander aboard the Chinese carrier *Shandong*, who dispatched J-31 fighters to deal with them for the same reason he also left *Fujian* to deal with the Americans *Admiral Sokolov*'s Sky Saker detected moving south out of Hawaii.

He had not wanted to show his hand to the Americans too soon by revealing the frigate's long-range strike capabilities. He was waiting for a juicier target: the American AWACS aircraft they had detected flying north and south of Hawaii, which they would very soon be in range of.

Very soon became *now*. The vertical launch tubes in the foredeck of the *Admiral Sokolov* punched two Axehead missiles into the air, their first-stage boosters ignited, and they streaked away toward the horizon. Inside a minute, they were traveling at Mach 5 and would cover the distance to the already doomed AWACS inside three minutes.

Which was why the AWACS in the north did not answer the page from the Aggressor fighters taking off from Hawaii.

Shandong's J-31s made quick work of Outlaw's first LongShot, and *Admiral Sokolov* was ordered to take down the second.

It was just about to launch on the LongShot when Outlaw's 20 JASSM-ER missiles were detected by the Sky Saker, flying at wavetop height just 20 kilometers from the *Admiral Sokolov*.

A less-capable radar might not have seen them at all.

Admiral Sokolov could track up to 100 air targets at the same time and engage as many targets as it had ready interceptor missiles in its vertical launch tubes.

That number was *12*.

Sokolov had 64 vertical launch cells, but 40 were loaded with Tsirkon cruise missiles for the imminent attack on Oʻahu. Ten cells were loaded with Tsirkon hypersonic anti-ship missiles and the remaining 14 with Axehead interceptor missiles, of which it had already used two.

Which was when the inexperienced air warfare officer aboard *Admiral Sokolov* made a mistake. Just a small one.

He allocated one of his 12 Axehead missiles to Rory's LongShot and the other 11 to the incoming JASSMs. He trusted that the frigates' short-range quad-packed missiles and CIWS autocannons would deal with the rest.

But the JASSM ship killer had been designed specifically to defeat the optical-infrared targeting systems of Russian and Chinese warships.

Fifteen kilometers out from the *Admiral Sokolov*, its Axehead missiles found their targets, destroying 11 JASSMs.

447

Outlaw's second LongShot was knocked down too, but it was a waste of an Axehead since it wasn't a threat to the frigate.

Ten kilometers out from the frigate, *Sokolov*'s short-range interceptors began launching and one by one whittling away at the JASSM swarm. But it took precious time because, in its terminal phase, the JASSMs not only started jinking radically in three dimensions to make interception difficult; they began jamming the Russian interceptors with laser sparklers.

Two kilometers out from the *Admiral Sokolov*, the two 30 mm Shipunov autocannons opened up on the remaining four JASSMs.

They killed only *three*.

The final JASSM made a terminal popup maneuver, rose 100 feet over the top of the *Admiral Sokolov* and plunged right through its deck, penetrating two levels down, where it exploded right inside the vessel's combat nerve center, the CIC. The frigate was still seaworthy, its sensor, hull and propulsion systems uncompromised, but without its CIC, it was suddenly blind and deaf.

The Russian air warfare officer inside the CIC didn't live long enough to reflect on the fact he should probably not have wasted an Axehead missile on Rory's LongShot.

The question was moot. The reality was Russia had lost the use of *two* of its ships to the actions of Outlaw and *Canberra*, and with them, the Sino-Russian fleet lost its long-range air strike capability and *Sokolov*'s inventory of 40 cruise missiles.

And the crew of Outlaw didn't know it.

"LongShot Two down. All signals from the JASSMs lost," Rory's EWO said. "No change in Chinese radar signal distribution."

"Dammit," Rory said. Their second Rapid Dragon combat launch, and their second fail. He'd lost another two LongShot drones too. As a proof of concept, he would not have won the AC-130X–Rapid Dragon combination any fans.

They were down on the deck again, circling over the waves, staying out of detection range of the Sino-Russian fleet but still close enough to pick up its radio and radar emissions so that they could track its progress. They had mapped even more vessels as the enemy fleet approached. "That's 32 now," Rory said despondently. "We achieved *nothing*. Hickam is going to have to send some seriously heavy harm at that fleet if it wants to make a dent." He looked at his map screen, and a feeling of impending doom came over him. They were so *close* to Pearl.

Uncle put his dread into words. "To paraphrase Churchill, Chief, I think the Battle of Taiwan may be over, and the Battle of Hawaii is about to begin."

17. Epilogue

The Egress

Bunny's plan was inspired by the conversations she'd had with Wu and Xu about brooms and pipes attracting a slaughterbot's lethal attention.

As she and Zak affixed the plastic piping to the semi-autonomous aircraft tug—a low six-wheeler with a grapple out front and a big battery at the back—she wondered whether the two special operatives, and the Marine, Cruz, had made it to Chiayi with Jackson. Given what she'd seen of the chaos at the clinic in Dongshi, and on the road north to Taichung, she wasn't giving them much chance.

They finished duct-taping the plastic pipes onto the tug. Bunny stood back and admired their handiwork. "That look to you like an uncrewed ground vehicle armed with twin TOW launchers?" she asked the aircraft technician.

Zak shook her head in the negative but was trying not to verbalize it. "Totally. I would be terrified if I saw that thing trundling toward me, for sure."

"Not sure a slaughterbot can be terrified," Bunny said. "But I appreciate the positivity, Zak."

"That monstrosity is supposed to fool a slaughterbot?" Chief Delray said, walking out from under the Gulfstream, wiping his gloves on a rag on his belt. Working in the MOPP suits had not been easy for any of them, and Bunny would have to take hers off to fit in the pilot's seat. Delray gave the modified tug a bleak look. "We're all gonna die."

"Then I'll take Zak's opinion over yours," Bunny said. "We good to go?"

"Got it rigged for a fast start," Delray said. "Suggest we don't open the outer blast doors until we have the engines powered up though. Slaughterbots seem to have audio sensing, or maybe they pick up on vibrations, I don't know. I just know that as soon as you open the throttles on our girl here, it will get them all riled up."

"Noted," Bunny told him. She turned to Zak. "Can you run the tug remote from inside the cabin?"

"Sure."

She went over the plan with them one last time. It had sounded so much more convincing in her head than it did when she explained it out loud. She could see that in their faces, but they'd already committed to it.

"Once the engines spool up, I'll pull the cables and chocks and let you know I'm aboard," Delray said. He looked at the tug again. "Times like this, I wish God believed in me."

The sound of the Gulfstream engines starting up was deafening inside the confines of the underground steel and concrete hangar. But the hangar was designed for exactly the type of takeoff they were about to attempt—a rolling start from the hangar, up the ramp to the taxiway outside and then a fast departure, potentially under fire.

Designed for jet fighters of course, not commercial jets, but the Gulfstream 650ER was just about the closest a business jet could come to the specifications of a fighter without mounting weapon pylons. No doubt that was why their billionaire owner, Aaronson—a former Swedish fighter pilot himself—enjoyed flying it.

Zak had boarded, and Bunny stripped off her MOPP gear and sat herself in the cockpit, plugging in her headset. The noise from outside increased again as Chief Delray climbed aboard, then decreased as he closed and secured the passenger door. He tapped her on the shoulder and gave an overly cheerful thumbs-up.

Bunny hit the button for the internal intercom. "Alright, Zak, door down, roll the tug."

A moment later, the big blast door at the top of the ramp, which had protected the hangar for the last several weeks, slid into a slit in the ground. Before it was even halfway down, Zak had the remotely operated tug moving at its best pace—a not-so-impressive 20 kilometers per hour—out in front of them.

Bunny let the brakes go and followed it up the ramp, then stopped at ground level, just inside the hangar, engines idling.

The tug headed out across the taxiway, then bumped over some grass as it made a low-speed run for the other side of the airfield. It passed the midpoint of the runway without provoking any reaction.

Delray was still hovering behind her shoulder. "I thought you said the perimeter was thick with slaughterbots?" Bunny asked. She wasn't disappointed the tug was sailing along unimpeded, just surprised.

"Maybe they aren't buying your plastic pipe missile launcher ploy," Delray yelled in her ear.

Then the first slaughterbot appeared. It had been sitting inside the wreck of a C-5 and rose into the air to get a better look at the tug. But it didn't open fire. It started moving closer to the tug, circling around it.

"It's confused," Bunny guessed. "Trying to make a 3D map so it can identify it."

And that was the point at which their great plan went right off the rails. The slaughterbot was supposed to engage the tug, allowing Bunny, Delray and Zak to bring the Gulfstream out of the hangar and power into the sky while it was busy.

452

What happened was that a Taiwan Army sniper across the airfield, who had clearly also been waiting for a slaughterbot to appear, opened up on the drone with a heavy rifle. Bunny couldn't hear the shot over the sound of her engines, but she saw a spark fly off the slaughterbot where it was hit.

It spun, facing the direction from which the shot had come, and began spraying 20 mm cannon fire in that direction. A second, missile-armed slaughterbot appeared from between two buildings and sent a Hongjian missile toward the sniper's firing position.

"Get moving!" Delray prompted. "Now or never."

Then a US MANPAD, fired from somewhere to their left, lanced toward the cannon-firing slaughterbot and knocked it from the sky. The second drone spun its turret, aimed and sent a missile in *that* direction.

Delray was right. *Now or never.*

Bunny eased the throttles forward, the twin Rolls-Royce engines responding smoothly. They started rolling, and she lined up the Gulfstream's nose with the taxiway. It was littered with burned-out vehicles farther down, but that was a problem for later.

Right now, as she shoved the throttles to the wall and the whine of the engines rose to a roar, the question wasn't whether they had enough taxiway ahead of them to take off.

The question was whether they'd be obliterated by a Hongjian missile before they got another 10 yards.

The sudden acceleration sent Delray waddling backward and landed him on his ass in the aisle of the passenger cabin. Zak had shown a little more forethought and buckled herself into her padded leather luxury seat.

The slaughterbot reacted to the sound of the jet engines, started to spin its turret, but then their new friend, the unknown sniper, sent another round at it. This one hit a rotor, which didn't bring the bot down but slowed its rotation. Now it had to decide which target to prioritize, the jet or the sniper.

It chose the sniper.

As the Gulfstream rocketed down the taxiway, the slaughterbot sent another missile toward the sniper's position. Bunny didn't see it hit but uttered a silent prayer of thanks to their guardian angel as she unstuck the nose of the Gulfstream and lifted it over the top of a burned-out fire truck, her wheels clearing it by what could only have been a couple of centimeters.

The Taichung control tower had been destroyed, and the airfield's radar with it, but her departure hadn't gone unnoticed. A voice broke in on the radio, and it wasn't happy.

"This is ROC AF Taichung for unidentified civilian aircraft; you have violated standing orders. If you do not land your aircraft at a nearby airfield immediately, we must order your aircraft to be intercepted by Coalition fighters and destroyed."

Good luck with that, Bunny thought, turning the radio off. *You have no ground radar, no satellite, probably no AWACS, so no way of knowing where I'm headed and no way to coordinate a search.* She climbed out a couple hundred feet, then dropped the Gulfstream down almost to streetlight level over the highway she knew ran from the west coast to the east, through the mountains, to the sea.

I am a ghost, a ninja, and the only thing you are going to see is my shadow …

She got on the plane intercom again. "Ladies and gentlemen, boys and girls, welcome aboard Aggressor Airlines for this flight bound for Hawaii. You will definitely be arrested and quarantined on arrival, so I suggest you make the

454

most of our in-flight facilities. There are beverages in the
kitchen at the rear of the aircraft, and you will find a drinking
straw in the collar of your MOPP suits." She dropped one
wing and hauled the jet into a tight starboard turn between
two mountain peaks, following the winding road. Delray had
been in the process of levering himself to his feet and ended
up spread-eagled over a couch. Bunny continued, "Now,
please sit back and enjoy the flight ..."

The Bird Man

Lin Hungyu watched with doom-filled expectations as the
technicians from Yehliu Ocean World uploaded his *shārèng jīqì*
"slaughterbots" attack algorithm to their drone control
system.

Their small tests using the algorithm to kill Taiwanese
defense industry quadcopters had proven hit and miss, but
they were smaller than the slaughterbots. Taiwan's military
quickly decided there was no time for small-scale tests; they
needed to reclaim their skies and streets to enable them to get
a grip on the epidemic sweeping the island.

The Bird Man's algorithm would either work, or it
wouldn't. And today was the test.

Drone swarms from Taipei parks, usually used for
entertainment displays, had been deployed across the city and
nearby provinces. The tiny LED-emitting drones of Yehliu
Ocean World were usually used to create awe-inspiring ocean
vistas, with sea creatures swimming just above the heads of
the theme park's guests.

If the algorithm worked, they were about to become killer
bees.

The drones were laid out in case after case beside a major Taipei city junction—a known transit point for Tianyi drones moving from the coast into Taipei City proper.

The radio in Hungyu's ear crackled. "Bot sighted; moving toward your position. Estimate five minutes."

Hungyu and the technicians from Yehliu Ocean World were in a multi-story parking garage overlooking the intersection.

"Launch the swarm now," Hungyu told them. He was tense, but not because of any failing of the technicians; they were doing a great job. He was tense and angry all the time these days, ever since his father died, gasping and choking in the corridor of an overcrowded military clinic dug into a hillside in Nantou, before a medic could even see him.

Hungyu wanted to hurt China, and simply stopping its drone attack would not be enough. He wanted to find a way to turn his swarms from a defensive tool to an offensive one. If he could, he would send his swarms at China itself, to the very heart of Beijing, and have them scour clean the streets of that place so that not a single Chinese soldier or politician remained.

And even that would not be enough to slake his appetite for revenge.

"Shouldn't we wait?" a park technician asked. "Until the slaughterbot is in view?"

"No, the swarm will rise and loiter," he told them. "Then it will attack automatically."

They nodded and triggered the swarm launch. From beside the intersection, thousands of tiny bee-sized drones rose into the air, forming a thin cloud that covered nearly a football-field-sized area. Every drone was keeping position with the drones near it, but every drone was also looking out for its "queen bee"—the slaughterbot.

They'd learned not to make the swarm too dense to start with, or the slaughterbot would be reluctant to approach it. The bots were smart. They learned. They would skirt around anything that they didn't easily recognize. If something was unrecognized, it could be *dangerous.*

This slaughterbot did not see the thin cloud of drones. It came down the road and flew itself right under them. Even as it was approaching, the first of the tiny bees spotted it, signaled to the others and flew toward it. Soon it was surrounded by hundreds, then thousands. The slaughterbot disappeared inside the cloud.

Tiny drones came spinning out, the new proximity algorithm forcing them into contact with the drone's rotors. The slaughterbot tried to rise, to get clear of the cloud, but the cloud rose too, and even from the parking garage 200 meters away, Hungyu could hear the grinding, clattering sound of drones and rotors colliding as a veritable rain of tiny drones began falling from the sky.

This one was a missile-armed bot. Hungyu had seen autocannon-armed bots fire wildly into the cloud, trying to drive it away without effect. This one was trying to shake the cloud off by moving quickly up, sideways and down. But after a few minutes, the slaughterbot's rotors took too much damage for it to stay airborne.

It began falling, but before it hit the ground, it detonated, taking out a large number of swarm drones. Not enough to visibly diminish the cloud though. The wreckage of the slaughterbot fell to the road below, and the killer bee swarm rose into the air over the intersection again, waiting for another queen bee to come by.

Hungyu had a PC connected to a wireless node plugged into one of the parking garage's hard-wired internet ports, and he watched as the messages came ticking in from across the region.

Test successful. One destroyed.

Test successful. One destroyed.

Test successful. Two destroyed.

He typed in his own message, confirming the kill.

There was a certain symmetry to their success; he could see that. Using drones to kill drones. With the amount of commercial drone swarms available just on Taiwan, they should be able to overwhelm the slaughterbot invasion within days. And they could begin mass deployment of the solution, overcoming the shortage of ground-to-air MANPAD missiles that had been the military's only real answer to the scourge until now.

It was possible, even probable, that the *shārèng jīqì* would learn and adapt somehow. He had trouble seeing how they could defeat his swarming drones; it was more likely they would just learn to spot and avoid them, but even that would give Taiwan a way to set up longer-term perimeter defenses to keep the slaughterbots out of the main cities.

He might not be able to fight the virus, but he could fight this scourge. He was already thinking ahead, to the next iteration of his algorithm, unable to stay in this moment and enjoy it.

Because his enemy would not stand still, he could not stand still. And would not, until his father had been avenged.

The Hammer

458

Colonel Alicia Rodriguez, 615th Combat Operations Squadron, Space Launch Delta 45, had just delivered her report to the Joint Chiefs on the outcome of the 615th's assault on Tiangong Space Station and was driving home for some long overdue sleep.

She had not shown the Joint Chiefs the combat footage from the Space Marines' helmet cameras since even she found it harrowing. The first manned assault on an enemy facility in space had been brutal, and had shown her that war in space was going to be particularly unforgiving.

And the mission had only been a partial success. The Chinese nuclear-powered laser module had undocked from Tiangong and boosted itself to a new orbit, from where it could be recovered or repurposed. The Skylons had a payload module equipped with a robotic arm for recovering satellites, and one could have been sent up again, but the Tiangong module was too big to fit into the bay. Electronic intel showed the module was in regular communication with China ground stations for several hours after its escape, then communication levels dropped away dramatically, indicating there may have been a Chinese taikonaut on board when it undocked.

The laser module had no escape capsule attached to it, though the Tiangong core module did. The Chinese taikonauts would have had ample time to see the approaching Skylon; they had even tried to engage it with their laser. They could have fled in the escape capsule, abandoned their station and returned to earth.

They didn't. They stayed to fight.

It disturbed Rodriguez … the thought that whoever was in that laser module would only have survived as long as their air lasted. Even though they were enemies, she wouldn't wish

459

that lonely death on anyone. And the soldier in her hoped that one day, China would recover their body and give it the hero's burial it deserved.

She shook herself out of her reverie. She had other problems.

The runway extension at Wake Island was a Space Force enabler, intended to give US and British Skylons an operating base in the Pacific from which to land, rearm, refuel and take off. Skylons needed a long and reinforced runway, nearly double the length of the existing runway at Wake.

But all communication with Wake had been lost immediately after US forces there reported they were under attack by a Chinese amphibious landing force.

Similar reports were coming in from right across the Pacific, and even Hawaii ... *Hawaii* ... was under attack, with a hostile armada of unknown strength approaching. The few recon drones and aircraft Hickam got airborne to try to attack, or even just to quantify the Sino-Russian force, had been driven back or destroyed. And there was another force approaching from the south, which seemed to be based around that damned indestructible Chinese flagship, *Fujian*.

Tug Boatt's Skylon, 'Tiger,' was still making its re-entry, but her second Skylon, 'Mako,' had been prepped with an ISR module and was due for launch any minute, to fill the satellite gap and try to get reconnaissance images and data. The British RAF had also offered one of its Skylons to assist. It would take days, even weeks, for the US and its allies to replace the dozens of satellites China had taken down in its Tiangong offensive, but their Skylons would soon be providing essential imagery of the new Pacific battlefields.

No number of Skylons could fill the gaps in GPS or communications capabilities though. Space Force was about to embark on the most intensive series of satellite launches in its history, but for the next few days, even weeks, the US Coalition would be fighting the Shanghai Pact forces blindfolded, with mouths gagged, ears blocked *and* hands tied behind their backs.

Alicia Rodriguez had dialed into the Joint Chiefs meeting and caught the tail end of a sidebar discussion about tactical nuclear weapon stockpiles in the Pacific. Even the few words she caught gave her chills. Were they worried about them falling into Chinese hands, or were they actively considering *using* them, for example against the enemy fleet west of Hawaii?

To her mind, to do so would be suicidal, no matter how grave the threat to US possessions across the Pacific. In the Shanghai Pact, the US Coalition was not only up against a nuclear-armed China; it was also up against the largest nuclear arsenal in the world, Russia's, not to mention North Korea's new long-range nuclear ballistic missiles.

If there was a silver lining to this nightmare, it was that if sanity prevailed and all powers showed restraint in the face of mutually assured destruction, they might only be facing a conventional Pacific war.

If sanity prevailed. That was an "if" of shifting sands you couldn't build a victory on.

The Empress

Japanese Empress Mitsuko Naishinnō was revered as a god by older generations of Japanese, but in her own mind, she was just a woman in her late 20s, like many others. She listened to J-pop, binged trashy series like the comedy about a teacher who became Prime Minister, and she cried at the

461

Olympics when the Japanese dressage gold medal favorite fell from her horse in her last ever games.

But she was a Japanese woman unlike any other.

For example, when her country bled, she bled. She was holding in her hands a communique summarizing the results of several Chinese attacks on US Air Force and Navy facilities on Okinawa. It named all the known dead and wounded, and she read each name slowly, with veneration.

She handed the communique back to her Head of Imperial Security, Hiroshi Santoshi, with a heavy heart. Santoshi-san had been head of her security detail when she was a teenager, and became Head of Imperial Security when she was made empress. His white beard betrayed his age, and his once strong body was getting weaker by the year, but his mind was still sharp and his counsel fearless, which was what she most needed him for.

"Twenty-three citizens dead, Santoshi-san," she said. "Double that number wounded. This is just the beginning. Are we fools to have sided with the Americans?"

He nodded, but not in agreement. "China is our ancient enemy. Now it is America's too. They will come at us like a tsunami, but with America at our backs, we will not fall."

"Then we need the people to believe," Mitsuko said. "We need an early victory." Mitsuko had been brought up in Tokyo public schools by a father with a desire to modernize the Imperial House. Having walked the streets and malls and frequented the city's cafes as a younger woman, she still had a sense for what the person on the street was thinking and feeling.

War had come, and her people needed hope.

"Shall I ask the Minister of Defense what is possible?" he asked.

"Yes, but wait until we have met our next guest," she said.

"Ah, yes, very wise," Santoshi agreed.

She stood. She had chosen to dress for her next appointment, not in her royal *junihitoe* kimono but in Western clothing. Black shoes. Sheer hose. Matching navy-blue trousers and jacket over a white silk blouse. No makeup, but pearl earrings and a simple string-of-pearls necklace. Like the leader of a powerful modern democracy, not ancient Asian royalty.

Like so much of what she did, it was signaling, and she was sure it would be noticed by their guest.

"How long have we kept him waiting?" she asked, standing by a window and looking out over the gardens.

Santoshi looked at his watch. "Two hours and twenty-eight minutes," he said. "He will have nothing to say that you don't already know. In fact, you probably know more than he, since he has been sitting out there without any telephone all this time."

She smiled, but the smile didn't linger long on her lips. Her guest was the Ambassador of China in Japan.

And he had come to present her with an ultimatum.

The drowning man

With Pearl Harbor-Hickam under slaughterbot attack, Outlaw was diverted to Hilo on Big Island. They were debriefed about their inconclusive attack, given billets and told to grab some food, a shower and some rest. With *Fujian*'s fighters intercepting reinforcements from the US mainland, assets like Outlaw were few and far between in the sector, and they'd be needed again sooner rather than later.

Uncle Lee didn't see Rory slide away, but he noticed he didn't join the rest of the crew for chow in the Hilo mess. He looked for him back at Outlaw, half-expecting he would be there supervising refueling or running a systems check, but he wasn't. His kit bag was gone from the storage space behind the pilot's seat.

Uncle got some coffee, had a shower, had something more to eat, then went to his bunk for a couple hours' rest. Rory's door was closed and locked from inside. Uncle figured Rory was sending a message, and he decided to leave him alone. He lay down on his bunk and was asleep in seconds.

He was woken by his cell buzzing. They were being called back to readiness. He looked at his watch. He'd slept three hours! It felt like three minutes. It was starting to get dark outside.

Rubbing his eyes, he slipped his flight uniform on again. They hadn't been given fresh kit, and he wasn't about to go hunting for it. There might be something in a locker on Outlaw; he couldn't remember. A T-shirt, at least.

Emerging from his bunk room, he went two doors down and saw Rory's door was still closed. He knocked. There was no answer. He tried the door. Locked. But like a bathroom door, it was designed for someone outside to be able to open it without breaking it down, and Uncle reached into his trouser pocket for his multitool. Twisting the lock screw clockwise, he heard it click and pushed the door open.

The smell of urine and alcohol hit him before he even got the light on.

Clothes were strewn on the floor. Rory O'Donoghue was lying on the bed where he'd passed out, piss stain down the leg he had hanging over the bed, one booted foot on the floor. The other, boot half off, on the bed.

464

On the floor was an empty fifth of rum. On the bed next to Rory, an uncapped quart of whisky. Most of the contents had drained out onto the bunk. *So that's why he went back to fetch his kit bag,* Uncle realized.

Uncle stepped around the mess on the floor, girded himself and picked up Rory's leg, swinging it up on the bed. "Hey, Chief, they're calling reveille." He slapped Rory's cheek lightly. Then harder.

Rory stirred, hand to his face like he was brushing away a mosquito. He opened one eye, saw Uncle standing there. Took a breath and closed his eye again. "I am not … combat … I am not combat capable, Lieutenant," he slurred.

"I can smell that, Chief," Uncle told him. "I'm going to report you have diarrhea. They'll have to find another pilot for whatever they want us to do. You get yourself cleaned up."

Rory bent his forearm across his face. "No. Don't understand. You don't … I'm not combat capable, Uncle." He let out a muffled sob. "I'm not *capable*."

"Hey, Chief," Uncle said. "You just need a rest. Clean yourself up. You'll be …"

Rory turned away from him, curling into a ball with his face toward the wall. "No! I can't remember his name!"

Uncle frowned. "What?"

"The guy I killed. The guy … on Kiribati. What was his *name*?"

Uncle sat, put a hand on his shoulder. "I don't remember."

"It was in the news reports. Six kids. It was on the news …"

"I told you not to watch those," Uncle said gently. "No good can come of that."

Rory pushed his hand away. "What was his *name*?!"

Uncle stood, walked to the door and killed the light. He closed the door, blocking out the sound of the sobbing man inside.

As the door closed behind Uncle, Rory curled into a tighter ball, hands over his ears. But he couldn't stop the sound of the child crying.

He peeked over his shoulder at her, then turned back to the wall. She'd hidden when Uncle came in; they did that. But she started crying again the moment he left. She was about six years old, barefoot, black curly hair, wearing only a T-shirt that came down to her knees. She never said anything, just cried and cried, but he knew whose child it was. The name ... he couldn't remember the name of the guy on Kiribati, but it was *his* child. If he could just remember the guy's name, that was the key.

He'd tried an internet search but couldn't find the news report with the name in it. Had he read it, or just heard it on the radio, or seen it on TV? He reached for the bottle he'd been holding when he finally fell asleep, but Uncle must have taken it. No problem; he had another under his pillow. He pulled it out, uncapped it, took a few gulps before curling up again. He knew the child was an apparition, not real, of course not. But someone on that island, they must have cursed him, sent this weeping child to haunt him.

He started moaning to drown out the sound of her crying, took another slug of liquor. It wasn't the first time the children of the dead had visited him. After his last Syrian tour, he'd been haunted by an Arabic boy covered in chalky dust, as if hit by an explosion. He'd appear all times of day or night,

466

but only when Rory was alone. Rory knew if he told anyone—a medic, a shrink—he'd be given a diagnosis and would never fly again.

So he spent as much time as he could with other people—the boy never appeared around other people—and when he was alone, he self-medicated with alcohol and sleeping tablets. Then he'd gotten an idea. The boy must have died in one of Outlaw's attacks; that was obvious. But he knew the USAF wouldn't give him the information he needed; in fact, they'd probably want to know why he was asking.

"I want to get this damn ghost to stop haunting me." *Yeah, not a good idea to say that out loud to anyone.*

So Rory wrote the Red Crescent in Syria, lied about being a researcher looking into civilian casualties from US attacks, and he gave them the dates and places of all Outlaw's missions where civilians could have been hit. He got a reply, and on the list—thankfully not a long one—was a boy. Right age. So he *wasn't* going crazy. The apparition was real; the kid's ghost was real. It took another six months, but he eventually got the boy's name. He asked in a Muslim chat forum if there was a Muslim ritual of atonement and found out there was.

It was called Tawbah, or repentance. So he bought a Muslim prayer mat online and made an act of Tawbah, admitted his part in the death of the boy, named him by name so there would be no question, prayed to Allah for his mercy and forgiveness.

The next day, the boy's ghost was gone. Rory allowed himself to believe the curse had been lifted.

But he'd screwed up again. Different child, but it was the same curse. *The name, what was the man's name?*

The survivors

Commander Gary McDonald, Captain, and Lieutenant Carla Brunelli, Executive Officer, of His Majesty's RAN submarine *HMAS AE1,* had ghosts of their own to exorcise.

The *AE1s* small crew had sealed the uncrewed rear compartments of their stricken boat, and stabilized its backwards slide to oblivion. They still had power, but no propulsion, so McDonald decided to play dead until they were certain the Chinese attack submarine had resumed its patrol.

Then he'd blown ballast, called in a mayday, and been taken under tow by a US Coast Guard cutter.

Not to Pearl Harbor, as he'd expected, but to Hilo, on Big Island. When they got there, they realized why. And saw on the live TV feed from Honolulu, the cost of their defeat at the hands of the Chinese sub.

Because there was no doubt in the minds of the survivors of *AE1,* that it was their quarry that had launched the slaughterbot attack on Hawaii.

While AE1 was being put in dry dock, out of the fight for the foreseeable future, McDonald received a message from RAN Port Kembla regarding their next posting.

Needless to say, he wasn't being given another command. He called Brunelli to his quarters.

"We have our orders," he told her. "Both of us."

"Return home for a quick court martial and then a dishonorable discharge?" she guessed, sitting on his bed.

"Worse," he said. "We're being joined to a British boat."

"British?" she said, disbelievingly. "Which…"

"The *Agincourt,*" he told her. "Someone in the British Admiralty thinks we have lessons they need to learn."

468

HMS Agincourt was the newest and most potent attack submarine in the Royal Navy; possibly in the world. He could see the wheels turning inside Brunelli's head. *"Agincourt* was a part of RIMPAC wasn't she?"

"She was."

"So she's in theater, somewhere…"

"She's inbound Hawaii."

"Here?"

"Here. I can protest. We'll be under the command of *Agincourt's* Captain, and I've heard he's a right bastard."

She stood. "We're doing this."

Her reaction surprised him. "It's a demotion, a punishment detail. We'll only have observer status," he said.

"They want us because the Royal Navy is about to go to war, Skipper. It's a chance for payback. Don't tell me you aren't gagging for it."

McDonald nodded. "I am."

"Alright then."

The Eisenhower Play

For the second time during the Taiwan crisis, Carmen Carliotti found herself fleeing Washington. The first had been after the Raven Rock assassination attempt, where she'd circled over Puerto Rico for several hours until the Secret Service was confident it had a truly secure location she could be moved to.

And now, she found herself in Air Force One again, with half her cabinet, a detachment of signals and communication specialists and a handpicked group of White House functionaries.

The government's second Boeing 747 VIP jet was following behind them, taking a different route with the rest of the cabinet, family members and security and intelligence personnel.

From Ronald Reagan airport, Washington Dulles and Thurgood Marshall, other flights would soon follow with contagious disease specialists, nurses, emergency services personnel, police, Pentagon and Federal Emergency Management Agency coordinators, plus their family members, while from Andrews AFB, a conga line of C-5 Globemaster cargo planes was preparing to take off with the supplies needed to sustain the Continuity of Government operation for its first few weeks.

It was the biggest evacuation of critical government personnel since the 9/11 attacks, and Carliotti could not help but wonder if she had said "yes" to General Maxwell too soon.

But Carliotti had not cut and run immediately, nor had she waited for China to formalize its aggression. At the first opportunity, she made an address to Congress peppered with images of slaughterbots on the streets of downtown Honolulu. In drafting the speech, which she did herself, she leaned heavily on Roosevelt's speech to Congress on December 7, 1941, knowing that comparisons were inevitable anyway.

Mr. Vice President, Mr. Speaker, Members of the Senate, and of the House of Representatives:

Yesterday, June 18, 2038, China showed its true face to the world when it unleashed its autonomous attack drones on military and civilian personnel alike on Hawaii. Our casualties are at this stage unknown, but they will be heavy, even though we were prepared for this eventuality.

Until now, the United States has shown a steadfast determination to protect the right of the democratic island of Taiwan to determine its own future, while at the same time resisting provocation after provocation from the Chinese military over, on and under the Pacific. The United States has not sought war with China, and was still acting in good faith to find a negotiated solution to the Taiwan conflict. But China has now chosen to attack American citizens on American soil, and worse, far worse.

Yesterday, the Chinese People's Liberation Army also launched an amphibious assault on Wake Island.

Its stealth bombers and submarines fired cruise missiles at US facilities on Guam, the Marshall Islands, American Samoa, and Palau, and our bases on Okinawa and Luzon in the Philippines.

And a large amphibious force is approaching Hawaii. Our forces there are preparing to resist any attempt to land Chinese troops on those islands.

The nature and scale of these attacks indicate they have been long in the planning, and that China's intention in the Pacific, from the moment of its blockade of Taiwan, has been to set the conditions for it to wage total war on the USA and our allies.

But we are prepared.

There had been a long debate about her next message. Because it was intended for the leadership of China as much as it was for US citizens and America's allies.

As Commander in Chief of our armed forces, I had already mobilized a large part of our expeditionary forces in anticipation of this day, and I have now directed that further measures be taken for our defense. Let me clear about this: Though I have ordered our Joint Chiefs of Staff to prepare our nuclear forces for the possibility of a nuclear attack, the US will not be the first nation to use nuclear weapons in this conflict, and we counsel our adversaries to maintain similarly cool heads at this terrible time for the sake of all humanity.

The NSC had also debated how far to take the next element of the speech. Some had even counseled against including it due to the panic it would cause, but since the civil emergency restrictions she was about to introduce were among the most authoritarian any US president had countenanced, Carliotti had insisted.

As I said, should these terrible events not be enough, there is worse, for the USA and for all citizens of all nations. You may have seen media reports of an epidemic of deadly bird flu that has broken out on Taiwan. I regret to confirm that the rumors are true, that this virus— known as H5N1c—is both highly contagious and terribly lethal. We must prepare ourselves for a high number of casualties among our troops on that war-ravaged and now plague-ridden island.

Furthermore, we are certain, beyond any doubt, that China was behind the release of this virus, to which it apparently already has a vaccine. It began inoculating its politicians, citizens and soldiers even before the virus was released and is providing the vaccine to its allies Russia, North Korea and Iran.

My fellow citizens, China has unleashed a lethal biological weapon on the world, and it will, sooner rather than later, as with all such pandemics, arrive on these shores. That is why today I have signed a number of Executive Orders expanding the remit of the National Guard forces already deployed, and charging both FEMA and the Centers for Disease Control with the necessary powers to prepare our nation for the coming international civil and health emergency.

It was a double-barreled shotgun dose of doom, so she had to finish with a message of hope.

No resource will be spared to develop and distribute our own vaccine. It may take months; it will not take years. And China's perfidy will not go unpunished.

My fellow citizens, as President Roosevelt said at a similar moment in 1941, with confidence in our armed forces, with the unbounding determination of our people, we will once again win the inevitable triumph—so help us God.

I ask that the Congress declare that since the cowardly attacks on our people and territories of yesterday, a state of war has existed between the United States and the Chinese empire.

Treasury had been prepared, and both the stock market and financial trading channels were closed in advance. As were banks and cash machines. But when trading resumed, money flowed out of the US economy like blood from a gaping chest wound, seeking safe haven in gold and other precious metals, European treasury securities and the currencies of nonaligned nations.

The Secretary of Treasury and his officials assured Carliotti the market would correct within days when fears of nuclear Armageddon began to dampen and Treasury began messaging about the many precautions the US had taken over recent years to fireproof its economy against war with China—from re-onshoring production of advanced computer chips to securing alternate sources for metals and rare earth elements, such as in Canada and Australia. But Carliotti had more immediate concerns.

The first was the evacuation of her administration from Washington. She wasn't so much worried about her own personal safety as she was the power vacuum that she was leaving behind and the blowback as it became known that her administration had fled the capital.

And she had just come out of three intense hours of in-flight meetings on the state of their defenses, domain by domain, where the recurring theme was that despite the confident assurances in her address to Congress, the most battle-ready US forces in the Pacific theater had been caught out of position by China's coordinated Pacific thrust.

There were 50,000 of the USA's best troops on Taiwan exposed to H5N1c. At least half were expected to die. There were 64,000 US personnel in Japan, another 52,000 in the Philippines. The advice was to leave them in place too, and those nations were expected to be among the first to be hit by the virus when it inevitably escaped Taiwan.

Most of the USAF's expeditionary Air Force units were in the Taiwan theater. Four of six deployed USAF B-21s and nine of 10 B-2s had been destroyed on the ground on Guam, one B-2 while it had been refueling on Wake. After Congressional cutbacks in the 2030s, the strategic bomber force consisted of just 20 B-21s and 21 B-2s—many deployed in other theaters or the USA—and about the same number of B-1s and B-52s in boneyards stateside.

China, on the other hand, had deployed its own precious H-20 stealth bomber for attacks on targets delivered from outside its own borders for the first time. With a range of nearly 5,000 miles and payload of up to 10 tons, it was capable of striking targets from Hawaii to Darwin in Australia, unrefueled. ELINT and naval radar data indicated it had been used in the strikes on Guam and Wake.

The bulk of the Pacific Fleet was engaged in the Western Pacific, and the first reports of ship-to-ship combat between US and Chinese vessels were starting to come in. China had flooded the littoral waters of the Strait and South China Sea with more than 80 small Type 22 anti-air, anti-ship missile patrol boats that US war planners had assumed it was holding in reserve to support a Taiwan invasion. HUMINT reports also indicated China had surged the remainder of its 60 strong conventional submarine fleet into the Taiwan Strait;

East, Yellow and South China Seas; and the Sea of Japan. Together, the small boat and submarine force gave China immediate surface and subsurface superiority in the Taiwan theater and put all military and civilian shipping in those waters at risk, freeing its cruise-missile-armed nuclear attack submarines to range eastward, supporting operations in the central and eastern Pacific.

She might be Commander in Chief, but operational conduct of this war was now well and truly out of her hands. She had just agreed to appoint three Unified Combatant Commanders under General Maxwell, splitting INDOPACOM into two new commands, including one called PACOMWEST and the other PACOMEAST, with a four-star Marine general and an admiral each taking one command. The Marine General was overall commander for the Taiwan and South China Sea theater, and the Navy Admiral for the Central and East Pacific theater, including Hawaii. A four-star Air Force general had been given command of Guam and the rump of the INDOCOM theater.

General Maxwell's strategy for playing peacemaker between the services with these first appointments appeared to have been reasonably well received.

Carliotti's focus now was purely political, both at home and abroad. On the global stage, the US was about to invoke Article V of the NATO charter, bringing all NATO nations into the war in its defense. The US was going to withdraw from the UN Security Council and vote for it to be dissolved.

Despite the attack on Hawaii, China and Russia had only delivered formal declarations of war to Japan and the Philippines, citing the presence of hostile US forces in those countries. Notably, it had not done the same with the US or South Korea. Yet.

She had avoided naming Russia in her declaration of war, but that didn't mean the threat from the nation was any less.

Russia had made no diplomatic moves and refused to even acknowledge its military action in the Kuril Islands, or its participation in the attack on Hawaii. It called all claims that it was involved in any military action against the US "outright lies." But it wholeheartedly supported China's right to defend itself against "rampaging Western imperialism."

Like a small wooden Russian matryoshka doll hiding inside a larger Chinese one, its plan seemed to be to obfuscate, deny and bluff for as long as possible. But that could not last. It had taken losses in Japan and would inevitably take losses in the Hawaii action.

Russia's long game was entirely tenebrous to Carliotti.

With the war being almost entirely centered in Asia and the Pacific, getting the mostly European nations of NATO to actively support the US defense of possessions like Guam, Wake and bases in the Philippines and Japan was *far* from a given. Especially if they, like the US, were also about to be battered by a new global bird flu pandemic and face a belligerent Russia on their eastern border again. It had sounded ridiculous to her, but her Secretary of State had warned her that the first order of business would be getting the other members of NATO to believe that the US hadn't brought the bioweapon to Taiwan itself, for use against China. And, she was told, some wouldn't.

They'd also reviewed their pandemic response plan. Several opposition-aligned governors were already outraged over her National Guard callout. They were going to go stratospheric when her latest batch of Executive Orders hit their desks. And the first thing they would demand to know would be "Where is the President?!"

476

Well, she reflected wryly, *the President is standing by the forward galley in Air Force One, where she's just been served a cup of coffee and is looking out of the window at … a snow-covered wasteland.*

"Ladies and gentlemen, we will soon begin our descent to Pituffik Space Base …" the pilot said, beginning the landing routine she had heard a million times in her life but never quite in these circumstances.

Pituffik Space Base—what used to be known as Thule Air Base, Greenland.

More than 3,000 kilometers, or 1,600 miles, from Washington, and 2,500 from the nearest US city, in Massachusetts. Thousands of miles from anywhere, in fact, including the nearest populated part of Greenland.

Carliotti drained her coffee, then took her seat for the landing, next to HR, who was already buckled up. "Why the hell *Greenland*?" she asked.

He gestured out the window, where there was nothing but mountains of ice and plains of snow. "Isolation," he said. "Easy to control who comes in and out. Air Force is already here, along with the US Corps of Engineers, so we can quickly erect quarantine fences and control entry-exit points." He pulled a map from a pocket in the table in front of him and laid it on the table between them. "Proximity to China: 4,000 miles. Plus"—he started counting off his fingers—"we already have early warning radar, HELLADS, THAAD and Patriot batteries here for ballistic and hypersonic missile interception, with two *Virginia* class submarines patrolling permanently offshore." He took a breath. "Plus, the subzero climate is hostile to viruses …"

"Hostile to anything, by the look of it," she said without irony, staring out the window again.

477

"There is that, uh, inconvenience. But Pituffik also has an underground Governmental Continuity facility and advanced satellite tracking and communication links for when we restore our space capabilities."

She nodded. "Which is when?"

"Space Force reported a successful operation to neutralize the Chinese satellite attack. We're beginning an accelerated program of launches to fill the gaps. Maxwell says we'll have limited return of capabilities within 24 hours, rising to full capability in two weeks." He tapped the tablet lying on the table in front of him. "Space Force also has 10 proposals here for how we can retaliate against China for the satellite takedown, but we need to stay focused." He raised two fingers. "One, prosecute the war on China. Two, consolidate the situation at home."

"Sure, but put this on your list. I also want proposals for how to retaliate for the release of this virus, discreetly but immediately. You don't kill thousands of our troops, potentially hundreds of thousands of our citizens and our allies' citizens, and get away with it, HR." Her voice was shaking, and she tried to stop her hands from doing the same. "They will pay and pay soon. This revenge will *not* be served cold."

She turned away. Despite her bravado, it was easy to feel like the hand of history had delivered her a resounding slap across the cheek. She'd been blinded by the brilliance of her own strategy for breaking China in Taiwan, all the while playing into China's strategy for breaking the US in the Pacific.

Was this how Roosevelt felt in December 1941? she wondered. *And how did we—how did I—let it happen again?* She knew enough history to know that the attack on Pearl Harbor was just one of a dozen precisely coordinated attacks by the Japanese across the Pacific within 48 hours, all of which took the allied nations of the time by surprise with their ferocity and meticulous coordination. By January 1942, just a month after Pearl Harbor, the Japanese-controlled Hong Kong, parts of the Philippines, Wake Island, Guam, Malaya and Singapore, plus parts of Indonesia ... the list was astounding when you thought about it, and Japan at that time was a shadow of the power China had become since.

In its hubris, the US had not allowed for the possibility that China could repeat Japan's feat 100 years later. With the added threat of a pandemic that could emasculate Taiwan and wipe out half the US population, half the *world's* population, outside China, unless a vaccine was found, *fast*.

That particular threat made the nightmare of the Chinese "slaughterbots" pale by comparison. The tiny bright light on that horizon? Maxwell said he had just received a report from Taiwan that its defense scientists had come up with a way to neutralize the killer drones. They had sent it to CyberCom, who were urgently looking at how to deploy it on Hawaii. A bioweapon was something abstract, surreal. Killer drones were something she could relate to, and the thought of Chinese drones on the streets of Honolulu filled her with an incandescent rage.

Stay angry, Carmen, she told herself. *We might have found a defense against the bots. We* will *find a vaccine for the virus. And then you can turn your attention to what comes next.*

"NSC meeting the moment we land," HR said. "Maxwell needs a decision; Taiwan is out, but does *Fallujah* ARG continue east to reinforce Japan, or do we bring it back to Hawaii? The decision is as much political as it is military."

"That's a waste of discussion time. Of course we bring it back to Hawaii," she said, then appeared to listen to her own words. "HR, when we land, take off all personnel necessary for Continuity of Government, including the Vice President. But you stay onboard with me."

Rosenstern frowned at her. "Ma'am?"

"I'm not running to the Arctic, HR. I accept we need to take precautions; of course we do. But I will not abandon my post and leave our nation to an uncertain fate with its president in *hiding*."

HR looked annoyed. "Madam President, this is not some terrorist attack you can ride out inside a bunker. China has shown it is willing to do whatever it takes to eliminate us as a global power … deploy autonomous killer drones, biological weapons, unleash a full-scale war with Russia at their side. It is nonsense to say you are abandoning your post. You need time to deal with the situation at home, too. The Governor of Texas …"

His irritated tone was enough to get her hackles up straight away, but calling her instincts "*nonsense*"?

She turned around and called over her Secret Service Division head, Greg Kitchen. The man had been by her side at Raven Rock. He didn't even look surprised that she wanted to talk as the plane was beginning its descent; he simply unbuckled and came down to her.

"Greg, when we land, everyone will deplane except HR, myself, you and however many of your agents you think we will need for our next destination."

"What destination is that, ma'am?" Kitchen asked simply.

HR leaned over. "The President and I were just discussing … nothing is decided … Madam President, I …"

She put a hand right in his face to shut him up. "HR, in '52, Eisenhower ran on a promise that if he was elected, he would fly to South Korea to get a firsthand view of the war there. Our forces had been fighting and dying there for two years without Truman ever having visited." She was nearly shaking with anger as the words spilled from her. "He won the election, and he went to Seoul. The horrors he saw there gave him the resolve to say to China that the US would do whatever it would take to deny them victory in Korea. *Whatever it would take, HR*—unless they started peace negotiations. Which they did."

"You are not Eisenhower," HR said abruptly. "And this is not 1952."

She let that comment hang in the air a moment before she replied coldly. "You are right about that, HR." She turned back to Kitchen. "When we land, disembark all other passengers, *including* Mr. Rosenstern, Greg."

"Now, Madam President ..." Rosenstern began.

She ignored his protest. "Keep everything moving at the UN, NATO and on the home front, HR. I want no backsliding," she said, then turned back to her Secret Service Division Head. "Greg, speak with General Maxwell. We're going to fly wherever we need to fly, so he can put me on Hawaii."

END Volume III of Aggressor: SWARM.

18. Prologue: MIDNIGHT

A new front

The dormant volcano of Kunashir Island sliding past under the wing of the Ilyushin 112 transport aircraft struck Major-General Yevgeny Bondarev as something of a portent.

The dispute between Russia and Japan over the sovereignty of the Kuril Island chain northeast of Hokkaido had long lain dormant, with neither country doing much more than exchanging protest notes whenever their ships and aircraft approached too close to each other. Russia had upgraded the airfield and military base on Kunashir (Kunashiri in Japanese) in the early 2000s with Bastion-P anti-ship missile batteries giving it the hypothetical ability to strike at Japanese shipping plying the coast of Hokkaido, just 37 kilometers distant, but Japan had done little more than huff and puff on the floor of the United Nations.

Until now.

Japan's parliament, the Diet, had passed a law recognizing Taiwan's government and affirming the sovereignty of Taiwan. This was regarded by China as a de facto declaration of war, and it showed its displeasure with a submarine-launched cruise missile strike on Japanese troops on the disputed island of Outsuri Jima in the Senkaku Chain off the coast of Taiwan.

Alarmed by this and the announcement of the new Russia-China defense treaty and military exercises just a few hundred miles off its northern coast, Japan had declared a state of military emergency, and in a pre-dawn raid, landed a company of Marines at Kunashiri's airstrip, corralled and disarmed the paltry platoon of troops from the small Russian garrison west of the island's only town—the small fishing and tourism center of Yuzhno-Kurilsk—and then filmed themselves destroying the Russian missile batteries in the name of "protecting their territorial waters from the threat of China and its allies."

The Japanese Marines then dug in at the airfield and remained in place "to prevent further Russian militarization." The humiliated Russian troops had been forcibly dispatched by boat to Iturup Island, nearly 200 kilometers north.

Russia and China responded by making Iturup the focus of a huge Shanghai Pact air and sea invasion simulation exercise involving thousands of troops, hundreds of fighter and heavy aircraft and dozens of naval vessels.

Bondarev's flight was both an assertion of Russia's continuing claim to the airspace over the Kuril Islands and a reconnaissance mission. From the observation port behind the cockpit, he saw an island about 100 kilometers long, with the volcano rising up in the northeast of the island, Yuzhno-Kurilsk on the east coast, an abandoned military garrison in the west and the airfield in the middle of the island.

"We have company," the pilot said over his shoulder, pointing out of the cockpit to the north.

Straightening, Bondarev saw a pair of Euro-Japanese Tempest stealth fighters about a half click away, flying parallel with them. They were close enough he should have been able to see the pilots inside their cockpits, but the Tempest's cockpit glass was matte black, impermeable to light.

Despite the skyrocketing tensions, a shooting war between Japan and Russia had not broken out … yet.

"Two aircraft. Is that normal?" he asked his pilot, who was no stranger to the Kuril Islands.

"Usually, they only send a single machine," the man said with a shrug. "And they stay inside their own airspace. They don't recognize the island as Russian territory, but they usually don't come this far across."

"Any communication?"

"Just the usual: Please stay out of our airspace."

Bondarev smiled. "They say 'please'?"

"Not really," the man replied. "It's more of a command than a request."

"Then we should teach them some respect," Bondarev said. "Take us west."

The pilot raised an eyebrow. "We are only 20 kilometers from Japanese airspace, Major General," he pointed out.

"And they are inside *ours*, Lieutenant," Bondarev said. He nodded aft. "With your permission?"

"My bird is your bird, Major General," the man said. Bondarev saw his hand tighten on his flight stick.

He went aft, to a small cabin behind the cockpit. Bondarev's command aircraft was not a conventional IL-112 transport machine. It contained a sleeping compartment, which allowed the crew to double up for long flights, and its cargo bay had been shortened about 10 meters by the insertion of a C3I module from which Bondarev could supervise the operation of the entirety of his 12th Mginskaya Red Banner Military Transport Aviation Division.

Sitting in the module right now were the IL-112's four C3I crew members, the Lieutenant who was Mission Coordinator, two communications specialists and an electronic warfare officer. Bondarev's machine was less transport, more flying battlefield command.

He stepped into the module and stood at his Mission Coordinator's shoulder, making a quick survey of his status screens. "Do you have eyeballs on the Japanese aircraft?"

"More than eyeballs, Major General," the man replied.

"Make them go away," Bondarev told him.

A reasonable man

"I'm sorry, sir, but we got our orders," Corporal Ted Oberheim of the California National Guard said, as equably as he could. They'd checked they were talking to the right guy. "The order applies to all Chinese nationals or dual citizens. You got to put the bracelet on voluntarily, or we will put it on for you."

Ted and his squad had done dozens of "digital internment order" visits already, and he'd found most people just reacted with shock at the sight of a squad of armed Guardsmen in their driveway or stairwell. Some got pissed though. And word was spreading in the Chinese community, so some even had lawyers open the door for them.

Ted wasn't worried by lawyers. He just read the notice to them instead, like he'd been told, and if they tried to interfere, he shoved them out the way.

The guy standing in the door of the apartment looked about 30. His cell phone location told Ted and his squad he was home. Ted saw two mountain bikes hanging on a rack on the wall behind him. Some type of gig economy tech worker, he guessed.

"Are you shitting me?" the guy asked.

"Sir, do you wish to comply, or will we be required to use force?" Ted asked in a calm voice.

A female voice from the corridor behind the guy, someone hovering there he couldn't quite see. "Alex? What's going on?"

"I … I don't know," the guy said over his shoulder, then turned back to face Ted. "There's a storm trooper here with a

485

court order says I have to put on an ankle tracker because I'm a dual Chinese citizen."

Ted shrugged. "We're at war with China, sir," he said, reasonably. He motioned his man forward with the ankle cuff. He found it was best to act, not debate. If you moved with authority, before you knew it, the deed was done, and you were moving on to the next person.

"Get the hell away from me with that," the guy said, trying to close the door on Ted's boot.

Oh well, so this is going to be one of the hard ones. Ted knocked the guy's hand from the door with a downward sweep of his arm, swung the arm behind the guy's back and then hooked his legs out from under him. In seconds, he was face down on the floor. The girlfriend started screaming. That was annoying. But at least she wasn't carrying a weapon. There had been a couple of interactions with armed Chinese citizens that had not gone so well.

For the citizens.

"Cuff him," Ted grunted, as the guy struggled and cursed. When the cuff was securely in place around his ankle, Ted stood and stepped back, reading off the back of the internment notice as the guy crabbed backward on the floor and his girlfriend grabbed him. She looked like a nice girl. Same age as Ted's daughter, maybe.

Ted started reading. He was pretty sure he'd have the words memorized soon, but not yet.

"Sir, you have been placed in digital internment under the authority of the Homeland Security Act Amendment of 2038, Public Law ... uh, 199-27. You are now prohibited from knowingly coming within a half mile of any Federal or State government employee, office, building or installation. You are prohibited from leaving the State of California to travel to any other state, and you must notify local police of any change in your home address. You are prohibited from engaging in the full range of occupations and activities specified in this law and detailed on this notice ..." Ted turned the page over. "There's a bunch; I'm not going to read them all," he told the guy. "Any attempt by you to remove your digital restraint will alert local police, and you will be arrested and charged with a crime under the Homeland Security Act." He folded the piece of paper and tossed it on the floor in front of the guy.

"This is total BS. I work for the FBI, asshat," the guy said, still sitting on the floor.

"Not anymore you don't, dude," the private behind Ted said, and Ted turned, signaling to him to zip it, and to the others to hit the stairs. Job done.

Ted didn't blame people for calling him names. Not really. Some threw stuff: food, lamps, a knife even, earlier today. He had some advice for the ones he felt sorry for, like this guy, something that wasn't in the official script he'd been given.

"I'm sorry to hear that, sir," he said. "You know, the border crossing at Otay Mesa is still open to Chinese nationals who want to leave the country, and no one there is too worried about that thing you have on your ankle. As long as there's no warrant out in your name, you can pass into Mexico, get your cuff cut off, take a flight home to China from there. Or wherever you want. Might be a better option than staying, right?"

Ted closed the apartment door, the girl crying, the guy still yelling at him.

Oh well, some people just didn't want to be helped.

British understatement

Major Alison 'Blackadder' Addison, Royal Air Force 23 Squadron, Space Operations, never got tired of the view from the cockpit of a Skylon D4.

Ahead of her, the blue-black horizon of earth under a blanket of glowing white cloud. Behind it, the moon, hanging in the abyss like a gleaming gray pearl.

But underneath that cloud …

"SAR online?" she asked.

"Synthetic Aperture Radar online, and painting a big, mostly empty sea. Coming up on Hawaii in five …" her copilot, Captain Hardeep 'Headlamp' Singh, told her. The panoramic flat screen in front of Singh showed a gray-tone image of the Pacific as they passed over it at a low earth orbit speed of 15,200 knots, or 17,000 miles an hour. Using the speed of their passage to simulate a large aperture radar dish, the Skylon's radar penetrated the thick cloud to give them a pixel-perfect 3D view of the surface of the sea below.

Addison did a quick survey of the instrument display on her own screen and minimized it, keeping the collision warning display top and center. "Put it on my screen too, will you, Headlamp? Let's see what the fuss is about."

The RAF Skylon was already in orbit, updating its map of satellites and space junk around the equator, when their new tasking came through and Addison diverted them to overfly the central Pacific. GCHQ wanted urgently for them to map all air and sea traffic west of Hawaii back to the Kuril Islands in Russia.

Her display flickered and then mirrored the one Singh was looking at. She saw a few transport vessels heading toward Hawaii and what looked like a fat cruise ship beetling away from it. Their radar could cover an area of the earth's surface

700 miles wide and several thousand miles long, and the resolution was so sharp it was even picking up wave clutter. "Set object to 50 feet above sea level, would you, Headlamp?" she asked. "And run an intermittent scan to 40,000 feet to look for air traffic." They had been asked to not just map the ground and sea surface but also look for any aircraft above it. At the resolutions their SAR was capable of, their AI could immediately classify the images generated by ship and aircraft class, and a list was already starting to flow down the right side of their screens as the intel was collected, analyzed and compiled for their report.

"Hmm, nothing unusual," Singh said, scanning the list. "Civilian and military freighters, a couple *Arleigh Burke* destroyers inbound, cruise liner outbound. Flipping object through to 40,000... hmm, no civilian air traffic." He bent to the screen, stopping the data from scrolling. "Big flight of F-35s outbound California. Twenty-plus ... yeah, headed for these two tankers, I'd guess, then Hawaii."

Addison nodded. Their in-flight intel update had included reports that Chinese autonomous drones had attacked Pearl Harbor, and a Chinese amphibious landing was underway on Wake Island—payback for the US intervention in the South China Sea, she guessed. It made sense the US was pulling more fighter aircraft from mainland bases and sending them west.

"Coming up on Big Island," Singh said, continuing his running commentary. "AWACS to the South. Got a few military aircraft southwest ..."

Before she transferred to Space Operations, was type rated on the Skylon and put in command of 23 Squadron, Addison had been a Tempest fighter squadron commander in the Middle East, with two combat tours under her belt. She studied the group of aircraft on the screen southwest of Hawaii and checked the data scrolling down the screen. "What we are looking at, Captain Singh, is a full-blooded furball. F-22s and Chongming fighters, at least one Gyrfalcon …"

He didn't respond, and she looked over at him. He was leaning forward, looking at ground images, not at the cluster of aircraft she was studying. And he looked perturbed. The Hawaiian Islands were rolling toward the center of the screen now, aircraft and ships, civilian and military, painted by their radar—if there was a battle going on there, they wouldn't pick it up on SAR, but they were recording with other cameras too. "Switch to infrared?" Singh asked. "Just over the islands?"

"Just quickly," she said. "Until we lose Oʻahu …"

He was already doing it. The screen flicked from gray-tone to ghostly green. They lost their high-fidelity imagery and saw only dark green blobs of land on a dark green sea overlaid with artificially mapped land boundaries that marked the coastline, city limits and major roads.

But the camera picked up heat spots through the thick cloud.

Honolulu was *ablaze*.

"Good lord," Singh said, with an intake of breath. "It's 1941 all over again." There were only a couple of US aircraft airborne over Hawaii.

"Bring up SAR again," Addison said tersely. "We're already passing Kauai."

As they passed over the Hawaiian chain's westernmost islands, they hit blank sea and sky. Not a vessel or aircraft was visible for a full 30 seconds.

"That's … scary," Singh observed.

490

Then it started. 200 miles out: Gyrfalcon fighters first, in a semi-circle of spread pairs. Behind them, a Wing Loong ISR aircraft. Behind that, a Y-20 heavy, the size of a US Globemaster, either a tanker or electronic warfare aircraft. And where there were Gyrfalcons, there had to be …

A carrier strike group. The list of identified ships and aircraft began scrolling faster than she could read. A half dozen *Renhai* class missile destroyers, at least as many *Luhang IIIs*, 10 or more *Jiankai II* class frigates, more Gyrfalcons, flying combat air patrols over …

"That's a carrier," Singh said, voice low. "By the plan form, either the *Shandong* or *Liaoning*."

But the list of ships and aircraft was still scrolling, because behind the carrier strike group was a sight even more chilling.

"Three *Yushen* class landing helo docks," Singh said, stopping the list on his screen scrolling. "Good heavens, that ship's Russian—a *Kirov* class battlecruiser." He was nearly whispering now, almost speaking to himself as though he were afraid to speak aloud. "That whole group is *Russian*."

Addison's eye had been drawn to the same group of Russian vessels. The battlecruiser, two *Udaloy* missile cruisers, two *Gorshkov* frigates and one older *Grigorovich*. A brace of newer *Stereguschiy* anti-air/anti-submarine corvettes and, most disturbing of all, what had to be Russia's entire complement of *Ivan Gren* class landing ships.

They spotted only a single US vessel. A littoral combat ship, headed south at speed. *Away* from the sprawling Sino-Russian force. Addison judged its Captain a very wise sailor.

Behind the American LCS came a trail of Chinese supply vessels, more ISR, refueling and EW aircraft, and a KJ-500 AWACS, traveling inside another vanguard of destroyers and frigates.

"That, Mr. Singh, is rather a lot of ships. Find me a satellite," Addison told Singh.

He flipped to a comms screen and scrolled. "There are no secure military …"

"Find me a bloody *civilian* satellite then," she said sharply. "OPSEC be damned. Somebody needs to understand a storm of steel is headed for Hawaii."

**AGGRESSOR series volume IV of V: MIDNIGHT
will be released April 2024.**

19. Author note

I hope you are enjoying reading along as much as I am enjoying writing as we turn the corner on the halfway point in the series!

For this episode, I was inspired by three epic strategic events in history.

The first was the battle of Cannae, fought by the great Tunisian-born general Hannibal against the Romans in 216 BC. Yes, a story about war in 2038 inspired by a war 2,000 years earlier! I was recently in Sofia, Bulgaria, reading about Hannibal's Balkan campaign. There was a display at the museum illustrating Hannibal's tactical genius through a retelling of the battle of Cannae.

In this battle, the outnumbered forces of Hannibal formed a bowed line facing the Romans, with a seemingly weak element in the center of Hannibal's forces. When the Romans attacked the center, Hannibal let them come, then had his men fall back in the middle, while the intact outer edges of his line moved forward and enveloped the Roman force and Hannibal's powerful cavalry swept around to the back of the Romans to attack and destroy them from the rear.

As I looked at the display, I thought, *What if Taiwan was China's Cannae?* What if it used Taiwan to lure the larger part of the available US expeditionary land, sea and air forces into a battle focused on defending Taiwan while China's numerically superior naval forces and its invasion fleets flanked Taiwan and attacked US bases across the central and eastern Pacific instead?

For that strategy to be possible in the era of satellite surveillance and speed of light communication across vast distances, China would need to deal with the US and allied military satellite network without risking damage to its own. And it would need to suppress the US-NATO satellite surveillance and communications network for several days to prevent detection as it maneuvered its forces.

In 2038, that will, unfortunately, not be as difficult or unlikely as it sounds.

Enter the Chinese BX-1 satellite, first tested in 2008. A very small cube, approximately 40 centimeters on a side (16 inches) and weighing around 40 kilograms (90 lbs.). During this test, it was released from an orbiting spacecraft; then, it maneuvered dangerously close to the international space station, returned to its mother ship and matched orbit with it. Fast forward to 2022, when China announced it was planning a test mission to deflect an orbiting asteroid using a microsatellite suspiciously similar to the BX-1, which would attach itself to the asteroid and *shove it* out of orbit. Couched as a "planetary defense system," military analysts immediately saw the offensive possibilities. If the microsatellites were able to shove asteroids out of orbit, then it was a small leap to see how they could be used against enemy satellites in low earth orbit. China's "planetary defense system" could become a very effective "anti-satellite offensive system" that overcame the biggest drawback of kinetic antisatellite weapons: the enormous uncontrolled debris fields that result and which can damage your own space assets. China's parasite satellites are a near-term reality.

The next major strategic event that inspired this story was the sweeping string of victories achieved by the Imperial Japanese Army and Navy in late 1941, early 1942. Listening to historian Dan Carlin's fantastic podcast series *Supernova in the East* brought home to me the enormity of Japan's ambition and capabilities at this time: coordinated attacks, almost simultaneous in strategic terms, against targets thousands of miles apart in China, Malaysia, Indonesia, the Philippines and the central Pacific. At the time, the Imperial Japanese armed forces had fewer warships and personnel under arms than the Chinese PLA already possesses today.

It achieved its early victories against the combined navies of the USA and the British Empire. The British navy in 1941 was by far the strongest in the world, but it has far fewer ships today, mostly concentrated in the Atlantic and Mediterranean, with few in the Pacific. Numbers matter. China's fleet already outnumbers the US and UK fleets combined, which are spread across the globe while the Chinese fleet is concentrated in the Pacific.

Again, my thinking here had a "what if" character. *What if China adopted a similar strategy to Japan*, in an effort to dislodge the US from the Pacific? We all know how that went for Japan, but China in the 2030s will not be the oil- and resource-starved Japan of 1941. It is an industrial powerhouse in its own right, with the biggest navy on the planet, technologies approaching parity with Western militaries in many areas and exceeding them in some, and a numerical advantage in air, sea and ground forces that cannot be ignored.

Would China be able to push US forces out of the Pacific, and keep them out?

Final inspiration came from the geopolitical earthquake that was the Warsaw Pact, with inspiration in a visit to Hungary I made late last year. Countries like Hungary and Bulgaria are living contradictions—one foot in the EU but one foot still stubbornly anchored in their eastern-bloc past. It isn't beyond the realm of fantasy to imagine a new Warsaw Pact emerging today involving the Central Asian Republics,

Serbia, Bulgaria, Hungary and Russia. So what is the link to an Asian conflict?

Officially known as the Treaty of Friendship, Cooperation and Mutual Assistance, the Warsaw Pact came into being in May 1955 as a counter to the formation of NATO in 1949. Seeing the close collaboration of Russia, China, North Korea and Iran over Ukraine, it is not hard to imagine Russia emerging weaker from that conflict, rather than stronger, and in need of friends. The incentive for it to seek formal alliances will grow, as will China's, if it sees a war with Western powers in its future.

Taking on China alone in the Pacific will be difficult enough, and the temptation to use nuclear weapons overwhelming. But if China's campaign in the Pacific is backed by not just its own nuclear arsenal but those of Russia and North Korea as well, the nuclear calculus changes dramatically, and the near certainty of *any* nuclear exchange resulting in mutually assured destruction is obvious. I believe that in a conflict between NATO and a new Warsaw—or "Shanghai Pact"—there would be no rush to a nuclear option, and a brutal conventional war would be more likely.

I accept that irrational actors can arise, and the threat of nuclear Armageddon is ever-present.

Now, another historical side note. I mentioned in passing in this novel the story of the USS *Yorktown* as it related to *Fujian*, but it is worth telling in full here to highlight that you should never count a carrier out until it lies on the bottom of the sea. Swarmed by Japanese aircraft in the Battle of the Coral Sea, *Yorktown* was hit in the center of her flight deck by a 550 lb. bomb, which penetrated four decks before exploding, causing severe structural damage to an aviation storage room and killing or seriously wounding 66 men, as well as damaging the superheater boilers, which rendered them inoperable. Up to 12 near misses damaged *Yorktown*'s hull below the waterline. The Japanese considered her sunk, but she made it back to Pearl Harbor.

She arrived at Pearl Harbor on 27 May 1942, entering dry-dock the following day. The damage the ship had sustained after Coral Sea was considerable and led to Navy Yard inspectors estimating that she would need at least two weeks of repairs. However, Admiral Nimitz ordered that she be made ready to sail to assist in the defense of Midway. Further inspections showed that *Yorktown*'s flight elevators had not been damaged, and the damage to her flight deck and hull could be patched. Yard workers at Pearl Harbor, laboring around the clock, made enough repairs to enable the ship to put to sea again *in 48 hours*. Joining the battle of Midway, *Yorktown*'s pilots attacked and destroyed the Japanese carrier *Soryu*.

So yes, *Fujian* repairing its flight deck and a catapult while underway using cannibalized parts, then docking for just six hours to take on more parts to complete more repairs underway, is a stretch—but compared to the heroic efforts of the crew and shipyard workers who put *Yorktown* back in action, not an impossible one!

A sad postscript to this heroic effort was that *Yorktown* did not survive the battle of Midway, and 141 sailors lost their lives.

Whether *Fujian* survives the Battle of Hawaii is a question to be resolved in MIDNIGHT, episode 4 in the Aggressor series!

FX Holden, Copenhagen, December 2023

MIDNIGHT: Coming April 2024
Volume 4 of 5 in the Aggressor Series

The night is always darkest before the dawn. But the surviving Aggressor Inc. pilots are asking themselves, **"What if the dawn never comes?"**

Taiwan's population and its defenders are decimated by H5N1c, and its government dissolved after accepting an offer for vaccine supplies from China. From their hiding place on Xiuguluan Mountain, a resistance cell wages a guerilla drone war on newly arrived Chinese forces.

Is their resistance futile?

Under the icy waters of the Northwest Passage, Russian, Chinese and NATO vessels engage in a deadly dance as NATO tries to choke off the new Russian lifeline to China.

Is Russia's intent finally revealed?

NATO and the Shanghai Pact nations face off as the battle—for the Pacific and for the very soul of America—rages. At home, rioting and unrest force US President Carliotti to consider extreme measures.

Can China's march across the Pacific be stopped, or is the era of US global domination at an end?

Glossary

For simplicity, this glossary is common across all FX Holden novels and may refer to abbreviations or systems not in this novel. As such, it is useful as a reference beyond this book! Please note, weapons or systems marked with an asterisk* are currently still under development or speculative. If there is no asterisk, then the system has already been deployed by at least one nation.

3D PRINTER: A printer which can recreate a 3D object based on a three-dimensional digital model, typically by laying down many thin layers of a material in succession

AC-130X*: a variant of the AC-130 series of special operations aircraft and follow-on to the AC-130J Ghostrider. Stripped of all heavy weapons to make room for two Rapid Dragon* palletized ordnance dispensers, it is envisaged as a signals and electronic intelligence, surveillance and reconnaissance aircraft with drone and standoff strike capability.

ADA*: All Domain Attack. An attack on an enemy in which all operational domains—space, cyber, ground, air and naval—are engaged either simultaneously or sequentially

AI: Artificial intelligence, as applied in aircraft to assist pilots, in intelligence to assist with intelligence analysis, or in ordnance such as drones and uncrewed vehicles to allow semi-autonomous or even fully autonomous decision making.

AIM-120D: US medium-range supersonic air-to-air missile

AIM-260* Joint Advanced Tactical Missile (JATM), proposed replacement for AIM-120, with twin-boost phase, launch and loiter capability. Swarming capability has been discussed.

AIS: Automated identification system, a system used by all ships to provide update data on their location to their owners and insurers. Civilian ships are required to keep their transponder on at all times unless under threat from pirates; military ships transmit at their own discretion. Rogue nations often ignore the requirement in order to hide the location of ships with illicit cargoes or conducting illegal activities.

AIR TROPHY*: 'Trophy' is an Israeli-made anti-projectile defense system using explosively formed penetrators to defeat attacks on vehicles. It is currently fitted to several Israeli and US armored vehicle types. In 2023 the US Navy announced it was testing the Trophy system for naval defense. Use as an air defense system is speculative.

AGGRESSOR/ADVERSARY: Fighter squadrons that provide training against adversary aircraft are known as 'Aggressor' squadrons. The US Air Force has several in-house No. 9 Squadrons (including F-16s and F-35s) which it uses to train fighter pilots and joint tactical air controllers. In the US Marines and Navy these are known as 'Adversary' units. In 2022, the USAF confirmed that Aggressor aircraft in Alaska had been used to intercept Russian aircraft off the coast of Alaska, and No. 9 Squadrons had been used to backfill regular USAF squadrons deployed overseas. Many air forces including the USAF and RAF, also use private contractors to provide these services, and several large private military aviation contractors exist, fielding recently retired F-16 and F-18 fighters. The most advanced private air force in the world, Air USA, claims to be able to field three No. 9 Squadrons including 46 ex-RAAF F/A-18 Hornets.

ALL DOMAIN KILL CHAIN*: Also known as Multi-Domain Kill Chain. An attack in which advanced AI allows high-speed assimilation of data from multiple sources (satellite, cyber, ground and air) to generate engagement solutions for military maneuver, precision fire support, artillery or combat air support.

AMD-65: Hungarian-made military assault rifle

AN/APG-81: The active electronically scanning array (AESA) radar system on the F-35 Panther that allows it to track and engage multiple air and ground targets simultaneously

ANGELS: Radio brevity code for 'thousands of feet'. Angels five is five thousand feet.

AO YIN: Legendary Chinese four-horned bull with insatiable appetite for human flesh

APC: Armored personnel carrier; a wheeled or tracked lightly armored vehicle able to transport troops into combat and provide limited covering fire

ARMATA T-14: Next-generation Russian main battle tank

ASFN: Anti-screw fouling net. Traditionally, a net boom laid across the entrance of a harbor to hinder the entrance of ships or submarines. Can also be dropped from a fast boat, or fired from a subsea drone to foul the screws of a surface vessel.

ASRAAM: Advanced Short-Range Air-to-Air Missile (infrared only)

ASROC: Anti-submarine rocket-launched torpedo. Allows a torpedo to be fired at a submerged target from up to ten miles away, allowing the torpedo to enter the water close to the target and reducing the chances the target can evade the attack.

ASTUTE CLASS: Next-generation British nuclear-powered attack submarine (SSN) designed for stealth operation. Powered by a Rolls Royce reactor plant coupled to a pump-jet propulsion system. *HMS Astute* is the first of seven planned hulls, *HMS Agincourt* is the last. Can carry up to 38 torpedoes and cruise missiles, and is one of the first British submarines to be steered by a 'pilot' using a joystick.

AUKUS class submarine*: AUKUS is a trilateral security pact between Australia, the United Kingdom, and the United States announced on 15 September 2021 for the Indo-Pacific region to counter China's influence. The AUKUS submarine deal signed in 2022 will provide Australia with access to nuclear-powered submarines, which are stealthier and more capable than conventionally powered boats. The total cost of the deal is estimated to be $100 billion, making it Australia's biggest defense spend. According to media reports, Australia will first buy US-designed Virginia-class submarines as a stopgap, before acquiring a future UK-designed boat under a multi-billion-dollar deal. The UK-built submarines are currently in the design phase and are set to replace the Astute fleet. The *AE1* featured in this novel is speculative.

ASW: Anti-Submarine Warfare

AWACS: Airborne Warning and Control System aircraft, otherwise known as AEW&C (Airborne Early Warning and Control). Aircraft with advanced radar and communication systems that can detect aircraft at ranges up to several hundred miles, and direct air operations over a combat theater.

AXEHEAD: Russian long-range hypersonic air-to-air missile, identifying code R-37, designed primarily to shoot down large aircraft at long ranges. Used in combat in Ukraine. The Royal United Services Institute stated: "The Russian Air Force fired up to six R-37Ms per day during October 2022. The extremely high speed of the weapon, coupled with very long effective range and a seeker designed for engaging low-altitude targets, makes it particularly difficult to evade." The

Ukraine Air Force disputes this assessment. The Axehead effectiveness is therefore assumed high, but impossible to verify.

AUTONOMOUS vs SEMI AUTONOMOUS: In drone warfare, an autonomous drone is one which can conduct its mission completely independent of human interaction once launched. This reduces its vulnerability to jamming as no signals pass between its operator and the drone which can be jammed. A semi-autonomous drone is one which relies on a wireless/radio/satellite link for communication with its operator but can make some decisions on its own if contact with the human operator is lost or unnecessary. Due to the reliance on a communication link to the operator, such drones are susceptible to jamming.

B-21 RAIDER*: Replacement for the retiring US B-2 Stealth Bomber and B-52. The Raider is intended to provide a lower-cost, stealthier alternative to the B-2 with expanded weapons delivery capabilities to include hypersonic and beyond visual range air-to-air missiles.

BARRETT MRAD M22: Multirole adaptive design sniper rifle with replaceable barrels, capable of firing different ammunition types including anti-materiel rounds, accurate out to 1,500 meters or nearly one mile

BATS*: Boeing Airpower Teaming System, semi-autonomous uncrewed combat aircraft. The BATS drone is designed to accompany 4th- and 5th-generation fighter aircraft on missions either in an air escort, recon or electronic warfare capacity.

BATTLE-NET: Generic name for tactical data sharing systems such as the US The Tactical Targeting Network Technology (TTNT) system; a high-bandwidth, secure data sharing network that enables real-time sharing of targeting and situational awareness data among aircraft, ground vehicles, and command centers, allowing for faster and more effective decision-making on the battlefield.

BELLADONNA: A Russian-made mobile electronic warfare vehicle capable of jamming enemy airborne warning aircraft, ground radars, radio communications and radar-guided missiles

BESAT*: New 1,200-ton class of Iranian SSP (air-independent propulsion) submarine. Also known as Project Qaaem. Capable of launching mines, torpedoes or cruise missiles.

BIG RED ONE: US 1st Infantry Division (see also BRO), aka the Bloody First

BINGO: Radio brevity code showing that an aircraft has only enough fuel left for a return to base

BIRD-DOG*: An 'autonomous foraging drone' or uncrewed aerial vehicle which can locate its own sources of power resupply and operate completely independently of human interaction when ordered to.

BLACK WIDOW (P-99)*: Several companies were competing in 2023/4 for the Next Generation Air Dominance (NGAD) air superiority initiative. The Black Widow is a purely speculative platform combining what is known about the requirements issued and the designs in testing. NGAD is described by the USAF as a "family of systems," with a stealth fighter aircraft as the centerpiece of the system, and other parts of the system likely to be uncrewed escort aircraft to carry extra munitions and perform other missions. In particular, NGAD aims to develop a system that addresses the operation needs of the Pacific theater of operations, where current USAF fighters lack sufficient range and payload. The successful NGAD aircraft is therefore unlikely to resemble current US stealth fighters such as the F-22 Raptor or F-35 Panther.

BLOODY FIRST: US 1st Infantry Division, aka the Big Red One (BRO)

BOGEY: Unidentified aircraft detected by radar

BRADLEY UGCV*: US uncrewed ground combat vehicle prototype based on a modified M3 Bradley combat fighting vehicle. A tracked vehicle with medium armor, it is intended to be controlled remotely by a crew in a vehicle, or ground troops, up to two miles away. Armed with 5kw blinding laser and autoloading TOW anti-tank missiles. See also HYPERION

BRO: Big Red One or Bloody First, nickname for US Army 1st Infantry Division

BTR-80: A Russian-made amphibious armored personnel carrier armed with a 30 mm automatic cannon

BUG OUT: Withdraw from combat

BUK: Russian-made self-propelled anti-aircraft missile system designed to engage medium-range targets such as aircraft, smart bombs and cruise missiles

BUSTER: 100% throttle setting on an aircraft, or full military power

CAP: Combat air patrol; an offensive or defensive air patrol over an objective

CAS: Close air support; air action by rotary-winged or fixed-wing aircraft against hostile targets in close proximity to friendly forces. CAS operations are often directed by a joint terminal air controller, or JTAC, embedded with a military unit.

CASA CN-235: Turkish Air Force medium-range twin-engined transport aircraft

CBRN: Chemical, biological, radiological or nuclear (see also NBC SUIT)

CCP: Communist Party of China. Governed by a Politburo comprising the Chinese Premier and senior party ministers and officials.

CENTURION: US 20 mm radar-guided close-in weapons system for protection of ground or naval assets against attack by artillery, rocket or missiles

CHAMP*: Counter-electronics High-power Advanced Microwave Projectile; a 'launch and loiter' cruise missile which attacks sensitive electronics with high power microwave bursts to damage electronics. Similar in effect to an electromagnetic pulse (EMP) weapon.

CHONGMING CH-7 Rainbow*: A stealthy flying-wing uncrewed fighter aircraft similar to the US F-47B, with a 22-meter wingspan and 10m length, and a maximum take-off weight of 13 tons. Reportedly able to fly at 920 km/h or 571 mph, with an operational radius of 2,000 km or 1,200 miles. Can carry air to air or air to surface missiles in an internal bay. Prototypes have been photographed and production was due to begin in 2022 but deployment has not yet been confirmed.

CIC: Combat Information Center. The 'nerve center' on an early warning aircraft, warship or submarine that functions as a tactical center and provides processed information for command and control of the near battlespace or area of operations. On a warship, acts on orders from and relays information to the bridge.

CO: Commanding Officer

COALITION: A US-led Coalition of Nations.

COLT: Combat Observation Laser Team; a forward artillery observer team armed with a laser for designating targets for attack by precision-guided munitions

CONSTELLATION* class frigate: the result of the US FFG(X) program, a warship with advanced anti-air, anti-surface and anti-submarine capabilities capable of serving as a data integration and communication hub. The first ship in the class, *USS Constellation*, is expected to enter service mid-2020s. *USS Congress* will be the second ship in the class.

CONTROL ROOM: the compartment on a submarine from which weapons, sensors, propulsion and navigation commands are coordinated

COP: Combat Outpost (US)

C-RAM: Counter-rocket, artillery and mortar cannon, also abbreviated counter-RAM

CROWS: Common Remotely Operated Weapon Station, a weapon such as .50 caliber machine gun, mounted on a turret and controlled remotely by a soldier inside a vehicle, bunker or command post

CUDA*: Missile nickname (from barraCUDA) for the supersonic US short- to medium-range 'Small Advanced Capabilities Missile'. It has tri-mode (optical, active radar and infrared heat-seeking) sensors, thrust vectoring for extreme maneuverability and a hit-to-kill terminal attack

CYBERCOM: US Cyberspace combatant command responsible for cyber defense and warfare.

DARPA: US Defense Advanced Research Projects Agency, a research and development agency responsible for bringing new military technologies to the US armed forces

DAS: Distributed Aperture System; a 360-degree sensor system on the F-35 Panther allowing the pilot to track targets visually at greater than 'eyeball' range

DEWS*: Directed Energy Weapon Systems. Various laser and microwave energy based systems are in development or have seen experimental use by militaries including US, UK,

Japan, Russia, China, India and South Korea. The US Navy has deployed the 60+ kilowatt HELIOS laser system on several vessels, which is claimed to be capable of long-range Intelligence, Surveillance, Reconnaissance (ISR) and Counter UAS operations, including optical-infrared jamming. The US Army has announced the BLUEHALO 20 kilowatt anti drone system will be mounted on light tactical vehicles and a 50 kilowatt MSRAD (Maneuver Short Range Air Defense) laser on Stryker vehicles. It is also experimenting with a truck mounted 50 kilowatt HEL-MD (High Energy Laser Mobile Demonstrator) laser for cruise missile and artillery defense.

DFDA: Australian armed forces Defense Forces Discipline Act

DFM: Australian armed forces Defense Force Magistrate

DIA: The US Defense Intelligence Agency

DIRECTOR OF NATIONAL CYBER SECURITY*. The NSA's Cyber Security Directorate is an organization that unifies NSA's foreign intelligence and cyber defense missions and is charged with preventing and eradicating threats to National Security Systems and the Defense Industrial Base. Various US government sources have mooted the elevation of the role of Director of Cyber Security to a Cabinet-level Director of National Cyber Security (on a level with the Director of National Intelligence), appointed by the US President to coordinate the activities of the many different agencies and military departments engaged in cyber warfare.

DRONE: Uncrewed aerial vehicle, or UAV, used for combat, transport, refueling or reconnaissance. Militaries and manufacturers twist themselves in knots to avoid using the word 'drone'. For example, 'loitering kamikaze drones' such as the Switchblade and Lancet have been described by the

UK military as 'One Way Uncrewed Aerial Attack Vehicles'. Let's just call them drones.

ECS: Engagement Control Station; the local control center for a HELLADS laser battery which tracks targets and directs anti-air defensive fire

EMP: Electromagnetic pulse. Nuclear weapons produce an EMP wave which can destroy unshielded electronic components. The major military powers have also been experimenting with non-nuclear weapons which can also produce an EMP pulse–see CHAMP missile

ETA: Estimated Time of Arrival

F-16 FALCON: US-made 4th-generation multirole fighter aircraft flown by Turkey

F-22: The F-22 fighter is a stealth aircraft with low radar cross-section (RCS), long range, and high weapons payload capability, introduced in 2005 and currently planned to be retired in the 2040s. Though intended primarily for air-air combat it is capable of carrying a variety of air-to-air and air-to-ground weapons, including missiles, bombs, and rockets, with a maximum weapons payload of approximately 2,000 pounds.

F-35: US 5th-generation fighter aircraft, known either as the Panther (pilot nickname) or Lightning II (manufacturer name). The Panther nickname was first coined by the 6th Weapons Squadron 'Panther Tamers'. There is much speculation about the capabilities of the Panther, just as there is about the Russian Su-57 Felon. Neither has been extensively combat tested, though the F-35 has reportedly been used in combat by the Israeli Air Force.

F-47B (currently X-47B) FANTOM*: A Northrop Grumman demonstration uncrewed combat aerial vehicle (UCAV) in trials with the US Navy and a part of the DARPA

Joint UCAS program. See also MQ-25 STINGRAY. The Fantom is used in these novels as an example of a possible uncrewed combat aircraft, and should not be taken to reflect the actual capabilities of the X-47B.

FAC: Forward air controller; an aviator embedded with a ground unit to direct close air support attacks. See also TAC(P) or JTAC

FAST MOVERS: Fighter jets

FATEH: Iranian SSK (diesel electric) submarine. At 500 tons, also considered a midget submarine. Capable of launching torpedoes, torpedo-launched cruise missiles and mines

FELON: Russian 5th-generation stealth fighter aircraft, the Sukhoi Su-57. There is much speculation about the capabilities of the Felon, just as there is about the US F-35 Panther. Neither has been extensively combat tested. Unlike the F-35 however the FELON has not entered large scale production and few flying production airframes exist. Capabilities discussed in these novels are speculative.

FINGER FOUR FORMATION: a fighter aircraft patrol formation in which four aircraft fly together in a pattern that resembles the tips of the four fingers of a hand. Three such formations can form a squadron of 12 aircraft.

FIRESCOUT: an uncrewed autonomous scout helicopter for service on US warships, used for anti-ship and anti-submarine operations

FISTER: A member of a FiST (Fire Support Team)

FLANKER: Russian Sukhoi-30 or 35 attack aircraft; see also J-11 (China)

FOX (1, 2 or 3): Radio brevity code indicating a pilot has fired an air-to-air missile, either semi-active radar seeking (1), infrared (2) or active radar seeking (3)

GAL*: A natural language learning system (AI) used by Israel's Unit 8200 to conduct complex analytical research support

GAL-CLASS SUBMARINE*: An upgraded *Dolphin II* class submarine, fitted with the GAL AI system, allowing it to be operated by a two-person crew.

G/ATOR: Ground/Air Oriented Task Radar (GATOR); a radar specialized for the detection of incoming artillery fire, rockets or missiles. Also able to calculate the origin of attack for counterfire purposes.

GBU: Guided Bomb Unit

GPS: Global Positioning System, a network of civilian or military satellites used to provide accurate map reference and location data

GRAY WOLF*: US subsonic standoff air-launched cruise missile with swarming (horde) capabilities. The Gray Wolf is designed to launch from multiple aircraft, including the C-130, and defeat enemy air defenses by overwhelming them with large numbers. It will feature modular swap-out warheads.

GREYHOUND: Radio brevity code for the launch of an air-ground missile

GRU: Russian military intelligence service

H-20*: Xian Hong 20 stealth bomber with a range of 12,000 km or 7,500 miles and payload of 10 tons. Comparable to the US B-21.

GYRFALCON, J-31: The Shenyang FC-31 Gyrfalcon, also known as the J-31, is a Chinese prototype mid-sized twinjet 5th-generation fighter aircraft developed by Shenyang Aircraft Corporation. It has a length of 16.9m, height of about 4.8m, and a wing span of 11.5m. The aircraft has a maximum speed of 1,200 knots, a combat range of 670 nautical miles on internal fuel or 1,042 nautical miles with external tanks, and a service ceiling of around 65,616 feet3. It has a maximum payload of 8,000 kg (four missiles in internal bays and six missiles or bombs on external hardpoints) and a maximum take-off weight of 28,000 kg. The first prototype took flight on October 31, 2021, and reached operational capability in 2020. It is being made available for export and is expected to replace the J-15 Flying Shark as China's dominant carrier aircraft.

HACM*: Hypersonic Attack Cruise Missile. A two-stage missile with solid fuel first stage boosting the missile to supersonic velocity after which a scramjet engine takes over to drive the missile to speeds of Mach 5 and above. The contract to develop HACM was awarded to Raytheon in September 2022.

HARM: High-speed Anti-Radar Missile; a missile which homes on the signals produced by anti-air missile radars like that used by the BUK or PANTSIR

HAWKEYE: Northrop Grumman E2D airborne warning and control aircraft. Capable of launching from aircraft carriers and networking (sharing data) with compatible aircraft.

HE: High-explosive munitions; general purpose explosive warheads

HEAT: High-Explosive Anti-Tank munitions; shells specially designed to penetrate armor

HELIOS*: Laser weapon. See DEWS

HEL-MD*: High Energy Laser Mobile Demonstrator) laser. See DEWS.

HELLADS*: High Energy Liquid Laser Area Defense System; an alternative to missile or projectile-based air defense systems that attacks enemy missiles, rockets or bombs with high energy laser and/or microwave pulses.

Currently being tested by US, Chinese, Russian and EU ground, air and naval forces. The combination of HELLADS with HPM defense systems is logical but speculative. See also DEWS.

HIMARS: High Mobility Artillery Rocket System, is a highly mobile artillery rocket system developed by Lockheed Martin Missiles and Fire Control that offers the firepower of MLRS on a wheeled chassis. It carries a single six-pack of rockets or one long range GPS guided ATACMS missile on a 5-ton truck, and can launch the entire MLRS family of munitions. It has a shoot-and-scoot capability that reduces the enemy's ability to locate and target it.

HORDE*: Drones, missiles or smart bombs with onboard AI and the ability to coordinate their actions with other drones while in flight, either autonomously or using preselected protocols. 'Horde' tactics differ from 'swarm' tactics in that they rely on large numbers to overwhelm enemy defenses. See also SWARM

HPM*: High Power Microwave; an untargeted local area defensive weapon which attacks sensitive electronics in missiles and guided bombs to damage electronics such as guidance systems. Chinese weapons developers using a pulse-HPM or EMP weapon were reported in 2023 to have brought down an uncrewed aircraft flying at 5,000 feet. The US Air Force Research Laboratory's (AFRL) Tactical High Power Operational Responder (THOR) system is a shipping-container-sized HPM weapon designed to bring down drone swarms. All HPM systems can currently be regarded as prototypes, and squad level or miniaturized HPM systems do not yet exist.

HSU-003*: Planned Chinese large uncrewed underwater vehicle optimized for seabed warfare, i.e. piloting itself to a specific location on the sea floor (a harbor or shipping lane) and conducting reconnaissance or anti-shipping attacks. Comparable to the US Orca.

HYPERION*: Proposed lightly armored uncrewed ground vehicle (UGCV). Can be fitted with turret-mounted 50kw laser for anti-air, anti-personnel defense and autoloading TOW missile launcher. See also BRADLEY UGCV

HYPERSONIC: Speeds greater than 5x the speed of sound. Often used in relation to missiles. Ballistic missiles are by nature hypersonic. Examples in use include the Russian Kh-47M2 Kinzhal, or "Dagger" in Russian: a Russian hypersonic air-launched ballistic missile that is claimed to have a range of 2,000 km (1,200 mi) and Mach 10 speed. It can carry either conventional or nuclear warheads and can be launched by Tu-22M3 bombers or MiG-31K interceptors. It has seen use in the Ukraine conflict with US forces claiming a 100% interception rate using the PATRIOT missile defense system (unverified).

ICC: Information Coordination Center; command center for multiple air defense batteries such as PATRIOT or HELLADS

IED: Improvised explosive device, for example, a roadside bomb

IFF: Identify Friend or Foe transponder, a radio transponder that allows weapons systems to determine whether a target is an ally or enemy

IFV: Infantry fighting vehicle, a highly mobile, lightly armored, wheeled or tracked vehicle capable of carrying troops into a combat and providing fire support. See NAMER

IMA BK: The combat AI built into Russia's Su-57 Felon and Okhotnik fighter aircraft

IONIC BOUNCE: a technique used by air defense radars to detect stealth aircraft by bouncing radio waves off the boundary to the ionosphere, striking the aircraft on their larger upper surfaces.

IR: Infrared or heat-seeking system

ISIS: Self-proclaimed Islamic State of Iraq and Syria

J-7: Fishbed; 3rd-generation Chinese fighter, a copy of cold war Russian Mig-21

J-10: Vigorous Dragon; 3rd-generation Chinese fighter, comparable to US F-16

J-11: Flanker; 4th-generation Chinese fighter, copy of Russian Su-27

J-15: Flying Shark; 4th-generation PLA Navy, twin-engine twin-seat fighter, comparable to Russian Su-33 and a further development of the J-11. Currently the most common aircraft flown off China's aircraft carriers.

J-11 AI variant*: *Zhi Sheng* (Intelligence Victory); 4th-generation, two-seater twin-engine multirole strike fighter. In 2019 it was announced a variant of the J-11 was being developed with *Zhi Sheng* Artificial Intelligence to replace the human 'backseater' or copilot.

J-20: 'Mighty Dragon'; 5th-generation single-seat, twin-engine Chinese stealth fighter, claimed to be comparable to the US F-35 or F-22, or Russian Su-57. Aviation experts believe it would have a larger cross section than its western counterparts, not just because of its larger size, but also because it employs nose-mounted canards. The first operational squadron of J-20 fighters was stood up by China in 2018. As many as ten squadrons exist today.

J-31: See Gyrfalcon.

JAGM: Joint air-ground missile. A US short-range anti-armor or anti-personnel missile fired from an aircraft. It can be laser or radar guided and has an 18 lb. warhead.

JASSM: AGM-158 Joint Air-to-Surface Standoff Missile; long-range subsonic stealth cruise missile capable of fielding multiple warhead types (e.g. electronic warfare, high explosive, cluster, anti-armor.) JASSM-ER is the Extended Range variant which can travel up to 580 miles or 930 kilometers. JASSM-E is an electronic signature attack version designed specifically to attack enemy command, control and intelligence targets. Other variants include electronic warfare and anti-radar capabilities.

JDAM: Joint Direct Attack Munition; bombs guided by laser or GPS to their targets

JOE*: "Joint Outcome Evaluator." A natural language learning system (AI) used by the DIA to conduct sophisticated analytical research support. The DIA has publicly reported it is already using AI for analytical support and to explore machine learning potential, but the JOE system in this novel is speculative.

JLTV*: US Joint Light Tactical Vehicle; planned replacement for the US ground forces Humvee multipurpose vehicle, to be available in recon/scout, infantry transport, heavy guns, close combat, command and control, or ambulance versions

JTAC: Joint terminal air controller. A member of a ground force–e.g., Marine unit–trained to direct the action of combat aircraft engaged in close air support and other offensive air operations from a forward position. See also CAS

K-77M*: Supersonic Russian-made medium-range active radar homing air-to-air missile with extreme maneuverability. It is being developed from the existing R-77 missile.

KALIBR: Russian-made anti-ship, anti-submarine and land attack cruise missile with 500kg conventional or nuclear warhead. The Kalibr-M variant* will have an extended range of up to 4,500 km or 2,700 miles (the distance of, e.g., Iran to Paris).

KARAKURT CLASS: A Russian corvette class which first entered service in 2018. Armed with Pantsir close-in weapons systems, Sosna-R anti-air missile defense and Kalibr supersonic anti-ship missiles. An anti-submarine sensor/weapon loadout is planned but not yet deployed.

KC-135 STRATOTANKER: US airborne refueling aircraft

KINZHAL: Russian air launched ballistic missile. Deployed in Ukraine conflict. Claimed to fly at Mach 10, Russia asserts the Kinzhal is both hypersonic and impossible to intercept. Ukrainian Patriot missile crews claim the Kinzhal travels only at Mach 3.6 (not hypersonic) and has been successfully intercepted. It is impossible to verify these competing claims.

KRYPTON: Supersonic Russian air-launched anti-radar missile, it is also being adapted for use against ships and large aircraft

LAUNCH AND LOITER: The capability of a missile or drone to fly itself to a target area and wait at altitude for final targeting instructions

LCS: Littoral combat ship. In the US Navy it refers to the *Independence* or *Freedom* class; in Iran, the *Safineh* class; in other navies it may be considered equivalent to a frigate or corvette class. Has the capabilities of a small assault transport, including a flight deck and hangar for housing two SH-60 or MH-60 Seahawk helicopters, a stern ramp for operating small boats, and the cargo volume and payload to deliver a small assault force with fighting vehicles to a roll-on/roll-off port facility. Standard armaments include Mk 110 57 mm guns and RIM-116 Rolling Airframe Missiles. Also equipped with autonomous air, surface and underwater vehicles. Possessing lower air defense and surface warfare capabilities than destroyers, the LCS concept emphasizes speed, flexible mission modules and a shallow draft.

LEOPARD: Main battle tank fielded by NATO forces including Turkey

LIAONING: China's first aircraft carrier, modified from the former Russian Navy aircraft cruiser, the *Varyag*. Since superseded by China's Type 002 (*Shandong*) and Type 003 (*Fujian*) carriers, the *Liaoning* is now used for testing new technologies for carrier use, such as the J-31 stealth fighter.

LIBERATOR II*: Also known as the 'Liberty Lifter'. The Liberty Lifter is a concept for a long-range, low-cost seaplane that can carry heavy loads across oceans by flying close to the water surface using the ground effect. The concept was launched by DARPA in mid-2022 to develop a new plane that could combine the speed and flexibility of airlift with the runway-independence and endurance of SEALift. The concept aims to revolutionize heavy air lift for maritime operations and logistics. DARPA awarded contracts to two teams, Aurora Flight Sciences and General Atomics, in February 2023 to design their own versions of the Liberty Lifter. The final designs are expected by mid-2024, and the winning design will proceed to build and test a full-size prototype. DARPA hopes to have the Liberty Lifter flying within roughly five years

LOITERING MUNITION: A missile or bomb, able to wait at altitude for final targeting instructions. Example: The AeroVironment Switchblade is a miniature loitering munition, designed by AeroVironment and used by several branches of the United States military. Small enough to fit in a backpack, the Switchblade launches from a tube, flies to the target area, directed wirelessly by an operator and crashes into its target while detonating its explosive warhead.

LONG-RANGE HYPERSONIC WEAPONS (LRHW)*: A prototype US missile consisting of a rocket and glide vehicle, capable of being launched by submarine, from land or from aircraft.

LONGSHOT*: Air launched drone, first flight expected 2024. According to manufacturer "able to be launched by manned fighter jets, transports or other aircraft and capable of venturing deep into hostile airspace to effectively engage enemy targets. Able to conduct a fighter sweep ahead of a strike wave and join human-crewed aircraft on a mission, effectively bolstering the firepower of the forces."

LRASM: Long Range Anti-Ship Missile is a stealth anti-ship cruise missile developed for the United States Air Force and United States Navy by the Defense Advanced Research Projects Agency (DARPA). It is a precision-guided missile designed to meet the needs of US Navy and Air Force Warfighters against maritime capital ship targets, with a long range that enables target engagement from well outside the range of direct counter-fire weapons.

LS3*: Legged Squad Support System–a mechanized dog-like robot powered by hydrogen fuel cells and supported by a cloud-based AI. Currently being explored by DARPA and the US armed forces for logistical support or squad scouting and IED detection roles.

LTMV: Light Tactical Multirole Vehicle; a very long name for what is essentially a jeep.

M1A2 ABRAMS: US main battle tank. In 2016, the US Army and Marine Corps began testing out the Israeli Trophy active protection system to provide additional defense against incoming projectiles. Improvements planned for the M1A3 are to include a lighter 120 mm gun, added road wheels with improved suspension, a more durable track, lighter-weight armor, long-range precision armaments, and infrared camera and laser detectors.

M22: See BARRETT MRAD M22 sniper rifle

M27: US-made military assault rifle

MAD: Magnetic Anomaly Detection, used by warships to detect large artificial objects under the surface of the sea, such as mines, or submarines

MAIN BATTLE TANK: See MBT

MANPAD: Man portable air defense missile, such as US Stinger, Chinese Crossbow or UK Starstreak.

MASS*: Marine Autonomous Surface Ship, or autonomous trailing vessel. Not to be confused with Uncrewed Surface Vessels such as kamikaze drone boats, which have already seen action in Ukraine.

MBT: Main battle tank; a heavily armored combat vehicle capable of direct fire and maneuver

MEFP: Multiple Explosive Formed Penetrators; a defensive weapon which uses small explosive charges to create and fire small metal slugs at an incoming projectile, thereby destroying it. As used in the Israeli Trophy armored vehicle defense system.

MEMS: Micro-Electro-Mechanical System

METEOR: Long-range air-to-air missile with active radar seeker, but also able to be updated with target data in-flight by any suitably equipped allied unit

MIA: Missing in action

MIKE: Radio brevity code for minutes

MIL-25: Export version of the Mi-25 'Hind' Russian helicopter gunship

MOP: Massive ordnance penetrator. A 30,000 lb. bomb with a hardened steel casing using GPS guidance to enable precision targeting. It can be launched at 'standoff' ranges and glide to its target.

MOPP: Mission-Oriented Protective Posture protective gear; equipment worn to protect troops against CBRN weapons. See also NBC SUIT

MP: Military Police

MQ-25 STINGRAY: The MQ-25 Stingray is a Boeing-designed prototype uncrewed US airborne refueling aircraft. See also F-47B Fantom. Already in service.

MSRAD: Maneuver Short Range Air Defense laser. See DEWS.

MSS: Ministry of State Security, Chinese umbrella intelligence organization responsible for counterespionage and counterterrorism, and foreign intelligence gathering. Equivalent to the US FBI, CIA and NSA.

NAMER: (Leopard) Israeli infantry fighting vehicle (IFV). More heavily armored than a Merkava IV main battle tank. According to the Israel Defense Forces, the Namer is the most heavily armored vehicle in the world of any type.

NAMICA: The Indian NAMICA (NAG Missile Carrier) is an Infantry Fighting Vehicle (IFV) equipped with a 30 mm automatic cannon, a 7.62 mm machine gun, and a launcher for anti-tank guided missiles, designed to provide fire support and transport for infantry troops.

NATO: North Atlantic Treaty Organization

NAVAL STRIKE MISSILE (NSM): Supersonic anti-ship missile deployed by NATO navies

NBC SUIT: A protective suit issued to protect the wearer against Nuclear, Biological or Chemical weapons. Usually includes a lining to protect the user from radiation and either a gas mask or air recycling unit.

NORAD: The North American Aerospace Defense Command is a United States and Canadian bi-national organization charged with the missions of aerospace warning, aerospace control and maritime warning for North America. Aerospace warning includes the detection, validation and warning of attack against North America whether by aircraft, missiles or space vehicles, through mutual support arrangements with other commands.

NSA: US National Security Agency, cyber intelligence, cyber warfare and defense agency

OFSET*: Offensive Swarm Enabled Tactical drones. Proposed US anti-personnel, anti-armor drone system capable of swarming AI (see SWARM) and able to deploy small munitions against enemy troop or vehicles while moving.

OKHOTNIK*: 5th-generation Sukhoi S-70 uncrewed stealth combat aircraft using avionics systems from the Su-57 Felon and fitted with two internal weapons bays, for 7,000kg of ordnance. Requires a pilot and systems officer, similar to current US uncrewed combat aircraft. Can be paired with Su-57 aircraft and controlled by a pilot.

OMON: Otryad Mobil'nyy Osobogo Naznacheniya; the Russian National Guard mobile police force

ORCA*: Prototype US large displacement uncrewed underwater vehicle with modular payload bay capable of anti-submarine, anti-ship or reconnaissance activities

OVOD: Subsonic Russian-made air-launched cruise missile capable of carrying high-explosive, submunition or fragmentation warheads

P-99 Black Widow (Pursuit Fighter)*: Concept aircraft. Several companies were competing in 2023 for the Next Generation Air Dominance air superiority initiative. The Black Widow is a purely speculative platform combining what is known about the requirements issued and the designs in testing. NGAD is described by the USAF as a "family of systems," with a stealth fighter aircraft as the centerpiece of the system, and other parts of the system likely to be uncrewed escort aircraft to carry extra munitions and perform other missions. In particular, NGAD aims to develop a system that addresses the operation needs of the Pacific theater of operations, where current USAF fighters lack sufficient range and payload. The successful NGAD aircraft is therefore unlikely to resemble current US stealth fighters such as the F-22 Rapiére or F-35 Panther.

PANTHER: Pilot name for the F-35 Lightning II stealth fighter, first coined by the 6th Weapons Squadron 'Panther Tamers' due to the unpopularity of the official name 'Lightning II'. There is much speculation about the capabilities of the Panther, just as there is about the Russian Su-57 Felon. Neither has been extensively combat tested.

PANTSIR: Russian-made truck-mounted anti-aircraft system which is a further development of the PENSNE: 'Pince-nez' in English. A Russian-made autonomous ground-to-air missile currently being rolled out for the BUK anti-air defense system.

PARS: Turkish light armored vehicle

PATRIOT: An anti-aircraft, interceptor missile defense system which uses its own radar to identify and engage airborne threats

PEACE EAGLE: Turkish Boeing 737 Airborne Early Warning and Control aircraft (see AWACS)

PENSNE: See PANTSIR

PERDIX*: Lightweight air-launched armed microdrone with swarming capability (see SWARM). Designed to be launched from underwing canisters or even from the flare/chaff launchers of existing aircraft. Can be used for recon, target identification or delivery of lightweight ordnance.

PEREGRINE*: US medium-range, multimode (infrared, radar, optical) seeker missile with short form body designed for use by stealth aircraft

PERSEUS*: A stealth, hypersonic, multiple warhead missile under development for the British Royal Navy and French Navy

PHASED-ARRAY RADAR: A radar which can steer a beam of radio waves quickly across the sky to detect planes and missiles

PL-15: Chinese long-range radar-guided air-to-air missile, comparable to the US AIM-120D or UK Meteor.

PL-21*: Chinese long-range multimode missile (radar, infrared, optical), comparable to US AIM-260

PLA: People's Liberation Army

PLA-AF (PLAAF): People's Liberation Army Air Force, comparable to the US Air Force, with more than 400 3rd-generation fighter aircraft, 1,200 4th-generation, and nearly 200 5th-generation stealth aircraft

PLA-N (PLAN): People's Liberation Army Navy

PLA-N AF (PLANAF): People's Liberation Army Navy Air Force, comparable to the US Navy Air Force and Marine

Corps Aviation, it performs coastal protection and aircraft carrier operations with more than 250 3rd-generation fighter aircraft, and 150 4th-generation fighter aircraft. There is speculation the PLA-N AF is considering the J-31 Gyrfalcon* (a prototype stealth fighter) for its aircraft carriers.

PODNOS: Russian-made portable 82 mm mortar

PUMP-JET PROPULSION: A propulsion system comprising a jet of water and a nozzle to direct the flow of water for steering purposes. Used on some submarines due to a quieter acoustic signature than that generated by a screw. The most 'stealthy' submarines are regarded to be those powered by diesel electric engines and pump-jet propulsion, such as trialed on the Russian *Kilo* class and proposed for the Australian *Attack* class*.

QHS*: Quantum Harmonic Sensor; a sensor system for detecting stealth aircraft at long ranges by analyzing the electromagnetic disturbances they create in background radiation.

QING* class submarine (Type 032): A class of diesel-electric submarine currently undergoing testing in China's People's Liberation Army Navy. It is said to be the world's largest conventional submarine, at a submerged displacement of 6,628 tons and is able to submerge for a maximum of 30 days. It features torpedo and vertically launched missile tubes and is believed to be capable of firing nuclear armed ballistic missiles. Only one of this class is known to have been deployed. It is speculated China built only one of this type of submarine because it was struggling at the time to build small nuclear reactors, having relied on Russia until this point to supply nuclear submarine power plants. This may also be why China's aircraft carriers are not nuclear powered.

RAAF: Royal Australian Air Force

RAF: Royal Air Force (UK)

RAPID DRAGON*: Palletized Munition Deployment System, in testing with USAF. A disposable weapons module which is airdropped in order to deploy flying munitions, typically cruise missiles, drones or glide bombs, from unmodified cargo planes such as the AC-130J Ghostrider.

REUNION* (Operation): Secret Chinese project to develop the Tianyi (Wing of Fate) armed autonomous drone and associated deployment technologies such as the TLV drone mothership and launch sites. Equivalent in scope to the US Manhattan project to develop the atom bomb, it is intended to supplant traditional invasion by ground forces, allowing control of enemy territory without the massive cost and risk of a conventional invasion.

ROCAF: Republic of China Air Force. The air force of Taiwan.

ROE: Rules of Engagement; the rules laid down by military commanders under which a unit can or cannot engage in combat. For example, 'units may only engage a hostile force if fired upon first'.

RPG: Rocket-propelled grenade

RTB: Return to base

SAFINEH CLASS: Also known as *Mowj/Wave* class. An Iranian trimaran hulled high-speed missile vessel equivalent to the US LCS class, or the Russia *Karakurt*-class corvette

SAM: Surface-to-Air Missile; an anti-air missile (often shortened to SA) for engaging aircraft

SAR: See SYNTHETIC APERTURE RADAR

SCREW: The propeller used to drive a boat or ship is referred to as a screw (helical blade) propeller. Submarine propellers typically comprise five to seven blades. See also PUMP-JET PROPULSION

SEAD: Suppression of Enemy Air Defenses; an air attack intended to take down enemy anti-air defense systems; see also WILD WEASEL

SENTINEL*: Lockheed Martin RQ-170 Sentinel flying wing stealth reconnaissance drone

SIDEWINDER: Heat-seeking short-range air-to-air missile

SITREP: Situation Report

SKYHAWK*: Chinese drone designed to team with fighter aircraft to provide added sensor or weapons delivery capabilities. Comparable to the planned US Boeing Loyal Wingman or Kratos drones.

SKY THUNDER: Chinese 1,000 lb. stealth air-launched cruise missile with swappable payload modules

SKYLON*: With capabilities similar to the US Space Shuttle and a modular payload Skylon is designed to take off and land like a normal aircraft. The vehicle design is a hydrogen-fueled aircraft that would take off from a specially built reinforced runway, and accelerate to Mach 5.4 at 26 kilometers (85,000 ft) altitude using the atmosphere's oxygen before switching the engines to use the internal liquid oxygen supply to accelerate to the Mach 25 necessary to reach a 400 km orbit. The high temperature test of the Reaction Engines – Rolls Royce precooler took place in 2019. Testing of the core engine components and pre-burner took place during 2020 and 2021. Uncrewed test flights in a "hypersonic testbed" (HTB) are planned for 2025.

SLR: Single lens reflex camera, favored by photojournalists and enthusiasts

SMERCH: Russian-made 300 mm rocket launcher capable of firing high-explosive, submunition or chemical weapons warheads

SOSUS: Sound Surveillance System. A chain of underwater listening posts located across the Arctic and Pacific Oceans. Used primarily for detection of submarines. US Navy recently announced it was upgrading SOSUS into the Deep Reliable Acoustic Path Exploitation System (DRAPES)* which is expected to have active low frequency sonar and magnetic anomaly detection capabilities added.

SPACECOM: United States Space Command (US SPACECOM or SPACECOM) is a unified combatant command of the United States Department of Defense, responsible for military operations in outer space, specifically all operations above 100 km above mean sea level

SPEAR/SPEAR-EW*: UK/Europe Select Precision at Range air-to-ground standoff attack missile, with LAUNCH AND LOITER capabilities. Will utilize a modular 'swappable' warhead system featuring high-explosive, anti-armor, fragmentation or electronic warfare (EW) warheads.

SPETSNAZ: Russian Special Operations Forces

SPLASH: US Navy and Air Force Radio brevity code showing a target has been destroyed. In artillery context splash over means impact imminent, splash out means rounds impacted.

SSBN: Strategic-level nuclear-powered (N) submarine platform for firing ballistic (B) missiles. Examples: UK *Vanguard* class, US *Ohio* class, Russia *Typhoon* class.

SSC: Subsurface Contact Supervisor; supervises operations against subsurface contacts from within a ship's Combat Information Center (CIC)

SSGN: A guided missile (G) nuclear (N) submarine that carries and launches guided cruise missiles as its primary weapon. Examples: US *Ohio* class, Russia *Yasen* class.

SSK: A diesel electric-powered submarine, quieter when submerged than a nuclear-powered submarine, but must rise to snorkel depth to run its diesel and recharge its batteries. Examples: Iranian *Fateh* class, Russian *Kilo* class, Israeli *Dolphin I* class.

SSN: A general purpose attack submarine (SS) powered by a nuclear reactor (N). Examples: HMS *Agincourt*, Russian *Akula* class.

SSP: A diesel electric submarine with air-independent propulsion system able to recharge batteries without using atmospheric oxygen. Allows the submarine to stay submerged longer than a traditional SSK. Examples: Israeli *Dolphin II* class, Iranian *Besat** class.

STANDOFF: Launched at long range

STINGER: US-made man-portable, low-level anti-air missile

STINGRAY*: The MQ-25 Stingray is a Boeing-designed prototype uncrewed US airborne refueling aircraft

STORMBREAKER*: US air-launched, precision-guided glide bomb that can use millimeter radar, laser or infrared imaging to match and then prioritize targets when operating in semi-autonomous AI mode

SU-57: See FELON

SUBSONIC: Below the speed of sound (under 767 mph, 1,234 kph)

SUNBURN: Russian-made 220 mm multiple rocket launcher capable of firing high-explosive, THERMOBARIC or penetrating warheads

SUPERSONIC: Faster than the speed of sound (over 767 mph, 1,234 kph); see also HYPERSONIC

SWARM: Drones, missiles or smart bombs with onboard AI and the ability to coordinate their actions with other drones while in flight, either autonomously or using preselected protocols. 'Swarm' tactics differ from 'horde' tactics in that swarms place more emphasis on coordinated action to defeat enemy defenses. See also HORDE

SYNTHETIC APERTURE RADAR (SAR): A form of radar that is used to create two-dimensional images or three-dimensional reconstructions of objects, such as landscapes. SAR uses the motion of the radar antenna over a target region to provide finer spatial resolution than conventional beam-scanning radars.

SYSOP: The systems operator inside the control station for a HELLADS battery, responsible for electronic and communications systems operation

T-14 ARMATA: Russian next-generation main battle tank or MBT. Designed as a 'universal combat platform' which can be adapted to infantry support, anti-armor or anti-armor configurations. First Russian MBT to be fitted with active electronically scanning array radar capable of identifying and engaging multiple air and ground targets simultaneously. Also the first Russian MBT to be fitted with a crew toilet. Used in combat in Syria from 2020 and claimed by Russia to have entered combat in Ukraine (but not verified independently). Very few examples are believed to exist and the last time they were paraded in public, three were seen, but one broke down and could not complete the parade.

T-90: Russian-made main battle tank

TAC(P): Tactical air controller, a specialist trained to direct close air support attacks. See also CAS; FAC; JTAC

TAIFUN*: Speculative iteration of the Zhu Hai Yun class drone mothership. The Zhu Hai Yun, launched in 2022, is the world's first drone carrier vessel, capable of launching and recovering up to 50 autonomous uncrewed vehicles.

TAO: Tactical action officer; officer in command of a ship's Combat Information Center (CIC)

TCA: Tactical control assistant, non-commissioned officer (NCO) in charge of identifying targets and directing fire for a single HELLADS or PATRIOT battery

TCO: Tactical control officer, officer in charge of a single HELLADS or PATRIOT missile battery

TD: Tactical Director; the officer directing multiple PATRIOT or HELLADS batteries in ground air defenses, or interception operations aboard an AWACS aircraft.

TEMPEST*: British/European 6th-generation stealth aircraft under development as a replacement for the RAF Tornado multirole fighter. It is planned to incorporate advanced combat AI to reduce pilot data overload, laser anti-missile defenses, and will team with swarming drones such as BATS. It may be developed in both crewed and uncrewed versions, and a version for use on the two new British aircraft carriers is also mooted.

TERMINATOR: A Russian-made infantry fighting vehicle (see IFV) based on the chassis of the T-90 main battle tank, with 2x 30 mm autocannons and 2x grenade or anti-tank missile launchers. Developed initially to support main battle tank operations, it has become popular for use in urban combat environments.

THERMOBARIC: Weapons, otherwise known as thermal or vacuum weapons, which use oxygen from the surrounding air to generate a high-temperature explosion and long-duration blast wave

THUNDER: Radio brevity code indicating one minute to weapons impact

TIANYI (Wing of Fate) autonomous drone*: A speculative design based on the TIKAD/SMASH DRAGON prototypes; gyro stabilized flying gun quadcopters which can be fitted with automatic weapons or a 40 mm grenade launchers.

TIANGONG: Chinese space station launched in April 2021 and currently comprising 3 modules. Planned expansion to 5 modules by 2025, the station is seen as a step toward a crewed Mars mission. With the International Space Station (ISS) due to be decommissioned in 2031, China will have the only functioning space station. There have been no discussions about international missions involving Tiangong, primarily because China was excluded from ISS participation by the USA.

TLV: Tianyi Launch Vehicle, a supersonic drone mothership launched by maglev, which glides to its target before engaging an electric engine and dispersing a swarm of autonomous Tianyi (Wing of Fate) drones.

T-POD*: Trauma-Pod battlefield medical assistant. A speculative merger of ongoing research into battlefield trauma treatment which aims to enable AI assisted rapid diagnosis and stabilization of the most common battlefield injuries (blast injury, projectile weapon injury, cardiac failure).

TOW: US wire-guide anti-tank missile, fired either from a tripod launcher by ground troops or mounted on armored cavalry vehicles

TROPHY: Israeli-made anti-projectile defense system using explosively formed penetrators to defeat attacks on vehicles, high-value assets and aircraft. It is currently fitted to several Israeli and US armored vehicle types. Use in aircraft is speculative.

TSIRKON*: (aka Tsirkon), scramjet powered anti-ship missile claimed by Russia to be capable of Mach 9 or 9,800 km an hour. Because it flies at hypersonic speeds within the atmosphere, air pressure in front of it forms a plasma cloud as it moves, absorbing radio waves and making it difficult for radar to detect. Russia claims to have deployed the missile on its Admiral Gorshkov class frigates but it has not been observed in use e.g. in Ukraine. See also Zmeyevik (air launched variant).

TUNGUSKA: A mobile Russian-made anti-aircraft vehicle incorporating both cannon and ground-to-air missiles

TYPE 054, TYPE 055: Chinese fleet defense destroyers. The Type 054 destroyer is a multi-role frigate equipped with anti-ship missiles, air defense missiles, torpedoes, and a 76 mm gun based on the old Soviet *Sovremenny* class; while the Chinese Type 055 destroyer is a more advanced guided missile destroyer with a more powerful armament that includes advanced air defense systems, land attack cruise missiles, anti-ship missiles, torpedoes, and a variety of guns, similar in role to the US *Arleigh Burke* class.

TYPE 95*: Planned Chinese 3rd-generation nuclear-powered attack submarine with vertical launch tubes and substantially reduced acoustic signature to current Chinese types

UAV: Uncrewed aerial vehicle or drone, usually used for transport, refueling or reconnaissance

UCAS: Uncrewed combat aerial support vehicle or drone

UCAV: Uncrewed combat aerial vehicle; a fighter or attack aircraft

UDAR* UGV: Russian-made uncrewed ground vehicle which integrates remotely operated turrets (30 mm autocannon, Kornet anti-tank missile or anti-air missile) onto the chassis of a BMP-3 infantry fighting vehicle. The vehicle can be controlled at a range of up to 6 miles (10 km) by an operator with good line of sight, or via a tethered drone relay.

UDV: Underwater delivery vehicle. A small submersible transport used typically by naval commandos for covert insertion and recovery of troops.

UGV: Uncrewed ground vehicle, also UGCV: Uncrewed ground combat vehicle

UI: Un-Identified, as in 'UI contact'. See also BOGEY

UNIT 8200: Israel Defense Force cyber intelligence, cyber warfare and defense unit, aka the Israeli Signals Intelligence National Unit

UPWARD FALLING PAYLOADS (UFP)*: A DARPA research project of the 2020s, now shelved, to develop deployable, uncrewed distributed systems that lie on the deep-ocean floor in concealed containers for years at a time. These deep-sea nodes could be remotely activated when needed and recalled to the surface. In other words, they "fall upward." Payloads could include sensor packages, canister-launched aerial drones, mines or torpedoes.

URAGAN: Russian 220 mm 16-tube rocket launcher, first fielded in the 1970s

U/S: Un-serviceable, out of commission, broken

USO: United Services Organizations; US military entertainment and personnel welfare services

V-22 OSPREY: Bell Boeing multi-mission tiltrotor aircraft capable of vertical takeoff and landing which resembles a conventional aircraft when in flight

V-280* VALOR: Bell Boeing-proposed successor to the V-22, with higher speed, endurance, lift capacity and modular payload bay

V-280* VAPOR: Concept aircraft only. AI-enhanced V-280 with anti-radar absorbent coating, added rear fuselage turbofan jet engines for additional speed, and forward-firing 20 mm autocannons

VALKYRIE (XQ-58)*: an experimental uncrewed stealth fighter designed and built by Kratos Defense and Security Solutions to support a USAF requirement to field an uncrewed wingman cheap enough to sustain losses in combat but capable of supporting crewed aircraft in hostile environments. In January 2023 it was announced the USAF had purchased two Valkyrie demonstrators for $15.5m USD, shortly after which the US Navy announced it had done the same.

VERBA: A Russian-made man-portable low-level anti-air missile with data networking capabilities, meaning it can use data from friendly ground or air radar systems to fly itself to a target

VIGILANT CLASS COAST GUARD CUTTER: The Vigilant-class Coast Guard cutter is a medium-endurance cutter with a displacement of approximately 1,000 tons, a sensor suite that includes radar, sonar, and electronic surveillance equipment, a weapons system that includes a 25 mm Mk 38 chain gun and various small arms, as well as a flight deck and hangar capable of supporting helicopter operations for search and rescue, law enforcement, and other missions.

VIRGINIA CLASS SUBMARINE: e.g., *USS Idaho*, nuclear-powered, fast-attack submarines. Current capabilities include torpedo and cruise missiles. Planned capabilities include hypersonic missiles.

VORTEX*: 'Quantum Radar' technology that generates a mini electromagnetic storm to detect objects. First reported by Professor Zhu Chao at Tsinghua University's aerospace engineering school, in Journal of Radars, 2021. A quantum radar is different from traditional radars in several ways, according to the paper. While traditional radars have on a fixed or rotating dish, the quantum design features a gun-shaped instrument that accelerates electrons. The electrons pass through a winding tube of a strong magnetic fields, producing what is described as a tornado-shaped microwave vortex.

VYMPEL: Russian air-to-air missile manufacturer/type

WIDOW*: P-99 Black WIDOW (Pursuit Fighter). Concept aircraft. Several companies were competing in 2023 for the Next Generation Air Dominance air superiority initiative. The Black Widow is a purely speculative platform combining what is known about the requirements issued and the designs in testing. NGAD is described by the USAF as a "family of systems," with a stealth fighter aircraft as the centerpiece of the system, and other parts of the system likely to be uncrewed escort aircraft to carry extra munitions and perform other missions. In particular, NGAD aims to develop a system that addresses the operation needs of the Pacific theater of operations, where current USAF fighters lack sufficient range and payload. The successful NGAD aircraft is therefore unlikely to resemble current US stealth fighters such as the F-22 Rapiére or F-35 Panther.

WILD WEASEL: An air attack intended to take down enemy anti-air defense systems; see also SEAD

WINCHESTER: Radio brevity code for 'out of ordnance'

X-37C*: A successor to the US X-37B uncrewed re-usable space craft, itself a scaled down version of the X-40 space shuttle intended to put small payloads in orbit. First observed in 2010, it set a record for the longest time in orbit for a re-usable spacecraft in 2022, with a flight of 908 days. The X-37C is a conceptual armed variant that will carry a 250kW High Energy Liquid Laser to enable it to conduct satellite interceptions.

X-95: Israeli bullpup-style assault rifle. Bullpup-style rifles have their action behind the trigger, allowing for a more compact and maneuverable weapon. Commonly chambered for NATO 5.56 mm ammunition.

YAKHONT*: Also known as P-800 Onyx. Russian-made two-stage ramjet-propelled, terrain-following cruise missile. Travels at subsonic speeds until close to its target where it is boosted to up to Mach 3. Can be fired from warships, submarines, aircraft or coastal batteries at sea or ground targets. Claimed to be operational but has not been seen in use in the Ukraine conflict.

YPG: Kurdish People's Protection Unit militia (male)

YPJ: Kurdish Women's Protection Unit militia (female)

YUAN WANG class tracking ships: Ships of 18-21,000 tons displacement, used for tracking and support of ballistic missiles and satellites, aircraft and for signals interception.

Z-9: Chinese attack helicopter, predecessor to Z-19

Z-19: Chinese light attack helicopter, comparable to US Viper

Z-20: Chinese medium-lift utility helicopter, comparable to US Blackhawk

ZHU HAI YUN class vessel: Aka Zhuhai Cloud (pinyin: Zhu Hai Yun) is described by China as an autonomous 'oceanography research vessel' designed for uncrewed operations in open waters and as a mother ship for uncrewed vehicles. It has been described in media as the first Chinese "drone mothership" and the first "uncrewed aircraft carrier." It is capable of hitting a top speed of 18 knots (about 20 miles per hour) and can carry 50 flying, surface, and submersible drones that launch and self-recover autonomously. A semi-submersible variant which can launch surface-to-air missiles is speculative.

Zmeyevik: air launched near-hypersonic ballistic missile. See also Tsirkon (Zirkon).

Printed in Great Britain
by Amazon

34540817R00297